Ordinary
Springs

This Large Print Book carries the
Seal of Approval of N.A.V.H.

FARMINGTON COMMUNITY LIBRARY

IN MEMORY OF:
JUDY PEIFFER

GIVEN BY:
CARRIE PEIFFER

Ordinary Springs

Lenore Hart

Thorndike Press • Waterville, Maine

Published in 2005 by arrangement with The Berkley Publishing Group, a division of Penguin Group (USA) Inc.

Thorndike Press® Large Print Core.

The tree indicium is a trademark of Thorndike Press.

The text of this Large Print edition is unabridged.
Other aspects of the book may vary from the original edition.

Set in 16 pt. Plantin.

Printed in the United States on permanent paper.

Library of Congress Cataloging-in-Publication Data

Hart, Lenore.
    Ordinary Springs / by Lenore Hart.
       p. cm. — (Thorndike Press large print core)
    ISBN 0-7862-7661-4 (lg. print : hc : alk. paper)
    1. Young women — Fiction. 2. Divorced men — Fiction. 3. Single fathers — Fiction. 4. Fathers and daughters — Fiction. 5. Dating (Social customs) — Fiction. 6. Large type books. I. Title. II. Thorndike Press large print core series.
PS3608.A786O74 2005b
  813'.6—dc22   2005005318

For David,
who, like many other best things,
only improves with keeping.

As the Founder/CEO of NAVH, the only national health agency solely devoted to those who, although not totally blind, have an eye disease which could lead to serious visual impairment, I am pleased to recognize Thorndike Press* as one of the leading publishers in the large print field.

Founded in 1954 in San Francisco to prepare large print textbooks for partially seeing children, NAVH became the pioneer and standard setting agency in the preparation of large type.

Today, those publishers who meet our standards carry the prestigious "Seal of Approval" indicating high quality large print. We are delighted that Thorndike Press is one of the publishers whose titles meet these standards. We are also pleased to recognize the significant contribution Thorndike Press is making in this important and growing field.

Lorraine H. Marchi, L.H.D.
Founder/CEO
NAVH

* Thorndike Press encompasses the following imprints: Thorndike, Wheeler, Walker and Large Print Press.

Do you think that the things people make fools of themselves about are any less real and true than the things they behave sensibly about? They are more true: they are the only things that are true.

— George Bernard Shaw
Candida

Acknowledgments

Never believe that any book is the work of just one person. I offer my thanks and gratitude to the following individuals and organizations, all of whom helped in some way to bring this novel into being. First of all, novelists and friends Janet Peery and Sheri Reynolds, for encouraging an earlier incarnation of "Madame Vera," which writer Eugene McAvoy then put on the Web. My good friend, writer Terry Perrel, was a master of structure and poser of astute questions. Tom and Jean Wescott offered an undisclosed location for work when chaos ruled at home. Ina Birch, Lisa Carrier, Celeste Clevenger, Doris Galen, Claudia Johnson, and Bruce Jones were insightful early readers. Also, the Virginia Center for the Creative Arts at Sweet Briar and the Virginia Commission for the Arts provided me with a working writer's paradise and the time to get my act together at wonderful, wonderful Mt. San Angelo.

Finally I must thank David Poyer, husband and friend, always my first reader, for love and encouragement — and keen, no-nonsense editing. And my daughter, Naia, for having a good sense of humor about mislaid laundry and a few late dinners.

Once the book left my hands, it landed in the highly capable ones of my terrific editor, Susan Allison, my equally terrific publisher, Leslie Gelbman, editorial assistants Anne Sowards and Jessica Wade, and copy editor Christy Wagner. *Ordinary Springs* could not have asked for a better home. Any mistakes or omissions in the story are strictly my own.

Late at night outside Marianna, Florida, in the Pine Hills School for Girls, I wake to screaming. The room's dark, but when I sit up in my narrow, sagging single, a light hurts my eyes. Not the moon, but a yellow security bulb outside the mesh-screened window.

More screams, blows, footsteps pounding down the corridor. The voices belong to two girls who share the dorm room down the hall. Tonight each claims the other stole her lipstick, her magazine, her boyfriend, her life. I lie back and try not to hear. To listen instead to the soft breathing of my roommates, who seem to sleep like babies, untroubled at least by night.

Past time to sleep, yet I can't seem to rest. I want to go back to the beginning, back to Ordinary Springs, and start my life over. But I'm not that same Dory Gamble, the sixteen-year-old girl hustled from town by the sheriff in the middle of one night. The nosy, awkward girl who didn't fit in, who screwed up her life. And others along the way.

Wish I could turn out that damn light.

I'm sixteen and pregnant, soon to be a mother. Why do I still feel like a two-year-old sometimes? I need sleep, have to get up early in the morning. Shouldn't be lying awake thinking about the far-off past, another town, a time when I was a baby myself. But then, that was the last night I still had a mother of my own.

I am two years old, lying in my crib. The door to my room opens a crack, then wider, and finally a woman comes in. Holding back her long dark hair with one hand, she bends to look at me. Almost asleep, I open my eyes and raise my arms.

"Sweet girl," she says and lifts me out. Then we sit in the rocking chair while she tells me a long story I don't understand. No fluffy bunnies or talking bears in it, though she gets my attention when she mentions Baby. I like the feel of the words, their soft tickling buzz murmured into my hair. When my head droops, she lays me back in the crib. Maybe thinking I'm asleep, but I'm not — just so drowsy and comfortable it's too much trouble to make a lights-out fuss.

She doesn't leave. Instead, she stands watching, a hand resting on my head. I can't see her face, her hair's in the way, but I think she's smiling. From somewhere else in the house I hear another sound: someone is crying. But it sounds so far away, I'm not worried. At last she lifts her hand from my forehead, gently squeezes my foot, and turns to go. That's when I notice, through the bars of my crib, that she's carrying something square and bulky by a handle.

The door closes softly behind her.

"Mama," I say, missing her then, wanting her back. But I must fall asleep instead, because the next thing I know sunlight's streaming across the floor, warming my face. Dust motes drift over the crib, and I'm trapped in a wet, sagging diaper. I chin up on the top rail, and my yells bring Daddy. He looks half-asleep still, eyes red, face creased. But he folds a dry cloth and pins it on, crooked. Then takes me to the kitchen, where he feeds me toast wedges with strawberry jam.

Each time I ask, *Mama?* he bounces me on his knee or we go out in the stroller or I'm handed a toy or a well-gnawed book, but no answer.

The next day he dresses me in a flowered sunsuit with bows at the shoulders and takes me in the big-finned Pontiac to the store. He ties clothesline around my waist and knots it round the wooden pillar near the cash register.

The first customers come in. Some pat my head or tickle me under the chin, but I sense something — pity, sadness — behind these gestures. One old lady's horrified by the rope, even after my father makes her feel how soft it is, how loosely tied. I don't understand what's going on. I sit on the floor and play with sanded blocks of wood, a rubber mallet, a fistful of paint stirrers. I am suddenly rich in the mysterious, once-forbidden currency of hardware.

We do this day after day until it becomes routine. After a few weeks I don't ask for Mama anymore. After six months it might have always been just the two of us, Dory and Owen Gamble, working and playing side by side in Gamble's Hardware. Sufficient unto ourselves, a holy duo no one could sunder. Hard to remember, after a few years, we ever had a woman in the house.

Years later, when I'm six, snooping in a back closet in the unoccupied bedroom at the end of the hall, I find a cardboard box of clothes, costume jewelry, high-heeled shoes with flowers or bows or rhinestone buckles. And a special prize: a shiny compact of real brushed gold.

I run my fingers over some fancy letters etched into the top: V-E-R-A. When I push the catch I find inside, along with traces of pink powder, a saw-edged photo of a couple, their arms wrapped around each other. My father, but with no gray hair, and looking happy. The woman beside him looks even younger, a stranger. Yet she has long dark hair and a round stubborn chin like mine. She's laughing, face turned to the sky.

I've seen such compacts and other cosmetics at my friends' houses, because they have mothers. Mostly nice women with full skirts and curled hair and red toenail polish who tell us to play nice and not fight. Sometimes they look at me and say *tch* and shake their heads; then go find a comb and replace the barrettes my father has clipped on crooked again.

Overjoyed at my find, I pull everything out into the light. Then dress in as many of the garments as I can pull on, slide my feet into the wobbly heels, and sashay up and down in front of the crazed glass of Grandma Gamble's pier mirror, which I love. She had left it to us when she passed, the only grandparent I ever knew.

I'm too absorbed to hear my father

calling, or his footsteps coming down the hall. So I'm shocked when he grabs my arm and jerks the dress-up clothes off my shoulders. One look at his face silences the protest knocking at the back of my throat.

He tells me to stay put as he bundles all the stuff back in the box and carries it out, into the backyard. Panting, I run to keep up. At the open back door I hear a shovel slice through grass into clay, a grunt, the *ching* when the blade strikes rock. Then the hiss of air sucked deep to send oxygen to the muscles lifting and slamming the blade down again.

The thick old backyard azaleas hide me from view, but it's hard to see what's going on. I know those digging sounds from when our dog Rascal got hit by a car and Daddy had to send him back to Jesus. I make myself hold still and don't whine or scream or cry. And I'm old enough by then to understand that if I cover my ears, it won't change anything.

I brush cobwebs from my face, scoot on elbows and knees to the edge of the bushes, and pull one branch back slowly so I can see. Across from my hiding place, a grassy slope of lawn runs from the clear cold Springs up to our old white clapboard house. Centered in that big green rectangle, a sweaty back gleams in the sun, muscles knotting and stretching under the skin like angry cats in a sack.

Daddy draws the shovel back again, raises it. Chops at the tough grass like he's killing a water moccasin. At his feet is the box, its cardboard patched together with yellow and black electrical tape, like a crazy quilt. Something pale pokes from one hole. I squint. Mama's thin, long-fingered white hand, her narrow foot with the crooked little toe . . . I freeze, surprised. *Mama.* Where'd that come from? I squeeze my eyes shut, afraid, until I realize the thing I see is just a yellowed ladies' glove.

The digging sounds drag, stop. My father pushes the box toward the doorway in the ground. It bumps along clumsily, soggy from the rain-drenched grass. He shoves with one foot, and it disappears. Some of the things have fallen out, and he kicks them in, too. I almost giggle, except it's too strange to be funny. Nobody in Ordinary Springs puts their old clothes in a hole in the backyard. They send them to the Baptist Ladies' Thrift Shop or put them on the curb for the lid-banging, hymn-singing Tuesday garbage men to pick up.

My father pats his pockets for a lighter, then leans down and a flame flickers up from the dark. He stirs the fire with his shovel, and a tornado of sparks swirls. A glowing scrap drifts by my hiding place and I grab it, forgetting for a moment that fire is hot. It's that picture, the edges charred now. Only the woman is left, her face and one bare shoulder. Haloed by scorched edges, she looks ancient and mysterious, a saint — or a witch — from centuries past.

My father jerks the shovel up again and again. Dirt thrums like hail. Soon there's just an oval of clay in the grass, a raw cut on green skin. He stands back from it and straightens, one hand cupping his chin.

I slip the scrap into the waistband of my shorts and crawl out of the bushes to stand beside him. His breath is ragged as he takes my hand. He looks back at the house, then over at the Springs, the dock at the foot of the yard. I worry that if I accidentally step on that dirt patch it might collapse, leaves and pebbles and dry broken twigs tumbling along, sucking me in, too.

But I understand. I pulled things into the light that should have been left in the dark, so he had to deal with them. These things belonged to a bad person, to the woman who left us.

I wonder for the first time, as I watch

him sigh and wipe his face, if her leaving was my fault. And whether I'll be bad, too, when I grow up.

As if he can read my thoughts, he looks down and says, quietly, "Never be a fool if you can help it, Dory Gamble. No good ever comes of it."

I shake my head, then nod, unsure which is the right answer. I want to ask about the woman. But then I remember: He set her on fire. So I close my mouth and we go back into the house. I know better than to tell that, tucked into the elastic of my cotton panties, is that scrap of photo, the face of the bad woman named Vera.

Remembering it all again, I sigh and turn over. Beat on my pillow, kick the sheet away. Because despite all warnings, help, and good sense, I have been the worst kind of fool imaginable. A walking, talking cautionary tale, a regular parable. Take a lesson from me.

1

A freshwater spring makes a path nearly as twisted as the ones people choose. It flows underground, then above. Sometimes pure, sometimes tainted with dirt or poison or trash. But though its course is neither straight nor predictable, the spring must keep on flowing whether it wants to or not.

My name is Eudora Gamble, and I was born on the same day a great war ended. My hometown is a droplet in the navel of Florida called Ordinary Springs. In spots, the icy water that gushes up from deep caverns will take a swimmer's breath away. When I left there on my sixteenth birthday, you could see hundreds of striped, colorful fish as clear as anything in those glassy waters. I didn't want to leave so soon and didn't plan to be gone long. But the rocks in the ground don't care which way the water wants to go.

The heart of Ordinary Springs is a wide brick street with plenty of parking in the middle, and everything you'd ever need right there, lining the sidewalks: the Leader

Department Store, Dove's Appliances, Crockett's Drug Store and Soda Fountain, the Corner Market, Nock's Diner, the Ordinary Cut 'n Curl, the post office. And Gamble's Hardware, my father's store. I grew up in its dusty aisles, teething on door knobs, stacking scrap lumber building blocks, scattering my coffee can full of bent, unusable nails like a galvanized *I Ching*. Sometimes ladies who came in were shocked by that, but my father knew I'd never put them in my mouth.

"Dory's clever," he'd say, from behind the counter. "Got a knack for the nature of a tool long before you explain it to her." That was the highest praise anyone could expect from Owen Gamble, and I knew it. So I was happy to learn to properly sort screws and bolts before I was three; to know the right uses for a ballpeen as opposed to a claw hammer, a mason's hammer, a rawhide mallet, or a ten-pound sledge.

The store felt more like home than our house. I loved the feel of worn, smooth, unvarnished floorboards buffed to tan velvet by decades of shoe leather. I liked to sit with my fat childish legs stretched before me and feel grains of sand pleasantly gritty against the backs of my thighs. From that spot I could hear my father explaining to customers the right wrench to fix the pipes under the kitchen sink, or giving confidential advice on borax powder to wipe out an unmentionable invasion of German cockroaches.

The town ladies loved him. They called him Mr. Gamble, but even a child could guess from the way their tongues wrapped around those four syllables that they wanted to call him just plain Owen. Or better yet, Honey Bug or Sugar Pie.

Monday through Friday nine to five, Saturdays till one, straw hats and T-strapped heels and full-skirted cotton dresses tapped past me on their way to the front counter. The women leaned there and talked of brass hinges and porcelain knobs and rubber washers. But I could hear them sigh when Daddy disappeared into the back. I'd heaved such sighs myself for the jar of hard candy in the drugstore window and the porcelain lady doll at Leaders', which wasn't a toy at all and not meant for a child's sticky fingers.

When my father came out again he'd write on the bill pad and add the purchase to their account. Drop it in a crisp brown bag, neatly fold the top over. The ladies took it with hands that smelled of cherries and almonds, carefully smoothed with Jergen's. If his callused fingers ever touched their scented ones, I didn't see — and as I got older I watched close. I didn't mind them stroking my hair or asking for help choosing the right shade of paint. But I had no intention of sharing my only parent, the last one in stock. And he was what they really wanted to take home.

For instance, there was Peggy Soudermilk, whose nineteen-year-old husband had been drafted and killed by a bomb in France. "Vaporized," wheezed the old men who haunted the store's liars' bench, still shaking their heads over it years later. "Blasted to mist and fog just like *that*." Once, at a party at the Martin's fish camp on the other side of the springs, Peggy kept asking until my father danced with her on the roof-top deck of the boathouse. Then one giggling woman after another kept tapping her shoulder to cut in, and Peggy went off to scowl and have a cigarette. Mr. Martin kept flipping Frank Sinatra records on the portable player. Drinks sloshed in the moonlight, and the Martin's dog howled at the moon, but Dad didn't ask the Widow Soudermilk or any of those other women to dance again. Or to go out with him the next week, or the week after.

"It's tragic, the way the man grieves," I overheard an old lady say to her husband once, as they were rolling their new seed broadcaster out the door. "After all, she left him."

But I saw nothing tragic about our lives. I knew Daddy would always be in our store when I got out of school. That when we went home he'd be the captive audience for my fairytale skits and dress-up acts. *The Drama Princess,* he called me. And *Miss Dory Heartburn.*

I had become an entertainer once I realized how, even on the days or nights when he sat on the couch, or at the kitchen table, staring at his hands, my performing made him take notice of me. Applaud, or at least smile. If I could become someone else, someone new and unexpected, it brought him back.

I had the rest of our lives planned, too. When I went off to New York City to become famous, Daddy would watch me on the stage. We'd go out for ice cream after the play, me wearing a fur stole and red high heels.

In the meantime, the town ladies brought me crocheted hand puppets, hair bows with my name scripted in glue and glitter, still-warm sugar cookies in wax paper skirts. Once Sis Majors carried a hand-smocked dress into the store on a pink yarn-wrapped hanger. When I tried it on at home, the seams strangled my arm-pits and when I reached up to get a book off the shelf, the sleeves ripped clean out underneath. Dad said it was the thought that counted. But I'm sure he didn't mean the one those ladies had in mind.

A few nights each month he did go off, to Rotary meetings or Men's Bible Group, leaving me in the hands of a teenage sitter or the hymn-singing colored woman who came sometimes to do our ironing or what-ever town lady had volunteered to give him a break. He could have gone out dancing and drinking if he'd wanted — we were Baptists, but not the hard-shell kind. I never saw him slip any woman in after I was sent to bed, though I got up often for a drink of water or another pillow or to visit the bathroom down the hall, just to be sure.

And as the years passed and Owen Gamble smiled and chatted but otherwise kept to himself, the red-lipsticked mouths gradually pursed up like drawstring bags. The ladies' hellos became grim and businesslike and their shoulders stiff with disappointment.

Once I got to be seven or eight, I begged Daddy to take me out fishing on Saturday mornings. He made excuses but at last gave in, and it became our weekend habit to slip down to the Springs and shove off in the blue rowboat, loaded up with poles, rods, and bait.

"Okay. We'll hook us a couple bass for breakfast," he always said.

As we glided through the mist rising in lacy ribbons off the springs, I tore hunks of lettuce from a wilted head and fed the scar-backed manatee. He came each morning to lay off our dock like a small gray whale and even followed the boat if I had something nice to give him. My father said pets were nothing but a bother and a waste of money. So I made do with the manatee and an occasional wandering box turtle.

I enjoyed the outings a lot until my friend Pearce McMillan, who lived just up the road, told me that the cotton-mouth moccasins in the Springs were so mean they'd chase down your boat and climb right inside. "Bite you all over and leave you to rot. Just for fun," he'd said, nodding in satisfaction. "My uncle told me they find dead fishermen all the time in johnboats, snakes crawling all over 'em."

Moccasins hung from nearly every cypress tree in Florida. They curled up on rocks in the sun, and the Springs was loaded with them. Usually when we went out in the boat I looked at everything, especially the clear water where rainbowed neon darters

swam like submerged butterflies and sometimes shimmied to the surface to nibble
my fingers if I trailed them over the side.
But after Pearce told me that, any time
Dad and I went out on the water and
passed under a tree, I squeezed my eyes
shut and prayed for God and Jesus both to
pay attention and come save us.

Finally one morning Daddy stopped
rowing. "Dory, what on earth you doing?"

I opened my eyes. Told him I was praying.

"What for?"

"Not to be killed dead by a snake, for fun."

He stared at me a moment. "That's a
good one. Say, did I ever tell you about the
time a drought dried up the Springs?"

"No," I said, daring at last to look at the
next tree coming up. I didn't want to hear
a story. What I wanted him to tell me was
that we were safe, that everything would always be okay. But I stayed on my side of
the boat, because he never liked for me to
cling or hang on him.

"That summer, laundry dried five minutes after Mamaw hung it. All the tadpoles
evaporated along with the last drops of
springwater in that cook-oven heat. Until
one dog-day August afternoon, at three
o'clock sharp, it rained tiny, perfect frogs.
Women leaving the Cut 'n Curl ran

27

screaming, holding purses up to protect their perms. Cars collided on Water Street when their tires skidded over jumping green puddles of frogs."

I cried then, imagining the great-great-grandmothers of the peepers I caught down by the water smashed to tragic green paste beneath spinning tires.

He pulled again on the oars. "Every night, Pop sent me out on the flats with Ma's old tin bucket to pick up bass and perch longer than your arm. I went from mudhole to mudhole till that pail dug a groove in the mud all the way back. We ate fish till I grew a set of gills. You believe that?"

I swallowed, following the stilt-legged progress of a water spider. "No sir."

We were at our best fishing hole, and I realized I'd forgotten to worry about crazed man-killing snakes. If you looked down, you could clearly see rocks on the bottom, the sand bubbling and misting up around the Springs itself, as if a benign god lived and breathed beneath the surface, stirring it.

He frowned and gripped my chin. Tilted my face up to look at him. "Then don't believe every fool thing you hear, either. Lord God."

After an hour of casting and netting we rowed back, and he rolled the filleted bass in flour and salt and pepper and fried them in butter. Then set heaped plates before us on the black-and-white dinette table. We ate like the king and queen of a small, rich country, until our bellies could hold no more.

Any night I might get up and pass my father's room, I heard soft, low snoring or an occasional mumbled dream-word. His deep, steady breathing, even from down the hall, would lull me to sleep again once I was back in my own bed. I suppose he could've been meeting a woman elsewhere — at her house, while I was at school, or maybe along the wooded, moonlit shore of the Springs. But I saw no evidence and believed my special rung on my father's ladder would always be reserved for me.

In fact, I never wondered until the Fitzgeralds came to town. By then I was past sitting on the hardware store floor as the legs of customers scissored past. Too late then to keep an eye on the comings and goings, the plots and plans of small-town lady admirers. I didn't know then that danger is the thing that moves right in while you're busy keeping an eye on the rest of the world.

2

For the other children in our town, I served as living proof that the bad luck of children in fairy tales really could happen. Because of this, I could never truly be one of them. Invited over to play, sooner or later I'd creep away to search the house for their secret to a complete family. Was it in the toy cabinet, the hall closet, the medicine chest in the bathroom? Or did something as simple as the freezer chest of hand-labeled casseroles and pot roasts wrapped in foil set their families apart from mine?

If my classmates' mothers caught me snooping, they didn't say much. Maybe I never gave them enough credit for accepting me as I was. At least I didn't break or steal things. It may have seemed flattering that I thought happiness was stored in canning jars on their pantry shelves or tucked in the hatboxes in their walk-in closets.

I felt more in common with boys than girls, anyhow. I couldn't work up much enthusiasm for fussy doll clothes with pin-head buttons or tea parties where you ate and drank only air. With boys you could get your clothes dirty and never had to sit with your ankles crossed. The problem was that most boys agreed there was a stigma attached to playing with girls, known carriers of sissiness and cooties.

Except for Pearce McMillan, maybe because we'd been playmates since babyhood. His family was our only neighbor on Spring Hill Road except for Mrs. Violet Barrows, the nice old lady in the bungalow one lot away. Pearce's mother used to watch me sometimes while Dad was working. We played with blocks and trucks, dug in the sandbox, or splashed in his blow-up wading pool. Our parents had been friends before we were born and remained so even after my mother went away.

The friendship cooled a little one sweltering fourth of July. The McMillans were having their usual holiday cookout. They owned the Corner Market, so food always figured in their weekend plans. That summer I was six, Pearce seven, and it had been the hottest on record; too hot to cook indoors at all or take anything but an icewater bath. At last I gave in and jumped up from the table, right in the middle of barbequed chicken and potato salad, shucked my shorts and shirt and panties, every stitch, and jumped into the wading pool. Pearce immediately followed, still holding a chicken leg.

"Gracious! You all are too old for that," Mrs. McMillan — Miss Harriet to me — cried. She had quickly hauled her son out and hustled him, dripping and whining, inside.

When she came back out she scolded me, too. "Shame on you, Dory Gamble. Get some clothes on! You're not behaving like a little lady."

Miss Harriet's linen skirts and cotton blouses were always perfectly pressed, and you could have balanced a dictionary on her head as she came back down the steps. That day, as usual, her red hair was curled and her eyebrows neatly arched. Her mouth was lipsticked, but not too sinfully red. I knew she would always be charming and gracious, even if her hair was on fire. But I didn't care for her tone or her wagging finger, and I had never liked being told off. So I narrowed my eyes and, for the first time, told her a lie.

"A bee got under my shirt. I was only trying to get rid of it."

"Show me," she said, tapping her foot.

"It must've stung you."

"It flew away," I countered, crossing my arms over my chest, hoping she wouldn't check for marks.

After his wife cleared her throat and glared at him, Jack McMillan set his sweating bottle of Budweiser on the picnic table and mumbled, "I guess big boys oughta play with boys and big girls with girls, maybe."

"Exactly," Miss Harriet huffed, blowing a lock of hair out of her eyes.

"Be reasonable, Harriet," my father said at last. He kept his seat at the picnic table and didn't look concerned. "It's so hot you'd love to do the same." And he went back to gnawing a pork rib.

Miss Harriet collapsed on the picnic bench, fanning herself with a paper plate. She'd never been one of the ladies who hung over the counter in the store, worshipping my father with her eyes. "Oh, Owen. I know you do your best. I just wish Vera —" Then she put a hand to her mouth and looked stricken, nearly sick.

My father laid his fork back on the plate. He stared at it, his face hard and set. "We don't talk about that," he said, each word dropping like a stone. "As you well know."

She turned red in the face. "*Tch.* Of

course not. But . . . but a little girl needs a mama. And with all the women in this town —"

My father turned to me. "Tell them what happened to your mother, Dory," he ordered.

"She left us alone to take care of ourselves," I said, picking at my thumbnail. "And we can get along just fine." I could have said, *She was the wicked witch.* Or even, *She's nothing but a picture hid in my cigar box, under the bed.* But I knew when to repeat the party line and when to keep a secret.

From the corner of my eye I could see Miss Harriet press her lips together and close her eyes. Then Mr. Jack cleared his throat, and with a shaky hand spooned baked beans I didn't want onto my plate. Slowly, everyone began eating again.

After that, we didn't spend many weekends with the McMillans. But Pearce and I would slip into the house anyway and beg butter and sugar sandwiches from Delia, Miss Harriet's maid. Her skin was a creamy cinnamon color, and she smelled like biscuits and soap and some flowery cologne splashed liberally. She had a broad, pretty face and one gold tooth in front that seemed pirate-daring, glamorous.

Delia was the only colored woman, except for the few who came in the store, whom I'd ever gotten to examine close up. We sat at the table and ate our snacks while she sang and washed dishes in impossibly hot, steamy water. Our colored store customers were almost always men, solemn-faced in dusty pants and long-sleeved shirts, who'd just come from mowing lawns or painting someone's house. They smelled like gasoline or turpentine, not Florida Water. Unlike most of the town merchants, Dad let them buy on account and pay in installments. But I couldn't imagine one of them ever breaking into song in broad daylight.

I'd heard on the playground and even in the store that the Negroes who lived in the Quarters just outside town got reeling drunk and went after each other with razors on Saturday nights — even the women. Some of these razor-artists were known to attack white ladies, though the tellers of this information were always evasive about when and where this had ever happened. Besides, Delia lived in the Quarters, and Miss Harriet drove her home every afternoon. If Pearce's mother would venture there daily in her silky stockings and pillbox hat, it couldn't

35

possibly be the way folks said.

Even though he was always a grade ahead of me, Pearce and I had the same recess, plus the time between the last bell and dinnertime to climb trees, throw mud balls, build forts in the woods, and make firefly lanterns in the twilight glow of summer nights until our parents shouted us in.

Each morning I'd gulp my Cheerios and milk and head off to school. Where, first thing, we sang the song every student at Ordinary Springs Combined School secretly despised:

> *I like to wake up in the morning, where the*
> *orange blossoms grow.*
> *Where the sun comes peeping into where*
> *I'm sleeping and the songbirds say hello!*
> *I like the fresh air and the sunshine, it's so*
> *good for me I know.*
> *So I'll make my home in Florida, where*
> *the orange blossoms grow!*

Then we'd catch our breath and launch into spelling, coloring, and arithmetic. Through it all I looked forward mainly to reading the stories in my *Roads to Adventure* book and to the time after school Pearce and I spent in the woods or on the water.

Whatever else happened to me, whoever else had left, he was reliable and unchanging. A best friend who didn't expect me to sit a certain way or keep my dress from flying up or wrinkling or jam plastic barrettes in my unruly hair.

But the year I hit twelve and started developing, I guess even my father worried I'd grow up warped if I didn't become more girlish. He'd gotten out of having to explain to me why, at a certain age, girls become crabby once a month and begin to bleed into their white cotton underwear. In sixth grade we'd all been herded into a hushed-up, girls-only assembly in the gym to learn about cycles and periods and the proper positioning of belts. And cotton pads that sounded like a character from *The Day the Earth Stood Still*: "Kotex Barada Mikto."

After the lights came on again, the nurse handed out pink pamphlets with a drawing of a pony-tailed girl with a big question mark floating over her head. Inside it explained how we strap napkins between our legs. No, not the dinner kind, she'd assured one girl who raised her hand. "It's a wonderful thing," she gushed. "It means you all are nearly grown up."

While we were shooting embarrassed

looks at each other, our hands shading our eyes, pondering this further proof of the mysterious hell awaiting us as adults, she'd said, "Be sure and take this home. And discuss it with your mothers, girls."

Everyone cut their eyes at me. The nurse cleared her throat. "Well, your *parents*, I mean, of course."

Of course. What other girl in the room would be talking about menstrual cycles with her father at dinner that night? On the way home I stuffed the pamphlet in a trash can. When I was younger I had asked about babies — how they got out, how they got inside in the first place. But any mention of sex had always made sweat pop on my father's upper lip. He'd develop a stutter, a sunburned look about the ears and cheeks.

Owen Gamble was a silent, self-contained man, not given to confidences or complaints. Nor to offering advice on anything more personal than the merits of different screwdrivers. I knew my father must love me, only . . . Why, when I came up and grabbed onto his arm or hugged him in the morning, did he step back and hold me at arms' length, like some muddy, untrained puppy? He might smile, or in a rare case pat my head, but still put distance between us all the same.

As I got older he began to stiffen up, to scold me when I tried to hug him or sit too close on the couch when we watched TV. "You're a big girl, Dory," he'd say. "Big girls don't do that." And he would look away, distant and cold, as if we hadn't even been introduced.

Having no mother to instruct me in the arcane ways of makeup and hairstyling, or how to match skirts and blouses, or what things not to whisper about at slumber parties, I suppose I was fated to turn into a clumsy, lanky outsider. My father made sure I had a clean outfit every morning until I turned eight. He showed me how to do my own laundry and then he didn't have to handle girls' underwear any more. By sixth grade, I saw I needed to exchange my overalls, T-shirts, and jeans for skirts and blouses, and dresses. I wanted to pick out my own clothes, to go up to the register and put them on our account. But he continued to shop for me. And he didn't buy the accepted uniform, the pleated skirts and fuzzy sweaters and saddle shoes of my classmates. He decided he would shop in the women's section because I was tall for my age and I wouldn't outgrow the clothes as fast. And he knew nothing about fashion.

I liked the stuff well enough when I first tried it on. The bold colors and sophisticated styles suggested that new life waiting for me down the road. But at school, dressed in a pea-green sheath and red ballet flats or a geometric print dress with a wonderful twirlable circle skirt and ladies' lace-up spectator shoes, I realized I looked like no one else. And worse, I had no clue about how I could. Because it wasn't just clothes. The other girls had a different vocabulary, different priorities. They talked in hushed, religious tones about makeup and singers and older boys, as if these things turned the earth.

At the lunch table I dreaded the way conversations were heading. "Jabbo Partee's *so* cute," a popular girl might say. Then I'd nod and smile, trying to look interested, even if thick, crewcut Jabbo looked about as attractive as a shaved baboon.

The girl next to me would know the proper drill, though. "I know! He said *hey* to me the other day at my locker. I like to've died." Then all I could do was wait it out until the sighs and simpers died down. Most other girls had also mastered the art of giggling at the end of every declarative sentence.

By God, that stuff made no sense to me.

I couldn't blush and squeal and giggle on demand. Couldn't make myself cry when Elvis came on the radio, except by pinching the skin inside my elbow until it turned purple. Clearly someone had forgotten to hand me the script for the place and time I'd been born into.

On the other hand, by seventh grade I'd mastered the use of more tools than any boy in the Ordinary Springs Combined School shop class. But I soon understood my peers considered this an aberration best not spoken of.

Around my thirteenth birthday, I briefly tried to interest Dad in women. Whenever we went downtown to buy groceries or get haircuts or new socks, I pointed them out. But by then the young to middle-aged ones had given up on him, gotten married, or moved off. That left high school girls, Ladies' Auxiliary matrons, and confirmed spinsters like the Bradley sisters. Or Miss Chenowith, the elderly piano teacher I'd already been a great disappointment to.

So 1958 was not a fruitful year for matchmaking. Still, I pointed out one or the other, wondering aloud what kind of wife they'd make, trying for a tone that suggested scientific detachment or instructions for putting something useful together. My father only shook his head and put cereal in the cart or ignored me while the barber trimmed his neck. At last I had to concede that the pickings were slim. So the only events of note that year were that sweet old Mrs. Barrows from next door fell in the yard, broke her hip, and was taken north to Jacksonville by her daughter. And I got to play the princess's maid in our school play, *The Lady or the Tiger.*

By spring, just before my fourteenth birthday, we heard Mrs. Barrows wouldn't be coming back. Customers passed word over the counter along with plumbing and dry rot problems. It seemed an out-of-town couple, some Yankees named Fitzgerald, had bought the tidy bungalow one lot over.

It was a hot day at the end of June when a yellow-green Thunderbird with a white top pulled up next door. The convertible clashed horribly with the house's lavender clapboards — Violet Barrows had really loved her first name. My first sight of that racy green convertible made me suspect these new neighbors might not fit neatly into Ordinary Springs.

A long-legged, dark-haired woman got out from behind the wheel, dressed despite the heat all in dead black — turtleneck, tight capri pants, even a wide black head-band. She stood for a moment on the brick walk, tapping her foot. And then, an honest-to-God ambulance pulled up. I had to go out onto the porch and pinch dead leaves off the geraniums to get a better look. Ratfink, a cat that actually belonged to Pearce, jumped up to weave invisible ropes around my ankles.

Two big-shouldered men in white uniforms got out and opened the ambulance doors. They wheeled a stretcher over the grass and down the cracked brick walk to the front door. I was mesmerized. A tall, witchy woman in black; a mysterious body . . . I followed their progress, parting the leaves of the azalea by the porch to see.

"By the pricking of my thumbs, something wicked this way comes," I whispered to the cat. We'd read *Macbeth* back in eighth-grade English, and I'd picked those for my lines to memorize.

The scenes I'd cribbed from storybooks and novels, revised to star me, acted out first in sheets and towels and a plastic tiara and then costumes swiped from the school drama chest, suddenly turned flat as the notebook paper I'd copied them on.

"That new fella's a sick pup. He won't

be with us long," a customer told Dad across the counter the next day. "Just keeps hanging on, though. Cancer or heart trouble or some danged thing."

All that week talk in town centered on the Fitzgeralds. How he was a war hero. The way his wife tended him, faithful as an acolyte. In the weeks that followed we rarely saw her leave the house, so it seemed to be true. Occasionally she did work in the yard. One weekend she planted dwarf azaleas, stargazer lilies, dipladenia, and leather ferns. The next, variegated pothos, which rapidly climbed the trunks of the palm trees, their fanning yellow, white, and green leaves cavorting like hootchie-cootchie dancers in the least breeze. All this newly installed greenery had an aggressive, knowing air no native shrub would've dreamed of.

Ordinary Springs was a friendly town; people dropped in to chat on weekends. But our new neighbors never came over. Of course, no one expected a sick man to rise like Lazarus and go visiting. So my father told me to bake some brownies, carry the pan over, and leave it on their front porch after knocking politely.

Our old pan reappeared, scrubbed clean, a few days later. A thick creamy notecard inside it had Myra Cohen Fitzgerald printed at the top in purple. Someone had extravagantly scrawled THANK YOU! underneath in peacock blue ink. But she still kept to the house and yard, barely lifting her tapered, red-polished fingers as we left in the morning for school or came home from the store at night. In the Corner Market, she wore black toreador pants or pencil skirts with sleeveless white blouses and pushed her cart the way she drove her car — fast and confidently. But sunglasses hid her feelings about Jell-O and corned beef hash and cocktail olives. And the silky gray scarf that covered her hair gave her the pious, untouchable air of a nun.

By October, their yard was an Amazonian jungle, a wild, unpruned place that thumbed its green nose at our straight-edged rectangle of grass. So changed, so foreign, I had to sneak across sometimes to prove to myself the old Barrows house still remained under all that green. I could have sworn Myra Fitzgerald even controlled the weather there. She'd somehow made it warmer, steamier, as if you'd stepped through a portal into a rain forest just a few feet from our dry, heat-faded marigolds. I crept over to breathe the perfumes of blooming bushes and vines: dipladenia, red trumpet, gardenia, hibiscus, winter jasmine. Scents so strong I broke out in a sweat standing in the shade, toes curling into the spongy composted dirt, dark jungly fluids soaking into my white socks.

The Fitzgeralds had come from New York City, reportedly for the climate. Florida was so warm you could grow anything all year round, and as the Fitzgerald garden unfurled, old Mrs. Barrows's grass died for want of sun, curled up, and yellowed to ghost carpet in all the new shade. The sweet, spicy smells, the furtive rustlings of oversize leaves and grasses all made me want to take off running right then to faraway lands so I could discover strange animals while poling down the Amazon, or invent a miracle cure to save a handsome explorer. As the nights cooled, my dreams got more disturbing: Often I hovered at the bedside of some hazy, unidentified male, laying cool hands on his fevered skin, healing him with my touch. Yet by day I wished every boy in the tenth grade at Ordinary Springs Combined School would drop dead.

Then something funny happened. On a hot Sunday right before Thanksgiving my father got up early. He paced out the borders of our backyard, then yanked the rusted reel mower out of the garden shed. Now, Pearce had been taking care of our acre of grass for years, trundling the McMillans' big-wheeled Snapper down the road. And he'd been there to cut it two days before. But that dawn I woke to the scrape and screech of metal as Dad steel-wooled and oiled the blades, then shoved the old push mower, creaking and groaning, over grass that couldn't have been more than an inch and a half long.

He was still out there an hour later.

"What're you *doing?*" I yelled, chasing after him with a glass of iced tea. "This don't need cutting!"

"Exercise," he grunted. "Out of shape." Finally he stopped and took the glass. He wiped his forehead with the tail of his shirt.

After another half-hour of hauling and shoving he took a flat-bladed spade and began edging the thick beds of ferns out front. His red-splotched face made me fear for his heart as much as his sanity. He'd always hated doing yard work.

"Fresh air, Dory," he snapped when I came out again. "You should try it. A nice day, too."

"Dad, this is Florida. It's hot and buggy, not fresh."

Then I noticed Myra was out, too, tying up the drooping vines that brushed the sides of the house and draped her shoulders like a live green shawl; bending with her narrow rump in the air to dig new holes for spiky, dangerous Spanish bayonet plants; dividing clumps of red-hot geraniums and prim-faced white periwinkle so she could plant them in zigzag rows, a chorus line of saints and sinners. Occasionally she dabbed at her face with a bandanna, then sat back and lighted up a Kool. The smoke haloed her, shrouding the plants like rain forest mist.

And this day, instead of envying the graceful way she held her cigarette, I felt annoyed. Why did the saint next door have to sit out there puffing like a paper mill — to fumigate the bugs?

I went inside but stood at the window, watching. At last my father stretched elaborately, then bent and yanked a dandelion. Soon he was sitting on the dented weed bucket, taking a break, too. Not smoking, but throwing glances at Mrs. Fitzgerald like he felt a strong urge to start puffing, too. I flipped a pencil off an end table and practiced balancing it, an imaginary butt, between my fingers. I paced the hall before Grandma Gamble's silver-flecked mirror, copying my neighbor's slow, lazy walk. The way she slunk and wove through the pine needle–carpeted paths of her yard, bold as a cat who's sprayed all the boundaries.

The week of Thanksgiving got even hotter. When I had chores to do, sooner or later I'd get the urge and run down to the Springs, jump in clothes and all, just to float a while and cool off. But despite the heat, fat, perfect pumpkins and yellow-striped gourds appeared on the Fitzgerald porch.

I'd had to pitch the rotting remains of my October jack-o'-lantern, which was mushy on the bottom and drawing fat desperate flies. On the way back from the trash I noticed Myra kneeling in the side yard, talking to her plants. Her black capris rode down, showing the scalloped edge of her panties, the sheer fabric and creamy lace stark against the honey of her skin.

Maybe this was what my father had been staring at. He'd been working in the yard nearly every evening. His face and neck and legs, normally pale from spending all day inside the store, began to tan. He was building muscle in his shoulders from all the pushing and cursing required to turn the rusty blades of the reel mower. His graying brown hair showed new blond streaks from hours spent in the late afternoon sun.

As their tans deepened, my father and Myra worked closer to the shared border of our properties. Maybe it was the only space left to plant. And she'd begun to glance up from time to time. My father was still looking, too.

One still-warm December afternoon during Christmas break, as I carried a plate of burgers out to the grill, I saw they'd crossed some invisible line. Dad and Myra stood a few feet apart. They talked and talked as it began to get dark. I paced, cleared my throat, then tapped my foot on the steps.

"Hey, Dad!" I called once in a voice so whiny it embarrassed me. But nothing seemed to make him understand I was hungry, that it was time to go inside and eat. The burgers sizzled, blackened, charred.

I could have dropped like a famine victim if a sudden sharp ringing hadn't erupted from the Fitzgerald house. Myra had been laughing at something my father said. At the sound she froze, then wheeled and ran for her door.

3

New Year's passed before I found out what the ringing meant. It was Frank Fitzgerald, who would shake a little brass bell to let his wife know he needed water or a bowl of soup or a basin to pee in. I discovered this by sneaking up to the back of their house one day. I peered into all the windows until I spotted Myra bending over a crank-up hospital bed, holding a glass to the mouth of a very thin man who lay flat on the rumpled sheets in a T-shirt and striped undershorts.

His arms and legs were thin and pale, his knees and elbows swollen like the joints of a diseased sapling. He was slowly taking sips of water and staring up at Myra as if he'd rather be drinking a glassful of her. But her hair fell like a curtain over the side of her face, and I couldn't see her expression as she gazed down.

I'd never peeped in a window before in my life. I ducked again and walked bent along the hedge, out of sight. Obviously her husband was so sick they couldn't share a room. I wondered if Myra cared, or if she was glad to have a bed to herself. My childhood snooping had taught me that the parents of my classmates generally slept in the same room in double beds, or sometimes in a pair of singles. And thanks to health class, I had a good idea of what healthy married men and women got up to together at night.

Plus, early on I'd taken in talk at school, first on the playground. ("The man pees on the woman's belly," Sharon Tilden had stubbornly insisted, despite our nose-holding and disgusted groans. "And that makes the baby." She only curled her lip at Robbie Cooper's rebuttal: "No, no, stupid! The baby grows from a seed, then it busts out the mother's bellybutton." Shrieks, followed by nervous, disdainful laughter, hands clapped over stomachs.)

I knew better by then, of course. But I was still an eavesdropper, tolerated on the outer fringes when the more popular girls gathered in a circle, and I'd gradually gotten the upper-level course. So much so that formerly innocent verbs like *blow* and *suck* made my face burn when I heard them in otherwise boring conversations or read them in books. Even Pearce, by then working in the store afternoons and Saturdays, had started making comments under his breath about female customers while we sorted bolts and washers into the bins and drawers that lined the back wall. He did it to make me squirm, so I practiced my poker face and kicked him when I couldn't stand it any more. The week before he'd sprung a new one on me. When he was older, he said, he'd leave Ordinary Springs and work on the water. He wasn't interested in college, and he didn't want to work indoors in an office somewhere.

"My uncle runs trawlers in the Gulf," he said, flinging a hail of bolts into a drawer. "I'm gonna spend my days fishing, shrimping, and getting fried. Maybe drinking a little beer and having fun after."

"Yeah, right," I'd said, thinking, *No. No.* Did everything I'd always counted on suddenly have to become treacherous, changing on me? My lack of logic didn't escape me; why shouldn't Pearce have plans, too? I wasn't the only person in town who had different ideas about how life could be lived. So what?

But that wasn't all. Saturdays at the store, giggling girls came in to flirt with him while waiting to pick up stuff for their parents. They were a year older than me, and they chewed gum in a drugged way while constantly flipping back their hair. They laughed low and kind of sneery, like they knew things I didn't. Some wore boys' heavy ID bracelets that clanked like handcuffs whenever they lifted an arm.

One morning Pearce asked out of the blue whether I had a boyfriend. That took me by surprise, because lately I had been pretending he was it. That was too embarrassing to admit. I'd heard rumors he liked a cheerleader with muscular calves named Marylee Tyson. She'd been dropping by the store, too, in her short, pleated green-and-yellow skirt. Her tanned arms were covered with blonde down, and her smooth, golden legs bare even in winter, when sensible girls wore dungarees or at least knee socks. She seemed to glide around the store, even in clunky black-and-white saddle shoes, as she followed Pearce down the aisles, talking about basketball scores and away dates.

So his question surprised me. Had I been staring at him without realizing it? I shook my head. "I got better things to think about."

"Like what? Oh, I see, you like girls, then."

"Sure, I guess," I said, picking a scab on the back of my hand. Then I took his meaning. "Pearce, you retard." Maybe he had figured out I didn't really have any close girlfriends, only acquaintances I could sit with at lunch.

He just laughed, and when he walked past to slide another ship-lap 2×6 off the stack he patted the top of my head like I was a good dog. This annoyed and pleased me equally, but I'd be damned if I'd let him know it.

"Well, you're supposed to like *boys,* Dor." But he said it without any of the evil, slit-eyed malice popular kids packed their whispered insults with.

"As far as I'm concerned, boys suck," I said. "And who wants a baby? They smell like rotten milk and dribble spit, and you have to change stinking diapers full of yellow poop."

Now he did snort, because everyone knew that's exactly what women did: They got married, then changed a lot of diapers. I had other ideas, but no intention of sharing them. So I faked a yawn and left.

The next weekend, I was in the back cutting key blanks while Pearce sharpened saw blades, throwing a fountain of sparks off the grinding wheel. He started on me again.

"Got a boyfriend yet?" he yelled. This

obsessing on one subject wasn't like him. Suddenly, I felt nervous standing close. It was a new feeling, one I'd never had in connection with him. I looked around; my father was all the way across the store, mixing house paint for Mrs. Holland. I swallowed and stared at the key I'd just cut all wrong. At last I shook my head.

"So what gives? All the tenth-grade boys lost their balls?"

I sorted possible smart-ass answers in my head, unsuccessfully. The scorch of hot metal stung my nose. It suddenly seemed terrible that he, my best friend and playmate from even before school, was ragging on me about my shortcomings, my so-called life. Trying to make me into one of the giggling idiots who came around just to gaze at him.

"Well, let's see," I began. "Balls. You know, Whitey let me hold his last week." It happened that Whitey Johnson was a sports fanatic who carried a signed baseball to school with him every day. I congratulated myself on this sharp, true comeback, a double hitter considering absolutely no one touched Whitey's prized Spaulding without permission.

Pearce let the grinder whine to a halt, his face showing mixed amazement and respect. Checkmate.

That simple win goaded me on. How easy it was to make believe when you'd been playacting nearly from birth. "He won't let just anybody do that." I inhaled deeply, a ploy some girls used to make their chests look bigger. "I think he, you know, might like me."

"Huh," said Pearce. He gave the saw blade one more screeching pass on the grinder, then flipped off the switch. As he went by he bumped me, and it didn't feel like an accident. I reached out, jabbed him in the ribs, and ran off down the plumbing aisle.

"Hey!" He shot after and grabbed me from behind, then pulled me into the storeroom. He pinned me to the wall, like we were six again and out in the yard, having kumquat wars, playing tag, wrestling. We were laughing like loons, but quietly so my father didn't hear. I could barely get my breath. Then Pearce did something that took the rest of my air clean away. He yanked my shirttail out of my jeans and slid his hands up my ribs, brushing his fingers across the bra I'd just started wearing. I gasped and shoved him off.

He looked surprised himself and mumbled, "Sorry."

"Like hell." I pushed him hard against

the brass and aluminum machining stock and stomped out. I heard the crash of metal cascading off the rack and his muffled curses as he scrambled to pick it all up before my father came to see what was going on.

But I kept recalling his hot, baseball-callused fingers sliding over my ribs, up the soft skin of my belly, then the tiny shock when they brushed a nipple. I went back to the bathroom and lifted my shirt in front of the mirror. He must've had a broken fingernail, because a red scratch ran from under the bra elastic across and down to my navel. I traced the thin line with a finger. Then reached up, closed my eyes, and felt of myself the way he had. But it wasn't even close to the same.

When I came out he was hard at work and didn't look up. We avoided each other the rest of the day. Just unpacked and dusted, sorted, and shelved in silence until five o'clock, when my father turned the sign hanging in the door to CLOSED.

One Saturday, a hot April morning two weeks before my fifteenth birthday, I sat in the living room in my pajamas, watching a *Tom and Jerry* cartoon, eating corn flakes from a sauce pan because all the bowls were dirty and I didn't want to wash one, though dishes were one of my chores. Dad had gone off to the Corner Market before he had to open up. I was supposed to walk downtown in an hour or so, sweep the store and sidewalk, then carry the groceries home.

I heard footsteps on the porch, then a knock on the screen door. I glanced over my shoulder. Myra Fitzgerald was peering through the mesh. "Shit," I whispered. I set the pan on the floor and shuffled over in my fuzzy slippers.

"What," I said. "Uh, hello. What do you want?" I wasn't sure I liked her much anymore, sick husband or not.

"Hi, Dory. May I come in?"

"Okay, I guess." I opened the door and stepped back.

She was wearing a Villager shirtwaist that any popular girl at school would have killed for. And here it was Saturday, yet she had on shiny black kitten-heeled sandals with thin leather straps that laced up her calves like a Roman soldier's. She smelled more expensive than all five perfumes from the mirrored tray at Crockett's Drugs combined. I knew, because I had squirted all the testers while Dad shopped for aspirin and Band-Aids.

59

"Look at you." She smiled and wagged a finger playfully. "Not exactly the early bird today, are we?"

I wanted to ask what the point of this visit was, but couldn't. Too rude. "My father's not home right now," I said, crossing my arms over my braless chest. Not that there was much to see. I wished I was not still in my faded babydoll pajamas and pink slippers.

"Oh yes, I know," she said, turning her gold scarab bracelet around and around. "He asked me to come over today, actually. As a favor. To help out."

That seemed strange. "I can't think of a thing we need any help with."

She smiled as if I was the cutest thing she'd ever seen. "Well, let's go sit at the table, then." But this sounded more like a command than an invitation.

I dragged after without another word, trained to jump when an adult issued orders. I took my usual chair, but feeling ornery I turned it around backward. She sat at the head of the table, at Dad's place.

"My, you're really growing up," she said. "I think you're taller than when we moved in, and that's been, what? A year ago?"

I stiffened at that bright false tone some adults put on. You know. Maybe meaning well but about to screw you up nonetheless. Maybe she noticed how rigid I'd gotten, because she rushed on. "Anyway, uh, your father thought we might get acquainted. Have a little girl talk."

About what? I didn't even know this woman. I slid lower until my chin rested on the chair rail. But inside I was all ears and at attention. And mad. "Maybe I should take notes," I said. Jeez. Was that what the two of them had been talking about for months outside — me?

She blinked. "If you like." Her voice got quieter, softer, which was scary.

Yes, I was being difficult. And maybe she did mean well. But somehow I couldn't stop myself. She seemed at that moment the grown-up embodiment of all the girls at school I'd ever wanted to be like, or to be friends with, but never could. At the same time she seemed much too late to do any good, the image of all the mothers who had never been mine. The ones who knew what to say and do and even feel. Had she guessed what a loser I was, inside?

"So, girl stuff," I repeated, frowning. "Such as what?"

"Dory," she said, her eyes shining with excitement, or maybe just the satisfaction that at that moment she knew so much more than I did. "It's such a wonderful time for you right now."

I stared at her. What in the world? I was not cute, or smart, or popular. I had no boyfriend, and just that morning I'd woke up with a really big zit, a red bump on my chin that glowed in the dark and throbbed like a toothache when I'd poked it.

So I just grunted, an all-purpose sound that worked for getting my father to think I was listening.

"You've noticed your body changing, I'm sure."

Oh, for God's sake, Dad! So maybe he didn't know about that old assembly, where the school nurse had separated the boys into one bunch and the girls into another, and shown us film strips. Then we'd stared at slides, diagrams of human parts split like cross-sections of floppy, exotic plants, with little arrows to show how these various parts fit together in the reproductive mode.

Mrs. Fitzgerald jerked me back to earth again. "Or maybe —" She tried to hold my gaze. One manicured hand shook a little, and for the first time she looked uncertain. "Maybe it's already happened?"

Lord. Which *it* was she talking about? I wanted to slide under the table. "Don't know what you mean." I picked up a fork left out from dinner the night before and began using one tine to scrape crescents of dirt from under my fingernails.

She winced and laid a hand over mine, gripping so hard it hurt. "I'm talking about your menstrual cycle, sweetie. You know, your period."

Then I wanted to run away so bad it made me feel not just rude, but cruel. "Yeah, I *do* know. It's like, when you bleed and have to stick wads of cotton up your ass."

Her face went stiff, as if she'd reached for a flower and closed her hand around a slug. "Well . . . that's one way to put it, I suppose."

"Great. So now your job's done. I know everything."

"Well, you see though, it's not. Maybe we can plan something. A girls' day out." She took another deep breath. "Look, Dory, I don't have a kid of my own. But we can pretend like we're . . ."

I waited, silent, not helping her out. Curious what sort of relationship she was going to try to foist on me. Remembering all those conversations out in the yard, the way she'd smiled up at my father. I didn't believe it was *me* she was actually interested in.

She shrugged. "Oh, well. Like maybe, sisters."

"Yeah, maybe." On some cold summer day in Florida.

I said I had to get dressed and get on to town, and she finally left. I yanked on a pair of rolled-up jeans and an old white oxford shirt of my father's, the man I planned to brain with a five-pound rawhide mallet as soon as I got to the store. I jammed my feet into rundown loafers and bolted out the door, careful not to glance at the Fitzgerald's house in case my new big sister was watching. As I passed the McMillans', Miss Harriet straightened from weeding a flower bed. I waved. Her face was hidden by the broad brim of a straw hat, but I could feel her watching, even after I'd gone past.

I burst into the store, shoving through the double doors cowboy-style, and stalked past Mr. Hollander and Mr. Spurgeon, both older than Jesus and sprouting white bristly hairs everywhere but their shiny bald heads. The air was fogged with cigar smoke. They were fixtures, unremarkable as doorstops, harmlessly planted on that same bench by the front window all year round. Still, I glared at their gummy, unfocused smiles. They'd been fathers, too.

"*Sic semper tyrannus,*" I muttered as I swept past, not sure of the exact meaning. It just felt right. "Daddy! I need to talk to you."

He was ringing up someone. As he handed the man a gallon of paint, he nodded over at me. "It's a wise child who knows her own father. You have a good day, now, Bart." He turned back. "I got something to tell you, too."

"Okay then. You first." I'd save my tirade and have the last word.

He ran a hand through his hair. "Got you a sitting job."

This news took my breath away. I'd dreamed for years of getting steady work, of making money to squirrel away for my secret ambition. I'd need plenty to get to New York, to live on until I was a success. But all the families with little kids had long been sewed up by the middle and younger sisters of their previous sitters, girls who'd passed on the mantle like a family trade. I had yet to get more than a couple assignments, fill-ins for girls with dates, and one unlucky soul with mono.

Forgetting I'd planned to kill him, I lunged and managed to hug him around the waist. "Who with, who with, where, when?"

He stiffened and leaned away but patted my shoulder. "Whoa, tiger. It's tonight."

I forgot about the where and the who and began planning. I'd pull out the cardboard box of Little Golden Books and colored paper and mostly whole crayons I'd kept under my bed for a sitter's kit. I'd make those kids beg their parents to call me again. I'd bake chocolate-chip cookies, I'd even —

"Kind of a special situation," he said, busying himself sorting through the new plumbing and tile catalogs.

Special situation? Then it must be Tommy Cappelman. A smiling, sweet-natured boy with curly black hair, his body plump and square as a couch cushion. His parents owned the appliance store, and he spent most afternoons roaming the sidewalks on Water Street, dropping in on different shops, begging for old bike inner tubes. He liked to sneak up on people and stretch the deflated tubes like big rubber bands, then let go. They made a horrible, teeth-gritting *snap*. When he could actually make a newcomer flinch, or an elderly lady fling her letters in the air outside the post office, Tommy would clap for joy. When anyone in Ordinary Springs talked about "special kids" they meant Tommy, who would have to live at home with his two parents forever.

"It's for Mrs. Fitzgerald," Dad said. "I mean, for her husband. She wants to get out of the house, run a few errands, maybe take in a movie. But she doesn't want to leave him alone. In case he needs . . . a glass of water or something."

I stepped back. "You want me to baby-sit a *man?* A grown-up?" Then I frowned. "Which movie?"

"Uh, let's see — *A Summer Place.* And it's no big deal, Dory. She'll get him fed and ready for bed. He sleeps most of the time anyhow. But you'd be there in the house to help, you see, if anything happened."

If anything happened. A chilly finger prodded my stomach. "Why can't you watch him for her?"

"Because." He leaned over and straightened the pocketknives in the glass case under the counter, though they were perfectly aligned. "I'm driving her. She doesn't know how to get to Ocala."

I should have seen it coming: those long talks over the periwinkle bushes. "She found her way here from New York."

He cleared his throat. "I *know* that, Dory. I'm doing a favor for a neighbor.

The poor woman's exhausted, works non-stop taking care of her sick husband, never gets out."

Not much I could say to that. They'd been living in Ordinary Springs barely a year, but Saint Myra was admired from one end of town to the other.

"And she'll pay you a dollar-fifty an hour."

I inhaled sharply. Most sitters got half that for putting up with two, three, even four squealing brats. And so somehow, though I'd meant to put him on the spot, I forgot to tell him how little I appreciated Myra suddenly turning up on my doorstep to set me straight on the joys of being a woman.

4

When we crossed our yard at six o'clock sharp, who could've suspected how it'd change our ordinary lives. The only thing out of the ordinary was the new madras jacket my father wore. Perhaps he was already imagining how everyday things could be enriched, *If only.*

Instead of picture books and cookies, I'd brought math homework. Might as well get ahead, then use the rest of the weekend to loaf and read and watch my favorite shows on TV.

We ducked beneath the vines and palm fronds and climbed the steps. Dad knocked, cleared his throat, straightened his tie, and picked lint off his jacket. After a moment, the tapping of high heels approached. Myra appeared, hazy as a ghost behind the gray mesh of the screen door.

"Oh! Come right in," she said, as if we were a big surprise. We stepped back as the screen door swung open. She wore a black silky scoopneck top and narrow black slacks so snug they were almost tights —

an outfit that would never make it past the deacons at Ordinary Springs First Baptist.

I stepped into the purple-and-white tiled foyer, then into the living room. Poor Violet Barrows! If she could see her house now, full of sharp-angled armless furniture, all geometry curves and planes, upholstered boomerangs perched on pale stick legs. The lavender walls had been repainted a cold, stark white and hung with pictures made of blotched colors and shapes. I wondered if Mrs. Fitzgerald had been a kindergarten teacher and liked to display her former students' work. Except these pictures weren't kindergarten material. The biggest featured bloodshot eyeballs staring out from trees, from under rocks, even beneath the skin of a lake, which a pop-eyed bunny was lifting like a bed sheet.

"Well, well. Look at this," said my father heartily. "Just see what you've done to the place. It's so —"

"Weird," I suggested. "It's really —"

"Modern," he corrected sharply, giving me a poke.

"I just love abstract, don't you?" Myra said. "But now I'm leaning toward Surrealist work. You know, Dali, Ray, the challenge to the viewer? The way they seem to ask a question you can't really answer, like with something straightforward, some plastic bowl of apples or a fat cow stuck in a field, and yet it's not really that at all. And the way they manipulate *space!*"

As I took in the blobs of paint, the detached body parts, the grimacing people with bureau drawers in their stomachs, answers for what these artists had had in mind were certainly not coming easy. I tried to catch my father's eye to exchange a conspiring look of disbelief.

But he was staring at Myra. Admiringly, I'd have to say. And nodding like one of those plastic birds that bob and drink out of a water glass. "I took a little art history once, in college," he said. "But I got to admit I don't know much about abstract or — what did you call it — surrealness?"

"Ah, but I have books!" She grabbed his hand, then glanced at me and dropped it. "Oh, here we are chattering on about art when the movie starts in a half-hour, and I need to introduce Dory to my . . . to Mr. Fitzgerald." She crooked a finger for me to follow her down the hall.

I'd never been back into the bedrooms, even when Mrs. Barrows still lived there and we had shared afternoon teas of molasses lace cookies and Earl Grey, heavy on the milk and sugar, in transparent china cups with painted violets. I reluctantly followed Myra's swaying hips down the narrow hallway, relieved to see a framed row of Mrs. Barrows's hand-tatted doilies still hung there. I felt a little better.

Myra glanced over her shoulder, tossing her ponytail. She wrinkled her nose. "I know, the dusty old doilies. That Victorian tripe. Just awful, aren't they? But don't worry, babe, I've got plans for this hallway, too." When she winked, it hardened my heart against her. Because I hadn't understood till that moment what a loss it all was: the brown-sugar lace of those warm chewy cookies, the powdery touch of Mrs. Barrows's thin, gnarled fingers, which had betrayed her in the end when they refused to bend and flash a needle quick enough to make the tiny, spidery knots she'd been so proud of.

It seemed like my own childhood being stripped and modernized, painted over as if it had never been.

"But I just love this here," I said real loud, because there was a lot more sense and feeling in Mrs. Barrows's tatting than in all those crazy paintings combined. But Myra didn't hear. She was already six steps ahead, opening the door at the end of the hall.

I hung back. Some girls my age were candy stripers, giving up Saturdays at the Memorial Hospital in Ocala for prestige, to do good works, and the uniforms looked swell. But the reality of sick bodies and germs and smells had never occurred to me before. Maybe I'd feel sick and disgusted and want to hold my nose.

I took a deep breath and stepped into the room. I'd been trained never to stare, but now I stopped short. This man was so clearly on his way out of this world and halfway into the next, I couldn't help but gape.

He lay uncovered, because it was a hot night, wearing a striped pajama top and shorts. The material billowed around his emaciated arms and legs like the robes of a Chinese emperor. Which was what he reminded me of — skin yellow as parchment, eyes narrowed against the glare of the overhead his wife had flipped with one manicured finger.

"Look," she said, in that same bright, white-lie tone she'd used on me. "See who's here? Dory Gamble from next door. She'll keep you company while I run a few errands."

Maybe I frowned, because she shot me a half-warning, half-pleading look. Perhaps she hadn't mentioned *A Summer Place*, or my father driving her around.

Frank — Mr. Fitzgerald — lifted one arm, slowly, slowly. An effort so clearly painful that, even if he might smell of old cobwebs and mold and dark caves, I wanted to rush over and gently do it for him. A tightness in my chest made me keep smiling though I wanted to look away. He finally got the arm all the way up to his face and used a trembling hand to shade his eyes. And when he opened them wider, they were the palest green. Beautiful, manly eyes; enough to inspire any amount of nursing dreams.

He smiled. "Ah. Miss Gamble's my baby-sitter this evening." He didn't sound bitter or mean. Though his voice was weak, it sounded amused — laughing not at me, or even at himself, but at fate and the way it played us all.

"Now, Frankie." Myra bent to tuck his sheet under the mattress a little tighter. "Don't give the poor girl a hard time." She ran a hand down his skinny calf. I looked away. Her tanned gardener's fingers stood out on his thin white leg. Her voice went lower and sounded teasing, maybe even affectionate. But I looked away mostly because of how his free hand groped to catch hers, though it was weak and slow, too late.

She straightened again. Showed me a water glass and pitcher and told me he'd already had some pills for pain. She held up an amber bottle. "These are the ones. But he won't need more tonight. And if you need any, you know, help — call this number."

I took the slip of paper with the words "Cross Ambulance" and "Dr. Whitman" scrawled above phone numbers.

"But of course you won't," she said, brisk and loud, to convince us all.

" 'Course not," he said raspily, then cleared his throat. "I plan to be a dead weight on society for a while yet."

The casual way he talked about dying, like it was a game. His grin should have been creepy, with those sharp skull-like cheekbones. Except there were laugh lines crinkled above them. I had to smile back.

"Off with you, then," he said to Myra, and we headed for the door. Behind us I heard a soft, heavy sound. A sigh.

When we got back to the living room, my father was standing in front of the eyeball painting, nose almost touching the canvas. When he saw us he stepped back and cleared his throat. "So. All set?"

Myra nodded and turned back to me.

"Now, you don't have to sit in his room, Dory. But he might like that for a little while. And he tires easily, so don't try to entertain him all night."

I said I'd brought homework. Then my father ushered her out ahead of him, like two parents leaving for a child-free night on the town.

I stood at the screen, one foot propped on the other, as they headed into the green tangle of yard. As they moved away, it made my father somehow appear small to me. Neither looked back as the swaying elephant ears and palm fronds swallowed them.

A dark, rustling jungle had eaten my father. Suddenly an ache arrowed in from nowhere, pierced and clenched my belly.

I'd never been a wimp, but this was different. It didn't spring from a cut or scrape or bruise. For the first time I'd been left out of the circle. Even though I couldn't conjure up her face, the black-and-white image from the scrap of burnt photo I still kept hidden in my room, suddenly I wanted my mother. Wherever she was, if she even existed in this world any more, I wanted her to come back and tell them both off.

I turned and stumbled inside to the

kidney-shaped, liver-colored couch, grabbed a pillow, and hugged it while tears rolled down my cheeks. "Stupid," I hissed. "Stupid, stupid, stupid."

A few minutes passed. Mr. Fitzgerald didn't call out or ring his bell. At first I was glad. Not afraid, exactly, of him or his disease, whatever it was. Not since I'd seen he was just a person, not a horror movie zombie. But his room felt dark and sad, even with the light on. And I didn't want to heap one pain on top of another.

I wiped my eyes on the scratchy pillow, got out my math book, and tried to work the problems due Monday. It wasn't easy. Puzzling over numbers and symbols, I gnawed the eraser until it dissolved into pink crumbs. I ran into the kitchen to spit them into the trash.

According to the kitchen clock, sixteen minutes had passed. I set down my book and paced the living room. Stared again with disbelief at each awful painting. Eyeballs tracked me whether I stood, sat, or ducked behind the dining table.

A cough echoed down the hall. I waited, holding my breath, but he didn't call out. No bell rang to break up the hollow ticking of the clock over the sink. I chewed a thumbnail, wondering if Frank Fitzgerald was choking to death while I stood dumb as a lawn ornament in his kitchen.

Silence.

I bolted down the hall and dashed in, slapping at the light switch. He squinted against the glare, just like before.

"You all right?" I gasped. Then my face burned. As if somebody in this condition could be okay, even on a good day.

He cocked his head, considering. "Been better," he admitted. "But so long ago I hardly recall how it felt."

I nodded, as if I knew what he meant. "Would you like me to, uh —" Aside from bringing water, and he had a near-full glass, what could I do?

"I'd like," he said, "for somebody to tell me what's happening outside. What it's like out there." He motioned toward the window, but his arm fell short, dropped.

I frowned. "In the yard?"

"No." He chuckled. "I mean the rest of the world. Well, the town at least. See, I've spent the last ten years or so in hospitals. Until Myra the city girl gets this wild idea we need to live in the country, where it's warm. That fresh *air* will do me some good." His laugh turned into a cough. " 'Well hell, why not,' I told her. 'The VA can't do anything else for me. One place's as good as another to die.' "

I opened my mouth to say, *Oh, but you'll be fine by and by*. But I couldn't make my jaws work those words. Because he wasn't going to be fine. Why say it? Why be a two-faced liar? So I closed my mouth and nodded.

"And how about you, Dory Gamble? Let's see — you must be sixteen."

I shook my head. "Not quite."

"Ah. Got a boyfriend? No, you wouldn't fall for that lovey-dovey crap. How about school? I bet you're whip-smart. Sitting in the catbird seat. That's what you say down here, right?"

I laughed. "Not hardly. I don't even understand half my math homework right now."

"Math?" His eyes lit up. Their pale green light looked too lively to be a part of his wasted face. "Go get it and we'll take a look."

"Here," I said, laying the dog-eared, graffiti-scrawled textbook carefully on the bed. "It's this page."

"Graphing functions, is it?" he muttered, sounding sympathetic but eager, as if he couldn't wait to see more of the stuff.

"Yeah." I shook my head.

"I see. Now, this problem — think about

it like this. In a mirror, the object you see is the reverse of the real object. So here, what's on one side of the graph line —"

"Is just flipped from what's on the other side?" I asked, suspicious he was kidding me. That didn't sound hard enough to be math.

"You got it." And he proceeded to show me where I went wrong with integers and prime numbers, though he said I would have to work the actual problems myself. Then he checked everything and set me to correcting my mistakes. But he did it all in such a way I didn't mind. In class, Mr. Grimes always jabbed one thick finger like Judgment at my mistakes and said, "It's elementary, my dear Dory. *Elementary.*" But he never made it clear exactly what was so simple.

Mr. Grimes always smelled of onions, chalk dust, and Vitalis, a combination which, right before lunch, ruined what little appetite I'd ever owned for the mushy squash, overcooked greens, and steam-wrinkled hot dogs in the school cafeteria. As I sat near Frank Fitzgerald, I noticed his smells, too: medicine, starched sheets, Lifebuoy soap, and clean sweat. A bag hanging from the bed post was slowly filling with a dark yellow fluid I gradually understood must be piss. Even that realization didn't faze me as, wizardlike, he made integers into sense for the first time in my life.

But in less than an hour his hand started to shake. He couldn't hold the pencil anymore. I lifted his glass so he could sip water, then turned out the light and went back to the living room. I toed off my shoes and watched *Wagon Train*. Then had some Oreos and a glass of milk at the kitchen table. I was dipping a cookie when the front door opened, and it slipped out of my hand. I quickly dumped it, rinsed the glass, and came back into the living room, where my father was helping Myra out of a rose-embroidered shawl. When he saw me, he took a step to the side, as if he hadn't just been laughing and sliding slinky fabric off her shoulders.

"Hello, Dory," they said together, like a weird stage act.

"Hi," I said. And even though I hadn't wanted to come to that house and at first couldn't wait for them to get back, I felt kind of disappointed.

"How'd it go?" Myra asked. "Is Frankie okay?" Then she bit her lip, like maybe I'd think she was accusing me of something. "I mean, I'm sure he's fine."

I shrugged. "Yeah." I didn't like the way she and Dad exchanged glances, like they were both my parents, like Myra also had some power over me. "I finished my homework."

"Great!" said my father, grinning like I'd just won a college scholarship. "Well, we better get going. School comes early tomorrow." As I followed him out, I glanced over my shoulder, figuring Myra would be hurrying off to check on "Frankie." But she was still standing in the middle of the living room, a goofy smile on her face. When she gave me a finger-wiggling wave, I closed the door harder than I needed to.

5

Those Sunday dates with Dad and Myra got to be a regular thing. Not that they called them that. It was all about taking poor Myra out for a break. So she could do errands, or maybe see a movie, but only because she so desperately needed to get out of the house.

One Monday morning a month later, I sat stirring my corn flakes, thinking how I didn't want to go to school, much less go to the store afterward and sweep, dust, and wait on women who needed mousetraps and flypaper or men with bathroom drain problems. Dad came to the table whistling, sat across from me, and poured Grape-Nuts in a bowl. He ate quickly, jaw creaking as he chewed.

"What?" I said, because he was staring so obviously, a hand propping his chin.

"I guess you miss having a mother."

Had it just occurred to him that I was the only motherless kid in Ordinary Springs? The question frightened me. This had always been forbidden territory. I wondered what would be a safe answer.

"Well, yeah. I guess," I mumbled. "But what good does that do? I mean, I barely remember her."

He looked surprised.

My mother was a shadow, a laughing face in an old photograph, as if disappearing had been a good joke on us. The only thing I had of her was a memory of a woman who came to my room once and rocked me to sleep, then left. I didn't want to share that, not even with him. That was the only thing that was mine alone. I closed my eyes and thought hard. And to my surprise, images began to come, slowly. The way a Polaroid developed in a darkroom, slowly, out of nothing, from a faint blur to a face you knew. Maybe even your own.

"Well . . . seems like her dresses were long and straight, not all poofed out and full like my friends' mothers'."

He laid his spoon aside and nodded, reluctantly.

"And her shoulders. Kind of broad, smooth and tan, soft and round? Peachy, with a little fuzz, when she wore sleeveless tops in summer." I smiled then, excited because a new thing had come to me. A vague recollection of being carried, of eyeing those delicious shoulders close up, of resting my cheek on them, once biting down and hearing a startled shriek, getting a laugh and half-hearted scolding.

Dad stared without saying anything. Then he began to cry. No big gulping sobs, just silent tears that suddenly spilled over his lids and rolled down his cheeks. I was scared, fascinated, horrified. I hadn't even known men *could* cry. I sat frozen, upraised spoon dripping milk *plink plink* into my corn flakes.

He jerked a paper napkin from the holder and blew his nose, then balled it up. "Well," he said, not looking me in the eye. "Yes, that's right." The tip of his nose was bright red.

I got up and went around to his side of the table, reached out, and tentatively hugged him. This time he let me. For once, didn't pull away.

"It's okay," I whispered into the part in his hair, as if I were the parent. "It's okay. Really."

He had slipped an arm around my waist, but now I felt him tense up again. "But it's not," he said. "A man can't be mother and father both. I should never have . . . I should've . . ."

"What?" I prompted, curious. Because hadn't he been both, after all? Taking care of me, feeding me, even inventing a toddler jumper he'd hung from a beam in the store so he could keep me close and safe while he waited on customers. But the big spring he'd pried from a skeet trap gave me a frightening, exhilarating trajectory. So then it was back to the soft cotton rope around my waist. He'd sold tools and nails and siding and watched me all day. Made my meals and changed my diapers and taken my temperature when I was sick. He'd never been cuddly or what you'd call tender. No hugs or kisses or baby talk. But still.

"Nothing," he muttered. "I can't — you don't understand." He gave me a pat on the back. "Better get a move on, or you'll miss first bell."

I trudged down the street with an armload of books, wondering all the way what he'd meant. Then I was in homeroom being counted among the living, then in math class, taking the test. No time to ponder that morning's conversation. I went on to English and gym and forgot about it. I'd developed a whopper of a headache; tests always did that to me. Even with a subject I was good at, my neck and shoulders seized up. I gripped my pencil with white-tipped fingers that went numb as I tried to write.

In the warm, thick sweat-and-deodorant mist of the girls' locker room my head pounded worse. The funky canvas and rubber stink of old Keds, with the sweet overlay of Final Net and Tussy and Faberge made me gag.

But this was the day for drama class try-outs, for the fall play, *Our Town*. I wished it was something more exciting and foreign; the first act seemed like a recap of life in Ordinary Springs, and where was the drama in that? Why couldn't it be *Macbeth*, or even *Ten Little Indians* — something with murder and lust and revenge in it?

Still, no way would I pass up a chance to get onstage. I'd been practicing in my room, even, and then the past two Sundays with Frank Fitzgerald. He'd read the other parts so I could concentrate on perfecting my lines.

I must have looked as bad as I felt. Coach Floyd, a hard-assed whistle-blower, scowled at me. "Gamble, your face looks like a boiled egg. Which is it, cramps or cafeteria food?"

"A headache," I croaked, not even milking it. Weird glowy lines haloed her head, I couldn't focus on any one feature of her face. Whenever I tried, that part seemed fuzzy, like somebody had rubbed out her nose or eyebrow with an art gum eraser.

She sent me to lie down in the nurse's office. But at twelve-thirty, when the nurse left for lunch, I got up and dragged myself to the auditorium.

"Goodness, Dory. You didn't have to put on makeup for tryouts," said Mrs. Hawks, who taught English and drama both. "The cemetery scene isn't until Act III."

It hurt too much too explain. "Can I go first?" I whispered, wondering if I could keep from throwing up long enough to say my lines.

"Why sure, honey. Be my guest."

I climbed the steps, stopped in the middle, and turned to face the rows of empty seats. All I could see was the glare of the footlights and the dust motes floating over them, like millions of tiny planets. I shut my eyes, and through closed lids the light filtered a dull red. The color of blood, ugh . . . yeah, it should've been *Macbeth*. I opened my eyes again and nodded to show I was ready. Then took a deep breath, raised my clasped hands before me, and told myself: *Now I am Emily.*

Randy Ficquet stood across from me, playing the stage manager. He didn't look happy about it. I wondered why he was even there; he hated English. Probably all the girls trying out, that'd be a big draw. I wished he was Pearce, except he would've made me laugh when I was supposed to be serious.

I concentrated mainly on not getting sick, and actually groaned that last part of Emily's speech: "Do any human beings ever realize life while they live it? — every, every minute?"

I flung one hand away from me in despair and clapped the other over my mouth. I wasn't acting. *Don't be a wuss,* I told myself. Frank Fitzgerald probably would be thrilled to only have to deal with a headache and a basketball jock missing his cues across the stage.

And then . . . everything swayed and dimmed to black, like the end of the movie in a darkened theater.

I woke up back on the cot in the nurse's office. "You fainted, honey," said Mrs. Taylor, the school nurse. She was peeling a cool, wet cloth from my head. "Got a little carried away, it seems."

"Yeah," I said. "I should've saved it for *Macbeth.*"

She laughed like I was delirious. "Mrs. Hawks says she's gonna make you Mrs. Gibb. Now isn't that nice?"

I sat up and saw a burst of stars on black. "But who got Emily?"

She didn't need to tell me. I'd already seen Marylee Tyson smirk and giggle her way through the part in class, smoothing her blonde, flipped hair as she read too fast. Dr. Tyson, her father, donated the money to print the programs and always presented a dozen roses to the lead after the play. Often it was Marylee.

At least my head felt better. But when Mrs. Taylor said she was sending me home, I didn't argue. Who wouldn't want to find herself headed out at one-thirty on a school Monday? All that was left was a dull, vague ache at the top of my skull, a pillbox hat of pain. I left the school grounds, crossed Water Street, and headed down our road. But at our walkway, I stopped. I thought I'd done real well on a math test. And I had gotten a part! But I needed to tell *somebody*.

Maybe that was what Dad had meant. No one home to hear about my day, my social problems, my little victories over public education. Of course I could turn around and head into town, to the store. But if I was well enough to walk around gloating, he'd send me right back to school. Instead I could eat ice cream, watch TV, lie on the bed, read the dog-eared good parts in a James Bond paperback. And for instant praise I could do an end-run around Myra and high-five Frank over our math and drama triumphs. After all, he'd helped.

So I didn't go home. I headed through the yard next door.

Myra — as I could think of her in my head, though no one my age dared call an adult by her Christian name — wasn't in the yard. I knocked; no answer. Went to the front door to call out — everybody around here did that — but the latch was on. No one from Ordinary Springs bothered to lock up. I went around back, and the yard was empty. But a faint ringing, thin and hopeless, was sounding as I rounded the corner of the house. I walked over to where Frank's window overlooked the bird bath and feeder and the bacon-and-eggs lantana his wife had planted around them. I'd tap on the glass to let him know I was there.

The Venetian blinds were up, and the bed was empty. It sent a shiver though me, that empty stretch of white cotton, like a blank poster for death. The ringing came again. I cupped my hands to look through the glass and saw a bare, thin leg lying against mottled terrazzo. I stepped back as if someone had slapped me. Then looked again.

Yes, there was the top of his head. I saw him slowly raise his arm and shake the brass bell.

"Oh my God," I gasped, rapping on the glass. "I'm getting help!" then added, stupidly, "Don't move." I yelled it, but who knew if he heard.

I darted around the corner to the side where the kitchen door, the only other entrance, was also locked. Where in the world was Mrs. Fitzgerald? The green car was under the carport. I ran back to the front door and tried it again. Still locked. Wringing my hands, I hovered on the front stoop, then dashed back across the yard, slapping and tearing at vines that slashed my face. Clawing branches of azaleas and holly and photinia dragged on me like witches' nails. I arrived on my own porch, panting, and wrenched the front door open. And there, right on the living room couch, sat my father and Mrs. Fitzgerald. I opened my mouth to scream at them *Hurry over next door,* before it dawned they had their arms around each other.

Breathless, I bent from the waist and gasped, sucked air in hard. Then looked up again, sure I'd been wrong. By then Dad was standing, but his shirt was unbuttoned. His brown leather belt dangled from the pant loops like a dead snake. And there, to my left, a flash of black cloth and tanned flesh — Mrs. Fitzgerald's back disappearing down the hall, a streamer of dark hair, the tail of her untucked white blouse trailing surrender.

"Dory, you ought to knock . . ." Dad began, his face red.

"At my own house?" I said incredulously. "And, and while you were — whatever you were doing — Frank, I mean Mr. Fitzgerald, oh, he's dying!"

My father's mouth dropped. He bolted past me. I started to follow, then, in a burst of rage at them both, ran down the hall, banging on the walls as I went, shouting "Your husband's on the floor. He might be dying. In case you care!" Righteous anger propelled me. I felt justified in being mean, ugly, spiteful. Exhilarated by it. Invincible.

When I reached the bathroom at the end of the hall, the door was open, the room empty. No one in my room, or my father's, or the den, or the spare room we used to store old furniture and a dusty Singer I never used.

But the French door that opened off my

father's room onto a little patio wasn't latched. I slammed it so hard the glass shivered. Dropped onto Dad's bed, then jumped up again. Had they done the same stuff in here? Undressed, touched each other? Or maybe even —

I backed away, staring at the bed that, though made up with a spotless candlewick spread, looked somehow rumpled and soiled. Though everything was neatly tucked, even under the pillows, and I'd changed the sheets myself the day before.

I didn't go next door to see how Frank was, afraid to know the worst. When I heard the siren wail up the street I went to stand behind the screen, peering out. Two white-coated guys jumped out and raced into the house. When a couple minutes later they wheeled a stretcher out, it seemed like a film of that first day, run in reverse. They bumped it over the sidewalk fast and jerky. I raised a hand, wanting to tell them to stop, to slow down. Not to kill him.

They wouldn't have heard. The ambulance attendants shoved him into the back, slammed the double doors, and took off, siren wailing again.

I dropped into an armchair. After a while I snapped on the TV but couldn't make any sense of the sounds. I wandered into the kitchen and got an apple, then came back out and sat again, holding it.

At last I raised it to my mouth, but stopped mid-bite. My books were still dumped under the Fitzgeralds' window, where I'd let them tumble when I saw him lying there like a broken toy. But I didn't get up and get them.

The room gradually darkened. When I heard the screen thump shut, the slow heavy tread of footsteps; when without glancing up I saw my father's khaki pant-legs stop before me, I looked down, stubbornly staring at my lap.

"Dory," he said finally, his voice cracking like a high school boy's, like Pearce's still did sometimes when he tried to make me believe an outrageous fib.

"Don't talk to me." The acid in those words shriveled even my heart. Who would have known such an ugly voice lived inside me until that moment. "And don't," I said, as he reached out, "touch me. Not with those hands."

I could have been his wronged wife, except I wasn't. But I brushed away the illogic. They disgusted me, the both of them.

I jumped up and pushed past. Slammed

the door to my room and then slammed the barrel bolt into the cradle after two tries and a splintered fingernail. I'd never before used that stiff old lock; the need to shut out my father had never occurred to me. Then I sat on the bed, facing the closed door like a death row prisoner waiting for the last walk.

I woke sprawled on the bedspread, squinting against the glare of the ceiling light, a God-awful taste in my mouth. The orange-pink glow of the rising sun streamed through my window. Everything rushed back like a bad movie. I sat and clutched my head, even though the pain was gone. I wished it back; an excuse to stay in my room, to stay away from school. But humming and leg-crossing couldn't make a full bladder go away. I had to hurry to the bathroom, hoping not to meet my father in the hall. Wondering why *I* should feel guilty.

I pondered the injustice with a wad of toilet paper clutched in my hand. She was married; her sick husband was right next door. And my father . . . my face heated up. My father was mine, I'd almost said out loud.

No. No, I shoved the blame back at

Myra. There she'd been in my house, almost naked, doing the things scratched on doors in the girls' restroom, whispered on the bus from one smirking set of teenage lips to another. Sticky, gross sex stuff. All the while her husband was lying on the floor, maybe dying.

Oh, God. Could he have died? I wiped myself and rushed out to the kitchen. My father was reading at the table. I swallowed, then dragged out a chair.

"Morning," I said, settling stiffly on the seat.

He barely glanced up from the newspaper. "Uh-huh."

"What happened last night?"

He raised his head again, his face blank as when he inventoried shingles. But a flush crept up his cheeks.

I said, quick, "I mean, is Mr. Fitzgerald okay?"

"Well, he's gone and broken his arm," he said, as if the poor man had been out climbing trees against everyone's advice. "He was trying to get up, to . . . Dory," Dad said suddenly. "I know what this must look like to you, but have some charity. You don't understand. That poor woman has done nothing but take care of the man for years — *years* — and sometimes people

. . . I mean adults, well, everyone has weaknesses. We all make mistakes," he finished lamely.

A shrug was all I could make myself give back. I ate, brushed my teeth, got dressed, and quickly gathered my dew-soggy books from the Fitzgeralds' backyard. On the front walk I turned my head to miss my father's wave. Even if Myra had been out, even if she'd spoken, fifteen years of strict social training could not have forced me to acknowledge her.

I didn't forgive them, or plan on forgetting.

6

I was sure Myra and my father must be all over each other, all the time. And maybe it wasn't just in my mind. I began to overhear comments in town, to see knowing glances between customers in the store when the Fitzgerald name came up. If the whole town was talking, then only divine intervention was left. Sundays during Altar Call I waited, watching Dad slantways, willing him to rise and go up the aisle, to kneel before the congregation. To admit how far he'd backslid toward damnation. To rededicate his life to Jesus. But he sat upright in the pew, fanning himself with the bulletin, looking as innocent as a baby in a manger. I could fold my arms and scowl all I wanted while the choir sang hopefully, over and over, "Just as I Am." None of that seemed to matter to Owen Gamble.

I shuddered to think what perverted things he and Myra were getting up to while I was in classes or rehearsing after school. I made sure not to miss any practices, though. I wouldn't give up my hard-won part or disappoint Mrs. Hawks. I'd never have admitted it, but I enjoyed it when she made us memorize Shakespeare in English class. Even the sonnets.

And yet. "Mine eyes have drawn thy shape, and thine for me," I recited for the required memorization test, standing next to Mrs. Hawks's desk, head bowed like a nun. "Are windows to my breast . . . where through the sun, uh, delights to peep —" But I had to stop. I was practically gagging. Naked shapes, breasts, window-peeping. Too close to home.

"Start over, Dory," Mrs. Hawks said. She looked a little annoyed when it happened again. "Really, dear. The human form is a natural thing."

How wrong she was, when admiring it even from across a yard could lead to all sorts of horrible perversions. Like having to live with people who smiled in your face and betrayed you at every turn. Like a hurt in the heart so huge it could take a nice man who had already suffered too much and break him in two. And if Mrs. Hawks thought either of the villains might be blushing . . . it surprised me someone so hot on Shakespeare didn't seem to grasp what treachery human beings were capable of.

But soon the whole town would know. You simply could not keep a secret for long in a place like Ordinary Springs.

After school I went to the store. Swept and stocked sullenly, silently, ignoring anyone who spoke. Customers began to give me a wide berth, detouring through the paint section to get to the counter. I didn't care. Myra might come in one day. I'd be there, and do my best to push her into the nail barrel.

In my mind I disposed of her in various ways — dismemberment by the band saw out back, slicing her into a black-haired 2×4. Sticking her head in a can of Williamsburg Blue paint until her face turned the same shade. Pulling her bright red nails out one by one with a pair of size 20 pliers. Shocking how violent my fantasies got. They didn't fix anything, but were free and private, satisfying in a small way.

We went on working and studying and eating, but I didn't have much to say to my father. I kept away from the house next door. Fall became winter, which turned for a few days to spring before settling into the heat of summer, the main season in Florida. All others were so brief you could miss them if you stayed inside a whole day; then it was high June for ten months.

On a Saturday in May, as I was on a stepladder dusting the bird houses and feeders in the front display, Pearce slipped up behind me. I'd heard him coming and expected the usual poke in the ribs. But this time he grabbed my waist. They must have heard my shriek across the street, under the driers at the Cut 'n Curl.

I grabbed for him, but he ducked and laughed, holding his ears like my scream had deafened him.

"That was so funny." I went back to rubbing the cheerfully painted bird houses.

When he didn't say anything else, I glanced over my shoulder. He had a strange look on his face, eyes hesitant, lips pressed in a line, as if faced with a puzzle, or a test.

"Look, uh, Dory," he said, fiddling with some chisels. "Look. I guess the carnival will be coming to town. Next week."

"Yeah, so," I muttered. Every year, like clockwork, the motley assortment of carnival trucks came chugging up the road, flatbed trucks with cages of animals and disassembled rides and game booths. I had stopped getting excited about this. Season after season I'd seen the shows, ridden ancient Max the Elephant, played the ring-toss game and had a squint-eyed carny guess my weight. I had already eaten enough popcorn and cotton candy in this life to choke a giraffe. True, I was less familiar with the carnival's more sophisticated entertainments, the ones not meant for kids: the freaks and betting games and the cootchie shows. It was my misfortune just then to be awkwardly in between ages.

"Thought you might wanna go next Thursday night," he muttered, the words all run together.

I watched my hand stop polishing the copper roof of a purple martin house. "Do what?" But I'd heard plain enough.

He seemed to pick up courage. "Come with me. Next week. To the carnival."

I jumped down from the stepladder and clapped a hand over his mouth. Too bad it was the one holding the dust rag. He choked, then bent over sneezing, while I waited for his fit to end. "Not so loud," I said, whacking him on the back.

"What's the *matter* with you?" he gasped, wiping his eyes. "Damn."

I loved this cursing, and always had, though he usually confined it to the outdoors. I doubted a single cuss word had ever been uttered inside the store till then. One small thrilling revenge against my father. "You know good and well I'm not allowed to date till I'm sixteen," I whispered. Not that it had been an issue ever before.

"Huh. That's right." He frowned at the floor, as if the house rules were scribbled in chalk on the planks. "But you have a window in your room. Right?"

"Who doesn't?"

"You can sneak out."

I hesitated. "Oh. Sure." I'd never sneaked out of anywhere, much less to go to something as racy as a midway with a freak show, a shooting gallery, and a hall of mirrors. Not to mention the spook house, where you could scream and grab at the person next to you and pretend to be someone else in the dark. My stomach tightened the way it had when he'd jerked my shirt up in the back of the store. I wished he'd do it again, but there was my two-faced father, talking to a woman at the counter.

Well, why not, whispered a voice in my head.

"Why not," I announced obediently.

"Okay then." Pearce rubbed my head in short, hard strokes against the grain, the same way he'd annoy a cat. "Meet you at the front entrance at ten Thursday night. Unless that's past your bedtime."

Actually that was my bedtime, on school

nights anyway. "Oh, ha ha," I said. Did he think I was a fool just because I was a year younger? Sure, meet him out front, then maybe his girlfriend could use her cheer-leading muscles to tear every hair from my head.

"What about Marylee?" I flicked a speck of fly crap off the corner of a feeder. "She going, too?"

Pearce's face screwed up, and for an awful moment I thought he was going to cry the way my father had at breakfast. But then I saw he was laughing. "That cheer-leading dope? We only went out once, after a game. Then she latched on to Rusty."

Rusty Breedlove was tall and dark-haired, with bleached surfer bangs down to his nose. When he tossed his head so he could see, the hallway echoed with the sighs of sophomore girls. I thought he looked like a skunk's ass.

"All right. Maybe," I said finally to get Pearce to be quiet. He might as well ask me to hop on so he could carry me piggy-back to the state capitol. I couldn't feature slipping through the hot, frog-singing night to meet up with anybody. I had other plans, big ones, and they didn't include staying in this town with some local guy.

And yet, the idea of being linked with a

boy, the prestige that bought at school, the coolness of having an admirer a grade ahead, made me smile and smooth down my hair the way girls did when they leaned on their lockers between classes. Ugh, sickening. But I did it all the same, like I'd been conditioned in a laboratory.

And after that, what? Hands under my shirt might be only the beginning. I shivered again. Not fear, it felt better than that. I didn't think I wanted to go. And yet —

"Cool," he said, giving me a thumbs-up. "How late would be safe?"

I hesitated. "Ten o'clock is okay." By then Dad should be snoring.

Pearce ambled off, back to whatever chore my father had given him.

If I did go out with him it would be my first date. Not that I was going to keep it. Still, I couldn't help taking this milestone out and turning it over in my mind, admiring it like new jewelry.

For dinner that night I heated up leftover tuna casserole, tossed some iceberg lettuce with a sliced tomato from the wilting row planted against the house, and got out a bowl of Jell-O fruit salad. My father and I ate in silence, only speaking up for salt or mayonnaise dressing. After dinner I put away the food and washed dishes. He watched Walter Cronkite. I did algebra until I came to a problem that made no sense at all: geometric graphs. I had no recollection of going over such a thing in class.

Frank Fitzgerald was home from the hospital, but I hadn't been over to see him in a while. I threw down my pencil. "I've got to run next door," I said to Dad. "I don't get this problem, and they're due tomorrow."

He nodded without looking up, as if he didn't know who lived there. But what was running through his mind had to be the same things running through mine. Myra might not want to see me; Frank might not be well enough. But I walked out with the textbook under my arm, pushed through the jungle, and knocked on their front door.

When Myra came to answer it, she looked me up and down, very cool. You'd never know I'd got such a good look at her underwear. I asked through stiff lips to see her husband, focusing on her left shoulder.

"Sorry, babe. Frankie's tired," she said, crossing her arms and leaning on the door jamb. "He hasn't had a good day. Otherwise I'd let you go back. But it's nice you stopped by."

"Oh. Okay then." I couldn't think of a

reason to insist. But as I turned to go, she grabbed my arm and drew me inside, her nails biting like fish hooks into the soft skin of my upper arm. How could my father stand to let her run those claws along his face, his neck, his . . . ugh. I clamped down on any further thoughts in that direction.

"What do you want?" I said, pulling my arm free.

"Sit down." It sounded like an order, which made me want to stick out my tongue and run away. But since she wanted to talk woman to woman, I'd try to hold my own.

"Now listen to me," she said, with a cold stare. "I know you're giving your father a hard time about our friendship."

Friendship? My nostrils flared but I gritted my teeth and stayed quiet. Politely puzzled, that was me. I didn't intend to buckle under questioning.

She lit a cigarette and exhaled, waving the smoke away. Then she barked a short, ugly laugh. "Oh, you're good, honey," she said. "Real good." She leaned forward and poked a finger in the middle of my chest. "But you're not fooling me."

"Fine," I said, rising from my seat. "I don't get this, anyhow."

Myra picked a shred of tobacco off the tip of her tongue, which was small, pink, pointed like a cat's. "Oh, I think you do. I can tell a troublemaker when I see one. I used to be in store security."

That stopped me. "I thought you were an artist."

"That, too," she said, laughing a little. Then she was serious again, her tone sweet. She wanted me to like her. "Look. I don't want to hurt you or your father, sweetie. And of course I don't want to hurt Frankie. I just need to live a little, you understand? Otherwise I might as well be . . . come on, I'm not asking for much, a little of Owen's time, some harmless fun. But you've got your father all upset. Look how he's raised you, taken care of you since you were a baby. Would it hurt to share?"

I thought it would.

She looked at me expectantly with a crooked little smile. A few months earlier it might've charmed me, like we were being girlfriends. I didn't say anything.

She frowned and tried another tack. "I hear you're in all the advanced classes."

"Yeah, right. Precocious." I made it sound like a disease.

"Only you don't apply yourself like you should."

I folded my arms and looked at the ceiling.

Her gaze skittered away like a chameleon. "So maybe we can help each other out," she whispered.

"I have to go." I got up and walked out the door. I didn't know the word for it then, but it felt like she was asking me to be some kind of pimp, a direct line to my father.

I stamped home through the bushes and flowerbeds, crushing and breaking things.

I lay on the bed, still in shorts and a shirt. The clock dragged its hands through molasses. My Keds lay on the floor, soles still dribbling dirt from Myra's flowerbeds. I was tired, but not sleepy. I read for a while, then threw down the book and rubbed my face. I felt hungry and rolled over to look at the clock. Ten-fifteen. How could I be starving? I'd had two helpings of macaroni at dinner. I got up and went down the hall to grab a glass of milk and some cookies.

As I passed my father's room, I saw his bed was empty, still made. He was an early riser, usually up by five, so normally by this time he'd be asleep. Maybe he was getting ice water; no television sounds from the living room.

But the kitchen was empty, too. The sink

light illuminated a lone palmetto bug that leapt down the drain at my approach. I poured milk and found the vanilla wafers.

Where was he?

I set down my glass, closed the box, and got up. The moon was nearly full, making it easy to see my way next door. I didn't stop to wonder why, or what I was doing looking in all the Fitzgeralds' windows like a Peeping Tom. I stopped at the one I figured must be the bedroom Myra slept in. The Venetian blinds were drawn, and I couldn't see inside. But the noises I heard — low voices, then a noise like a fist thumping the wall. I wanted to pretend I didn't know what was going on and just leave. But I stood there with a hand over my mouth, listening.

Could they do such things in his house, right under his nose?

Moving slow as a dream, as if there'd be no consequences, I sneaked around to the front and tried the handle. Someone had been careless. I pushed the door open slowly, slipped past the ugly pictures, the floor lamp with cone-shaped shades, the curved Danish modern couch. In the hall my damp dirty feet made faint sucking noises against the terrazzo. At least the Fitzgeralds didn't have a dog. A panting, whining dog breathing down my neck would have made it too real to bear.

I wondered what I was going to do — throw open the door and point at them with God's own finger? Throw a hissy fit? At the first room, the sounds of two people so lost in using each other they didn't even know they were being spied on came through the hollow-core. I stood listening to the pants and moans until my ears shriveled and curled and drew back inside my head. Until my heart hardened into splintered wood, until everything good my father had ever done for me crumbled into a heap of mold and dung and dust and I could hate him freely, without guilt.

I would never, ever be like them.

Could Frank hear the sound of his life being squashed between the two of them? That pleading, adoring look I'd seen him give his wife the first day we met burned me now. I tiptoed down the hall, to the room that waited like a gas chamber at the end. The light was off, but in the dark I could hear him, breath hitching as if he couldn't quite catch it, then couldn't bear to let it go. Was Dory Gamble stealthy, smart, and good enough at fooling people that he'd never realize she'd come to his room late at night, to stand outside and pity him?

The breathing stopped.

Oh dear Lord, he's dead. I took a quick step back and bumped one of Mrs. Barrows's framed tatting pieces, which pendulumed on the wall. Then took a step into the room, and another. He levered himself up to get a look at who was standing at the foot of his bed. I had forgotten he'd been lying there a long time, eyes long since adjusted to the dark. And the hall light was behind me.

"Dory," he said calmly, as if he'd invited me to turn up around this time. But he was breathing like a man running from something he didn't want to glimpse over his shoulder anymore.

"Hi," I said, looking at the floor, the walls. "I, uh, I just —"

"Never mind. It doesn't matter." He laughed a little. "I think when you get really sick, people assume none of your parts work anymore. Even your ears and eyes."

"I guess." I couldn't look him in the face.

"Do me a favor?" he said suddenly. He reached out but winced and let his arm fall back again. "I can't quite . . ."

"Oh sure, what, anything," I babbled. A glass of water, a book, a tissue? Something in my power to fix, fluff, deliver; how wonderful.

"My pills," he said. "They're over there."

He pointed to the dresser. "I can't pry the cap off myself."

"Oh. Sure. Water, too?"

He nodded. First I poured half a glass from the plastic pitcher on the bedside table. Then I thumbed the cap from the brown bottle. It popped off easily, doing its damnedest to be helpful. I tried to make it look harder, though, because it seemed insensitive to let Frank see he couldn't handle a task a five-year-old could do with ease. "Oof," I said. "Ah, there we go."

I dropped one tiny white pill in his upturned palm. Now that my eyes had adjusted, too, I saw he was watching with an amused look. Amused, but sad.

"Usually I get two," he whispered. "But tonight, I need an extra one. For the pain." He glanced down at his arm, the one still trapped in a white plaster cast, shrugging as if it wasn't a big deal.

The arm, right. That must hurt, too. All he needed on top of the rest. I dropped a second pill beside the first.

When he looked up again, he smiled. But his eyes said something else.

"Oh! Oh, right." I nodded, watching my hand move in dreamlike slow motion. Too dark to read the typewriting on the label, anyhow. "That'd be three." I shook another tablet into my hand, then carefully slid it between his lips. They were dry, warm, a little chapped. "There," I said.

He swallowed that one, too, then closed his eyes. When he opened them again, he was smiling at me. "Thanks, Dory. I'm sorry I have to . . ." But he trailed off, didn't finish.

I stood, hands hanging at my sides. Didn't he wonder what I was doing in the house? I guess we both knew. At that moment, I felt like we understood everything. More than both of us had ever wanted to know.

He reached over, took my hand, and held it. Not tight; I don't guess he could've done that even if he'd wanted to. It hurt me. My whole hand burned.

"She appeared like an angel in the sick man's room," he said, as if quoting somebody in a movie or an old book.

" 'Palm to palm is holy palmer's kiss,' " I blurted out, as if Mrs. Hawks had poked me with a ruler. Heat spread up my face and down to my bare grimy feet.

Frank stared at me for a long time. I looked away first. "That's right," he said at last. "That's right, Dory. But the thing is, I'm tired now. You can leave in a minute, it's okay. Just . . . just one more pill."

I opened my mouth to say maybe that wasn't a good idea.

But he went on. "That way if the pain gets to be too much, I'll be ready."

I shivered with the prickliness of things being not right. Time for me to go, how stupid, how embarrassing creeping around his house like a thief. While my father, his wife . . . the whole shitty mess laid out before us like a bad play.

He sighed and patted my hand. "Or, if you could just go get Myra." His fingers twitched toward the fat little bell, which squatted like a brass toad next to the water glass.

"No," I said, too loud. Anything but that. "I mean, it's okay. Here." I shook another pill from the bottle and set it next to the bell. "See? Right there if you need it."

"I need it now," he said harshly. Then he sank back against the pillows.

I swallowed hard.

And see, here's the thing. At this point, I could have left. Because the pain wasn't my problem, at least not in the way it was his, or even Myra's. But I didn't leave. I sat down on the edge of the bed and when, in a little while, he asked for another pill, and then another, I gave them to him. I didn't have to do it. I know that now. And I guess

I knew it then, too. But it seemed to be the right thing at the time. The one comfort I could offer. A gift to make him stop hurting. As he lay back and his eyes lost their focus, I began to hum a song my father used to sing when he put me to bed, back when I was little. I didn't know the words, or the name of it.

" 'Parting is such sweet sorrow,' " he whispered in the dark after the fifth or sixth tablet. Then he squeezed my fingers hard, startling me into silence again. I'd thought somehow he was already asleep. But after that he mostly lay quiet, still breathing, but so soft I had to lean forward to be sure.

I gave him pill after pill, as a loud cry came from down the hall, then another. Hard to tell, through walls and doors, if the sounds meant pleasure or pain. At least they were coming farther apart and getting fainter. I sighed aloud without thinking. Then, unbelievably, it started up again. Frank's fingers twitched, pressed mine. I flinched and shook the bottle. Held the water glass and helped him raise his head. He swallowed slowly, choking a little as it went down.

The last one.

"No," I whispered. Stared down at the

bottle, shook it as if it was trying to deceive me. How could the thing be empty?

I stood abruptly and unlaced my fingers from his. Laid his hand across his chest, then tiptoed back, past Myra's bedroom, past my traitorous father who lay in there. Past the awful art and mean modern furniture, out the door, across the wet spongy ground and night-blooming plants, back to my own front porch. All I had to do was turn the knob, step inside, wash the dirt off my feet, and climb in bed. But these familiar chores seemed to take forever, and I was crying the whole damn time.

7

At dawn an ambulance sat in front of the Fitzgerald house. But that was no surprise. Last night the man who lived there had been alone, sick enough of pain and living to let — no, to *persuade* a fifteen-year-old girl to help him stop it all. Of course the girl wasn't blameless; I knew what I'd done. But when I'd been sitting there in the dark, it'd felt more like the right thing to hand over those clean, white pills, one by one, than it had to think of reasons why I couldn't, shouldn't, wouldn't do it.

No flashing lights, no siren. That told me all I needed to know as I watched with a hand on the pane, my breath fogging the glass. I stepped out onto the porch as the boxy white van started up and rolled down the street. The screen banged shut behind me.

My father, no doubt groggy from a sleepless night spent in his neighbor's bed, came stumbling out then. "I heard — Dory, what's wrong?"

"Like you don't know." All their fault,

his and that woman's. I ran down the steps, landing hard, letting the blows to my bare feet punish me. One, two, three. Counting again a trickle of little white tablets, their numbers ringing like a jump-rope song in my head. I tossed my hair, shook my head, shook it away. I wasn't to blame. They were.

"Dory, wait. I need to talk to you," my father called. But I ran away, toward the Springs, as if I hadn't heard, then turned and crashed into the pine woods. He didn't call me again or come looking. I heard the screen door close with a thump, like the lid of a casket.

After school the next day I ducked out of the alley and came up the sidewalk to the store. Pearce was sweeping, which was my job. But it didn't matter. He was welcome to the broom, the dirt, the concrete, the whole damn store.

He pointed the handle at me. "Pop that screen outta your window yet?"

I didn't understand at first. Then remembered our so-called date. "No, I couldn't budge it," I said. "Old screens, rusty frames. Maybe I can't make it."

He raised an eyebrow, knowing me too well. I turned away to go inside.

"Hey. I heard about your neighbor. Think the old lady killed him?"

I stopped and stared. He didn't know anything about anything. Why couldn't he stay where he belonged, in the old world of treehouses and games and jokes? Instead of trying to change a perfectly good friendship into something else, something that might turn as ugly as what was going on at my house.

Pearce shook his head. "Man, do you ever get out? That sick guy, what's-his-name next door to you. He died last night. Shoot, Dory, if my neighbor croaked off, I'd know about it."

My stomach did a flip-flop, a carnival-ride loop. "Oh yeah," I said. "How'd you hear about it?"

"My cousin — the one drives the ambulance for the county hospital. He said there was an empty bottle right on the bed. He thinks the wife got tired of changing diapers and fed the guy too many sleeping pills." Pearce spun the broom like he was dancing with it.

I clenched my fists. "But I —" That was when, all in a rush, I understood what I'd done. What I'd been. Not an angel of mercy, delivering a man from pain, but a murderer who might as well have taken a hammer from the store and hit him over the head. No one would ever understand why it'd seemed right to hand over those perfect white bits of forgetfulness, one by one. In daylight, on a sidewalk in town, there was no way to explain.

It was me who handed him the pills. I did it. I actually opened my mouth to confess to Pearce, used to telling him whatever came into my head. In the future I'd have to be more careful.

Now Frank Fitzgerald was entertainment, the latest gossip. I couldn't pretend it was a bad dream out here in the hot sun, watching the sweat bead on Pearce's forehead while he spun a witch's broom in his hands. No one would believe what I'd done was noble or innocent. That it wasn't really me who killed Frank Fitzgerald, but the hurt of knowing his wife would do anything, leave him alone to fall and break bones, just so she could have the man next door.

He'd looked silent and brave in the dark, dying of a broken heart, its sharp edges grating against his ribs.

"I, uh, guess I knew about it," I stammered to Pearce. "I just forgot."

Come on, Dory. No one died of a broken heart except in country western songs. I'd

122

put those last white tablets in his mouth myself. Not Myra, not my father. But had it been kindness, or had it just been easier to kill Frank Fitzgerald than look at his reddened eyes anymore, at his unanswerable plea for help?

I pressed my hands over my mouth, cold despite the sun on my head, my back, my sweating face.

"Hey, you okay? Look like you're gonna puke."

I pushed past, through the doors into the dim interior. Cool as a tomb must feel. Dust motes drifted in the bay display windows. The faint tang of machine oil in the air, the damp earthy smell of hardwood mulch. Usually I liked to get inside when the sun had beat down all the way from school, ironing my cotton blouse to my back. Today I shivered.

My father was deep in conversation with an old couple about leaky copper pipes. He didn't look up or issue any chores when I dragged past.

I stumbled around in a pretense at working, knocking rolls of toilet paper off the shelf when I restocked the bathroom, scrubbing out the rust-stained sink until my hands were raw, opening boxes of shiny outdoor faucets and white rubber sink stoppers. I dropped, knocked down, or tripped over paint stirrers and rakes and mailbox posts until my father came around the counter. "Dory, what on earth?"

I looked up from where I had squatted to scoop up handfuls of metal washers. They glinted dully, like all-seeing eyes, not-so-magical coins in a dim cave. I clawed at the rolling discs, forcing splinters and grit under my nails, pushing the washers one by one back into their stupidly tiny box.

"Fine. I'm fine," I muttered. The need to tell someone nearly made me scream. But nothing I could say would make anything right again. The world I'd taken for granted was gone. "I just, you know, I'm upset about, about . . . Mr. Fitzgerald."

Dad blinked and glanced away, rubbing the back of his neck. "Of course you are, honey. But maybe now he's —"

". . . in a better place," I finished, my voice flat, the words rushed together, because I didn't want to hear my own father mouth such a stupid cliché. Hypocrite, fornicator, a one-man band of all the evils Reverend Hardy named in sermons. Once every decent woman in town had been innocently in love with sad-eyed Owen Gamble. Now, when the sun went down he slunk next door like a dirty dog. His daughter poisoned sick men in their beds.

"Dory!"

I flinched, glanced up blindly. Grit and a bitter taste on my tongue. I coughed, gagged, and metal washers hit the floor with a dull *ping*. I didn't recall stuffing them in my mouth. Maybe I had to bite down on something real, something round like the world was supposed to be. But it would take more than nuts and bolts and washers to keep our family secrets screwed down. There wasn't enough duct tape in Gamble's Hardware to make me keep quiet. I'd be looney before nightfall, blurting our guilt all over town.

My father hauled me up as if I were three again and carried me to the back. He set me on the cot in the storeroom where I used to take my afternoon naps. I wanted to hang on his neck and cry into his shirt collar until it was pasty with melted starch. If he'd sing to me again in his awful cracked tenor, maybe it would blot out the evil we'd both done. I didn't mean to hurt him, I'd only wanted —

To stop it. To not see anymore.

Well, I'd done a bang-up job; everything was hunky-dory. I groaned and fell back against the pillow. My head hit the plywood wall and the pain felt like a friend. So did the throbbing that set in, because both made it harder to think straight. I closed my eyes and laid an arm across them.

"You just lay there now," my father was murmuring. If I lowered my arm and looked at him, maybe he'd have more wisdom to hand me. Like, *The ways of adults are mysterious and stupid . . .* or, *It's okay to kill someone if you really didn't mean it.* Or maybe, *I can't possibly care more about you, Dory, than this strange woman who's changed everything in our lives, who comes complete with terrible paintings of dead eyeballs. A woman I want enough to steal from a dying man, to lie and cheat and break my word.*

But when I looked his eyes just seemed tired, maybe from working hard to guard his secret thoughts. All he said out loud was, "I'll take you home soon. Poor little girl."

Little girl. But I was a killer. A nosy, clumsy, stupid teenage assassin. Cheesy paperback murder novels about me should be in the revolving rack at Crockett's Drugstore. I began to cry, snot leaking from my nose. My father sat down again. I didn't expect him to touch me or give me a hug or a kiss. But he laid a hand on my shoulder.

Then he said what seemed the most chilling thing I'd ever heard, as he patted my up-flung arm.

"I know, honey," he whispered. "I know."

I'd hoped Myra would get on the train and take Frank away to some veteran's cemetery. I imagined a hero's sendoff, with horses and uniforms and guns. Then she could go be a widow somewhere else. But the day after I fell apart in the store, I read the obituary in the Sumter *Banner*. Francis Sean Fitzgerald, a decorated veteran of the Korean War, had died at home after a long illness. He'd be interred at two o'clock the following day.

Interred. As if he'd been whipped off the tree like a dried seed pod by the impartial wind, to be planted in our good red dirt. But where? Here you buried your dead in the family place, where you, too, planned to spend the rest of your days.

The Fitzgeralds hadn't been religious as far as I knew. But the black-bordered notice said there'd be a service at our church, then a burial at Springs Cemetery, where all good Baptists eventually went. He was survived by Myra, his loving wife of ten years; a brother, Patrick, and two nephews, who all lived in New Jersey.

The photograph was the worst. A smiling man in uniform, with a strong jaw, broad cheekbones like an Indian's, and thick black hair. This could have been Frank's son. Except he'd never got to have one.

The next day when I came home from school, the tan sheriff department cruiser was parked in front of the Fitzgerald house. I went inside quickly and sat hunched in my room, expecting any minute to hear Sheriff Burney's thick knuckles rapping like doom on our front door. But the sound never came. When I finally got up and looked outside, the car was gone. I began to wonder if I'd imagined it, if I hadn't willed it there myself.

That night I drifted off to jerk awake again, gasping and clutching the sheets to keep me from falling off a cliff, from drowning, from being buried in soft red dirt that sifted into my mouth and eyes. In the dark, I drew the sheet up to my chin but kept my eyes shut tight. I felt surrounded by sad-eyed ghosts and avenging angels. Tomorrow Frank would lie beneath a few hundred pounds of red clay and leaf mold. But every night his eyes would be open, staring with disbelief at his coffin lid. Through it, and beyond. Past the thick red clay veined with narrow tunnels made by beetles and the wider passages of moles and voles. Through the heavy concrete capstone and all the way down the streets his gaze flew, to pin me where I huddled in the dark. One thing comforted me. I believed he was too good a person to frighten children, and I'd never felt more like a scared kid in my life.

At dawn I slumped to the kitchen and stirred a bowl of Cheerios and milk to tan mush. I didn't want to go to this funeral. And yet I did. To repent. To atone by reliving the terrible thing I'd done. To set eyes on the Black Widow, who hadn't come out since the ambulance had pulled away. When I woke in the night now, I didn't hear anything to indicate Dad was sneaking out, creeping over to lie with his neighbor's wife.

I'd thought for a while he'd known my sin, too. That the words he'd whispered to me in the back room of the store meant he understood the part I'd played. But then I wasn't so sure. Even if he did, he wouldn't tell. I was family. This didn't make me feel better.

When we pulled up to the church, the

hearse was already idling there. No green convertible Thunderbird in the lot, but then a black Cadillac big as a tuna boat pulled in beside us. Its windows were tinted dark.

The funeral director got out, looking tall and pale in a black suit, his white shirt spotless as an untroubled soul. He came around to open the passenger door of the Caddy, opened it, and held out a hand. Then drew the elegant length of Myra Fitzgerald from the deep back seat, like a snake from a conjurer's basket. She was in black from veiled hat to sheath dress to sheer stockings. She leaned on his arm as he escorted her up the brick walkway.

The side doors of the church flew open, and two of Mr. Small's assistants and a couple other men trudged out. They slid a mahogany box with brass handrails from the hearse. The heavy coffin looked too big for the frail body I recalled sprawled against rumpled linen, thin arms and legs pale as the sheets.

Frank had finally gotten into town. Funny how he felt larger, more powerful dead than alive. As if his spirit would hang over us always, gray and mournful as Spanish moss.

My father took my arm, but I pulled away. "I can walk."

He pressed his lips tight, then bowed his head, shoved his hands in his pockets, and went on ahead.

The church's white clapboard, red doors, and green trim looked too cheerful. A row of gargoyles would've suited me better. Spires and towers gray as guilt, a dirty hunchback to toll the bells in the loft. The narthex was musty with the sweet rot of flower stems dissolving in stale water, the sugary sulfur of burnt wax. I hadn't lingered outside, but everyone seemed to be seated and the service had begun. Folks in the pews all craned to stare when the doors shut behind me. My father was up front, sliding in beside Myra, who was otherwise alone. The townsfolk there were merchants, mostly. A few strangers, too, wearing clothes too heavy for our summer days. They must be the relatives from up north, but they sat a half-dozen rows back, on the other side from the widow.

I lowered my head and slipped into a back pew. The rustle of my skirt seemed too loud, my patent shoes squeaked, the wood plank bench groaned under my weight. Sweat trickled down my sides until I suspected the faint metallic stink was coming from me. *That's what fear smells like,* I told myself, and dropped to my knees on the pine floorboards. I said a prayer for Frank's soul, then one for mine.

Halfway through the service, someone began to cry — a string of harsh, dry sobs drowned out by Reverend Hardy's droning baritone, and the rumbling lines of the Lord's Prayer. We sang "The Old Rugged Cross" and "Rock of Ages." Then it was over. A thin tide of people surged up the aisle. I scrambled to beat them out the door, rushed to the car, looking back in time to see the coffin riding on the shoulders of six men Frank had never met. I turned away before they slid it into the hearse.

My father nosed our station wagon out behind the Cadillac, which in turn followed the black hearse. We traveled Council Bluff Road at a crawl, a paltry string of five cars with headlights glowing weakly in the sun. Funerals in Ordinary Springs were usually a big deal — the sermon and eulogy, the dignified last journey through the cemetery gates, the hugs and hands clasped over condolences, the neighbors' spice cake and rice and noodle casseroles and fried chicken and iced tea at the family's home. None of that would happen today, I thought.

As usual, cars on the other side of the

road pulled off respectfully. People on the sidewalks took off their hats and watched somberly until we passed. But none had come to the church or actually joined the procession. I glanced at my father, steering one-handed, staring through the windshield as if everything he owned rode in the car ahead. Did he notice we were already set apart from those people we'd known all our lives? The adulteress, the fornicator, the murderer. Parading through town, the final act of our shame. Frank's brother and nephews were behind us; if only they knew. Then a new thought struck me: maybe they did.

The rusted iron gates were open. The grave site was all the way back, near the fence that separated the grounds from Meadowmarsh, a decayed, empty mansion from the timber and turpentine days, its gingerbread porch sagging like a rotted hammock. I wondered why the grave was so far off. Springs cemetery was huge; surely all the front and middle plots couldn't be spoken for.

I got out and stumbled on the slope of a sunken grave. I kept my eyes down, not wanting to meet anyone's gaze — Myra's, the funeral director's, my father's.

Reverend Hardy cleared his throat,

mopped his forehead with a hankie, and began in a deep mournful voice. "I am the Resurrection and I am the Life, says the Lord. Whoever has faith in me shall have life, even though he die. And everyone who has life . . ."

Would God forgive me? I closed my eyes and tried to ask Him but couldn't quite put my question into words. The humid air rang with the sawing of katydids. The harsh grating sounds bored into my brain.

"In the midst of life we are in death . . ."

Someone began coughing as if he might be the next to leave us. A mockingbird called in the hedges. A lone fly buzzed my face.

If God's mercies could not be numbered, then couldn't He make up to Frank all he'd lost? I could pray for that, anyway. Maybe He'd consider having mercy on us, while He was at it. But I wouldn't have blamed Him for striking us all dead.

". . . and comforts us with the blessed hope of everlasting life."

Without knowing I would do it, when they began to lower the casket into the raw, red clay rectangle hacked into the heat-faded grass, I turned and bolted for the car. No footsteps came after me, and for that I was grateful. I ripped open the back door and threw myself full-length on the seat, feeling as sick as if I'd just ridden a twisting back road, curve after curve.

Dad slid in and leaned back heavily against the seat. He sighed, and I squeezed my eyes shut, hoping he wasn't going to *talk* to me. But keys jingled, and the starter gave a grinding screech when he held it too long. With a lurch we crunched onto the gravel drive and left the cemetery faster than we'd entered.

At home I went into my room, stretched out on the bed, and laid a magazine next to me to look at instead of Dad if he came in. I heard his footsteps going down the hall, away from me. Then the front door slammed. I pulled a pillow over my head. If he was on his way to console the grieving widow, I didn't want to know.

In movies, when faced with tragedy, teenage actresses smiled through their tears. They squared their shoulders and carried on. In my real-life experience, gathered in locker rooms and from after-school arguments, girls screamed and cried like lunatics, and blamed somebody else. I felt too worn out to do either. I put my head on the pillow and laid the magazine down. When I woke much later, lines of useless advice were smeared on my forehead, inked there by my own sweat and tears.

8

Saturday morning I managed to stay in bed until almost noon. When I was sure the house was empty I went to the kitchen out of habit and hung on the door of the Fridgidare. Milk, juice, water, green Jell-O salad with brown-edged bananas trapped in it like fossils, leftover tuna casserole. I shuddered and closed the door. As I turned away I caught a flicker through the kitchen window.

Was Myra out planting flowers again? She'd been staying inside since the funeral. I slipped out the kitchen door and walked around the house to see. When I reached the back corner I felt stupid. What in the world would I say to her? So I ducked behind the azaleas and then crawled along the hedge until I could get a clear view.

She was out there in her nightgown, face smeared with dirt, digging like a maniac. Throwing shovels-full every which way. In her grimy white nightie, her fuzzy soil-crusted slippers, she no longer looked cool or artistic or superior. Her long black hair was tangled; she was sweating and grunting and heaving clods like a human backhoe. Some bundles lay near her; they looked like stuffed laundry bags. One had burst at the top, things had spilled out: shirts, slacks, something khaki colored, a crushed military hat with a shiny black brim.

I was stunned at this messy replay of my childhood. I sat back on my heels, wondering if this was standard adult mourning behavior or if Myra and my father simply had more in common than I'd imagined. In a movie, it would have proved only one thing — that she'd killed Frank. But this was life, and I knew who had. So why bury his clothes, as if they'd died, too? I knelt there watching until my knees were embossed with twigs and pebbles and my hands had gone numb from leaning on them. When I tried to shift I lost my balance and fell against the azaleas.

Myra paused in mid-stroke. The face she turned my way looked so crazy I nearly screamed. She could've been about to brain me with the shovel and throw me in the hole, too. Except she was staring over my head, not at me, as if she couldn't believe her eyes. I took that chance to scramble backward on hands and knees but slammed up against some hard, immovable object.

I did scream then. But it was only my father, looking paralyzed at the sight of Myra rooting like a crazed hog, at the shame of his only child crawling around in dirt-smeared pajamas at high noon. His arms hung limp, his face was slack. He backed up a step, then croaked, "Came home. To see if you were okay."

He glanced again at Myra and winced. "You know, I thought maybe —" But he didn't finish the sentence.

"Daddy," I whispered, but I had no sensible explanation to offer next. If we'd had more neighbors, they could talk about us over coffee: *That's right, a crazy woman lives next door to Owen Gamble on Springhill Road, but so what, because his daughter — the one who crams nuts and bolts in her mouth when she's upset? — fifteen if she's a day and she crawls around in the dirt like some white-trash toddler.*

Well, maybe this was a good thing. We could have our own altar call right now. I'd confess what I'd done, and they could tell their sins, too. I sat up and rubbed the dirt off my hands, ready to start. And then we could — all right, not go back to the way it had been before — but at least be a team again, a family, Owen and Dory Gamble.

Daddy reached out and took hold of my hand, looking down on me like Jesus come again. But as he lifted me to my feet, Myra wailed. She threw her shovel down and fell to her knees on the edge of the hole she'd made, as if it were Frank's open grave. She screamed and tore at her beautiful black hair.

My father's face twisted. His grip loosened on my hand. Slowly his fingers slid away from mine. With a shuddering sigh he stepped around me, then across the grass to her. He pulled her up tight against him and whispered in her ear, and after a moment she stopped screaming and gasped, "Huh huh huh."

He wrapped an arm around her waist and half-carried her to her back door. They disappeared inside.

After the door banged shut, I staggered to my feet. My torn knees hurt and blood threaded my shins. My palms were pocked with scrapes from gravel and pine cones and sandspurs. I dragged a shaking arm across my sweating face and turned to go in. What else could I do? I hadn't been chosen.

The next week passed slowly, in excruciating detail. I didn't see much of my father, because he'd taken on a second job: making Myra Fitzgerald feel better about being a widow. Nearly every night the bedsprings creaked as he rose and went quietly down the hall, out on another mission of mercy.

Each morning after I got up Dad waited until I'd gotten dressed and left for school. But he hurried me along more than usual. Why else if not to have time to go next door before he had to open the store? Shadows grew under his eyes from lack of sleep. At the same time he looked younger, happier than I'd ever seen him. Afternoons I went straight to our front door, careful not to look over at the other house. I threw my books in a pile on the couch and locked the front door. Not that Myra would stroll in, but I wanted to feel sure.

I did my homework first, then made dinner. While I chopped or stirred or thawed, I imagined that night turning to him over meatloaf and mashed potatoes, and asking, *Do you love her more? And what about me? Do you still love me?*

But when we finally sat down at the kitchen table, neither of us had much to say, besides "Pass the salt, please" or "Did you finish your homework?"

We lived like strangers in a motel, polite but separate, for at least two weeks. Then one day, I came home in a better mood and didn't lock the door, made banana pudding, took out the leftover pot roast, and put some peeled potatoes on to boil. I even sang while I worked.

Who knows why. Maybe I was incapable of holding a grudge longer than fourteen days. But I think it was because we'd gotten up to dress rehearsals. Mrs. Hawks had made me Marylee's understudy after she'd noticed me backstage mouthing Emily's lines. She said they needed a backup, that Marylee might fall and twist an ankle cheerleading, God forbid. Even if I never got to be the star, I could replay Mrs. Hawks's look behind her cat-eye glasses as she glanced between me and Marylee, who was gesturing like a farmer sowing rye grass. She mumbled her lines; no one past the third row would hear.

"I can do the part," I said quickly, when she'd told me I'd be understudy. "I mean, I could. If you ever needed me to."

She smiled and patted my cheek. "You know, Dory, I think you could do all the parts in this play at once, if you set your mind to it." The touch of her cool, dry fingers lingered on that cheek like a blessing.

141

A promise that someday things might be normal again. Or what passed for it in the world.

So remembering there was a future to look forward to had finally convinced me of one thing. Whatever my father chose to do, I could make a life of my own. I would still have my dreams and plans. The world wouldn't end because it no longer centered around him. He'd raised me, but I couldn't be Owen Gamble's baby girl forever.

So I hummed and mashed the potatoes in a hurry, because we usually ate between five-thirty and six. By the time I poured the steaming saucepan of hot pudding over the sliced bananas and vanilla wafers, it was after five.

At five-thirty I turned the burners to low so the food would stay warm. Sometimes a customer came in the store at the last minute needing lumber cut to size, and Dad was never one to say no to trade.

At six I called the store, but there was no answer. At six-fifteen I turned off the burners. At six-thirty I took the pans off the stove. But it was a quarter to seven, getting dark outside, before I heard the front door open. He came in whistling, something he'd done a lot when I was little. When had he stopped? I couldn't recall.

I hovered in the kitchen, wondering whether to act mad or relieved. Maybe he'd had to do inventory and forgot to tell me. It was weird to feel like an angry housewife, sulking in my chair at the dinette.

When he appeared in the archway between kitchen and dining room, I tried to keep my face blank. But then I saw Myra. Smiling bravely, her face paler than before. She looked thinner, but instead of widow's black, she had on a bright orange sweater, soft and expensive looking, like cashmere.

"Dinner's ready," I blurted out. "Since two hours ago." I stood up and turned to leave. Let them eat the burnt roast and cold mashed potatoes. I wasn't hungry.

"Now, Dory," said Dad, but he sounded tolerant, kind of amused.

I swung back around, arms folded tight across my chest.

He smiled and his mouth twitched, as if he knew a secret. "Sit down. Just for a minute. We have some news."

I didn't want to obey, but it's hard to go against training. They pulled out chairs across from me. I looked down at the flowered oilcloth.

"Now, this won't happen right away," my father began. "But —"

"*What* won't?"

"I'm trying to tell you." He reached over and patted my hand. "Something we decided tonight. We wanted to tell you first."

Myra leaned across the table and clasped her hands in front of her. It was the same pose from our girl talk that Saturday ages back. She took a deep breath. "Yes. So you can have time to . . . to get used to the idea. Sweetie," she added, and gave my father a sappy smile.

Oh, God. God. *God.* I sent a glare back, then fiddled with my butter knife. "Let me guess. She's moving away," I whispered.

Dad frowned. "No, no, Myra loves it here. See, Dory, that's the news. I've asked her to marry me. So we'll be a real family at last."

And I'd thought we had been a real one all along. I opened my mouth to say so, but he held up a hand, palm out, before I could squeeze out a word. "I know, I know — it hasn't been that long. I know she's only just widowed. But we're not teenagers, why I'm not young anymore at all. Besides, we're just making plans. It won't happen for a few months, that'd only be proper."

I stood so quick I didn't realize the tablecloth was still gripped in my clenched fists. Plates, glasses, and silverware tumbled. A

144

cup hit the floor and shattered. "I hope you didn't just say *proper*. Not if you're going to marry a black widow spider. I mean, did you know they kill their mates?"

Maybe they actually didn't, I might have got that mixed up. But why didn't he understand it was Myra who'd really killed Frank? That they both had, day by day, inch by inch, not caring what he saw and heard and felt. My hands shook, my face scorched as I stood glaring at the two people I hated most in the world. Though not long before I had loved one of them maybe beyond reason.

"Here's the thing," I said. "I don't understand why the sheriff doesn't arrest somebody for killing him." Myra's eyes widened and she shrank behind my father, looking around as if ready to bolt. "You know what I mean. She neglected a helpless man. She treated him like dirt. Now you're going to give her another chance."

My father shoved back and his chair toppled. He came around the dinette so fast he might have been on wheels. I was glad, thinking he'd seen the light and was leaving her. Like the song, coming to stand by me.

Instead, he grabbed my shoulders and shook me like a rat in a dog's mouth. Then gripped my chin hard, so it hurt too much to pull away. He slowly forced my unwilling head on its stiff neck to turn toward Myra. I squeezed my eyes shut to refuse the sight of her, all black and orange like a Halloween witch.

But I couldn't block the sound of his voice saying calmly, dangerously, "I didn't raise any daughter to be rude and spiteful. And a liar to boot. Eudora Gamble, are you my child?"

I tried to say no. But I could barely open my mouth. The only sound that would come out was a strangled sob. *"Yes."*

"Then you'll apologize and beg forgiveness. So we can sit like decent folks and eat dinner together."

I shuddered. At last I opened my eyes and looked at Myra's white face. She wasn't smiling, but her eyes told it all. *I won,* they said. *Me. Not you.*

What point, then, in not giving in? So I swallowed and nodded.

"Go around the table, now," my father said softly, easing his grip on my chin. "Go to her and shake hands. Because if it kills —" He stopped, cleared his throat. "I mean, it surely won't hurt any of us to be civil to each other, to get along and adjust to changing circumstances."

Before he let go he gave my arm a last little shake.

I leaned on the table for a second, breathing like I'd just run the fifty on the track and come in last. But I wasn't going to let anyone know how beaten I felt. I took a step, then another. Even before I rounded that table I knew I wasn't going to adjust, not to any of this.

I stopped in front of Myra and twisted my mouth up into something like a smile. I glanced down at the hand she held out. And though I'd never done such a thing before — even as a toddler, the age when it was common and expected — I hawked up a wad of spit. And let it fly right into her outstretched palm.

She screamed and yanked her hand back so fast my saliva could have been acid.

"Dory!" My father lunged around the table again. Dishes flew; the roast hit the floor.

He yanked me around and backhanded my face. Then did it again, as if he had only a few seconds to knock a life's worth of discipline into me. He pulled my arm up behind my back and frog-marched me to my room.

"A Gamble never behaves that way."

"Oh, that's right." I was bent, maybe,

but not ready to give in. "We just sneak over to other people's houses and fuck them while —"

He slammed me against the wall in my room. It didn't hurt so much as knock the breath out of me. He pushed his face right up next to mine. It had turned such a dark shade I could imagine his head exploding in a shower of blood and brains. My hands shook, my knees trembled, but I was still mad. So I pressed on, seeking the thing that'd hurt most.

"See," I hissed in his face. "This must be why my mother left. No wonder she hated you so much. Enough to leave me, too!"

He opened his mouth. I wouldn't have been surprised if he'd howled like a wolf, then taken me apart and eaten the pieces.

Instead, he let go. His squared shoulders slumped. But it seemed he wasn't finished, either.

"Your mother? You want to know about her? She didn't care about you or me. Only herself. She had to have everything she wanted. I should've known," he said slowly, "you'd turn out just as bad."

I stared at him, eyes burning. I was sinking into a pit, sucked down by the very quicksand waiting around the corner for me all my life.

He took a deep breath. "Don't even think of leaving this room tonight."

"I hate her," I said. "And I hate you."

He shook his head. Turned away. "You heard me," he threw over his shoulder. "Maybe you're not my daughter, after all."

He slammed my door without another word.

I couldn't get enough air down to my lungs. I'd stopped feeling triumphant after the first slap. My father had never before laid a hand on me in all my fifteen years. I fell back onto my bed, face stinging, eyes burning. We'd just clawed each other bloody. Not honestly, like animals, but with the worst, the most cruel things we could think to say. Things that were unforgivable and had no good answers and would never be fixed by an apology. No one could mend such rips and tears, not in a hundred years.

Maybe I didn't want to try. And I refused to stay locked in like a bad dog, while they ate, and touched each other, and made plans. I shoved up off the bed and paced the room, side to side, ready to snap and growl again if I had to.

I stopped in front of my window. The screen I'd never actually tried to pry out of the frame, despite what I told Pearce, was clotted with dust. Dried bugs hung there, feet death-locked in the rusted mesh. The metal edge was snug in the wooden frame. If Pearce believed I could be an escape artist, then I could do it. I could be anyone, play any part at all. Mrs. Hawks had said so.

I touched the dusty mesh like a blind person feeling for a braille message. I was no saint; I made mistakes, got carried away, and exaggerated. Wanted people to notice and praise me. I'd wanted to please my father from the time I could walk and talk. To make him proud of me. But that would never happen. I'd been doomed from the start by the tainted blood in my veins. Only half his, and now he'd disowned me.

Fine. Then I'd be someone different; dark, dangerous. Someone not to be messed with. I could start now.

My alternative was to apologize, to creep out and humbly wish them well. To hug my father and cry, to happily lick the crumbs from the table — and it was my own table, food I'd made myself. Could I take Myra's hand and practice calling her Mother?

No. My fingernails scraped the screen. I'd rather be locked away, sent wherever bad girls go. I gripped the flimsy metal strips, curved my nails under the edges, braced, and tugged. The screen popped out so easily I staggered backward like a dancing bear. Then got my balance, leaned it against the bed, and hauled myself up onto the sill. I perched a moment, looking down at a clear spot between thick clumps of plumbago. Then let go and dropped, landing light as a dancer, as a thief. Until I lost my balance and pitched over sideways. I rose, a little scratched, and rubbed my dirty hands on my shorts. Pearce had been right, nothing to it.

I stepped out of the flower bed and onto a new road. I would be Dory, but not Dory. I decided no one would ever really know me again.

A choir of crickets and cicadas buzzed and scraped in the trees. Rabbits froze like forgotten toys on the grass as I slipped around the house. They scattered when I took off running, then cut through the woods and orange grove to the road.

The unpaved clay of Springhill Road was gritty under my Keds. The perfume of Confederate jasmine was thick and sweet. I passed the driveway that led down to Pearce's house. Suddenly a shape rose on the side of the road. My heart squeezed and I bit back a scream. But it was only a fat racoon who'd been raiding the garbage cans. He was staggering on his hind legs, trying to bat a potato chip bag off his head. I laughed then. Imagine all the things I might see, loose on the town like an outlaw after dark.

When I reached the crossroads where Springhill meets Water Street, it occurred to me that I'd also be seen. Everyone in town knew Owen Gamble's daughter, from the store if nowhere else. They only had to mention they'd waved to me late on Wednesday night, and he would know. So I shot across the intersection and ducked into the paved back alley that ran behind the drugstore, the Corner Market, the post office, the Cut 'n Curl, and of course, Gamble's. In a small town you don't stand on ceremony. Everyone comes in the back way.

I stopped at the end of the alley to catch my breath, glancing at the back entrances of the stores, each flanked by garbage cans, to the backs of the white frame houses that faced the next street over. A marmalade cat slithered up and rubbed my ankles, meowing, but I had nothing for him. I stooped to scratch his ragged ears.

"Now what?" I asked the cat.

I looked down the alley, to the west, and that's when I noticed the glow. A faint orangey tint, like the heat aura above a campfire. Down that way lay the Seaboard Railroad Depot. But no trains ran this time of night, at least not any that'd be stopping. What could it be, that light in the sky? I started that way, not afraid of the night, the empty alleyway, of being alone. I knew exactly where I was; I had known all my life. That new things might be waiting ahead was only a vague, exciting idea.

The green-and-white depot was lit up like a carnival. Not by a passing train, but a caravan of trucks pulled up in front, their headlights a double chain of full moons lighting the roadway. Some big as semis, snorting and hissing their brakes. Smaller ones painted with bright flowers and animals. Some even had carved wooden doors and tiny shutter-edged windows, like Swiss chalets on wheels.

I hung back in the shadowline of trees and watched. A man jumped down from the lead semi and stomped to the third truck back. He spoke to someone up in the cab, though all I could see was one beefy tattooed arm resting on the edge of the window. The man pointed beyond the station, then waved. Trucks honked. I heard a muffled roar and a trumpeted reply, then a symphony of screeching straight from the Amazon jungle. And I finally understood that it was here: the carnival. The one I'd been to every year for as far back as memory reached. I'd just never been up and out late enough to see it actually arrive.

These folks had come like gypsies in the middle of the night. That alone was exciting enough. I peered down the line at flatbeds hauling metal struts and cross braces jumbled like the folded legs of giant spiders. Swaying seats jingled from chains, swinging from what I now saw was bringing up the rear — the crescent rails of a small Ferris wheel.

The man who'd talked to the driver began waving like a traffic cop. One by one the trucks peeled off, circling the station and pulling out of sight. They were heading to the fairgrounds, the flat, weedy, paper-littered cucumber field that once or twice a year was transformed into something rich and strange and festive.

I was absorbed again in the scene, the chaos of painted trucks and junker cars backing and turning. I didn't hear anyone come up behind. But suddenly someone jabbed my ribs, and when I went to scream muffled it with a hand clamped over my mouth. Then dragged me back further into the darkness of the woods.

I was suffocating, obviously about to die. Then Pearce whispered in my ear, "You got the screen out."

When he let go I turned and shoved him hard. He fell on his ass, laughing, still looking pleased with himself. Lord God, did he stink of beer.

"You stupid creep! You scared hell out of me."

"Sorry, Dory." He didn't look it.

"I got to go. Dad's up, he'll miss me."

"But you just got here." Pearce scrambled to his feet. He shoved his hands in his pockets and stuck out his lip. "Ain't you gonna watch them unload?"

I looked over at the fairgrounds. I could see now that a few townsfolk were scattered here and there in the dark, watching the trucks bumping out onto the field. The whole motley assortment of vehicles spun wheels and hissed brakes and blew horns like a herd of discombobulated mastodons. Town children would be dreaming of jungles tonight. Though how anyone could still be asleep, unaware of all the goings-on, was hard to imagine.

"No," I said sharp. "I have to go home."

Pearce grabbed my arm, right at the spot where Dad had twisted it before, and I yelped.

"Come on now, Pee. Let go," I said, using my old, old name for him from when we were little. Taking a page from Miss Harriet's book, trying a different voice, more teasing than sharp, since he was drinking and maybe unreasonable. The strong smell of alcohol on him shocked me. Of course high school boys drank, that was a local hobby. But I'd gone skinny dipping with Pearce in the old horse trough behind our house when we were two or three while our parents looked on. I could out-climb him up the biggest oak tree by the Springs. Had beat up on him more than once, even bloodied his nose. I wanted him to play my husband in *Our Town*.

"What'll I get if I do?" He pulled me tight against him, closer than I'd been since we were little and wrestled over toys. Or that day he'd slid hands under my clothes. Beer breath, not so great, but also the smells of aftershave and soap. And something else that was the essence of him: a mysterious, peppery scent. Pushing back against him, I felt his flushed skin radiating heat through his shirt. And the muscles of his chest, which, I knew from hot days when he took off his shirt to load lumber in back, was no longer hairless. All this still news to me, close up. A different experience I was reluctant to cut short.

I pushed hair out of my eyes and glanced up at him. "Come on, now. Let go, and I'll meet you tomorrow night."

"You will?" He shook me a little, teasing. "Out front?"

"No." I thought quick. "By the Ferris wheel."

"Okay," he said. But just before letting go, he swooped down, bent me backward, and kissed me. Surprised, I started to kiss back. Then he pushed his tongue in my mouth.

I broke loose and bolted from the trees, back into the alley behind the main street. The noises pursuing me through the dark might've been owls hooting, carnival roustabouts shouting and cursing, or Pearce laughing himself silly.

On Water Street again, I slowed to a walk and untucked the tail of my blouse to wipe my mouth with it.

"Ugh," I kept repeating. "Oh, gross."

But no matter what I said, my heart pounded and my stomach was doing empty thrill-ride flips. I darted quickly across Water Street, making myself one of the shadows again.

9

Every year for my birthday Dad always ordered a Red Velvet cake from the Springs Bakery. We had dinner at Nock's Diner, where I could order anything I wanted. After our plates were cleared, Red the cook sang "Happy Birthday" and the waitresses, Martine and Alma, who both were old enough to be my grandmothers, would kiss my cheek. This had been our tradition since Dad had to seat me on a stack of county phone books so I could reach my plate.

This birthday couldn't be the same, and I told myself I didn't care. All that was over. But I did care, and this fact, plus all the talk about the carnival and disturbing thoughts of Pearce, made it hard to concentrate at school. Lots of kids were planning to go to the carnival, the older ones in mixed groups. No one asked my plans. If they wondered they probably assumed I'd be, as usual, with my father.

When I got to the store after school, the roar of the paint machine was deafening. Dad was mixing up a gallon of something for Mrs. Roper, the only other neighbor on our road. She smiled and patted my cheek and asked if this heat wasn't just killing me.

"No, ma'am. It's not so bad," I said, piling my books behind the counter. The weather didn't interest me, but I remembered to ask, "How about you?"

"I can barely go out in the yard anymore. Elizabeth said she'd carry me to the carnival tonight with the little ones, but I'll stay put. Walking makes my arthritis flare." She turned back to squint at the sample my father had dipped with a stir-stick. "I don't know, Mr. Gamble. That looks mighty dark."

I heard honking out front just before closing and looked out. Jack, the Burgess's rheumatic old yellow lab, had sat down in the middle of the street to scratch a flea. He often slept there, on the yellow line. Everyone knew to steer around him. He was a good dog. On a rare baby-sitting job I'd come into the Burgess's kitchen in time to save him from the littlest Burgess boy, who was thumbtacking Jack's ears to the linoleum as the dog lay suffering in dignified silence.

A flatbed truck was trying to back into the alley between the post office and the store. Dad must've ordered some lumber, and this looked like a different driver. He honked again.

My father didn't look up from the ledgers spread across his desk.

"Delivery," I mumbled.

Dad jerked a thumb over his shoulder, as if I didn't know which end of the store was front or back. I walked out, letting the screen doors bang shut.

He didn't yell the usual, "Take it easy on my hinges!"

Jack thumped his tail, flopped down, sighed, and closed his eyes. Across the street in front of the drugstore, three teenage boys in blue Future Farmers of America jackets scuffled and shoved. My spirits sank. Neither those bumbling, pimply guys nor the impatient truck driver knew today was my birthday. Yet it seemed depressing no one noticed me at all, except maybe as the hired help who'd take care of annoying details.

Jack levered up suddenly, pursuing another flea, ignoring the certain death casting a truck-shaped shadow over him. I imagined how the Burgess kids would feel if their much-loved mutt was pulped. I shook off my self-pity, shoved off the curb, and ran to where fat old Jack lolled with a

stupid grin as his hind foot finally connected with the right itchy spot. I'd never
be able to move him, so I dug in my
pockets, found an old peppermint, and
thrust it under his nose. He sniffed and
grudgingly lifted his butt off the asphalt. I
dragged him by the collar onto the sidewalk, where he licked my hand and peed
on my shoes.

"Oh, Jack." It seemed like everyone had
the same idea for marking my birthday. I
balanced on one foot and yanked off my
dripping shoe. The truck driver gunned his
engine and without even a wave of thanks
rumbled between the buildings to the
back. I hobbled back there, too, to go show
the guy where to unload in the lumber
shed out back. Everyone here took short-
cuts; they ducked down alleys, cut across
streets, even cut through the store, in the
front door and out the back. No privacy,
no surprises, no mystery left in this town. I
wanted to be taken by surprise again. As-
tonished, the way I had by been by Pearce.
To be thrilled and mystified.

I signed a receipt, and the lumber truck
roared off. Then I limped barefoot around
to the front again, holding my pee-soaked
tennis shoes out in front. I flipped the door
sign to CLOSED, locked up, then went on

down the aisle and past the counter. Dad was hidden by stacks of catalogs and mail and green clothbound ledgers. The old black adding machine squatted like a toad at his elbow. He was so deep into the monthly statements he didn't notice me. His shoulders were so hunched and thoughtful I knew better than to disturb him.

In the bathroom I tossed my reeking shoes in the sink and ran cold water over them. I left them to soak. The phone rang, and I headed for the front again, because it was my job to answer when Dad was busy. But he beat me to it. For lack of anything better to do till time to go home, I went over to the plumbing aisle and began slicing open new boxes of faucet sets. Some company would've been nice. I'd hoped Pearce would come in, but maybe Friday was softball practice. Or maybe he was off with a bunch of renegade Future Farmers.

The phone rang again, and before I could even twitch Dad picked up. I wasn't paying much attention until he raised his voice to a near-shout. "What? That's ridiculous!"

He wouldn't speak to a customer like that. I moved to the garden aisle and straightened the rakes. In paint and refinishing I took a leaking tin of linseed oil off the shelf. I could hear Dad again. Either he'd gotten madder or forgot he wasn't alone. His voice kept rising.

"Okay, okay. Try to calm down. When did he come?"

Silence for a moment as he listened. I did, too, forgetting I wouldn't be able to hear anything. Then Dad cleared his throat. "Well, I don't understand that. The coroner said right out and plain that it was suicide."

I didn't have to hear a name then. I knew who was calling and why Frank had been buried so far from the other graves.

"Ah, that's just standard procedure. They got to do their paperwork. What? No one thinks you had anything to do with —"

He was tapping something, maybe a pen, on the desk.

"Now, look. If he comes back to the house, you tell old Tom Burney if he has any questions about what happened that night, to talk to me."

Another pause. More tapping.

"What? Dory! Well, if that doesn't beat — what does he want to see her for, a child? Why it's just . . ." His voice trailed off until I could no longer make out the words.

I gripped the leaky linseed oil can so tight more oil oozed from it, thick and sticky, smelling of rush seats and newly finished wood. I was making a mess. Tom Burney was the county sheriff, an old friend of my father's. If he wanted to know what'd happened the night Frank Fitzgerald died, then folks were talking. Were they saying my father and Myra had killed him? Maybe they had, but not any way they might imagine, with a gun or rat poison or even those deadly white pills. They'd done it slowly, from the inside, by carrying on together as if Frank was a ghost already. Pills were only a tool he'd used to stop the pain.

Or maybe a tool to show the world what they'd done to him.

I hadn't thought of that before. That Frank might want to hurt people, to have revenge, even if he had to die to get it. Another thought came, a regular epiphany afternoon. What if the pills hadn't finished him? He'd been breathing when I left. What if, after my father left, Myra had decided she was tired of mopping up pee and carrying water glasses. Of rolling a wasted body from side to side as she changed the sheets. Maybe she was tired of waiting on a husband, a grown man who'd never get better or be able to do the things married folks like to do?

She had to have thought these things sometimes. Suddenly I could understand that. Because I would have.

She'd want to be free to see Owen Gamble in broad daylight. To go out in public, arm in arm. To be known as his lady friend.

I'd put those pills in his mouth, but other people had reasons to be rid of Frank. To send him out of this world, far from his ailments and injuries. That felt comforting. It felt like the truth, and I hugged it to me.

10

But Dad hadn't forgotten my birthday. When we came home from the store he handed me a little package off the hall table. The box's crooked corners were thick, warped with extra tape. So I knew he'd wrapped it himself.

"Go on, open it," he said, not looking at me.

Slowly I peeled tape and striped paper, then pried the lid off the white box. Inside, nestled in batts of cotton, was a silver ring, set with a big chunk of turquoise and bits of red coral. I didn't want to like it, but it was the one I'd admired in the window of the drugstore for months. Imported all the way from Mexico, the cashier told me. I couldn't remember mentioning it to Dad. But in a small town, people notice and remember things.

At last I put it on. My hand suddenly looked more grown up, the fingers long and slender. I loved the ring, but couldn't say so. My left cheek still tingled from his slap. My arms had bruises. No, he couldn't buy me off.

"Come to the kitchen," he said gruffly, not remarking on my manners for once.

The table was set, though dinner was in white cardboard cartons on the counter. He must have had Nock's Diner make it up ahead. Fried okra, roasted chicken, mashed potatoes and cream gravy, a seven-layer salad. Without thinking, I gave him a quick squeeze. No Myra, just the two of us. Maybe it was an apology of sorts.

But we'd only just sat down when a knock on the door caught us. My father frowned, wiped his mouth. "Sit, I'll get it."

I kept eating salad leaf by leaf, spearing bright green peas two or three at a time, too wound up to enjoy it. What if that was Myra at the door?

I set down my fork and contemplated the hand-painted flowers on my plate, one of the old Stangl set that must have been chosen by my mother. I wondered if she'd loved these dishes like I did.

I heard the door open, and my father saying something. I squinted at the wild-flowers and vines on my plate, the red border licking the edge. If a person stared at some special, left-behind object long enough, would they go into a trance, maybe into some other world? Perhaps if you could look long and hard enough, that much-loved object could reveal some kind of message. I didn't know my mother was dead, but otherwise why had she never come back for me?

The flowery pattern blurred, the vines seemed to twist to turn snaky and sinister. Snakes, eels, dragon tails. Maybe I was halfway to some kind of trance because not until Dad cleared his throat behind me did I notice he'd come back. And that he wasn't alone. With him was Tom Burney, hat in hand like a gentleman caller.

We'd known him forever; he was often my father's fishing partner. When I was little he'd bounced me on his enormous knees and chucked me under the chin before I could talk well enough to tell him I didn't like it. In all that time his size hadn't seemed important. He wasn't just tall but broad shouldered and towering. I had a glimmer, just then, of how a criminal might feel to look back and see Big Tom Burney closing in.

What's more, he'd lost his left hand to a grenade in Korea. By now there were more advanced, jointed gadgets to wear instead of a hook. But Tom had told my father that when he went banging with it on someone's door, no matter what the person was doing — beating his wife, owing money, hiding stolen radios, fixing to be evicted — he opened up and came out like a lamb.

"Because of this, Owen," he'd say, tapping the steel sickle on the counter. "Nobody lies to the Hook."

Looking at that shiny curve, familiar yet threatening, you could feel how fragile life is, how the fabric of it could rip and tear on something so sharp.

Yet Tom also helped old ladies cross the street. He'd pick up stray kittens on the road and ride them around till he found a good home. When he sat in the dunking booth at the fall festival every October, no one threw straight because they didn't want to knock Tom Burney into a vat of cold water.

"Hey, Dory," he said, smiling.

"Have a chair, Tom," said Dad, pulling one out. When the sheriff sat, the joints of the old chair creaked in distress. I caught his smell: hair tonic and cigars and oiled leather.

"Just dropped by to ask a couple things about this Fitzgerald situation. You spare a minute? I hate to interrupt." He spread his ham-size hand, fingers blunt as toes, on one knee.

I glanced at my father, who still stood

behind his own chair, gripping the top rail. "Well sure, Tom. Go ahead."

It amazed me that my hand didn't shake when I laid my fork down neatly on my paper napkin. "No sir. It's no bother."

"We're just having a little birthday supper," said Dad. "Won't you join us?"

I folded my hands in my lap and looked Burney in the eye. I'd had an opportunity to practice this in the principal's office once or twice. All a mistake, my expression was meant to say. I got nothing to hide. Even if the dark corners of the room shifted and moved, even if my life quivered with ghosts.

"Thanks. Maybe just a bite." Tom reached across and helped himself to a hunk of cornbread. I'd thought for a minute he was going to chuck me under the chin. But because he was here on business, maybe this time with the cold curved back of the hook, not his warm, cat-savior hand. I turned my shiver into a shrug.

"You liked Mr. Fitzgerald, didn't you, sugar?" said Tom, the words muffled by cornbread.

I smoothed my shorts with both hands, pressing my trembling legs into stillness. "Yes sir. He was nice. He helped with my algebra homework. And sometimes, when Daddy —"

I stopped just short of saying, *When Daddy and Myra went out, I used to baby-sit him.*

We had never called it that, just a job. Or, "helping out the Fitzgeralds." But Tom Burney's tan uniform and unblinking gaze made me realize how it would sound. Leaving such a sick man in the care of a high school girl. I must've understood that all along, of course. Because I'd never told anyone what I did those weekends. Even Pearce. People would have talked, no matter they had no clue what was really going on.

"Go on, honey," said Tom Burney. "Go on." He slipped a cigar out of his shirt pocket and clamped it between his teeth, but didn't light up.

I glanced at my father, suddenly horrified by the power in my hands. Did I really want him to be arrested for his time spent with Myra, to be talked about and stared at in town? To lose the only parent I had left? I coughed, and took a sip of water from my glass.

"Well," I said slowly, as though I'd nearly lost the train of the conversation. "Dad tried to help the Fitzgeralds out when he could."

" 'Course he did," said Tom. "I guess you did, too."

"Uh-huh."

"Mrs. Fitzgerald tells me you spent a good bit of time talking to the . . . to her husband. Did you know he was on some real powerful medication? You know, stuff for when you're in bad pain. You ever pick up the room, tidy things to help out? Maybe move those pill bottles around?"

So she hadn't told him about the sitting arrangement. Now I was only a visitor. I held very still. Myra didn't know I was there that night, but maybe she'd like to blame me. To save herself, dig her claws deeper into my father. Here was a chance to take my burden away, explain what had happened, clear up a mystery. Except . . . maybe Tom, or even Dad, wouldn't believe me. How wicked a crime was it to hand deadly pills to a man who wanted to take his own life? Would they put a girl just turned sixteen in jail for it?

My tongue tasted bitter. I swallowed with a click in my throat and glanced at my father again. He stood staring down, frowning, as if he'd just noticed a flaw in the Formica.

"No sir," I finally said, a little too loud. "Mrs. Fitzgerald told me plain, never mess with his medicine. That she was the only one who could give him pills. That was why she kept them on a table across the room. In case he got confused, took more when it wasn't time."

Burney nodded sympathetically. "Did he seem confused sometimes, to you?"

No one had been sharper, clearer, sounder of mind than Frank Fitzgerald. "Sometimes he was in a lot of pain."

Burney grunted. He took the cigar out and slipped it into his shirt pocket. "Do much baby-sitting these days?"

I stared at him. I'd never done much sitting for anyone, not even the Burgesses. Only for Frank. "No sir," I said slowly, running my thumb up and down the handle of my fork, making a cloudy smudge on the silver. "The Burgesses don't go out much lately, since that new baby."

My father laughed a little. "Why, Tom? You and Joyce need a sitter?"

A joke. The two big Burney boys played football for Florida State. But Tom didn't laugh. "Harriet McMillan, down the street, said she'd heard Dory sometimes would sit with the husband, Fitzgerald, when the missus was out running errands."

My father pulled his chair out and sat down at last. He looked stricken, as if not until this very moment had it occurred to him other folks might notice such things.

"You like some coffee, sir?" I said suddenly to the sheriff.

"Why, thank you kindly. Coffee! She's a big old girl now." He nudged my father, but was watching me, eyes narrowed, head tilted. Like he was considering me and what I'd told him, trying to make the two fit together without seams.

"Excuse me." I shoved my chair back, took my plate to the sink. After starting the percolator, I scraped and rinsed dishes with my back to them. They kept talking as if I wasn't there. My hands tightened on the slippery china. I was sixteen years old today. Did grown men still think I didn't understand big words?

"Now I know you'd never put your girl in any bad situation, Owen. I expect Harriet's a bit fuddled. You know how gossip runs like brushfire around here. It's just, what with the coroner's report — he thinks this Fitzgerald couldn't have squashed an ant, much less pried the lid off that pill bottle. It's at the lab now. So everyone's confused."

I glanced over my shoulder. My father nodded, too long. I wanted to give him advice, some acting cues: Loosen up your shoulders. Raise your head. For Lord's sake, look the man in the eyes.

Tom Burney drank his coffee in long swallows, hot as it was. Then scraped his chair back and jammed his hat on. "Well, you all take it easy. I'll be getting on home to supper now, before Joyce thinks I'm out to the roadhouse."

He clapped Dad on the shoulder. My father followed him out. "Expect you're done with all this business now."

At the sink I shook my head. Dad ought to try to sound less hopeful.

"Oh, I will be, by and by," said Burney noncommittally. He called over his shoulder, "Good coffee, miss."

Then my father was shutting the door behind him while I held the edge of the sink to keep myself upright.

Dad didn't come back. When I looked into the living room, he was standing, head bowed, deep in thought.

"Dad?" I said. "Should I cut the cake?"

"What? Oh, no thanks. I'm going out to the shed. Need to oil some tools."

He'd already forgotten it was my birthday. "Thanks for the ring."

He smiled. "Myra said you'd like it."

Then he pushed open the door and went out. I went back to the kitchen and tugged the new ring off my finger. I set it on the windowsill above the sink. He hadn't eaten any dinner. And though he sold hardware, Owen Gamble never oiled anything at home. Not door hinges. Not rusty tools. Only that squeaky, balky mower when he'd decided to get out in the yard and impress Myra.

I reached for the next dirty thing and held it under scalding water. As the steam rose, and my hand began to sting, I thought: *This is the way it'll be from now on. My father and I in different rooms, not talking. Or only speaking about safe things. Saying nothing.*

I stared at my double in the window pane. It should have reflected the rags of my childhood, hanging in shreds.

11

My father wasn't back an hour later, nor was he out in the shed. I went to my room and tried to read my assignment for English, "The Minister's Black Veil." But I couldn't concentrate on the story or the character. What use was it to wear such a getup? Might as well turn the bathroom mirror around and pretend you had no face.

I kept hearing creaks, like footsteps in the hall. Finally I got so spooked I threw the damned book in a corner and turned on all the lights. I sat on the sofa with my feet pulled up under me, watching variety shows, loud comedians, anything to take my mind off a grieving, faceless man who howled like a banshee in the woods.

I wasn't interested in *I've Got a Secret*. The stuff those folks behind the screen were trying to hide was nothing, nothing. In the middle of the show, I suddenly realized the sheriff and Nathaniel Hawthorne had scared dates and times right out of my mind. Here it was Friday, opening night at the carnival. I'd promised to sneak out and meet Pearce at the Ferris wheel.

The stove clock said nine-forty. And this moth-eaten outfit might not even have a Ferris wheel. But how hard could it be to find red-haired Pearce McMillan in a field lit up like day? I put on loafers without socks, found my wallet on the dresser, and looked at the window again. Why bother to climb out like a monkey; who'd see or care? I checked my cash, counted fifteen ones and a ten — my baby-sitting savings. I stuffed it in the pocket of my dungarees and felt under the bed for the pint bottle of Wild Turkey I'd taken from the cabinet the day before and hidden there. Pearce would like that; we'd have a birthday celebration.

My hand hit something square and dusty first. I pulled it out: the HavaTampa box I used to keep my treasures in. I opened the lid. A chunk of pink quartz, some Indian head pennies, a Cover Girl compact, and the charred photo of my mother. Old treasures and forbidden things. I dabbed powder on my nose and cheeks. It smelled of faded violets, too sweet. I clicked the compact shut and slipped it in my other pocket. The whiskey was farther back. My fingers finally stumbled over the neck of the bottle. I drew it out and tucked it into my waistband.

Then I left by the door. If my father could make up lies and still walk bold-faced out the front, so could I.

The west side of town held a warm gold glow, as if someone had buttered the siding on all the buildings. I streaked down the back alley like a stray, breaking into a flat-out run as I neared the depot. Getting back some of the excitement I used to feel each year when I was little and the carnival midway opened up.

I went up to the ticket booth, an outhouse shape painted turquoise. The man perched inside needed a shave; his eyes were shadowed by the brim of a greasy fedora. I pushed a crumpled dollar into the pocked metal slot, and yellow-stained fingers jabbed back a ticket and my change: twenty-seven cents.

That was weird. "Isn't it seventy-five?" I asked. "Like on the sign?" But the impatient tilt of his head and the harsh reek of old cigarettes seeping from the box made me gather up the two dimes, one nickel, and two pennies and go on in.

I passed a faded clown face painted on plywood sheets, its red jaws the gaping entrance to a show tent. The popcorn and candy stands were empty. The younger kids had probably been taken home already, and the teenagers and young marrieds were just getting there.

Here was all I'd expected: flapping posters of elephants and fat ladies and a one-eyed man called Cyclops. Everything shimmying like a fever dream in the wind that had kicked up across the field. I passed soldierly racks of candy apples so impossibly red they seemed to glow from within. I craned to see over booths and games and tents for the way to the Ferris wheel, lit up but still on the far side of the grounds.

A chorus of recorded shrieks and groans meant the Tunnel of Horrors was ahead. That'd been my favorite the past few years, and usually a recording of a honking, wheezing organ played in the background. But this was no recording. Someone, somewhere was actually mashing on the antique toes of a senile pipe organ. Cheap yellow lights winked and pulsed around everything, except spots where a broken bulb or empty socket broke the wavering line like a missing tooth. I turned at the bottle knock-down booth, shook my head and dodged the barker trying to lure me in. And found the heart of the midway, and the crowd, at last.

Gawking youth snickered and nudged each other's ribs while the barkers egged them on to *Come in, come in justa one thin quartah, what you chicken boys?* Some older guys in JV jackets were stopped before a bored, tattooed worker with skin bronzed the color and texture of a wallet. He tossed a ball up and down in front of a pyramid of wooden milk bottles. I looked, but Pearce wasn't among these T-shirts and leather jackets. Giggling packs of girls stomped past in saddle oxfords or flatfooted Capezios. Some wore capri pants like Myra's, others tight jeans with the cuffs rolled. Some even wore angora sweaters, despite the heat. Here and there a circle pin gleamed like a silver bull's-eye. Tonight I despised these groups as much as I longed, for once, to belong, to stride arm in arm down the midway with nothing on my mind but making boys want me.

I passed another booth, its glass smoked with steam and the sweat of the man who labored over the rotating popper. I inhaled the thick, buttery scent of exploded kernels and suddenly felt starved. The air was misty with oil droplets, sweet with melted sugar. The vender tweezed up my quarter with the only two fingers left on his hand. Sticky ice cream papers and greasy bags windmilled past my legs. I bent to peel a Popsicle wrapper from my ankle, and when I straightened, a hairy arm thrust a cone of popcorn out the little pick-up window, right under my nose.

I crammed a handful into my mouth right away, not caring how it looked. I was going to enjoy myself, because I had a dim feeling, not yet strung into words, that somehow this might be my last chance.

Up the midway loomed a painted wooden castle, flat cartoon turrets poking a strange combination of Jolly Rogers and Cinderella pennants into the night sky. Beyond that a wheel whirred like a mill, blurring the horizon. I pushed through laughing, shrieking crowds who left a scent trail of sweat and flowery perfume and sizzling sausages in their wake. Past the plywood castle and over a shaky footbridge. I stopped at the turnstile to the Ferris wheel. Maybe Pearce was already on the ride, but the faces I saw peering down, swooping past, were all unfamiliar.

"Ticket, girlie?" The old man hunched over the lever resembled a mummy in jeans and checked flannel.

I shook my head, then there was Pearce, grinning at me.

"Tickets, kids?" repeated the mummy man.

Pearce reached in his pocket, but I shook my head. "Baby stuff. Come on." And just like when we were kids, I led him by the hand.

"Back here," I said, pulling him behind a trailer. I slipped the flat bottle out of my waistband and showed it to him.

"Cool," he said, and tilted it back for a long swallow. I watched his Adam's apple go up and down, first impressed, then alarmed by how much he was putting away.

"Okay, here," he gasped, wiping his mouth on the back of his sleeve.

I took it doubtfully, eyed the two inches still swirling inside.

"Bottoms up," he said. Then, "Oh, wait." He wiped the neck carefully on his shirt tail, presented it again. He had nice manners when he wanted to.

I lifted it, threw back my head, and tipped an amber stream of molten fire down my throat. *"Gah,"* was all I could gasp, handing over the rest, no longer eager to keep up. "All yours, buddy. Come on."

We stopped in front of the Tunnel of Horrors, a squat Quonset hut painted flat black. Compared to the neon-shiny Wild Mouse and the space-agey Rocket Deluxe, it looked rigged up. But still creepy. At the ticket booth I didn't even reach for my wallet; just stood by as Pearce pushed a dollar into the hands behind the window. He handed me a red stub and we made for the wooden stairs leading up to a bridge where you boarded the cars. The splintery rungs were silvergray with rot, they shuddered under my heels. It was like climbing a living backbone.

For some strange reason, the cars were shaped like little Viking boats. The attendant had a nibbled mustache and an undershirt stiff with ketchup and mustard droppings. He spit into an empty Vienna sausage can, then squeezed my arm so hard I yelped as he handed me into the next car. Pearce jumped in and laid his arm across the steel backrest. The attendant shoved a bar across our laps and winked.

As we headed for the dark maw, I suddenly wanted to bail out. Too bad I'd had no mother to pull me aside before my first date. Maybe I would've rolled my eyes while she lectured about how young ladies behaved. No scrambling on all fours through the Fun House, no riding the Wild Mouse in a skirt, no sitting next to boys on the Bobsled where centrifugal force would stick us together like airplane glue. Any taboos I needed to know I would have to teach myself.

There'd always been gruesome rumors about rides like this one. I'd heard them on the playground as far back as grade school, between ups at softball or waiting in the cafeteria line. Horrors hissed into my ear or sent zinging over my head so my ears heated and my stomach flopped: bodies sliced in two on the tracks, giant rats that leapt into cars from the metal girders, pranksters who substituted real axes for the rubber fakes.

The car lurched forward with a sawing and grinding of gears. The rusted prow jolted through a fringed curtain, and we slid into blackness. Immediately a chattering skeleton, leg bones tinted pink by the red lights, dropped from the ceiling. I gasped, laughed, and hid my face in Pearce's shirt sleeve. The bones cackled crazily, and a buzzer kept going off like we were late for something.

The tunnel smelled like mildewed towels. I slid low in my seat and looked over the side of the car. The tracks were clogged with wrappers, bottles, paper cones, and every now and then something I took at first to be pale, deflated balloons.

Pearce pulled me closer. I started to scoot away, but when hidden gears dragged a store mannequin wrapped in red-splashed gauze right into our path, I crawled onto his lap. Suddenly I was clawing spiderwebs from my face, choking on them. A hideous green thing with one yellow eye was leaning over us, staring down, her pointed black hat cocked like a jaunty beret. Lord God . . . but it must be nearly over. I saw a telltale seam of light, the exit doors.

But then we jerked to a stop. The hairs on my arms and neck rose quivering in the thin draft blowing through the door seam. I held my breath in the dark.

"We'll be moving in a second," said Pearce.

"I know." I could actually feel him thinking about touching my breast. The car hiccuped ahead a few inches and threw us together. When it jerked to a stop his free hand landed on my thigh. He lifted my chin gently, turned my face up, and kissed my mouth. His lips were dry, warm, a little chapped from the wind. I leaned into him, relaxing. This was something new and all mine, a thing my father would never dream I was doing. So I didn't push Pearce's hand off my leg, and after a moment it slid

186

higher. His other hand cupped my breast, his fingertips grazed the nipple, sending sparks shooting to my stomach. I wondered if he'd learned all this, or if it was wired into him like a machine.

Then he leaned over and probed my ear with his tongue. I had liked everything else, but that hot, wet squirming in my ear was awful. I turned my head and bit down on his wrist.

"Damn!" he said, pulling away. "What's the matter?"

I wasn't sure. Except what we were doing, and how much I wanted to keep on proved I couldn't really blame Myra or Dad for their sins. Because now I was caught up in the same white-hot kindling, juice and heat building in my lower parts that could not be ignored or denied. All of which must've driven them on to craziness. I didn't want to understand it, why they might have needed each other. Why they could not stop.

It seemed Dad had been right. My mother's tainted blood was in my body, which had passed through hers, which she had made. Her bad thoughts were in my mind, and my father's weakness, too. If he saw all this ugliness in me, and I saw it in him and in Myra, what abominations in us all must Almighty God — the One who knew everything — see everywhere, all the time?

To go any further would ruin our lives. Then Reverend Hardy could put us in one of his sermons about eternal hellfire. Then Pearce's dreams of the sea, and the acting career I wanted, all of it would warp and twist and melt, burn out, and flow away downstream of us, like ash sprinkled on water.

I yanked at the safety bar despite the peeling warning sticker on the car's dash. The lock gave with a screech and the bar flew up. I jumped out, skidding on something I didn't want to see, and ran, slipping and sliding in trash. Someone was shouting, maybe Pearce, but I was already hitting the exit doors with outstretched hands. They burst open and I stumbled out onto the platform, fifteen feet above the upturned faces below.

The wind was clotted with burnt popcorn and waffle grease. I bent over, hands on my knees, sucking it in like an ocean breeze. Behind me again the mocking buzzer, the rattle of bones, of snapping cables, maybe. I looked down on a fortune-teller's booth, a gypsy with hair wild and black as snakes; her eyes, mouth, upturned face unperturbed as she stared back. She was too elegant to be sitting in a box beneath an elevated track where ticket stubs and abandoned underpants and broken hula dolls and crushed peanut shells littered the packed dirt.

"Dory!" Behind me Pearce sounded half-mad, half-apologetic. I stepped to the edge and jumped. Into a madness of yells, shouts, carnival music, barkers crying *hurryhurryhurry girlie four chances only a dollah!* I hit the pebbled ground hard enough to skin both hands. Then I scrambled up and ran, pushing through the crowd that had swelled so I couldn't see more than a few feet ahead. I didn't care, just stumbled on, wanting to be home. Afraid of this new Pearce, his roving hands, the groping I liked too much. I had to get away from the whole sex-musky, sweet rotten-apple and smoke stink of carnival. Too much like real life, after all.

I don't know how long it was before I slowed to a walk, then leaned against the back of a tent to catch my breath. I meant to go home as soon as I found my way out. But the carnival, which had seemed rinky-dink when I'd come in, seemed to have grown to Barnum & Bailey proportions. I finally spotted a ticket shack like the one near the entrance. I took a deep breath and walked toward it.

As I went on the crowd thinned. It seemed to part before me. Then I saw why. A familiar figure was striding through the entrance: Tom Burney in uniform, face set so I knew he hadn't come for cotton candy or rides. He flashed his badge at the ticket taker without breaking stride. I ducked behind a cutout magician, then peered around his rabbit-stuffed top hat.

The blaring music stopped for a moment, replaced by a crackle, a blat of static. A nasal voice droned over the loudspeaker: "Dory Gamble, report to the front ticket booth. Dory Gamble, front ticket booth."

I crouched lower, scared out of all reason. Maybe teenage girls could be arrested and thrown in jail with the cons and murderers and dangerous tramps movies had taught me about. We had no jail in Ordinary Springs, so I'd be taken to the Sumter County lockup or to Ocala. Maybe the logical thing would be to give myself up and tell what'd happened. It was very bad, but not murder, not really. Yet I had no faith I'd be believed or even listened to. Hadn't my father just disowned me the day before, condemned me as bad from birth?

So I ran. Away from the booth, pushing through the crowd, to where old trucks and junker cars and caravans and generators squatted like rumbling dinosaurs. I skulked along without a plan. No good to take off across an empty field; I'd be spotted immediately. But how could I go back to town where everyone knew me?

I heard voices coming and ducked beneath a semi. Scrabbling in the dirt, crawling under the wheels of a truck, I spotted an empty metal compartment, a deep, fair-sized shelf. I squeezed in, surprised to find a couple smelly old blankets, as if someone bunked there. The wool was rancid and greasy, but it padded the metal under me. I stretched out, heart thudding and jerking, and waited for the voices to pass. Another bunch came by, laughing and shouting, and then another; girls giggling and chanting football cheers.

It had to be getting late. I crawled out and stood, stiff and cramped, pins and needles shooting down my legs. I glanced around, but before I took a step, a hand clamped my shoulder hard. The fingers tightened and dug in. I turned slow as doom.

It was Pearce. "Dory!" His face was red, he was panting. "What the hell? I've been looking all over. Thought you went home or something."

"No. Not home."

"What's the matter, how come they're looking for you?"

I put a hand up to his lips, and he stopped talking. Ready to hear me out. My friend Pearce. What had all the fuss been about, over a kiss? I could barely recall. He appeared at that moment the most reassuring, the dearest thing I knew.

I knelt in the dust and litter of the grounds and drew him down with me. "Today is my birthday."

He smiled. "I know. That's why I —"

But I shushed him again and pointed beneath the truck. "Look under there," I said. He did, then laughed, sounding delighted, as full of admiration as when we'd built our tree house or found a new hideout in the wooded hammock by the Springs.

"Come on," I said, and we squirmed beneath the greasy undercarriage. "See. There's room for both of us."

We squeezed into the shelf side by side, angled around to get comfortable, and discovered the best way was face to face with his arm beneath me, mine over him.

"Pretty cool place you found here," he said.

I didn't want to talk anymore, because then I might have to explain why I was being paged, why the sheriff was looking for me. So every time he started to ask, I put my mouth over his. His breath was sweet with whiskey and Juicy Fruit.

"Hey," he said, when we had to stop to breathe. "What're we doing?"

I'd tried to avoid thinking about that. I hadn't believed sex could seem bigger, more important than anything or anyone in the world. But now I had to admit it was nice lying so close, in the warmth under the truck, in that confined space. Gradually we managed, by squirming around like contortionists, to shuck most of our clothes. We'd run around naked together before, though it had been a long time. A lot had changed.

It was warm under there, but the heat that came off his smooth, tanned skin burned my fingertips. He closed his eyes and ran his hands over me as if he'd been struck blind and wanted to map each curve and hollow of my body, to hold forever in his mind. And when he pressed on, I pressed right back. Even if it hurt worse than any skinned knee or sprained arm or fall from a tree — and that first unimaginable pain, in such an unimaginable place,

193

did paralyze me a moment.

But Pearce McMillan had never yet bested me in a dare or an adventure, in anything we'd done. I didn't figure to let him start then.

As it grew darker and the circus noise thinned out, I realized lights were being cut off. Part of the show must be closing down. I shook Pearce, who'd dozed off as if we were spending the night curled in blankets in our old treehouse by the springs. He grumbled and turned over, the sharp molasses tang of whiskey still on his breath. I couldn't wait for him anyhow, because I'd decided what to do. Go home, slip in, and gather up some things. I had the fifteen dollars in my wallet and ten silver dollars tucked in my sock drawer. Not much, but they might take me north to New York City. So what if I was ahead of schedule. I was tall for my age and betting I could pass for eighteen. Get a job in a diner or a drugstore or maybe even in hardware. They must need such stuff even in a big city.

I leaned over and kissed Pearce's sweaty forehead. He mumbled and swatted at me. I looked on his face a long time, because who knew when I'd ever see him again? By then I'd be a different Dory, and he'd have changed, too.

I slipped through the thinning crowd, out the front gate. Everything about Ordinary Springs looked different, because I knew what I was going to do. Leave, leave it all. There was a junior, a girl a year ahead of me in school, who was always bragging about how her aunt, or maybe it was her second cousin, had become a model just by turning up in the same drugstore in New York every day, sitting on a stool nursing a Coca-Cola, letting the ice melt, until one day she was spotted by a big agent. Then she became a dancer and finally the Revlon Girl. And like Cinderella, she met and married some rich Hollywood actor. Or so this girl claimed.

Sheer fantasy. The practical side of me dismissed it. The practical side worried twenty-five dollars was peanuts. Would it even buy a bus ticket? Well, it'd have to do, being all I had in the world.

In the alley behind Water Street, near the back door to the hardware store, I stopped, looked around, and listened. I found the old crack in the door's window glass in the left bottom corner. Funny how my father sold repair stuff to people, gave them advice, and yet this window had been broken for years. Not that it mattered much here, a place where crime was so low Tom Burney had to go out into the woods to look for moonshiners or hide behind a billboard on Highway 44 to trap speeding tourists just to keep busy. No one local would dream of pushing that glass in the rest of the way, of reaching inside and turning the knob, then walking through the back storeroom and up behind the big oak counter, where the register sat, unlocked.

It would be wrong. Worse than theft, stealing from a blood relation. On the other hand, I'd worked at Gamble's Hardware for years, worked hard, and had never been paid a cent. I had helped earn that money in the cash drawer. I wrapped my fist in the tail of my shirt and punched out a pane in the bottom corner.

The store was dark, so quiet it was creepier than the Tunnel of Horrors, after all the noise and lights and crowds. When I pulled out the unlocked cash drawer it screeched on its tracks. I clawed out a wad of bills without counting and stuffed them deep in my jeans. Then dumped the rest of the drawer and swept everything — change, paper money, hardware catalogs, account ledgers, an empty coffee cup, a jar of stubby pencils, the tin of paper clips —

onto the floor to make it look like a real robbery. But truly I enjoyed the crash, the broken crockery, the scattered papers. The disorder of our lives made visible. I kicked Dad's old ceramic coffee mug. It rolled across the floor and stuck under a bin.

Then I turned and ran out the back. No need to go home now. I could simply hit the road and never look back. In fact, a brilliant idea was forming. I wouldn't leave on the bus; it wasn't due till tomorrow afternoon anyhow. No, I'd hitch a ride out with the carnies.

No one gave me a second look as I bought another admission ticket. The mysterious hat-shadowed guy was gone; the new ticket taker was a pudgy woman who sat filing her nails to daggers, chewing gum double-time.

"Uh, excuse me, ma'am," I said, glancing around. "Where do I go to sign up?"

She stopped filing and chewing and looked at me for a moment, mouth open. "Do what?"

"The carnival," I whispered, looking over my shoulder. "I need to join the show right away."

She hooted. "G'wan wit you, babyface." She jerked the file over her shoulder, then reached past me for the money the next person in line was handing over.

I walked away, forcing myself not to run till I'd reached the back lot with the trucks and caravans again. I had known for years that I'd leave this place anyhow. I'd thought after graduation. Why not now? The carnival seemed like a good way out. I was fairly smart, I could act. There had to be something here I could do.

There was the truck I'd crawled into before, or one just like it. If Pearce was still here, maybe he'd want to come along. I was hopped up, so antsy I could hardly keep from jittering right out of my skin. The wad of money dug into my hipbone. I dropped to my knees and was about to crawl under the truck when a heavy hand gripped my arm. This time, I knew it wasn't Pearce.

A quarter-moon glint of curved steel. "Your daddy's been worried about you, Dory." Tom Burney's deep voice in the dark. "So let's walk."

I didn't make a fuss because he was in uniform, and there I was with a pocket full of cash and glass shards on my clothes. "Just wanted to see the carnival," I said. "Guess I shouldn't have gone without permission, but —"

Burney's lips stretched in a humorless smile as he herded me out the front gate to his car. He didn't bother to answer. Just opened the door and told me to get in back. When I saw the deputy in the passenger seat, I knew things were too bad to fix with an apology.

12

Burney prodded me into the house when I balked at the front door. Dad was sitting in his favorite armchair under the good reading light. But I couldn't tell from his face how mad he was.

"Found her, Owen. Now let's sit down and talk."

Dad nodded but didn't look right at me.

Burney hooked some ladderback chairs from the dining room. He set one by me, and I dropped into it obediently. He straddled the other backward, his arms resting on the top rail. The hook was a gleaming thing that drew the eye, even against my will.

"We got a problem, folks." He looked over at me. "You know what fingerprints are, Dory?"

I almost laughed. What did he take me for? Anybody who watched TV, shows like *The Naked City* or the *Untouchables*, knew that. Then ice water trickled down my arms and legs because we weren't talking about TV. I swallowed and nodded.

He stared at me silently a moment, waiting for a comment, maybe a confession. "We took the empty bottle my deputy found near Fitzgerald and sent it to the lab in Gainesville. Guess what? They found three sets of prints on it. One belongs to Mrs. Fitzgerald, who always gave her husband his medicine. One belongs to the pharmacist. But the last set, they couldn't tell me who those belong to."

My father frowned. "So what're you saying, Tom? You don't think Myra —"

Burney took off his hat and ran a hand through his hair, which was thinner than I recalled, the scalp showing in places. "Owen," he said sadly. "Wake up. You got your mind on one thing, and here Rome is burnin' up all around you."

Dad opened his mouth, then closed it. They both looked at me, and I shrank back, pressing my backbone to the chair's hard slats. Burney said, "What would you say if I told you, Miss Dory Gamble, that I was gone drive you over to the office and take a set of your fingerprints?"

"That I don't want to go," I whispered, gazing at the floor. The seam of my jeans rubbed uncomfortably between my legs, my underwear felt damp and sticky. I wondered if he could look through me like an

X-ray machine and tell what else I'd been up to.

"Well then," said Burney. "You better look me in the eye and say what happened the night Frank Fitzgerald died. And don't leave nothing out."

So I did. For some reason it was easier to say what I'd done myself than to get out the parts about my father and Myra. Burney asked me to speak up at those points, and I did, but I couldn't look at either of them. Yet none of that seemed to shake him. It was like he'd already known. Perhaps there was a secret men's social club, or a special Rotary meeting where they shared such things. It was me Big Tom was most interested in.

When I reached the part where I gave the pills to Frank, one by one, my father said, "Dory!" He looked at me with such surprise and grief, I knew he hadn't had a clue after all. Hadn't *known*, no matter what he'd said to me in the back of the store. But then even Tom Burney said he was too stuck on Myra to notice much of anything else.

"So here's the thing, Owen. I won't fingerprint your girl, but we'll have to get her out of town. Fitzgerald was too weak to open that bottle. The widow has you for an alibi. You don't want that to come up in court, though, do you? Or to have Dory take the stand."

Dad rose and paced to the dining room and back. I kept waiting for him to yell at me, maybe to slap me again like he had over the dinner with Myra. Instead, he just looked beat, shoulders slumped like a man who's just lost everything on a Jai Alai serve or a single hand of cards.

Burney and I watched like he was on stage and we didn't know the script. At last he came back and stood in front of the sheriff. "I have a second cousin in Savannah," he said. "A retired librarian. She might like to have Dory stay for a while."

I was opening my mouth to protest. What had I done wrong that he hadn't a hundred times more? Why was I going to be punished if he wasn't? But Burney shook his head impatiently. "I don't think so. You've lost control of the girl, Owen. She's been all over town, late at night. She's committed something, manslaughter at least. You think some spinster librarian's gonna keep her straight? What's called for is structure, discipline. I can drive her to Marianna tonight if you'll sign the papers."

My protest over being shipped to an elderly cousin died in my throat. *Marianna.*

If a delinquent boy or a wild girl was sent up there, everyone knew what that meant. We'd all heard horror stories about knives and gangs and nutty kids who'd killed other kids. About girls who were proud of their scars and carried razor blades under their tongues, praying for a fight.

Now it was Dad's turn to stare at Burney. "Damn, Tom. She's a good kid, she just got caught up in all this . . . this . . ." His face was red. "Maybe she slipped out once, but Dory isn't the kind you send off to a place like that."

"No? Go look at her bedroom window. You think this house don't need screens to keep out the bugs?"

My father frowned, then disappeared down the hall. He came back, the bent screen in his hand. "It was under the bed," he said in a flat voice. "Dory, what's the meaning of this?"

"She's been sneaking off to meet boys at night," said Burney. "You didn't know that."

I could see the battle taking place, plain on my father's face. If he slipped out to fornicate with a neighbor at night, was it a crime if his child imitated him? At last he shook his head. "I can't cast any stones," he muttered. "We'll just keep an eye on her, we can —"

"You think this is some kind of phase?" Tom Burney's huge head swung over to stare at me again. "Stand up, Dory."

I got up, tried to look him in the eye.

"Turn out your pockets," he said.

I stood there, not moving. Willing with all my heart and mind, please Jesus, for him to drop dead at my feet. So maybe I was a born killer, maybe I should be sent away.

Burney thrust two beefy fingers into the front pocket of my jeans. He fished out the green wad. Then slowly, methodically counted it. When he got up to seventy-five, my father held up a hand, astonishment on his face.

"Dory, where'd you get all that?"

I shook my head and began to cry then, furious with them, with my own stupidity, snot running from my nose like a three-year-old. I wiped it on my sleeve.

"It's from the store, Owen. You're gonna have to fix the glass on that back door. She's breaking and entering, she's going with boys, she's stealing from you, and if those prints on the pill bottle match she'd be in a world of trouble. Trouble we can't do nothing about."

My father kept looking between me and his friend, as if he didn't know either of us anymore.

"Don't take my word for it," the sheriff went on. "If you want to go see for yourself, we'll wait. But don't dawdle. It's late, and it's a long drive to Marianna."

In the end, my father nodded.

I tried to stall. "I need to change clothes. Wait, I got to have a different pair of shoes, these are giving me blisters."

Most of all, I tried not to look at my father's cold, stony face, as he stood across the room, arms folded, like all this had nothing to do with him anymore. Maybe I was no daughter of his, after all. We weren't the inseparable father and child who went everywhere, did everything together. We hadn't been that for a long while.

Finally Burney lost patience and prodded me out the door barefoot. "They got a whole set of clothes for you there, honey," he said.

He hustled me to the car with his hands clamped to my shoulders. The deputy, who'd fallen asleep, rubbed his eyes and sat up straight. I didn't know him, but he was almost as big as Tom, and he looked cranky and used to getting what he wanted. Tom pushed me into the backseat, a hand on top of my head so I wouldn't bump it on the frame. He shut the door and got in. A roar of the engine, and the county car fishtailed out of our driveway.

"I'm real sorry to see you fall this way, Dory," Burney said in his deep, rumbling voice. Then he was silent the whole four hours it took to drive north and then through the panhandle to Marianna.

I didn't have much to do but sweat between the rolled up windows, to shake with terror at the thought of where I was going. I counted the minutes at first; the dashboard clock was visible through the mesh screen that separated the back seat from the front. And then, despite my terror, at some point after Tallahassee, I fell asleep.

When I woke we were pulling through a chain-link fence topped with barbed wire, then up a long curved drive to a bank of flat-roofed brick bunkers. It took Burney and the deputy both to pull me out of the backseat. They hustled me through the front door, down a pale green hall floored with cracked linoleum, and into a little gray room. "Sit there," said the sheriff, "I got paperwork." He closed the door behind him.

I looked around at the empty room, the tiny high windows. I thought of Pearce. Was he awake yet, had he gone home thinking he'd see me at the store in the morning? I wondered if he'd believe all the things he'd hear. I'd been right to suppose I'd never see him again. But I wouldn't cry about that; I was done scrubbing tears off my face. They'd be the last ones anybody wrung out of me, ever again.

After a while the door slammed open again and a huge square-faced woman came in. She nodded but didn't say anything at first. The nametag pinned on her blouse said MATRON CAMBER.

"Stand up," she said. I did, and then she turned out my pockets. As she was writing something on a clipboard the cops came back, along with another man in a suit. Nobody was smiling, and I couldn't think of a thing to say. I looked at them once, then stared straight ahead. Nodded when they asked if I understood the questions and understood where I was at. A different cop sat outside the door, I guess to keep me from escaping.

As dawn broke they took me to a cavernous old courthouse that smelled of disinfectant and years of body odor. The yawning black-robed judge was called Donofrio. He had a hooked nose and a mane of white hair, and he looked like he'd been born with them.

"Do you have an attorney, young lady?"

he asked in a soft drawl.

I swallowed, brushed the hair out of my eyes. "No," I said. Then added, "Sir."

"The court will appoint one for you, then."

I started to ask why, then just nodded. That seemed nice, because for all he knew I was guilty of everything he'd read on the sheet Burney handed him.

Then the cops took me straight back to the jail. And in the same room, the grim and square-jawed Camber came out again to pat me down. I tried to smile, to catch her eye, to figure how to charm her like Harriet McMillan would. But the matron never looked at my face, just ordered me to strip off my clothes as impersonally as an undertaker. Beneath my jeans and button-down shirt I had only a cotton bra and a pair of underpants. I took off the bra and crossed my hands over my chest. When she motioned for me to take down the Fruit of the Looms, I shook my head. She stepped forward and jerked them to my ankles in one quick, economical yank. I stepped out in a clumsy dance, and she bundled everything up together.

"Regulation shower," she said.

Arms crossed, shivering, I followed her down a hallway floored with gray linoleum, then into a smaller room with open shower stalls and a huge drain in the middle of the sloping floor. Sinks and toilets against the walls. But no curtains, and nowhere to change or hang your clothes.

First she made me lean over while she got out a special comb and checked my head for lice. She pawed through my hair for a minute or two, then grunted as if satisfied. While she fiddled with the shower knobs I was drawn, like nails to a magnet, to the mirror. It wasn't glass but some kind of wavy polished metal, pimpled with rosebuds of rust. I looked long and hard at myself; it had a distorted funhouse effect. So this is what she looks like, I thought. A loser-girl who kills invalids and robs her own father. A teenaged sleaze who goes all the way under the belly of a carnival truck. My eyes, swollen and red-rimmed, were naked and pink as newborn mice.

Like a bobcat in a trap, I'd chewed myself free of Ordinary Springs. Only the result was not what I'd imagined.

Matron turned on a shower and a sudden spray spewed out, steaming in the cool air. She nodded at me to get underneath.

I was beginning to understand by then that there was no point in refusing to do whatever this official uniformed world demanded. I stepped under the lukewarm spray and gripped a grime-cracked cake of soap. It kept squirting away onto the tiled floor. Matron Camber scowled each time she had to bend, then hand it back. The warm water felt good on my chest and back, though the rest of me was cold. Finally she grunted, flipped off the levers, and handed me a towel thin as a lace curtain. I could see through it in the dim light.

"This way now," she said.

We walked back to the first room, me stark naked, goose-pimpled, and shivering. She pulled the kind of rubber gloves a doctor used out of her dress pocket, then squatted before me like she meant to pray. She lifted my feet, checked between my toes and under my arms. "What're you doing?" I asked, flinching away. "What you looking for?"

"Just open your mouth." She looked inside, at my teeth and under my tongue. Grunted as if satisfied. "Okay, turn around. Hands on the table."

Ears to armpits, she checked every inch and fold of my skin, humming as if she were shopping vegetables. At first I was so shocked by the cool rubbery fingertips that poked and pulled so impersonally, I just gripped the table and gasped once or twice. But then she bent and slid a hand up the inside of my thighs, to my crotch. Without even thinking I twisted around and kicked her.

She cursed, shoved away, and yanked the door open. A uniformed cop came in with a thick sandwich in one hand, brushing crumbs out of his moustache. I backed off, trying to cover my crotch and my small naked tits.

"A real live one," Matron Camber said. "Lend a hand, okay?"

The cop swallowed his last bite of ham and bread, wiped his hands on his pants, and came for me.

My room was in a wing off the main hallway. Its four beds were made of iron with railings for the headboard and footboard that looked like they'd been welded from recycled cell bars. Humped shapes in two of them; my new roommates, sleeping. The room had a tiny sink of stained porcelain and another wavy metal mirror. I wondered about a toilet; by then I had to go bad. I finally whispered this, and Matron Camber took me down the hall. Told me to leave the door open while I lifted the shapeless blue shift she'd given me to wear. That's when I understood it wouldn't let up, that in this place I'd be allowed no privacy or dignity. I could not conceal any act, no matter how personal or embarrassing.

She walked me back and pointed to one of the middle beds.

"There's a nightgown in the chest," she said. Then turned on her heel and left.

I opened the drawer of a plywood chest and lifted out a white sack, pretty much a double of the faded blue I wore. So I took that off, put on the white gown, and slid between the sheets. They smelled of bleach yet felt gritty. I laid my head on the flat thing that must have once been a pillow and closed my eyes. I lay like that, not moving, letting silent tears leak from the corners of my eyes and drip into my ears, till they overflowed and were soaked up by my hair and the coarse cotton of the pillowcase. So much for my brave claims.

After what seemed a week, dawn light came through the thick window glass embedded with mesh. Then a bell went off out in the hall, and I met my roommates.

As the clanging died away, someone groaned in the bed to my right, while another voice uttered a string of curses from the bed one down on the left, next to the wall. I opened my eyes and, without meaning to, sobbed. The hoarse voice from the far bed complained, "You cried us a river, honey. Now give it a rest."

That, I learned, as we all rolled out of bed, was Letitia. She was milk pale, thin as wire, with lank blonde hair and a mountain-twangy voice. She looked me up and down, snorted, and went to the sink to splash water on her face.

The girl on the right was olive-skinned with a soft, rounded face and baby fat on her arms. She looked pleased to see me, as if I'd been invited for a sleepover.

"What's your name?" she asked. "I'm Ardis."

She had little blue-green and yellow bruises all over the tender flesh of her upper arms. I found out later some of the other girls liked to pinch her because she cried so easily. She put out her hand to shake but drew it back when I didn't reach out right away. I hadn't mean to be rude, just felt shell-shocked, and it didn't occur to me to respond until she'd already pulled away.

We went down the hall with a bunch of other girls, and after watery oatmeal and cold toast at long cafeteria tables, the others went in various directions. I was collared by Matron Camber again and herded to a waiting police car, this time a local one. The cops drove me back to the old courthouse in Marianna, where I was hauled in front of a different judge. The charges were delinquency, breaking and entering, and theft. This judge, to my surprise, was a grandmotherly looking woman with a bad perm. Not that I looked so hot myself, lacking a comb and encased in a blue feed-sack. I tried to take deep, calming breaths. I needed to get my act together and make these people see I didn't belong there.

A man in a suit was telling the judge I was an escape risk, sure to abscond from any training school or detention center. "The Pine Hills School is the only secure placement, your honor." He handed her some papers. "The father has signed away rights. He agrees she's incorrigible. There's the theft, the breaking and entering — oh yeah, and she goes out the window at night."

I was no longer his daughter. Now it was official. I sat there on the hard wood bench and realized I was helpless. A gush of pure panic unhinged me. I lurched up from the bench and tried to run. The cops imprisoned me with hard, thick arms while I thrashed like a hooked fish. The judge banged her hammer, shook her head, and ordered them to take me out.

Then they decided my fate without the inconvenience of my presence, behind closed doors.

13

The first few weeks at Pine Hills, at night after lights out, sometimes I heard voices just beyond my bed. Pearce, who sounded amused. *Dory, you nut. What mess you got into now?* Or sometimes it was my father, calling me Eudora Heartburn, telling me not to talk about the bad woman who went away. Those nights I pulled the thin pillow over my head to block them out. Then the only one I could still hear was Frank Fitzgerald. That scared me the worst, because I wasn't crazy; I knew he was dead. But I listened anyway, because his voice was the only one not laughing or yelling or telling me off. He seemed to be saying, *Chin up, Dory. You can work this little problem out. Might take time and figuring, and I can't do it for you, but work at it and you can get the answer.*

I still liked Frank and felt comforted by the sound of his voice — soft, but deep and friendly — even though he was part of the reason I was in such trouble. But I had to disagree with him. No. Sorry. This time you overestimated me.

★ ★ ★

A couple weeks later a public defender came to talk about my charges. He introduced himself and said I was in trouble, all right, but he thought we could work something out. I just had to be straight with him.

"Okay, I did sneak out. But I didn't kill my neighbor," I said. "He wanted to take those pills, because of my father and his wife."

He stared at me silently. Perhaps I wasn't being clear. But what else was left to confess — that I was a menace to myself, a lousy liar, not a virgin anymore? That was nobody's business but mine.

He picked lint off his lapel and nodded like he was humoring me. "It's not important to me whether you're guilty or not." That sounded strange. He said the fact of Frank Fitzgerald's death was "inconvenient," which was such an understatement I had to bite my tongue not to bark out a laugh.

Then he said, "The good news is, Judge Fariello's waiving trial in favor of commitment to the girl's school. Which is good, because then you get your high school diploma and maybe some kind of rehabilitation. The way she sees it, you're a victim, too, in a sense. So don't blow it. Then you turn eighteen and — poof! You're out of here."

I registered what he'd said: Commitment. Diploma. Rehabilitation. But I had just turned sixteen; I still had two and a half years of school to go. Did they mean for me to spend it all here? I looked up at him through my hair, which still needed combing. "That's the good news?"

He shuffled papers and looked anxious to move on. "Take it or leave it, kiddo," he said, glancing at his watch.

I screwed up my face to show I was considering it. What the hell. If I followed their rules, did like I was told for a change, maybe they'd let me out sooner.

"Hey, it could be worse," he said in a buck-up-kid voice. "After that flip-out act in the courtroom, she could've ordered you committed to Chattahoochee."

The state hospital was in another panhandle town called Chattahoochee. Parents often mentioned it as a threat, a sort of reverse-boogeyman tactic. If my father said, "Dory, if you don't stop tapping your feet sixty to the dozen you're going to drive me to Chattahoochee," I knew it was time to quit, to straighten up. Now I was the one who'd narrowly avoided being driven there.

So it was back in the white state car; down the rural twisting two-laner, highway 90 northeast; past muslin-shaded tobacco fields and ramshackle wooden barns; through little towns with names like Bayou George and Sawdust.

Then the aide was parking the car, tucking the keys in the visor. The guard was pulling me out.

I was back at the school, where the staff didn't smile much, and the way you said anything, even "Good morning," was taken very seriously. Even after you'd earned the few privileges possible, like owning a belt and shoelaces again, the rule was always no glass, because it could be broken into shards. And no metal, because it might be sharpened into knives. And especially no ballpoint pens, which, I was soon informed by Letitia, made great zip guns.

"Hell, yeah," she told me. "Huh, where'd you grow up, girl, Sunnybrook Farm? Even a sharp *pencil* make you a good stabbing knife."

Because we were sharing a room, I worried about how she'd done her research. She told me one night that she'd been married off at thirteen to a friend of her father's, a man thirty years older than her. He had branded his initials into her upper arm with a length of hot iron.

"But they all done that, to show them other men to keep hands off," she said. I had to believe it; when she lifted the sleeve of her blue dress, there were the crooked, crude letters COW in raised scars, for Cory Otis Wainwright. "He made me his heifer, all right," she snorted.

When I asked her how she'd gotten from the Appalachian mountains in Tennessee to a reform school in Florida, she'd only laughed.

"This place is a dream vacation for me, honey." And to take it, she'd had to burn down the house around Cory Otis, who'd graduated from knocking out her front teeth to renting her body to his friends to keep him in shine. Then she'd hooked up with another guy. "A big mistake," she admitted. "Cory all over again."

When he'd stopped in Weewahitchka to rob a 7-Eleven and got caught, she was sent here for being the getaway driver. He'd told her he just needed smokes and a quart of beer, but hadn't mentioned the cash drawer.

I marveled at the lives of my fellow detainees. Most had broken some law, but most had also been beaten, burned, raped, shot, or stabbed. One girl had been in thirty-two foster homes. I didn't have time to consider what all this meant, because the staff kept us pretty busy. When we weren't taking classes in the big room at the back that held all ages from eleven up to eighteen, we were put on housekeeping duty, which meant scrubbing out the rows of ancient rust-stained commodes with eye-watering bleach. Or washing the scuffed, curled linoleum tiles on our knees with a sponge and bucket.

True, it wasn't all work. Every now and then we'd go out in escorted groups for walks, if it wasn't raining or too hot and the matrons felt like getting some fresh air. We could go to the school library, a dingy little room with secondhand *Nancy Drews* and *Reader's Digest Condensed Books*. Reading even such mildewed, out-dated stuff was heaven compared to being sentenced to the whining daytime soap operas that held most of the girls in thrall. I began to devour stories: *Wuthering Heights*, what a sorry couple. *Jane Eyre*, who I felt sorry for and proud of all at once. *Little Women*, fatherless girls who all, except for Jo, made me roll my eyes and yawn.

Sometimes I still dreamed my own father would come to his senses, come save me, if only I could be patient. Other days, I imagined his face as part of the ground beneath my hoe, as I chopped and slashed weeds from the school vegetable garden. By then I'd been at the school long enough to have learned the girls' motto: *I am responsible for my own decisions. I control my own actions.*

Well then, God help us, was all I could ever think as we dutifully recited this, standing in a motley, imperfect circle.

Almost against my will — because it might imply I'd be there long enough to need one — I also made a friend. My other roommate Ardis, a large-boned brunette from Crystal River, wouldn't talk about why she was there. It made no difference; I didn't have much call to be self-righteous about anyone else's sins. We often ended up side by side in line to go to the hospital library, though her taste ran to gothic romances and *Trixie Belden, Student Nurse.* The hospital books had sticky plastic covers, stained with what I hoped were chocolate smears or coffee stains and greasy fingerprints. The nicotine-yellow pages were grimy and dog-eared.

We talked when it was allowed and ended up at meals giggling like school girls — which of course we still were. I'd always wondered what had been so funny to those packs of girls at Ordinary Springs Combined School, who were always leaning head to head, snickering, bursting into sudden high laughter. Now I knew: nothing, and everything.

Like the way Ardis could imitate Matron Camber, right down to the nasal drawl and her secret nose-picking method of rubbing inside one nostril with a thumb. Ardis would talk about how when we got out we'd get a roomy apartment with tall windows at the top of a building in New York. We'd start our own beatnik coffee house with little round Frenchified tables.

When we talked about this world to come, even on the bad days when I hung my head thinking of how long I had to be shut away in Marianna, I could get up and do things, even smile a little. Which was good, because then the staff wouldn't feel obliged to write in my file that I was being uncooperative or sullen.

Ardis was also my first vegetarian. I'd never heard of such a thing, but all it meant was that she didn't eat meat. I didn't care, but for some reason the cafeteria staff did. They had special orders not to serve her any meat, which was no reflection on them personally. Perhaps it felt like some kind of insult to their menu or their cooking skills, which weren't advanced.

But then just about anything I ate those days made me feel sick. I woke up sick, and the smell of burnt oatmeal that seeped down the halls made me gag. As the weeks passed, more and more often I had to run over and retch into the sink as soon as I got out of bed. Some days I felt puny morning to night.

Just how much Ardis's preferences were resented was made clear one afternoon in the cafeteria, as she and I pushed our trays down the line, pointing out what we wanted. She got anxious before meals, believing it was not just unhealthy but a mortal sin to eat animals or wear their skins. She was always after me to get shoes that weren't real leather, though I kept pointing out I had to wear what the school gave me, because all my own clothes were back in Ordinary Springs. Besides, it was too cold for rubber thongs in February, even in north Florida.

"What's in that dish?" Ardis asked the worker behind the glass divider that day. She pointed at a steaming steel tray. The server, a wizened little woman with no front teeth and a dried-apple face, said, "Just green beans, honey, you eat on up. Get you some —" She hesitated, lips pressed together, then grinned and finished, "Some curves on those bones!"

Ardis flushed, because she had plenty of curves already. Being a vegetarian didn't rule out pies and cookies and cake, and she loved desserts. But she nodded and held out her plate for green beans.

We sat and dug in because we'd been for a long walk around the grounds after Horticulture Class, which was really just all of us pulling weeds and planting stuff around the grounds while a bored guard followed. For once I didn't feel sick, but starving. Still, I set down my fork when I noticed crescents of dirt under my nails that washing my hands hadn't got rid of. I was cleaning them with a corner of my paper napkin when a tall black guy wearing a cafeteria smock walked over. He started wiping down our gray Formica table, though it looked cleaner than the greasy rag in his hand.

While he was making flat, wet circles right next to our trays he glanced at Ardis's plastic plate, the three sections of different vegetables, plus a side dish of apple sauce. He smiled and shook his head. "Hey, girl. Din' they tell you that pink bit floating in the beans used to be part of a pig?" Then he snorted to demonstrate, in case we hadn't gotten the picture.

Ardis covered her mouth and moaned. When she bolted from the table, Camber and another matron looked up, forks stopped in mid-bite, like *Now what?* She didn't make it to the bathroom door before losing her lunch on the checkerboard tiles.

I got up then, too, because that was just the last straw.

"Where you going?" asked Letitia, whose age and school seniority entitled her to act as a sort of house mother to our wing.

"To tell somebody about what they did to Ardis." I tried to pull my arm free.

"Sit," she said in her calm, flat, cracker drawl.

"It was on purpose!"

"Those people got they hands on your food bowl, honey. They control what go in it and what don't. They c'n take it away. An' they think you and me and her are trash. Now you better *sit.*"

One last jerk against her hard, bony fingers, then I dropped back onto the bench. When the matrons finally half-carried Ardis back to the table, her hands were crossed over her chest, she was sour with vomit, and her face gleamed with snot and tears. Letitia draped one bony arm over her shoulders without even stopping the steady, up-and-down rhythm of eating.

But I couldn't look at Ardis, for shame. Me, her friend, and I'd done nothing.

One night the next week she came to my cot, crying. Said they'd been poisoning her, putting slivers of horse hooves in the bean soup. Hiding live maggots in her rice. I sat on my cot and rocked her, my rage building. She was a nice person, and this place was driving her crazy for entertainment. I myself was wrong-headed and stupid and full of bad choices, but I'd never set out to deliberately torment somebody just to laugh about it later. If we had to wait to be released before we got out to share a place, Ardis would be crazy before then. Driven in the white panel truck to Chattahoochee before we even got high school diplomas.

"Hey," I said, lifting her face to look up at me. "Don't cry. We're getting out of here soon."

She sniffed and smiled at me, her face uncreasing until it seemed like a hopeful child's. Looking down, I felt a nudge of impatience. Would I have to be the parent, always the one to figure things out, after we escaped? I wished for a minute . . . but I pushed that thought back down. Afraid it meant I wasn't her friend at all, that I was no one's friend but my own. I hugged her harder, but the desire to let go felt more like the God's truth.

At last she stopped crying and only sniffled. I lay back against the rail headboard. She smiled and patted my arm, then frowned. "Hey. You got a little belly, Dory."

I looked down and saw what she meant. I'd always been tall and thin, my stomach nearly concave. I hadn't noticed under the baggy dresses we always wore, but now my lower belly had a distinct curve.

"All that white bread and potatoes and rice," I said. That was mostly what I ate, because the other stuff, the gray, boiled gristle they called meat, the lumpy green pastes labeled lima beans and spinach, with bits of fat pork floating like meal worms, disgusted me.

Ardis stared at me fearfully. "When you got your period last?"

I laughed in disbelief but began counting up the weeks from when I'd been sent away. I'd bled a couple weeks before that. I got to almost three months, the whole time I'd been there, and sat up abruptly.

"I had a baby once," said Ardis dreamily. "But they took it away."

"You said you were in here for stealing stuff," I reminded her.

"I stole a lock at the Western Auto and put it on my bedroom door," she said. "But it didn't keep my brother out." Then she looked at me again. "Oh no, Dory. They'll send you away."

"Don't be stupid," I snapped. "They already did that. They sent me here." But I felt sick again and cold despite the hot, stuffy room. Ardis leaned her head on my arm, stroking it.

Breathing hard, feeling a fluttering panic, I pushed her away.

"Sorry," she mumbled, her hair over her face. She scooted backward like a crayfish, then slid off the bed and was gone. I closed my eyes. Thought about going after her to say, *Never mind, it's okay.* But it wasn't. If I'd been sent here already, because Sheriff Burney had got my father to say I was incorrigible, what would they have in store for a girl who got pregnant to boot? And how could I have a baby? No, it was impossible.

But I couldn't deny what Pearce and I had done, after we'd peeled off most of each other's clothes in the crawl space beneath that truck. As far as I knew from schoolyard lore, we'd done everything needed to make one. I wanted to get up right then and run away, climb the chain link and barbed wire that held me there. But I couldn't run from a thing so tiny it was part of me, floating in the universe of my body. I laid a shaking hand on my stomach and felt with my fingertips, like a blind person. But carefully, because suddenly that stretch of me seemed alien, strange. Then I quit, in case somebody saw me doing it. I picked up my book. Turned pages, but didn't understand a word.

That night I heard rubber soles pounding down the corridor, someone shouting orders, and, far off, the wail of a siren. I stumbled out to the common room. Girls were out of bed, humped together like cows in a cold pasture, wiping sleep-crusted eyes, and whispering. I found Letitia and tugged at her sleeve. She always knew what was going on. But this I couldn't take it in; something about Ardis and bedsprings?

"God damn, are you deaf," she finally said. "Your little friend gone and swallowed them. Cut her insides up so bad, they say —"

I spun away and ran back to my cot. Pulled the pillow over my head and bit down on bitter foam rubber. By lunchtime I'd heard all the rest. How Ardis had crawled under an empty cot in one of the other rooms, lain hidden there in the dark. Had sawed at the bedsprings with a metal butter knife she got who knows where, bending little bits of spring with determined fingers until she snapped off enough pieces to do the job. My throat closed up imagining this, something like cat claws scraping, sticking in my windpipe.

Now Ardis was on her way out of here, to the "real hospital," as some of the girls called it. Where you went to have tonsils, and tumors, and though I'd never thought about it before, babies taken out. Then you got to go home. Unless, of course, you were one of us.

14

Over the next few days, as a homecoming surprise for Ardis, I planned our escape — if she lived, if I saw her again. I thought of hiding in a laundry basket, like I'd seen prisoners do in a movie. But our laundry was done in one of the outbuildings here on the grounds, so I wouldn't get far. I thought of stealing the keys and walking out, but that was a long shot. All the matrons and guards kept their heavy rings of keys clipped tight to their belts.

So what was I good at? Two things: playacting, being someone else. And I knew a lot about hardware. If I could somehow impersonate a matron or guard, I could walk out. But that required a uniform, and the only way to get one of those seemed to be to take it off a staff person's back. Most of the matrons were large women, their upper arms padded with fat and muscle, big around as one of my thighs. I'd swim in their clothes; that wouldn't fool anybody.

That left hardware. I began to take an interest in the heavy mesh window fittings and door knobs and lock assemblies around me. The windows were rectangular, probably large enough for a body to slip through. But they were set high up and covered with metal mesh. Still, that hadn't grown there; someone had installed it. Some kind of fittings held it in place. Those could also be taken off.

One day on our way to class I told the matron I had terrible cramps. She narrowed her eyes, but I was good at twisting my face into a mask of subtle pain and suffering, like I'd once done auditioning for Laura's part in *Our Town*, under the influence of a headache. When I recalled that, my muscles and tendons also seemed to remember the exact lines of that pain. I was grateful for my baggy dress, which hid the growing bulge of my stomach and the fact I hadn't had any period at all for months.

She sent me back to the dormitory with an aide. After the woman walked me through the locked outer doors and left me in my room, I climbed up on the bed and examined the window screen. It was held in place by smooth-headed rivets at each corner, and in the bottom center a key lock. Even if I managed to open it somehow, there remained the problem of getting off the grounds. But I had realized something during our horticulture sessions outside, while yanking weeds and throwing them in a big bushel basket. That although the place was locked up tighter than a tick at night, the gates were open in the daytime. I supposed they figured no one could slip past during the day, without the concealing cover of darkness. So I either had to leave at night and get past the main gate, or find a good disguise that in daylight would prove them wrong.

Two weeks later, Ardis came back, thinner and very pale. She'd always been quiet, but now she hardly said a word. I took her aside the first night, just before lights out and before Letitia got back from the bathroom, and whispered my plan in her ear.

After I finished, I sat back. "What do you think of that?"

She smiled. "Sounds real good, Dory." But her voice didn't sound enthusiastic. She didn't laugh or clap her hands in delight the way she used to.

"What's goin' on in here, some big powwow?"

We both jumped, but it was only Letitia, a thin grayish towel draped over one arm, a frazzled toothbrush in the other hand.

"Just girl talk," I said, faking a yawn.

"Say, you think I should get it cut short?" I grabbed the ends and mashed my hair all up on top of my head.

Letitia looked at me like I was an alien. We had no beauty parlor there, no way to go into town for such things. "Yeah, why not," she muttered, making a disgusted face. "Bring me back a manicure and a bleach job while you're at it. And a good-looking man." She clomped across the room and flopped on her cot.

The lights-out signal buzzed, and I felt my way back to my own bed. I crawled in, but I didn't go to sleep for a while. For the first time in months I was excited about something, a chance to beat the system that punished some folks and not others for the same transgressions.

One thing I was learning at the girl's school was patience. Not to leap before I looked, and then to look again. I could wait patiently as an aide unlocked the big metal door that led to the outside. Because now each time I walked through and heard it clang behind me, I swore it soon would be the last time I ever heard that sound.

One day I had a piece of luck. Taking a crape myrtle seedling out of a nursery pot one afternoon in the yard, I found a bent piece of rusty wire stuck down in the soil, roots twined around it. I slipped it into a little pocket I'd made in the hem of my dress by ripping out a dozen stitches. The matron was laughing, listening to the security guard tell a joke. "What you doin' over there, Gamble?" she called out when she saw me bent over.

"Just tying my shoe, Ma'am," I called back, fiddling with the laces on one of my tennis shoes, tightening the bow.

I also knew Letitia had a pair of tweezers, serious contraband, because one day I had walked into the bathroom between leather shop and math class, and there she was working on her eyebrows. They had a nice arch; she was real vain about them. She whispered a curse and stuffed them in her pocket, but I looked away and pretended I hadn't noticed.

With these two possible tools, I thought I could make some headway. At night, after the breathing of my roommates had slowed and deepened, I got up and worked on the window lock with my wire pick. The school routine, so stifling and deadly in the daytime, became my friend. I had to listen for footsteps because the night matrons always did a couple bed checks. If I heard anything I threw myself back on the bed, yanked the covers up to my chin and turned away from the door. Then went back to work after the flashlight had probed around the room, knowing I had hours left to work at freedom. Like most of us, the staff were creatures of habit.

The window lock was similar to a set my father had once special ordered for old Mrs. Roper, who had a morbid fear of Communists breaking into her house while she slept. Pearce had found that hilarious and had made it his mission to pick the locks before they were installed. He'd finally done it, while I kept an eye out for my father, though Pearce had used a thin flat piece of metal to trip the lock mechanism.

On the sixth night, I heard a faint click. Sweat was running down my arms and into my eyes. I blinked it away and wedged my fingernails under the bottom of the frame. I exerted pressure slowly, and it moved out — only a little, because the four corner bolts were still in place. But it was no longer locked. I got down, stuck the wire into the side of my mattress under the ticking, and fell sound asleep from sheer exhaustion. I'd barely slept in five or six nights and was worried the staff would notice the darkening circles under my eyes.

Next, the rivets. I couldn't get a grip on

them with my bare fingers or nails; they were smooth and too flush with the frame. But with Letitia's tweezers, I might be able to undo them. The seventh night, I went over to the hook on the back of the door where Letitia hung her dress. I felt in both pockets. No tweezers. They weren't wedged behind the mirror and the wall or tucked under the little ridge underneath the sink bowl, either.

I got up on the bed again and tried to force the wire under the rivets, but it bent and slid off the edges. I was near tears and cursing, and trying for the sixth or seventh time, when a hushed voice below me said, "You looking for these?"

Letitia stood by my bed, holding up her tweezers. I silently took them from her outstretched hand. "Just mind you don't break 'em," she warned.

"You won't tell anybody," I said, without thinking. She looked offended. "I mean, I know you won't," I amended. "Thanks."

"Don't thank me," she said. "They'll just catch you agin."

"No, they won't."

She looked interested for the first time. "How come you don't think so?"

"Because I don't plan to get in any more trouble."

She laughed soundlessly at that and went back to her cot.

I wasn't so sure about Ardis though. But I'd promised to take her. I worked at the rivets, wedging the tweezers under them first, then using them to lever the rivets up. I was afraid Letitia's prized grooming tools would bend, but Revlon knew what they were doing; they should've been in the hardware business. At last I got all four of them loosened and pried far enough to pop out by hand.

I climbed down and took the tweezers back to Letitia. "Why don't you go with us?"

She raised up on one elbow and looked at me hard. "I got only six months to get out of here. If I do anything else they can send me to Florida C.I."

"What? Where's that?"

"The Correctional Institution, the women's prison at Lowell," mumbled a sleepy voice. Ardis was up now, too. She yawned. "Hear they got a beauty parlor, Let. They'll train you to fix hair."

"Well, hallelujah," said Letitia, rolling her eyes at the ceiling. "Maybe we should all sign up." She turned to me. "How you expect to get off the grounds?"

I had thought and thought about that.

Having been transported around the area some, I had gotten a good look at the vehicles, and once I'd seen an aide tuck the keys in the visor. Maybe they didn't all do that, but he had. "The only thing is," I said, "I don't drive. Do you?"

Ardis shook her head, but Letitia guffawed. "Cain't be hard if Cory Otis could do it."

The next week the moon waned down to nothing. After the bed check, I took the mesh out and cranked open the window. Letitia boosted me up first. I wiggled through, the metal sill scraping my belly. Then I dropped. I waited for Ardis, looking around, expecting lights to blaze on and sirens to howl at any second. I wished I'd seen more prison break movies. Finally Letitia stuck out her head. "She ain't going," she said. "Says she's more feared of the outside than this place. Thinks her brother will find her again."

I couldn't wait around to talk her into it. "Look out for her, okay? And tell her good-bye."

Letitia nodded, and her head disappeared back inside. The window shut. I'd asked her to replace the rivets, too.

I turned away and slipped along the side of the building. I was wearing my blue dress because it was dark, but I'd bundled up my nightgown and brought it along. The aides and matrons wore white smocks. I figured in the dark, a woman wearing white, driving a state vehicle, maybe wouldn't look too suspicious. I crawled the last few yards to the packed-clay square that held a panel truck, a station wagon, and a sedan, all white, all with the Great Seal of Florida on the doors.

I reached up and opened the driver's door, pulled myself in, and shut it. I yanked the nightgown over my head and pulled on the hairnet I'd found in the trash and saved. It had holes in it; one of the cafeteria ladies must've thrown it away. "Yeah, that'll make you look old and ugly," Letitia had agreed when I showed it to her.

Then I felt around for the key. It wasn't in the visor. A bitter taste filled my mouth, acid flooded my stomach. Wait, I thought. Be calm. I felt around on the floor, on the other side, and finally there it was — in the passenger-side visor.

I jammed it into the ignition, and according to Letitia's instructions and my recollections of driving with Dad, pulled the gear shift down till the little red line was on P. "Make sure you don't make it jerk and buck," Letitia had warned me.

"Push on the gas real smooth like. That's the secret."

I did. It jerked a little at first, but I took a breath and made my trembling foot relax and press lightly. I turned the wheel and headed for the gate. It was so dark! Then I realized I hadn't turned on the headlights. I slapped around the dash, twisted and yanked, and got the wipers first. At last a light flared and bloomed ahead when I pulled the largest knob straight out.

I let off the gas as I neared the gate. The guard in the little shack was sitting on a stool, reading a paperback. He looked up as I drew closer, then came out and looked in my window. "Workin' late tonight?"

I nodded. Tried to squinch my face into the lines and furrows of a weary jaded woman who stood squinting over a steam tray three times a day.

"Well, take her easy," he said and went back inside.

I sat there, stunned. Then hit the gas and took off a little too sudden, laying rubber on the road outside the gate. I went fast as I dared, wrestling with the wheel, which always seemed to want to take the car across the yellow line or into the ditch. I only passed one other vehicle, excitement enough as I squinted into its headlights, fighting a desire to run my car off the side of the road.

I allowed myself only to look ahead, afraid of what I might see in the rearview, like someone coming for me, saying this only proved how dangerous and looney I was. That I had to be sent back. I drove the car down highway 90 through sleeping Marianna without stopping, taking any road that looked like it might go north, to Georgia.

But I hadn't reckoned on the lackadaisical nature of the staff when it came to keeping a gas tank full. I coasted to a stop in a stretch of shade tobacco fields just as the sun was pinkening the east. Then got out and ripped off the bottom half of my night-gown, hoping it would look like I was wearing a white blouse and blue skirt. Folks around there might recognize a re-form school uniform when they saw one. I left the car nosed in under a stand of live oaks, and kept on north. Mt. Pleasant was the next place. I would lose myself there and decide what to do next.

But this town was even smaller than Ordinary Springs. Getting lost wouldn't be easy. It was still early and I'd been hurrying. But now I made myself walk at a normal pace. I slipped inside an empty tobacco warehouse, the first building I saw.

A dry brown smell of crumbled leaf and dried mold greeted me, fine motes spinning in the light from high windows, a sticky resinous feel to the wood under my hands. A pile of faded burlap sacks looked inviting, and I flopped, heart thrumming, hands twitchy nervous, feet still wanting to fly on. I was so antsy and jangling I could hardly keep from running right out of my hiding place. But fatigue and lack of sleep caught up. I closed my eyes and slept like a worn-out toddler.

It was late afternoon before I woke. I walked down the narrow street slowly, trying to look preoccupied but purposeful, like I had an errand and belonged out on the street in this town. In the west a storm was drawing across the countryside like a stage curtain, nearing town — what I was able to see of the place with my head lowered: a post office mailbox, a farm truck, a general store window full of dusty odds and ends. Picket-fenced yards and brick houses. A lone sapling bent under the weight of an empty feeder. A bird pecking not very hopefully at thick, insect-free grass. Occasionally a pair of legs scissored by. I must have been successfully near-invisible, a skinny, awkward girl in faded clothes. The only living thing to address me was a stray dog investigating the trash cans on the curb, who thrust his gaunt muzzle into my hand, then hung his head when it proved to be empty.

Whenever I did glance up, wind-whipped flannel clouds had turned the sky the weak gray of fish broth, as if this special lighting was nature's way of sympathizing with my mood. I had escaped, it seemed. But now what?

In fact, life had suddenly become basic and uncomplicated, a simple progression. I'd need shelter, and food to keep from starving to death. That was about all. To get food I'd need money; to get money, a job. But this town felt too close to where I'd come from. My stomach was rumbling, but it would have to wait in line.

I walked all the way down the main street, and when I hit the end of downtown, the last boarded-up gas station, I ran again. Ran, then walked when I got winded, along a winding, cracked asphalt road, up and down hills, the crickets and peepers loud as farm machinery. It was so much like home I wasn't afraid. Not of the empty road, or of the animals who might be watching from the scrub palmetto thickets, or of the thin, watery light of the rising bitten-out moon. But I'd thought Ardis would be with me, that I'd have someone to talk to, to run plans past: How about this? Is that a dumb idea?

After spending months never alone, with some matron barking orders or another girl's face or elbow or ass in my way, you'd think I'd be pleased. But already I felt lonely. I wanted someone along who'd make jokes, tell me how brave I'd been, how everything would work out. Who'd cut up and make weird faces and distract me from the fact that I was a criminal escapee with no money in my pockets and a baby growing in my belly. Lord God, my life had self-destructed at the advanced age of sixteen.

I did run then, lolloping along panicked and ungraceful as a twenty-dollar mule. As the sky darkened the woods ended, and before me stretched flat dark quilts of fields. After a mile or so, I came to a T-shaped crossroads. One way led off into more dark, winding fields. The other, toward a faint glow in the distance. Maybe another town. I was hungry and thirsty and foot-sore, and needed some different clothes. I headed that way.

Around a bend I came across a camp of sorts. Two trucks were parked on pull-offs on either side of a dying campfire, and no one was stirring, probably asleep inside the trucks, one of which looked like a boxy house on wheels. Everything I'd been told about strangers since I could understand words came back. I ought to go on down the road, around this campsite, on into the town, whatever it was. But I was so tired, and my stomach was aching with emptiness.

I walked quietly around the trucks, one shaped very much like the one I'd hidden under at the carnival back in Ordinary Springs — and a real mess I'd ended up in thanks to it! But a light rain was beginning to fall, I felt light-headed, and my knees were turning to rubber. I bent and looked under the larger truck. Sure enough, a shelf, just like before. Which had brought calamity down on my head and, who knew, maybe Pearce's, too.

But I didn't want to think about him, what he might be doing, or how he might be feeling about his old friend Dory.

It was hard and uncomfortable under there, greasy and stinking of crankcase oil. No blanket like in the first hidey-hole, but the rain had begun, cold and fine as needles. I crawled in. If there's no food, there's nothing to do but sleep and dream of it. Yes, and I must have managed to sleep hard, because I only woke at loud noises outside. I jerked up, banging the hell out of my head, shivering, and though my clothes had dried, I smelled strong of sweat. I held my breath, huddled in my secret cave, as heavy footsteps descended from the cab. Some men and at least one woman were talking, arguing. I pressed as far back into the metal space as I could.

"What about the tomato stakes?"

"Beau forgot to pack 'em."

"I'm gone toss my stuff under there then," said the woman, who had a raspy smoker's voice. "Too damn crowded up front for it and Delmar, too. Who needs him a *shower*," she called louder, as if making a point to someone blocks away.

Another truck pulled up alongside, and I saw the wheels. More people got out. I heard shouts, grinding gears, snorting, idling engines, and even the high-pitched squeal of children's voices, but the sense of the words was drowned out. Then, when I least expected it, a face framed in lank blonde hair popped into view. A thin, wiry woman in a faded house dress who grunted and huffed, heaving a cheap fiber-board suitcase up beside her, tugging at the handle to angle it under the truck.

When she noticed me her eyes widened.

Her lips moved, she was talking, but I couldn't hear a word. I pushed so far back my spine scraped the metal wall. Her upper arm made mesmerizing arcs as she motioned someone over.

And then, out of all the racket of grinding machinery and idling engines and gray-truck exhaust, a pair of strong brown hairy arms reached in and gripped mine, which I'd crossed protectively over my chest. Sun-glow hit my face, blotting out everything. I gasped and stared up blindly, helpless as a newborn, dazzled as they pulled me into the light.

15

All I knew that morning, when I was plucked from beneath a rusted-out truck like a tick from a dog's belly, was that I was in trouble and couldn't figure what to do about it. Full of guilt and anger, terrified at what the future held for a knocked-up runaway. No epiphanies lit my brain; no angels chorused above, because revelation is really a slow, painful dawning of the sense we should've been born with. And for some, the jolts and bumps of living by wits and hustles.

The two men who pulled me out from under the truck seemed torn between delight and annoyance. This indecision made me more nervous than if they'd discussed calling the law or just dumped me there on the blacktop. The glow of the town I glimpsed the night before must've been farther off than I'd thought, maybe even a mirage. For all there was, I saw, when my eyes stopped watering in the glare of sun, was a long two-laner beside the open patch we were barely pulled off on. Ragweed and pinewoods beyond. That, and the trucks, plus an old Woody pulling a dented camper. And four men and two women staring down at me as I lay on the asphalt with my hands clamped over my face, gravel embossing my back, afraid to move.

"Lookahere," said a tall pimply guy, as if he'd spied a dollar on the sidewalk. He had a bandanna head wrap.

"Stowaway," said the short one next to him, who wore a black pork-pie hat and had a wet cigar clamped in his terrier jaws.

The other two just stared and grinned. I liked that least of all.

The thin woman looked sympathetic. "He'p her up," she ordered in twangy nasal accents, then tilted her head and smiled at me. She was missing two teeth in front, but her eyes were sharp and lively. And though she was pale as a white rabbit and wore no eyeliner or lipstick, somehow her face, bare-skinned and pitted with acne scars, was beautiful.

"Who're you, honey?" she said to me kindly.

"Yeah, how come you to be stuck under there, like some possum's baby?" The little man, puffing furiously on his cigar, looked more like a bulldog all the time.

"Shut your hole, Beau. Let her tell it."

"We gonna cross a state line. If the law

was to happen by —"

As these two began to argue, the two silent guys didn't waste any time. They hauled me up, backed me against the trailer, and started in on the buttons on my dress. "Show what all you got under there, sugar tits," said the one pinning my arms. He smelled like grease, BO, and tooth decay.

The one actually trying to figure out the buttons was so drunk his fingers couldn't get a grip. He tweezed clumsily at each in turn and had just torn off the top one when suddenly he flew backward as if plucked by the hand of God. The thin woman yanked him away by his shirt the way you'd do a food-stealing dog.

"Get lost," she said, the cords on her neck standing out. To my surprise, the men did. Then she walked me across the empty lot. "Pardon they manners, honey," she said. "They mommas din't teach 'em no better."

They were all fruit tramps, it turned out, and had had engine trouble. Strawberries and cucumbers were over, and now they were headed north for the tomato fields in Virginia.

She patted my shoulder. "So don't you mind them boys. They's bad as they seem.

Ain't got a lick of sense. Now it's your turn."

But what to say? I looked around. In the other trucks, small children who all looked related hung out the windows like puppies, panting and whining and gaping at me. Their parents regarded me with flat, noncommital stares. One thing was clear: I had no money, no place to go, and was in trouble with the state of Florida. It's hard to confide in a stranger that you're a well-meaning murderer running from the law. I sorted alternate stories in my head and settled for something in between. "I'm leaving home. My father . . . threw me out."

One pale eyebrow rose. "Do tell. How old're you?"

"Eighteen . . . almost," I amended as I saw her left eyebrow go down and the other shoot up.

"And what you planning to do?"

"Work," I said, lifting my chin. "I'll get along fine."

"Well, what can you do?" She walked around me in a circle as she snapped this out, as if sizing up the haunches on a plow mule.

I shrugged, feeling more and more hopeless.

She sighed, shook her head, and draped an arm around my shoulders. Her skin looked rough, but it felt soft, warm. Her tone so motherly I burst into tears.

"Ah, shit," said one of the men and spat over to the side.

"She gonna get us in trouble," growled the short one.

Suddenly my stomach growled, too — so loud everyone laughed.

The woman got out a split-oak basket and fed me a leftover biscuit with ham so salty I could hardly swallow it. She gave me half a warm, flat beer to wash it down with, all they had left. "Now you got something in your belly. That's all we can do."

"Please," I said. "I can't go home. My father will kill me."

She frowned. Her expression grew distant, thoughtful, as if seeing back to some bad thing in the past, some almost-forgotten hurt. "A ride, then."

At least she wasn't scowling anymore. "So you'll take me along?"

"Give you a lift far as the turn-off for Bainbridge. You ain't suited for pickin'. A nice, educated girl. Stand out like a busted thumb. We don't need the law on us, neither."

"But —"

"Take it or leave it."

I nodded. Seemed like the best deal I was going to get.

"Climb on up in the truck, then."

My savior, Sadie McElroy, was the buffer between me and the men, who were closemouthed, not talkative and hearty like most of the ones I knew back in Ordinary Springs. Their pale eyes and blank expressions made me nervous. She seemed to realize this, because she gave me a short pep talk about a woman traveling on the road, ending with, "So if'n you're ever skeered, don't you never show it, not to no one. Leastways a man."

I nodded and vowed to remember this. Still, I leaned away from Delmar, who was silently driving like a sun-creased, plaid-shirted machine. Finally we rolled past the town limits of Quincy, Florida.

"Stop right here, Delmar," Sadie said at an intersection in the middle of town.

He grunted and made a sharp left that threw me onto his lap. I levered myself up again, glanced up, and saw he was grinning. His teeth were all there but stained from either snuff or chew.

"Do that again, I'll whack me a piece offa you directly," said Sadie mildly. "Somethin' more important to you than a brain."

"Yeah, fuck, I ain't a-quarreling," he mumbled, scowling out the windshield.

Sadie jumped out and helped me down. I was feeling queasy from the twisting back roads, the warm beer breakfast, the half ham sandwich that seemed to have lodged halfway to my stomach.

She patted my shoulder so gently I nearly burst into tears again. I wanted her to stay with me. I didn't care if she talked like a mountain hillbilly. I'd have given her the job of being my mother right then and there.

"Lord sakes." She shook her head. "I didn't never ask your name!"

I'd already thought of this. I couldn't be Eudora Gamble anymore. Between the Pine Hills School, the sheriff, and my father, somebody in the state of Florida had to be looking for me, the runaway teenage killer. Maybe my father had been right. I was bad, fated to be just like my mother. I'd had to leave her picture when they dragged me from my own house, off to Marianna without even a pair of shoes. All I had left to take was her name.

Why not? I was on the edge of something. A new life.

"It's Vera," I said, looking her right in the eye.

"Yeah?" Sadie frowned and waited, giving me time to tell the truth, or maybe make up a last name.

"Just Vera," I insisted. "That's all."

She shrugged. "Suit yourself. Now give me some sugar," she ordered, as if I were three years old. She squeezed me in a hug that left me breathless but smiling.

"You gone make out fine," she whispered, out of earshot of the boys in the truck.

I nodded, then watched them pull away in a cloud of exhaust, leaving me on a sidewalk in downtown Quincy, a nice-looking, sizeable town with stores and cafes and white-painted two-story houses and a Civil War monument in the center of a little shady park. It was time to find a job, to get started on my new life as a woman named Vera.

The idea of looking for work might've scared me, except after being stared at, questioned, and stripped nearly naked just to get a ride, an interview didn't sound so bad. But it turned out no one in town wanted to hire a girl who had only a first name and no references. After three or four tries I got nervous at a five and dime when the manager went into the storeroom and I saw her pick up a phone. I'd given a song and dance about being on my own with a widowed mother who couldn't work because she was sick a lot. When the manager looked at me, then turned away, I left quick out the front and kept walking on out of town.

I walked all morning and most of the afternoon. Whenever a car passed I tried to look like I was just out for a stroll, that I didn't need help or a ride. Somebody worse than Delmar might stop. The sun beat down as if it had a long-standing grudge against me, heating the asphalt until the air smelled like scorched tar. I kept hoping to find something to drink, but the only water I saw was a pond green with scum. It gave off a spoiled-cabbage stink. I staggered on, telling myself I'd get someplace soon and would think of something.

I tramped through a couple places so small they probably weren't on the state map. At one crossroads called Gretna, it seemed like a hundred Negroes were gathered outside a big tar-paper shack, a jook joint with bluesy music blaring out the open doors and windows. I heard loud laughter and smelled hair tonic and cheap perfume. Some stared, but no one called out or flashed a razor or threw a bottle at me.

The next mile I passed the thick-pillared veranda of a down-at-the-heels *Gone with the Wind* mansion. Way up the walk, under its shade, two elderly ladies in flowered dresses rocked and petted cats. I considered going up their wavy brick walk and asking for help, or at least a glass of iced tea. But then a sheriff's car cruised by slowly, the star and shield of authority blazing like a brassy sun on its door. It might just be on its way to the jook, but I picked up my pace and left that place behind.

I knew from history class that this Highway 90, which crossed the panhandle, was just the Old Spanish Trail, paved over. Though the conquistadores wouldn't recognize parts of it now, the thick pinewoods and saw palmettos and loblollies, the cypress and tupelo swamps surely must be much the same, deep and endless. Once I saw a screech owl blinking down from a tree overhead, eyes like twin golden moons in the shadows. But it was still daylight, so I was probably getting delirious and feeling pretty weak by the time I saw a green highway sign that said MIDWAY 5. That felt like encouragement, as if it proved my ordeal was at least half over. Well, fine. I'd steal food and water if I had to, then find a place to hide out and rest.

After another mile or so I heard voices around a bend. Off the highway, down by a rickety rail fence and a muddy cow pond, two men were arguing. I had to stop anyhow; I had a burning stitch in my side.

"Hit was that damn gator of yourn got away last month," said one, a skinny guy in overalls. "See here, the skid marks where he drug my mule in the water."

"Now how do you know that?" The other man, a tall, sunburned cracker, wore a big straw cowboy hat. "You sayin' you c'n tell one big alligator from another?"

The skinny man stuck out his jaw. "You gotta admit, this un's uglier than the usual."

The big man laughed. "Well, he ain't there now, is he." He cleared his throat and spat off to the side. "But let's just imagine you're right. How much would I owe you then?"

The skinny man narrowed his eyes, scratched his head. "I figure about fifty dollar."

"Fifty! Hell's bells, here's twenty."

The other man scowled. "Huh. Well, it was a no-account mule, anyhow." He shoved the wad of bills in his pocket and went through the gate, muttering.

The big man in the Stetson shook his head, too, and kicked at a clump of ragweed. Then he started over to a red pickup. I decided it best to move on before he noticed I'd been eavesdropping. But when I started off again I felt wobbly. And suddenly the ground was rising up to meet me, instead of staying underfoot where it belonged.

As I fell I saw a flash of red, then green. Someone yelled, "Hey!" And that was all.

When I came to I was lying in the bed of a pickup. The old cowboy was pouring a thin trickle of water from a thermos bottle into his hand, then flicking drops in my face. His huge, pocked nose looked like a sunburnt potato, the rest of his face a collection of squint-lines and creases, like a farmer's. His eyes, brown and concerned-looking, were staring anxiously at me. And his dripping hands were huge. I was getting soaked, a waste of good water I could be drinking instead.

So I sat up, grabbed the bottle, and gulped the rest. It flowed down my dusty throat ice cold, better than anything I'd ever tasted in my life.

"You feelin' better now, Miss?"

I nodded.

"Where you headed? Look like you been walking a long ways." I followed his gaze down to the caked dust and leaking blisters on my feet. The cheap sandals I'd worn out of the Pine Hills School hadn't been meant for cross-country hikes.

"I'm on, uh, a nature walk," I mumbled.

He raised an eyebrow. "Huh. Well, my name's Clayton Sebring. You ever hear of heat exhaustion?"

I closed my eyes and nodded. "I'm Vera."

"Well, Vera. Would it be breaking some rule to accept a ride to a big glass of ice water?"

He was a stranger, but at least not a cop. And if he'd wanted to, he could've taken advantage of me already. So I shook my head. "Think I earned it," I whispered.

But we didn't go all the way into Midway. Instead, he pulled off the highway at a roadside place that made me sit up and take notice, beat as I was. A combination truck stop and diner, with separate tourist cabins squatting to either side. They were of white stucco and, for some reason, shaped like Indian teepees from a child's drawing, painted with stripes of red and blue around the base. The diner, instead of a plain old doorway, had an enormous alligator head for a porch, the gaping jaws forming the entrance. A huge neon sign arched over this announced SEBRING'S ORIGINAL YOU BETTER BELIEVE IT NATURE MUSEUM AND RESTAURANT. More signs were posted on both sides, yellow billboards with red lettering, that warned SEE BIG JAKE 13 FEET LONG! and TWICE A DAY — THE JUMPING JAWS OF DEATH!

Mercy.

I must have said it out loud, because Sebring nodded. Smiled with obvious pride. "It ain't Gatorland," he said. "Not *yet.*"

"You keep alligators here?"

"I farm gators, raise 'em myself. Sometimes we'll go out after one, if it's a real nice specimen."

We got out, and he took me into the diner. "Ruby," he called. "Look at what I found on the highway."

A tanned, sparrowish woman, her short brown hair set in tight waves, came out of the back, wiping her hands on a dish towel. "Sweet Jesus, Clayton. What've you drug home now?" She stopped dead when she saw me. "Oh, my. Now, she don't look too hot. Here, honey, set in that booth and I'll get you some water."

264

The diner had fake wood walls and a counter shaped like a boomerang. I scooted into one of the wooden booths, my sweating legs sticking to the red vinyl upholstery. The floor was red and black checkerboard tiles, and in the window was a sign: HELP WANTED. A thick strand of cobweb stretched like a lifeline from one corner to the window frame.

Ruby came and set a sweating glass of cold water in front of me. The ice cubes made a lovely tinkling noise. Then they both slid into the booth, too, opposite me.

"This's Vera," said Clayton. When Ruby cocked her head, he shrugged. "Just plain Vera."

"Drink it slow, now," she ordered. When I couldn't stop, she pried the glass out of my hands. "Take a breather. Then have a little more."

"Actually," I gasped, because the icy water was shooting pain through my sinuses, "I have a confession. I come about the, uh, the job."

Clayton frowned, his leathery forehead creasing into hundreds of lines. "Huh." He didn't sound excited. "Like at what, for instance."

This set me back. "Waitress?" I guessed.

"It's an old sign," he said gently. "We

don't get the traffic we used to. So —"

Ruby leaned forward and raised one hand. He winced and stopped talking. Maybe she'd kicked him under the table.

"You got any experience, sugar?" she asked briskly, folding her hands on the tabletop in front of her.

I crossed my fingers in my lap, where no one could see. "Sure."

"Now, Ruby," Clayton began.

She held up a hand. "Don't you always say you got to think big to get big? And my ankles ain't what they used to be."

"But I thought we decided —"

"I could use a day off now and then, Clayton Sebring."

I held my breath as they tossed my fate like a rubber ball between them. Clayton seemed like he'd be a hard sell.

But Ruby barely hesitated. She squinted until her eyes were nearly shut, as if she was getting some divine input, a spirit message from beyond. "A young waitress in a uniform. Something nice, eye catching. But not trashy. Maybe she could cook some days, and work the counter. Give ol' Ruby a break. Them truckers is tired of my face."

Clayton frowned. "I dunno. We cain't afford much."

I thought fast. Recalled the Ordinary Springs diner, its quilted stainless steel walls and counter, the two antique waitresses in hairnets chatting up the regulars, slipping quarters and dimes into the pockets of their matching aprons.

"I'll work for tips," I said quickly, "and one meal a day. And . . . a place to stay."

"Yeah. We got that," said Clayton, tapping a cigarette out of a crushed pack of Marlboros.

"If she can hold a tray, let insults roll off her back like she was greased, and count high as ten," said Ruby, "then I don't see no problem."

"Ruby, baby," said Clayton wearily. "Thought we agreed. No more strays, folks or animals. She ain't even old enough to serve beer."

But she rattled on as if he hadn't spoken. "She can learn the register, the Fry-O-Lator, the grill. And she'd look good in one of them tennis-type get-ups. Not too short," she finished and smiled at him. "Come on now, hon."

He sighed and bent the cover on a matchbook back and forth. "She's tall, all right, but she looks kind of puny. Can she haul a tray full of plates and stay on her feet all day?"

Ruby reached over and felt of my upper arm. Then said, "Show us some leg, honey."

Face burning, I looked pleadingly back. She only gave me a little nudge out of the booth. Feeling trapped in a bad dream, like the kind I used to have before math exams, I unfolded from my seat and yanked my dingy, smelly dress up well past my knees. But they both eyed my dirt-streaked thighs as wearily as housewives checking wieners in the Winn Dixie. Faced with such obvious disinterest, I felt almost bored, too.

"Good veins," said Ruby enviously, sticking her own stringy varicosed calf out for comparison.

Clayton sighed. "Yeah, okay, whatever," he said, flapping a hand. "Sure you ain't jail bait, now?" But he was already turning away, gazing out the window as if dreaming of a newly expanded empire.

I was assigned the last teepee on the far right end. Inside it was dim, the paint peeling a little on its tapering walls, the floorboards scuffed. But still, very clean. A tiny window over a double bed, a pasteboard dresser, a luggage rack, and a little bathroom.

"Yeah, I know, it's tee-niny," said Ruby, rolling her eyes.

"It's beautiful," I said.

She looked at me funny, then shrugged. "No place like home, honey." She fumbled in a pocket and pulled out a huge ring of keys bigger than what the matrons at the school had carried. She handed me a single numbered one with a flourish. "Don't lose it."

I was about to say I'd never let it out of my sight. But a hoarse bellow came from outside through the open window.

Ruby grimaced. "Ah, don't mind that. It's just Big Jake," she said.

I swallowed. "The Jumping Jaws of Death?"

"Yeah." She shrugged, smoothed the bedspread. "Been mad as a wasp in a bottle ever since Clayton caught him and dragged him home again."

So then I asked to see the setup out back: the alligator pits fenced with boards and chicken wire, the big enclosed pens that held a black bear, a family of sleeping racoons, and two orphaned deer. "We found 'em after last hunting season," said Ruby. "Raised 'em on baby formula, now they're too tame to go live in the woods. That's what give Clayton the idea to branch out into mammal exhibits."

She scratched the bear's head. He

smelled like wet dog and musk. "He ain't strictly native, now. Got him from a bunch of gypsies. He can't dance no more. Too old, like me." She cackled and crooned into his ear. The bear closed his eyes and grunted approval of her technique. "Oh, I'm afraid I've spoilt him now."

Then she showed me the alligator enclosures, which were really like fenced borrow pits. A smell of algae and musk and spoiled meat hit me in the face. Almost dark by then, so what I mostly saw, looking down, was dozens of glowing orange orbs, like car headlights. And they were all staring back up at me.

"Ugh." I shivered, though I'd seen plenty of alligators before in the Springs, sometimes even right under our dock. Yet for some reason, down in that pit, their glowing eyes seemed not natural but evil, much too aware; minor demons risen halfway from hell.

Back in the diner we sidled down a hallway so cluttered with stacks of boxes and crates of Coke bottles we had to turn sideways. The first doorway led to the kitchen. A pile of pots and pans and food-crusted plates sat on the counter. "Feel any better?" asked Ruby.

I looked away, because she seemed to be

staring at my belly when she said this, as if she'd already seen through the baggy dress, the too-loose cotton drawers, my flesh and blood and bone, to the secret little swimmer growing inside.

"Don't worry," she said. "Everything will work out. We'll figure out what you do best later." Then she added briskly, "In case you're wondering, ain't no funny business going on here. We run a clean place. But the next county over is dry, and folks will come a long way for a beer on a hot night. The truckers ain't so many since they built the new highway, but tourism's growing like a bed of weeds in Florida. We're just a little north of the action now, but it'll catch up."

It was both simple and complicated. I trained first as a short order cook. At lunch, truck drivers all stopped at Sebring's Original You Better Believe It. The menu was short: burgers, corndogs, fries, and one homemade special. Greens, coleslaw. Barbeque pork sandwiches on Wednesdays. I started out on the fry baskets. Jam the hotdog on the little stick, dip it in the sticky yellow cornmeal batter, drop it in the deep-fryer basket, and sink everything in the hot grease. Then jump back like lightning so you don't get some body part burned off. And keep the mustard, catsup, relish, and onion jars full. Easy, boring, and hot.

A week after I started Clayton also introduced me to Micco Poteke, a tall, bronze-skinned trapper who sometimes supplied him with new alligators or small animals for exhibit.

"Just Mick," he said to me the first day Clayton introduced us. Then not another word. He had glossy black hair that dipped like a crow's wing over one eye. His T-shirt was rolled to his shoulders, revealing thin, ragged scars all over his arms. Ruby told me he was half Seminole Indian, and that when someone needed a particularly big or dangerous alligator relocated or disposed of, they called Mick Poteke.

I knew when a gator got fed by tourists or any newcomer stupid enough to think the sight of a ten-foot lizard munching marshmallows was cute, it was forever spoiled for living near folks. A gator doesn't get the difference between the snack and your hand, or your poodle, or your two-year-old splashing in the shallows. Once its dim reptile brain has put the idea of *human* and *food* together, anything people-shaped just means a meal on the way.

So from time to time, a too-tame gator must be shot or at least moved from a suburban lake or river to a more remote home — like the Everglades. Up in the capitol, they were even talking about protecting alligators; that maybe every problem lizard shouldn't just be turned into a handbag and belts anymore — unless it had actually eaten something or someone important. In the meantime, it could still be shot or captured by a trapper with a permit. Some of the gators at You Better Believe It had got here that way. Big Jake had gobbled up three chihuahuas, a boxer, and a mixed breed hound, then treed a Yankee golfer at the Dubsdread Country Club in Orlando before he was permanently evicted. Clayton bought him from Mick.

It seemed Big Jake had also made a meal of the mule down the road, but Clayton didn't like to be reminded about it. Every time I imagined how the big scaled creature must've lumbered across the parking lot by my new front door, his evil slitted eyes alert for food, I felt a little cold inside. But Clayton had built him a stronger, deeper holding pen and had had no problems since.

At first I kept track of the days, of how long I'd been away from Ordinary Springs.

Maybe I'd think of a way to go home again once I was over eighteen and a success. Save my money and take a bus back; the Greyhound stopped twice a week outside Monk's Sinclair on the highway. Then I remembered: I was going to have a baby. What would I do with an infant while I made myself famous? So I made corndog after corndog. And basket after basket of fries, sweating my clothes into sodden rags on busy days.

Some nights at first I also prayed for Frank Fitzgerald and for Pearce. I left Dad and Myra out of it. Though weirdly enough, after two weeks away it was harder to remember why I'd been so scared of the girls' school, why I'd had to get away. Sometimes it seemed I could have explained everything well enough that they'd have let me go home, though I wasn't sure how. That was because I was doing my best to ignore the growing bulge in my middle, which was becoming all knees and elbows.

I began to fall into the daily rhythm of Clayton's place, which was a lunch stop and roadside attraction by day and a gathering place and bar by night. It was the biggest thing around for miles. I also fed the small black bear, Pasha, gray-muzzled and bleary-eyed in his huge shady pen out back behind the diner. He was more a pet; both Ruby and Clayton adored him. "But he farts worse than an old hunting dog," she complained. "Sometimes it drives away the customers."

About two months after I'd arrived, she decided I'd better shift to waitressing and running the register. My stomach was showing by then. The kitchen was close quarters, maybe she figured I'd get burned. I'd bought a couple loose gauzy dresses from a thrift shop in Midway, printed India cotton, nice and cool for summer nights. She'd told me to wear anything I liked.

I'd thought waitressing would be a breeze, literally, after feeling the heat generated by the grill and fryer. But I was wrong. Ruby had done short-order for thirty years. She could flip a pancake in the air and catch it in the cast-iron pan she kept oiled and ready on the counter next to the grill. She could dice a Vidalia onion into bits with a huge knife in about ten seconds. To me she looked like Einstein with a spatula, the rocket scientist of cuisine. She must have known from the moment I'd sat in the booth and lied my head off to the both of them that this was my first real job.

Not that I was lazy. I bounced around that diner like a pinball, juggling water pitcher, order pad and pencil, a tray, and anything else I'd forgotten the first three trips. I had no idea what I was doing except to find out what the people sitting in the booths wanted to eat, then try to get a plate of it to them. But everything took forever. I wasn't working in a restaurant, but slogging through a nightmare in which mouths moved, giving me directions, but the distances between things lengthened until I seemed to be wading through a congealing sea of grits.

I was constantly apologizing. The first morning when I dumped a plate of biscuits and gravy on a tattooed long-distance trucker, I threw my apron over my face and burst into tears.

The man reared back and opened his mouth to curse, blunt face red and twisted. One look at me, and he sank back into the booth. "Ah, hell," he said. "Just bring me a wet dish towel and another plate, honey. Make it toast; that's safer."

At least customers must've gotten the idea I was trying my damnedest. They all left tips, sometimes even dollar bills.

From the first day Ruby gave me advice, set up my orders in sequence so I could figure them out, grabbed my apron string and spun me around in mid-flight, heading me toward the walk-in cooler or the bread bin or whatever it was I'd just forgotten. "Consolidate your trips, honey," she flung over her shoulder as I desperately ransacked the refrigerated shelves for butter pats, the dishwasher for clean glasses, or the walk-in freezer for a tub of ice cream.

"I'm trying to," I gasped, not even sure what she meant.

That night I staggered out back to take a break, a bunch of vinyl covered menus still gripped in my sweaty hand. I wanted to get away from the heat and food for a while. I wasn't sick in the mornings anymore, but sometimes things smelled or tasted weird. Something as innocent as fresh-mowed grass could send me running inside, hands clapped over my nose. The smell and taste of salted peanuts made me retch.

I went through the kitchen, careful to avoid a greasy spot between the black rubber mats, and opened the back screen door. I went out back to Pasha's cage and scratched his forehead, which he pressed against the bars. "Hey, big fella," I whispered. He groaned with pleasure and butted my hand.

There was a lean-to set up to store feed

and dog chow and the mower. I heard thumping noises and figured maybe the raccoons had gotten out and were into the chow again. I snatched up a couple garbage can lids to bang together to scare them off. Instead I stumbled over a man and woman rolling around on an old blanket, half naked. I stopped, embarrassed, and tried to back away quietly. But I kicked an empty lard can, and it went over with a clang. The couple sat up. I didn't know the woman, but the muscular guy was Mick without his T-shirt.

The girl yawned, smoothed her bleached pageboy, tugged down her skirt, and stepped off, switching her rear end like a circus pony. Mick got up slowly, like he couldn't care less. He looked right at me, taking his time getting everything tucked back in his jeans again. He was the first male I'd actually seen naked since I was five and Pearce was six, and we'd been scolded by his mother for being too old to take off our suits in the pool any more — our groping and fumbling under the circus truck had been by feel, in the dark.

I told myself I should walk off, not showing I was scared, as Sadie McElroy had advised. I began backing up, but it was difficult to look away. How strange that every male — my father, Pearce, Clayton, probably the good Lord Himself — had this same awkward equipment. Why would a woman lie down in a dirty alley with a smirking roughneck like a cat in heat? All to be prodded and poked, pounded and kneaded like dough. All that bouncing and thrashing on the sacks reminded me of the way Mrs. Tucker had thrown bread dough around on the big floury board at the bakery back home.

But then I'd done the same, under a circus truck with Pearce.

"Want to see more?" said Mick casually, like he was demonstrating toasters. I turned and ran back into the kitchen, but his unembarrassed laugh seemed to follow me all the way to the coffee station, then to my room later, when I had to cross the dark parking lot by myself. Not that he'd likely be lying in wait for a skinny, pregnant teenager whose clothes and hair, whose very pores reeked of bacon grease and onions.

I saw him in the restaurant a few days later, biting into a barbeque sandwich. He looked me solemnly up and down when he came up to pay his check, but he never said a word. I refused to speak or meet his eye, yet it seemed important to keep the

now-obvious swell of my belly hidden behind the counter. I just handed him his
change and went back to counting out the
register, as if I didn't care, either.

No matter what I was doing, I'd see
Clayton Sebring strutting around, thumbs
in his pockets, walking, walking. Always
moving. Presiding over every detail of the
diner and roadside exhibit, no matter the
time of day or night, as if he never slept.
He loved constant motion, and he and
Ruby were devoted to each other. The four
well-fed, battle-scarred cats and the three-
legged greyhound who all lived in their
place, a three-room unit attached to the
diner, must've been the strays he'd protested about. But I wondered if she'd taken
in other girls as well, besides me. Because
whenever Clayton saw me, even months
after I'd arrived, he'd pop the ever-present
Have-a-Tampa cigar out of his mouth, ges-
ture at the place at large, and say, "Settling
into the family okay, kid?"

To pass the time during the slow, off-
season, Ruby decided to teach me how to
read palms. On rainy days, she sometimes
set up in a corner of the diner and told
tourists' fortunes for two dollars a pop.
She said it never hurt to have a backup
skill. So I paid close attention and learned

each finger has its own name, from thumb all the way to pinkie: Jupiter, Saturn, The Sun, Mercury, and Venus. And each hand has five main lines, also named, and these tell if the owner will have a long, happy, healthy life or a short, sickly one. Whether he'll encounter obstacles and misfortune, get married or not. The *linea naturalis* and the *linea mensalis* even gave away whether the owner would be reckless or unfaithful in love.

"If you got any talent for it, or at least some decent intuition, it's okay to take a little compensation, I think. But no crooked stuff! Never get greedy, and never be a fool." I nodded, both impressed and annoyed. I'd had the Don't-Be-a-Fool lecture way back, from my father. Some example he'd been.

And the longer I stayed and spent time with the Sebrings, the more at ease I felt. Gradually the idea of Ordinary Springs as home, of home as my father's house, became distant, faint, even ridiculous. Here I was taken as seriously as any adult. And why not? I was going to be a mother soon. That very fact had to prove I was grown, mature. Yet I hadn't bought any baby clothes, or diapers, or a crib. The notion of an actual child felt too fantastic. Each time the baby turned or kicked inside me I was startled.

In any case, there was no way I'd ever go back to live under the same roof with Myra, to pretend she was my mother. If Owen Gamble missed his daughter, let him find me. If he cared enough anymore. Surely he'd heard I'd escaped Pine Hills. I wondered if he'd ever looked for me or had worried my picture might turn up on a wanted poster to embarrass him. I sometimes imagined my face was tacked up on bulletin boards all over the southeast. But I didn't have the guts to go inside Midway's post office to find out.

16

I wrote to my father once, just a postcard. A hand-tinted shot of Sebring's Original You Better Believe It Nature Museum and Restaurant, with a garish pink and orange sunset behind it, from the revolving wire rack at the register. I'd written on the back:

Dear Dad,

> *I am alive, in case you care.*
> *Don't bother to look for me.*

> *Your former daughter,*
> *Dory*

Of course I couldn't mail it. A giveaway, a fool's move, unless I liked the idea of giving birth behind the concertina wire and mesh–reinforced glass of the Pine Hills School. So I only slid it into my waitress's smock and carried it around with me all of one evening. A corner kept poking my armpit, a small pain I endured like a penance. As long as it was in my pocket, I could pretend I might actually send it. But after my shift I took it back to my room and wedged it under the frame of the mirror, where it greeted me morning and night, cold reality.

Even so, I used to imagine a reply, a real letter from Owen Gamble. Would it say what I'd imagined, hoped for, feared? First tell me off, then tell me to come home soon, then, in smudged words (tears? yes, I wanted to imagine this part, too), it would end with a heartfelt "I miss you and love you, Dory." I, not we, because that would mean Myra and him together, that they both did. I even didn't like to think of the two of them living together. It felt different if I came upon Clayton and Ruby, who now and then necked with their arms around each other. Then Clayton would get red in the face, turn away, and clear his throat. But Ruby only laughed like a fast, go-to-hell teenager and then I had to grin, too.

I reread the postcard while I was brushing my teeth or combing my hair, which had gotten very long and thick, because of all the extra hormones, Ruby said. My own face had begun to look strange to me, reflected, with a shadow around the eyes and cheeks like a bandit mask. Even my body seemed to know I had to stay in hiding and did its best to disguise me. I was more than an inch taller, and my belly was getting huge. My skin had cleared up and glowed with good health even under the greenish bathroom fluorescents. I was turning into someone else.

I looked around at the curved walls and for a moment couldn't breathe. Was I far enough away from Ordinary Springs that my father, Sheriff Burney, and Matron Camber couldn't reach out and find me? Freedom was a gift I'd been given and nearly thrown away. I went to my bed and lay watching the ceiling. The movie of my life unreeled there. How wrong we had all gone! Made our paths and stuck to them, like mules circling in a rut, dogs in a wire run wearing everything away beneath our restless, restless feet.

But I couldn't sleep, so I got up and ran a bath in the claw-footed tub. Waiting for it to fill, I stared at my bloated, naked self in the full-length mirror on the back of the door. The original map of my body was lost, topography changed by a hill in the middle, swollen ankles, and an oddly racoonish face. I wanted to shrug, open my mouth and deny it, laugh it off. To ignore the coming baby, pretend my belly was a handy way to hold up skirts, a nice shelf to prop a book on while reading in bed. But my condition was clear, the once-skinny length of me now a naked, rounded Venus from a *National Geographic*.

I kicked the sweat-stained puddle of my dirty clothes across the room and climbed in the tub. I slid down the cool white enamel as water groaned and gurgled in the pipes. I turned the tap with one foot and let more hot gush in, probably emptying the tank outside. Then lay back and gazed at the ceiling, the flocked wallpaper, the fancy mirror. Anywhere but that wet hill of belly, that slippery island in a shallow sea.

An hour later I pulled the plug on the cooling water and dried my frame on a thin but soft towel Ruby had left. I was just reaching for a nightgown when the first pain ripped through my middle, followed by another, low and sharp. A sudden gush soaked my legs as if, spongelike, I'd soaked up too much bathwater.

"Oh, my," I said. My voice sounded loud, hollow in the room. I pulled on a nightgown and staggered weak-kneed across the parking lot to the Sebrings' unit.

"I think it's coming," I blurted out when Ruby opened the door. She had sponge rollers in her hair and a clownish, pasty white beauty mask on.

"Mercy." For once she sounded nervous. "We better get you to a hospital fast."

"No hospital," I said. "No police."

"Police?" She stared as if I'd lost my mind.

I dragged the towel off my head. "I'm not going anywhere."

"Are you crazy?" she said, pulling me into the room. It was small but cozy, with a green tweed couch and a slinking ceramic panther on top of the TV. "Come on, lie down."

"But I'm supposed to work in the morning."

She laughed. "I don't think so."

So there I lay, the small-town simpleton, arguing about being late for work, even as the next cramp seized me like a giant's fist. It shouldn't have felt like such a surprise. My turn to learn babies didn't come pink and clean in a cellophane-wrapped box, like a doll from McCrory's. I'd managed not to give much thought to how the baby would get out, only eyed and dismissed my growing belly each morning, as if one day I'd simply unbutton and take it off, like a prop from a play. Now I looked down, horror-struck, as it bulged and rippled with a mind, a life of its own.

In less than an hour, the contractions were coming five minutes apart. Ruby held the Big Ben alarm clock to time them. "We'll get a doctor," she insisted. "One who makes house calls."

"No! No doctor," I snapped. In my mind, the medical and legal worlds had somehow become intertwined. A doctor would want names and family histories, a list of shots I'd had, where I'd been born.

By two a.m., it was raining fit to drown a herd of alligators and poor Pasha in his pen. Past the museum's short sidewalks, the ground would be a gumbo of red-brown mud. As each pain arrived I clutched a bedpost with one hand, twisting the sheets around me. But the other kept a grip on Ruby until she nodded. "Okay, okay! No doctor."

Then she peeled my viselike fingers away, one by one, and ran out into the deluge. She reappeared after eternity plus a day, though by the clock it was only half an hour. Puffing along behind, shedding quarts of rainwater off a yellow slicker, came a dark, broad-faced woman wearing the rainbow-striped skirt of a Seminole Indian.

"This is the mama," said Ruby.

"Uh-huh," the midwife stated calmly. "Pretty young."

"Don't worry, hon." Ruby patted my arm. "Scilla's done this a million times."

But then the woman pushed Ruby toward the back. "You, out. Get boiling water, towels, some nice sharp scissors. You got any fry bread? Huh. Then some of them shortbread cookies. And hot tea."

"No, wait," I cried, fighting another pain. But Ruby was already down the hall, out in the kitchen, rummaging and banging and cursing, maybe dumping every drawer and cabinet she owned. Clayton stuck his head in once, then pulled it back quick. I heard the front door shut and the truck engine turn over.

Scilla whipped the sweat-soaked sheet off me. "Huh. No hips," she grunted, frowning as if this design flaw was my own fault.

While you're held prisoner by a long, hard childbirth, shut away in a room with pain and frightening smells and sweat running in your eyes, at a certain point you begin to resent the unfairness of life. While you labor endlessly, racked with hurt, elsewhere people are laughing, driving convertibles to the beach, eating chocolate ice cream.

That whole night, the next day, and on to the following dawn, any time I raised my aching head, I had this to focus on: Scilla ensconced like a queen on two chairs, stoically eating cookies, then powdered doughnuts. Ruby fading in and out, bringing tea I couldn't drink.

Finally, as orange sunrise outlined the blinds, I was seized with a contraction that dwarfed all the others. A giant hand squeezed my last breath away. All I could do was groan, too tired to scream anymore. Scilla brushed sugar off her lap and yawned, then bent and checked under the sheet. "Okay. Now's the time. Push with all you got."

I glared through my tangled, soaked hair, hating her calm face, her perfectly parted hair, her very Indian guts. But only for a moment, because suddenly, without my consent or participation, my belly muscles crunched and squeezed in a tremendous wave I knew would rip me in two.

"That's right," said Scilla. "Ain't so hard now. Come on, come on."

I wanted to hit her and would, as soon as I could walk. Then I'd show her *hard*. At the moment there was the stabbing in my back, the cramps in my quivering thighs, the red-orange flashes that dazzled my eyes. My mound of stomach rippled like a storm-ridden sea as I propped up on my elbows, gritted my teeth, and gave one more soldierly push to get it over with, so I could lie down and die in peace.

A strange, low pressure then, as skin and muscle surely parted. And the smell of fresh blood, oddly painless, leaving only a huge feeling of relief. I lifted my head with my last iota of strength, and peered through my shaking, parted thighs. Darned if Scilla wasn't right. The baby shot out so fast the midwife nearly dropped the wet new bundle. For the first time her face became animated, even excited, as she whooped and juggled, squeezing between the bed and wall to lay it on my exhausted belly.

Then Scilla clicked open Ruby's best sewing scissors and bent over me. I shut my eyes and lay back panting, arms wrapped around what I'd just birthed. Who knew which part of me she planned to amputate, who cared? When she called sharply for needle and thread, I decided with great detachment that she'd cut off the wrong thing and simply had to sew it back on.

Ruby appeared again and handed each tool over, solemn as an acolyte. Then she leaned over and lifted the baby.

"What is it?" I whispered weakly.

291

"Oh, that reminds me. Gotta get a birth certificate," said Scilla. I nodded vaguely, drifting off, nearly asleep. Ruby brought us a clean baby a few minutes later, bathed and wrapped in a bleached old undershirt that by its voluminousness must have belonged to Clayton.

"Your little girl," she said, holding her out. "Some beauty, eh?"

I lifted my head and saw a red, squash-muzzled face beneath a cowlick of dark hair. Its squint-eyed glare seemed to accuse me of some crime.

Oh, God I was tired. So tired. Shocked by all the blood and mess and smell. Dull thudding fatigue had chased away every feeling, even pain. I grunted and turned away. Could I stand to look at the cause of so much misery yet? Let me sleep for days and days first. Babies demanded too much.

"She needs her mother," Ruby cajoled, then scolded. She repeated this, less certainly.

I closed my eyes and shook my head, feeling jagged-edged and screamy. If I had never had a mother, why should she?

I slept for a while, woke, and spooned up lukewarm chicken rice soup someone had left covered on the table by the bed. Then threw back the covers and jacked myself up on shaky legs that threatened to dump me any moment. I tiptoed to the orange crate lined with old coats where my new daughter slept. She heard and turned her rose-pink face up as if I were the sun, then pursed her lips.

Imagine what she saw: a tall, bony girl with bruised arms and faded green eyes, who didn't know which end of a baby was up: Mama.

No wonder she wailed. I looked around for help. "Ruby?"

Faint snoring from down the hall, but nobody came. Hands shaking, I lifted my daughter gently as you would a soap bubble. My nipples hardened as she cried louder, and I hugged her to me, murmuring, *shh, shh.* She quieted and nuzzled my shirt front. My breasts, swollen to a respectable size for the first time in my life, ached and stung. Then to my surprise and disgust, they began to leak milk.

At last I came to attention, a sleepwalker waked. Lifted my shirt, and Rose — for that was the name that sprang into my head, that was who her pink, opening bud of a face seemed to be telling me she was — Rose did the rest.

Ruby was like a proud grandmother and two maiden aunts rolled into one neat package. She doted on Rose and me, maybe because she'd never had any children of her own.

"Look how she follows you with her eyes!" she said. "You're everything to her."

"But I never know what to do," I said, pacing, jiggling Rose nervously up and down, frightened by the depths of my ignorance, by the strange, heart-stopping sounds this tiny baby made.

"Just keep her fed and safe, hon."

When she cried, I was terrified. Though there seemed only three things a baby cared about: milk, a dry diaper, and sleep. But when she opened her mouth was she yawning or gasping for breath? Oh God, was she breathing at all? It took so long to figure the problem, the right want.

"Nobody knows at first. They don't come with instructions."

"Well, they ought to." I began to cry along with Rose. Suddenly, here I was a mother, and clueless as a post. Had my own been so flustered by endless, mysterious demands she'd finally turned tail and run? Plus, here my father had a granddaughter, probably the only one he'd ever get, and didn't know a thing about it. And Pearce . . . childhood friend and playmate, now a father. It was so strange! I could imagine what Miss Harriet would say. Could Pearce both love and fear Rose as much as I did? Would he ever meet her at all? He'd be graduating soon, going to sea with his uncle and cousins. Maybe he'd make a better job of leaving than I had.

Oh, I was tired of surging hormones and endless crying, of sour milk and ammonia smells, of the face-slapping line of wet diapers strung across the room. It had rained every day since Rose was born. "If I had a mother here I'd know what to do."

Ruby didn't look offended, though she probably had a right to. "Ah, maybe you're lucky. Mine stuck around. Birthed me at twenty-five, then waited twenty years to give me a brother. Held him long enough to name him Red, give him the colic, and break his arm before the state got the sense to take him away."

"Oh," I whispered, holding Rose closer. The state had taken me away, too. Did they also haul off helpless babies? "What happened to him?"

"Burnt up in a tunnel in Korea in fifty-one," she said, turning away to stack a pile of folded diapers. "Dead fourteen years now. Still got the lousy medal somewhere."

"What about your mother?"

Ruby threw her head back and laughed.

"Used to write her. Send cards with the same postscript: 'And who the hell was my daddy? It won't matter a damn after all these years who knows his name!' The old bitch never told. Died raving nuts in the county home."

"I'm sorry, Ruby," I said, shifting Rose, who was quiet now, to the other breast.

"Pish. I didn't cry when she died. And get this, they asked if I wanted an autopsy. 'I'll tell you what killed her,' I said. 'See that big hole in her chest where a heart shoulda been?'"

I reached up and patted her cheek, but she waved me off. Blew her nose on the corner of a dirty diaper. "Ah, forget it."

"Will you be Rose's godmother?"

"Of course." She smiled and wiped a tear off her cheek. "She's an angel! I love her already."

Rose grew less red and wrinkled. She even began to have a personality. Clayton called her My Pretty and kissed the top of her head, no longer squeamish once the soft spot closed up. He called her Baby Rosebud and Miss Pinky. He danced her around the lounge when the radio played old songs like "Boogie-Woogie Bugle Boy" and "Unchained Melody."

She grew and grew. I went back to work when she was three months old, and hired a nice woman, a middle-aged widow from up the road, to watch her. Soon Rose was crawling and into everything: the packed kitchen cupboards, the pots and pans she loved to bang with a spoon, Ruby's trunk of old clothes — some of it looking like it'd been through the Civil War. By the time she was nine months old, she could pull herself along the furniture. Sometimes I took her over to the restaurant with me, and she banged spoons in a playpen in the kitchen or rode my hip. But if it was too crowded or busy, I'd bundle her off to Ruby's or to the sitter's, where it was okay to get into all the drawers and chests.

At twelve months, Rose liked to push her fat toes into sequined high heels, wrap scarves or a feather boa around her waist, bend her knees, and bop to music on the record player while one of us held her hands. We'd laugh at the faces she made, the way the four cats looked offended and then panic-stricken at her birdlike coos and screeches. How joyfully she waved her arms and shook her diapered bottom. What rhythm! She hadn't gotten it from me.

One lazy Sunday afternoon just like that,

Ruby and I were watching Rose, smoking Kools and drinking Earl Gray fortified with rum.

The week before I had read Ruby's palm based on the lessons she'd given me, and she pronounced me a tolerable apprentice. "We can do it more like a full-time sideline now. Clayton'll love that! Oh — and hold on." She'd jumped up, dashed into the back, and reappeared cradling something wrapped in a black velvet cloth.

"Look here." She had folded back the cloth to reveal a gleaming, perfect glass ball. "Clayton got me this to hold down the bills in the office so the ceiling fan wouldn't keep blowing 'em off the desk. He spotted it in a little shop in Quincy, thought it was a paperweight. But it kept rolling off the desk. Finally I realized he'd bought me a crystal ball!"

So we'd made plans, chattering at the same time like excited girls, which I guess we were. I'd already bought some fake silk scarves in the Midway five and dime, but we couldn't find a real Tarot deck anywhere. Then, in the back of an old *Alfred Hitchcock* magazine, Ruby'd spotted a tiny ad for a set of instructions on how to tell fortunes with regular playing cards. It claimed they'd been written by somebody named Mademoiselle Le Normand, which sounded impressive. The thick manila envelope had arrived the day before.

Now we sat with the crystal on the coffee table, a deck of cards laid out beside it. We were looking over Mademoiselle Le Normand's blurry, mimeographed directions. Ruby kept rubbing her temples as she read, then the back of her head.

"Mercy," she gasped. "Oh my, what a pain. I've got the worst headache of all time."

"I'll get some aspirin," I said. But before my cup was even square in the saucer, she'd slumped against the arm of the couch, her hot tea pouring into her lap. Then she slid over sideways to the floor.

I rushed over and tried to lift her. She was thin and small boned but so limp a weight I couldn't get a good grip. I only managed to stretch her out on the floor and slide a cushion under her head. That looked peaceful, like she was sleeping. Except one eye was half open and only the white showed. This small wrong detail undid me. I backed up, a hand pressed to my mouth, and snatched up Rose, who howled at having her fun interrupted. I ran out the door and over to the restaurant, screaming for help. Behind me, Ruby's three-legged dog set up a howl, too.

I burst through the door so fast I skidded on the welcome mat and banged my hip against the counter. Clayton was in the back on the phone, talking loud and waving a smoldering cigar. He took one look at my face and hung up without even saying good-bye.

"Ruby," I gasped, trying to keep my grip on Rose, who was wriggling and slipping down my side.

He shoved back his chair, threw the cigar at an ashtray, and pushed out the door. I shrugged Rose up on my shoulder and ran after. Clayton was way ahead, moving faster than I'd ever imagined such a big, heavy-set man could. He disappeared into their unit. The baby was a sack of lead, pulling my hair, cooing in my face, all this running and shouting a new game she liked.

I went in slowly, panting, wishing it was still an ordinary day, that I was only just coming in from my shift, looking forward to spiked tea and cookies and Frank Sinatra on the record player.

Clayton knelt on the floor, holding her limp hand, patting it the way he always did if she got upset. Tears slicked his broad face, and he was whispering something. I started to back away to give them privacy, but when he raised his right hand and crossed himself, I realized he'd been praying.

"I'll call an ambulance, get on the phone in the office. Go get someone," my voice so hoarse I could barely get the words out.

But he shook his head. "It's too late, Vera," he said in a choked voice and went on with his prayers, his vigil at her side.

So I set Rose down and dropped to my knees, too. I didn't know any Catholic prayers, but I thought back to all the church services I'd been dragged to as a kid. Oh, why when I'd been there had I so often been thinking about homework, or the strange hats people were wearing, or what we'd be having for Sunday dinner? Finally, I began to whisper the Our Father — all that came to mind of a whole piece.

Clayton didn't look up. "We can't leave her," he whispered to me, then reached over and took my hand. He held it so tight it hurt.

My fingers went tingly, then finally numb, but I didn't pull away. He murmured prayers in some other language, Latin I guess, while in the background Rose la-la'ed nonsensically with the record that kept hitting the changer and replaying itself. My knees began to ache, and I wished they'd hurt even more, anything to take my mind off what we'd all just lost. I saw now how Clayton Sebring had been mad for Ruby, the loud, sassy south Georgia girl who'd rescued herself decades ago from a shotgun house in Valdosta. She'd made it her business to save other creatures in trouble. She always said she'd never been sick a day in her life, and I knew she'd never been mean to a soul. And now she would never be old.

When I was a child we always went to the First Baptist Church in Ordinary Springs. Each Sunday the reverend would quote homilies. His favorite was, "The Lord never asks us to shoulder a bigger burden than we can bear." He'd wag a finger at the choir and say, "The human soul's elastic, my friends. Purely one hundred percent elastic." I'd imagine a red rubber band hooked at the top of my head and the soles of my feet, holding me tight together. The day my friend and savior Ruby died, that band stretched as far as it could. It didn't break, but it lost a lot of snap.

At the funeral I kept a hand on Clayton's arm, because he looked suddenly smaller, less sturdy and wise. He'd shrunk like a mislaundered suit since we'd knelt together in that room and prayed for Ruby's soul as it brushed by us in a hurry to move on to the next, better place.

The baby-sitter, a sweet, round-faced blonde woman named Peggy, sat in the pew with Rose on her lap, keeping her occupied with a rag doll and a sippy cup of apple juice. I blew my nose on a tissue; Rose cooed and patted her face. We'd had to lock the dog in the house. It had tried to follow our car down the highway, as if it knew we were going away with Ruby for the last time. All her strays had loved her. Rose was the only one too young to cry because she'd never see her Aunt Ruby again.

Huge, stolid Clayton finally broke down in shuddering gulps, his face blotched like a child's. He kept blowing his nose on a hankie I'd handed over before I realized it was a nice one Ruby had given me, with a little embroidered R and a violet in one corner. I didn't have the heart to ask for it back, but wished I'd kept it. Anyhow, I still had the best of Ruby, what she'd taught me: to take on challenges, to try new things, to demand respect from customers but still be honest and fair. And that I shouldn't worry too much if I didn't have all the answers. It was more legacy than my own mother had left. It would have to be enough.

After I went back to work, the restaurant was haunted. Not by a ghost; our Ruby had left and gone on to better places. She'd never come back to frighten anyone, to rattle ghostly bangle bracelets in the night to make us feel guilty. It was haunted by her absence. Her furniture, her clothes, her costume jewelry, her special Zippo lighter with a flamingo on the front — everything was there waiting, but she wouldn't be back. Pasha drooped in his cage, his furry black cheeks matted with constant weeping. He mourned, too, barely touching his food, lying with his back to me when I came with fresh water or offered to scratch his muzzle.

Clayton sank into the deepest despair of all. He talked to Ruby's dog a lot, and he was getting forgetful. He didn't put the cats outside enough; they were shitting on everything. The only thing that seemed to bring him out of his funk was Rose. At the sight of her he sat up straighter; he smiled and bounced her on his knee. And she adored him. "Pap-Pa," she called him, and sometimes I felt a little jealous, a little resentful. She had a grandfather, a real blood one, down south in Ordinary Springs. Yet who knew if she'd ever meet him? Clayton wasn't really her Pap-Pa, but she didn't know that.

Then I felt ashamed. After all he and Ruby had done for me and for Rose, who was more kin, after all? What short memories people have, I thought. Then I got up and went back to work.

Over the next six months, I took up double shifts and cigarettes with a vengeance, though I went out in the parking lot or at least opened a window and blew the smoke outside so Rose didn't breathe it. I didn't mind poisoning myself, but not her. I hated going to the room alone on late nights, when the baby was already asleep or at the sitter's and it seemed the emptiest. Then I knew I'd lie awake, thinking about what to do with the rest of my life. I hadn't followed my own plan, simple as it'd been. Yes, I was still young. But late on a sleepless night, the weight of all your transgressions and mistakes can make a body feel like you've already used up your allotted span and then some.

I also allowed myself to notice men who came into the diner, even some of the tourists who stopped to gape at the animals at show time. Especially at the sobering sight of Big Jake launching himself diagonally skyward, like a faulty Cape Canaveral rocket, to capture a whole raw chicken suspended on the wire across his pen. I sometimes gave the preshow spiel, and often when I glanced at the crowd I realized some of them — the men, I mean — were watching me instead of the gator. I smiled at the ones who looked single and later cleared their plates and swept their extra tips into my apron pocket. But that was all. At night sometimes I'd run my hands down my sides and imagine one there with me. But I never felt moved enough to actually do anything about it.

Mick Poteke had been coming around again. He thought Clayton ought to expand the place. He was full of ideas, but Clayton only shook his head and sighed. He'd built the museum not just for himself, but also for Ruby. Now half his reason for hitting the big time, for being the next Gatorland, was gone.

But Mick kept coming around. Some nights he drank beer after beer, his long legs in boots and jeans stretched out in the aisle where I had to step over each time I passed. Staring at me harder than any tourist or trucker had yet; long past polite.

Even after I pointedly turned away, I could feel him taking stock of my body, which had gone back to its old shape, its old geography. Without looking, I could even feel him sliding out of the booth and walking confidently to the counter. He came up behind me but didn't say a thing. I began to feel skittish and foolish, standing facing the order window, sticking new tickets up on the revolving metal rack for the quiet, gray-haired colored man named Sweeney, who was our new cook. I grabbed up a stack of menus, wiped them off, evened them up like a deck of cards. And finally turned.

"You look different," said Mick. He didn't smile when he said it, just looked in my eyes as if there wasn't a counter full of hungry truckers and booths of tired Yankee tourists whose crying kids were waiting for their chocolate milk and corndogs. I tried to look away, but all I could think of was the night I'd stumbled across him in the back alley, out by old Pasha's cage, rolling half-naked on a blanket with some blonde tourist. I had to work to keep my eyes above his collar; they kept wanting to focus lower. I felt cornered, hot and red in the face. At last an order came up behind me. I turned gratefully to pick up.

Sweeney caught my eye over the plate of french fries and chicken fried steak. He didn't say a word, but I knew from the way he looked at me, then at Mick, that he was asking: Need help? And probably hoping like hell I didn't.

I shook my head and ducked under Mick's arm, swinging away with the steaming food.

Mick came up and took one plate and set it down in front of a woman with curlers under her scarf and two crying toddlers next to her. He smiled at her. "Hope you enjoy it," he said, his voice deep and smooth and cool as a lake on a hot day. As if he owned the place.

She smiled and touched her bristling head self-consciously. "Why, thanks." When she giggled, I turned away, not wanting to see her bat her eyelashes, too. Oh, brother.

"What time you get off?" Mick said behind me, trying to scoop up part of the next order. I blocked his arm and swept off again, plates balanced all the way up to my elbow. I shrugged, playing mysterious. Wishing he'd go away yet hoping he'd stay a little longer.

All that night he kept glancing over. I hadn't been much for this kind of game before. But without Ruby, the You Better Believe It had sunk into a slow-moving despair that made a person desperate to find diversion, some comic relief. So you didn't have to think about how empty some folks leave a place when they're gone.

"Thursday night," I said at last. "I get off at ten."

"Well, what do you know. She walks, she talks," he said, like a deadpan carnival barker. "But does she ever crawl on her belly like a snake?"

I couldn't help but burst out laughing then. "Don't push your luck."

Over the next few days I caught up on my sleep, painted my toenails. I sat outside in the sun, and even got Peggy the babysitter to fix up my hair and trim the ragged ends. I smoked continuously; it kept the mosquitoes away. As she clipped Peggy talked — mostly to Rose. And suddenly, in the middle of one of her long rambling stories, I realized with a pang that while I was daydreaming about Mick Poteke, Peggy was entertaining Rose, answering her questions, admiring her scribbled crayon drawings. It was clear from her voice: Peggy loved my daughter. But surely not more than I did! Yet Peggy was the one who was always patient, who never seemed to get tired. And from the way she clung to Peggy's hand, babbled new words over and over for her approval, and hugged her legs as she moved around me, clipping split ends, it was clear that Rose loved Peggy. As much as Ruby, it seemed. Somehow that seemed wrong. Like a betrayal.

No one would ever take Ruby's place in my heart, but Rose was so young she didn't think to play favorites and liked everyone. As she was rocked and petted and danced with and entertained, I was free for a little while to daydream. Why should I resent that? It was silly.

More and more I'd been reliving my first encounter with Mick. That crude, embarrassing, yet undeniably exciting scene behind the kitchen. In retrospect, it seemed to have more to do with me; the anonymous woman he'd been fooling with barely figured in at all.

I had dreamed one night of him stretched out on a bed, sleeping under a thin, weightless sheet. Somehow he looked more undressed than in the alley. Helpless and enticing. I imagined the rise and fall of his smooth, near-hairless chest, a tanned hand hanging over the edge of the bed, fingertips grazing the floor. The other tucked beneath him at the waist. Just where my own would rest if we ever happened to slow dance, which was pretty unlikely. While he slept, I memorized him like a scene from one of Mrs. Hawks's Shakespeare plays.

We met Thursday night in the diner. There really wasn't anyplace else to go. I was determined not to seem too easily impressed, but it was harder than I'd thought. This was much different than my only previous date, when I'd sneaked out and met Pearce at the circus.

My tongue felt heavy as a sock full of pennies, so I let Mick do most of the talking and learned that he trapped animals and sold them to zoos and nature parks. Once he'd been all the way to South America, with some rich man who wanted exotic additions to his private game preserve. I discovered Mick liked to play poker, and he talked nice to waitresses. He'd been to college for two years on the GI bill and never planned to go back. He wouldn't tell me what he'd studied. I began to like his sense of humor, the way he said just what he thought. And his laugh, a deep, infectious rumble I actually *felt* traveling through the air.

When he reached out and tried to capture my hand, though, I pulled it back.

He smiled. "I'm not the one with claws, the one who bites."

"No? What about out back of the kitchen, by the bear's cage? You were with someone. Another . . . date," I said, hiding a smile.

He didn't even look sheepish. "Oh, yeah."

I tilted my chin up. "So, why me now?" Did he know what I was thinking? Probably it showed on my face. I still didn't have the knack of being secretive, of concealing anything strangers or even friends might read there and use against me. "I'm kind of young for you. And I have a daughter."

"I like kids," he said, leaning back, running a hand down the knife-sharp crease of his pants, moving slow, like someone trying not to frighten a wild animal. "How old are you, anyhow?"

I shook my head. But then, seeing he wasn't going to talk until I said something and broke the spell, I finally gave in. "Nineteen." It didn't feel like a lie; surely I'd aged fast the past couple years.

"Huh. That old." Smiling again.

Maybe I looked scared then, showing my real age, because he laughed out loud. But he held up a hand. "I'm not laughing at you. Just seems funny, you knowing me so much better than I know you. And now here we sit, like a couple of statues. Aren't we a pair!"

I picked up the bottle of beer and wondered if I could get any down. The first time I'd tried I'd been twelve, when Pearce sneaked a couple of Old Milwaukees out of his parents' refrigerator and smuggled them down to our old treehouse at the Springs. I'd taken one bitter gulp and poured the rest over the side into the water.

I took a sip. Then another, which seemed not as bad as the first.

After an hour or so Mick got up and said he had to go. He left me at the front stoop, saying he'd had a nice time. He reached out and I stepped back, but he only shook my hand, then went whistling down the sidewalk. I felt a little relieved, but honestly, more cheated. My dreams that night were full of naked men, all just out of reach.

Yet he came back. I didn't have to work at making him take notice. He'd pass the counter or the register and smile and wink as if we were all too well acquainted. I wanted to feel offended, but it was hard. Weekend nights were still busy, breakfast shift seemed to come way too early, and Rose was teething and fussy, coming up on the terrible twos at one and a half. The attention Mick Poteke paid was an oasis, a glimpse of another life outside the close limits of my own. Was it already gone, my chance at excitement and admiration? I'd gone from high school to motherhood with nothing in between.

I meant to refuse to see him again. But as if he knew my thoughts, he disappeared for two weeks. The days he was away on the road, then suddenly turned up again I realized I'd missed him. Our daytime flirting turned to quick gropes and kisses behind the partition of the waitress station. Or out by the animal pens. Anywhere but in the alley behind the lounge, which he was careful not to even mention. One afternoon between breakfast and lunch shifts, while Clayton called my name, looking for me, Mick pressed me up against the wall of the walk-in freezer and breathed heat on my neck, my face as I shivered and goose bumps rose on my bare arms in the frigid air. He pressed himself hard against my pubic bone until he stiffened, shuddered, and whispered my name softly, like a mocking echo of Clayton's plaintive call, breath warm and moist against my ear.

I broke away first, telling myself, *That's enough, be careful.* But I didn't want to be careful. Who were we hurting? No one even knew. I was nearly eighteen. But the last time I'd been reckless, I'd paid with pain. That sobered me up and helped cool my longings for a while. But then I'd catch Mick's hot, yearning glances across the diner, and it got harder to remember.

I looked up from pouring a glass of sweet tea for an elderly couple and saw I had my own audience. Mick was watching me from the counter, swiveling around on his stool to meet my eyes. The jukebox played "Don't Be Cruel." He grinned and pointed at me, then swung back around. The farmers and truck drivers and people passing through on their way to Miami and Atlanta didn't notice any of this. But as the evening went on, his gaze followed, whether I was folding napkins, or filling salt shakers, or wiping down condiment bottles.

I began to smile to myself, a secret satis-fying smile, and made an effort to do these plain everyday things with grace and flair. But being so distracted I made mistakes, setting tables with two spoons but no forks; putting order tickets on the carousel backward so Sweeney couldn't read them;

mixing up a woman's order of a fried chicken basket with her husband's Salisbury steak, twice.

I did want to go off with Mick, right then and there. So bad I couldn't concentrate on the simplest part of my work. And he was waiting patient as a statue, nursing the same warm beer for an hour. At closing time, to give my hands a chance to stop shaking, I stacked all the menus, put a rack of clean glasses in the station, and filled three bins with folded napkins. Only then did I go back to tell Sweeney I was leaving.

He was scraping the grill clean. "Best watch yo'self," was all he said to my good night. But his voice was soft and kind. Not a warning, I thought, but a blessing.

When I came out, Mick was leaning on the giant alligator head that was our front doorway, his back propped against a six-foot tooth. He was smoking a thin black cigarillo, which seemed exotic. Without a word, we walked together across the still-warm asphalt. I heard Pasha circling his pen, slamming his bulk against the bars as he turned, growling soft and deep in his chest.

When we reached my concrete teepee I stopped. Mick put out a hand and ran it down the rough sloping concrete wall and snorted a laugh.

"Better put that out," I said, nodding at the cigarillo. "I don't smoke around the baby." Actually she was spending the night at Peggy's. Fridays meant late shift for me, and it was easier than carrying twenty-two pounds of sleeping child, trying to get her into a different bed without waking her.

I expected him to complain — it was a new one, just lit. But he smiled, flicked it onto the ground, and crushed the glowing red end under a boot heel. He gripped my arm above the elbow and firmly steered me up to the door. I made a little show of pulling back, but we both knew I didn't mean it. The metal doormat clanged under his boot heels. He unlocked the door, and we went in. At least the room was fairly neat. No unfolded clothes, no papers or hairbrushes or any dirty plates in sight. Only my bed, Rose's crib behind a little Japanese screen Ruby had given me, a straight-backed metal chair, a woodgrain Formica desk, and my pasteboard wardrobe with square corners.

It could have been anyone's room. Or no one's.

He looked at me, one eyebrow raised. "Beer?"

I shook my head. "All out."

He laughed again, softly, then unbuttoned

his shirt and, in one smooth motion, pulled it and his undershirt over his head. He stepped close, drew me up tight against his bare chest, and kissed me. Not like Pearce had done so long ago, fast and uncertain in the Tunnel of Horrors, then hard and desperate and awkward beneath the belly of a truck in the dark.

No, Mick took my face between his hands and worked my mouth open with his tongue. And he did this incredibly slowly, until my body felt heavier and heavier. Until it was a chore just to stay upright and on my feet. Tight, hot suspense grew in my belly, as thrilling, as gripping as fear. Except I liked it, didn't want it to stop. When he pulled back at last and slid his hands down my arms, I expected sparks to leap from under his fingers in the cool dim room.

His hands cupped my breasts as if to weigh them. He made an approving noise, like a satisfied storekeeper, and I laughed, because it was almost but not quite a game. Then he pulled me into a kind of slow dance that moved us over to the bed. Which I recalled now was unmade, a tangle of sheets and flowered spread and discarded clothes and an empty hot dog wrapper from a rushed lunch. Even a coffee mug, all of which he swept onto the floor like so much dust.

How many women had he been with before me? The nameless blonde, of course, and surely lots of others I didn't know. I opened my mouth to say, *Slow down.* To say who knows what, but he was already unbuttoning my uniform blouse. I wanted to leave it on, because after nursing Rose, even on the edge of nineteen, I was once again flat-chested. The bra I wore was padded. I crossed my arms over my breasts, but he pulled them apart, unhooked the bra, then kissed his way up and down my front, flicking out words in code on bare skin.

Finally, when I thought I'd scream if he didn't get on with it, he hiked my skirt up over my hips, then yanked my underwear down, leaving it to hang where it'd snagged around one ankle.

I lay back, snarled hair over my eyes, ashamed I was practically panting like a dog in heat. Mick stretched out beside me and unbuttoned his jeans. Took hold of my right hand and slid it under his waistband as far as it could go, which wasn't far — those jeans were tight. He wore no shorts, no underwear at all.

Of course we'd kissed before, and he'd put his hands on me. But I'd never felt his bare skin till now. All those other stolen times I'd held still, only brushing the angles and lines and bumps of his body through his clothes, eyes closed, while he guided my hand as if I were blind, showing me just what had made women willingly follow him into alleys. Why he could stand half-naked in front of a stranger, smiling, vain as a three-year-old, tucking every last bit of himself back into his clothes, holding my gaze as if I were a mirror made to reflect it all back. His eyes never left mine.

It was then, of all moments, that I knew suddenly I didn't want all this. Did not want him on top of me, molding me to the mattress, suffocating me. But that made no sense; I'd wanted him bad just an hour before. I'd had to have him, had insisted on getting my way, hiding in freezers and behind partitions, making Clayton go look for me during the day, frowning and rubbing the back of his neck, wondering where I'd disappeared to.

Now that I had Mick Poteke in my bed, a worm of doubt squirmed in my stomach. There was something else about him I didn't yet know, something important. But what?

As if he sensed my mind pulling back, he paused. Pulled my hand out of his jeans and captured both my wrists in one of his big hands. Then with the other, he peeled my remaining clothes away like gift wrap. My uniform skirt, chosen by Ruby to look like a modest tennis outfit, not too short. My beige lace slip with the stretched-out elastic waist; I'd worried all night it might slide over my hips and fall. My underpants, also white cotton, same kind I'd worn since elementary school. Then, as if he couldn't wait any longer, he rolled onto me, yanking at his belt, shoving down his pants.

He kneed my legs apart and ran his hands up and down my bare sides, groaning softly as if the very grain of my skin somehow hurt him. So I pushed away my doubts. A bit late for them, anyhow. I thought everything would be all right then. But to my surprise, a sudden liquid warmth spread over my thighs and seeped between them to the sheets. Mick cursed and rolled off as I reached down and touched the still-warm smear on one thigh. I laid a hand on his shoulder.

He shook me off. The back of his neck, the tips of his ears, and his sweating back gave off heat like the leavings of a bonfire. He smelled strong of beer and something else, maybe whiskey, maybe the shine I knew Sweeney sometimes drank back in the kitchen on slow nights. Maybe Mick'd had a bit too much, waiting for me all night.

So I decided to wait, too. Give him some time. Too much, I guess, because gradually his breathing became slower, deeper, until it was clear he was asleep. I reached over and turned on the shaded reading light mounted above the headboard of my bed. He looked uncomfortable, still tangled in his clothes like an exhausted little boy. So, carefully, the slow way you'd undress a sleeping child, I tugged off his rumpled jeans, his boots, even his socks, until I'd uncovered every inch of Mick Poteke. I could satisfy my curiosity, if nothing else.

He mumbled and turned on his back, snoring. I ran hands over his skin, still hot to the touch. Except for his legs and arms and the thick patch below his navel, his body felt nearly hairless. That seemed strange. Were all Indians so smooth-skinned, or was it possible he shaved more than his face? I pressed a fingertip to one of his nipples, dark and rosy and flat, smaller than mine. Ran a hand down his belly, testing the ridges of muscle.

I hesitated, then at last traced two fingers over the line of black hair, the road leading down from his navel. Mick groaned and swatted at the air, knocking some dream thing away. I moved one hand down to feel his cock slowly unfolding from its tangled black nest, obeying some silent order. I glanced up, but Mick sighed, and slept on. It seemed I could look all I wanted.

Really, up close the thing was pretty ugly. Drab and functional-looking, like a garden hose. Pinkish-yellow darkening to purple at the head, like a bruise. I stroked gently, velvety skin sliding beneath my fingers. It stirred again, stretching like an appreciative cat. Nodding approval, curving a bit to the right, to where I sat. I forgot Mick was asleep and laughed out loud. How funny it was, this fleshy thing drawn true as a compass needle, to me.

So occupied, only gradually did I realize his breathing had turned fast and uneven and that his eyes were open, watching me.

"Hey there," he said, gaze soft and unfocused as if still dreaming. Maybe he could see me for a moment not as I was; skinny, awkward, stubborn. Could imagine who and what I would be some day, and maybe it was good. Because he took hold of my arms, gently this time, and pulled me slowly, slowly up the whole hot length of him. Then Micco Poteke, four-times-great-grandson of old King Bowlegs of the Seminole tribe, began to teach me what all could be done with the greedy little monster I'd teased awake.

17

Once we got together, Mick got me into all sorts of things I'd never even imagined before. One night after work he brought a pouch of dry crumbled leaves to my room. Told me it made a cigarette that'd make anyone feel good, no matter how down they'd been before.

"You mean it's like dope?" I said.

He looked surprised, but I'd heard about such things at the Pine Hills School. I'd never had any, though. And I wouldn't let him light up with Rose there. But the next night we were alone, he pulled out a skinny cigarette with twisted-up ends and we smoked it. I hadn't felt particularly bad, but soon I was laughing at everything he said. Like, "It makes screwing better, too."

He insisted he could prove this. The main difference was, I was real hungry afterward. Giggling like loons, we sneaked back into the diner and raided the walk-in freezer to make hot fudge sundaes at two in the morning.

One Wednesday, my day off, he turned

up in a different car, an old Corvette with a convertible top that wouldn't latch down in back. When I told Clayton I was going for a ride with Mick, he looked at me funny.

"He's going to teach me to drive," I said.

"Huh. That so," was all Clayton said. He was frowning; maybe he didn't think much of women drivers.

So we headed south. When we reached a deserted stretch on Highway 267, nothing but turkey oak and lightning-struck pines, he pulled over, got out, and came around to my side. "Slide over. You get to drive now."

"But I don't have a license." My one drive had been escaping the school.

He grinned. "Neither do I."

I took a deep breath of air heavy with pine resin, a faint lemony sweetness from the blooms of wild magnolias and already a salt hint of sea. Mullets plopped and splashed in some nearby creek. Having never shifted gears, pushing in the clutch smoothly took all my concentration while he worked the shift lever.

"Come on, go faster," he kept saying. "You drive like an old lady early for Sunday school."

So I went fast, then a little faster. Until

on a sharp curve I panicked and didn't turn the wheel far enough. We ran off the road and stopped a few feet into the weed-choked shoulder, a telephone pole sitting inches from my door. I was shaking with the fear of just-missed death, expecting Mick to order me out and take over the wheel. I waited to be chewed out; almost longed for it.

But he hooted as if I'd done something charming, funny. "You lucky girl."

Then I felt, at least for a moment, a different fear. The kind that creeps up your spine and raises the fine hairs on your arms and the back of your neck. *Maybe,* it said to me, *there's something not quite right about your Mick.* Something those gliding, circling black turkey buzzards up in that blue sky already know. And if that were so, what did it say about me?

"I can't risk it," I said at last. "There's Rose. Who'll take care of her if I got killed?" I was actually more worried about being stopped by a patrolman. Maybe he'd know about me. Maybe send me back to Florida, to the school.

Mick seemed disappointed in me then. But I climbed over him and he backed the car onto the road again.

I suppose the warp of everyday life suddenly stretched to include a stranger comes as a surprise to everyone. I studied his profile. He looked like a wood carving, a hawk turned human, this mysterious man who disappeared silently as a Florida panther into the woods, then returned unexpectedly, bearing small gifts: a bunch of Shasta daisies, a tin of peppermint candy, a beautiful branched piece of coral. He wasn't much into clothes and wore khaki pants and jeans with a plain white shirt most of the time. But women of all ages — waitresses, cashiers, the usherettes at movies, high school girls in the five and dime — all couldn't help but stare at his glossy black hair, broad chest and shoulders, or his thigh muscles straining denim.

Every night he wasn't away, after I'd counted out the night's take and handed the drawer over to Clayton, gone to get Rose or come back to the room to watch her sleeping and kiss her sweaty little forehead, he'd turn up. Without a word, he'd grab my waist and tumble me onto the bed. And even if it'd been a bad day with bitching customers and grabby truckers and dog-flies biting when I took a turn at the animal tours, I'd feel a wonderful fullness rising in my chest and not be tired after all, but rested and rich and full of energy.

Of course it wasn't all gifts and love talk. In a bad mood, he'd slam out, crashing the door so hard dishes jumped to their deaths off the narrow shelves I'd nailed up. And one afternoon, just in from a trip down to the Glades, he'd come in unexpectedly, pushed me down, yanked up my skirt in short rude jerks, and thrust into me as if meaning to draw blood. It'd started out that way, yet soon I was right with him, biting and clawing, enjoying the contest. Because in this we were always matched, with nothing on our minds but each other. He wasn't around enough that we fought over little things, like who ate the last apple in the cupboard, who'd put the toilet paper roll in up or down, or who'd left the percolator on the stove to burn.

Did Clayton or Sweeney the cook or the new waitress I'd trained know all this? Perhaps. But when you live in the midst of folks and are thrown together daily, minding your own business is the only wall of privacy.

In Wakulla County, we passed peeling white board bungalows and Holiness churches and concrete block ranchers painted sun-bleached pink and green. The bushes were spread with drying laundry, because clotheslines cost money and clearly these folks had none. Abandoned fields were thick with wild mustard, tapped-out pecan orchards choked with mistletoe. Wild grapevine twined through the empty doors and window sockets of abandoned cabins, sprouted on collapsed roofs and around rusted tin chimneys. A few faded billboards listed on the roadside: SAVE OUR REPUBLIC — IMPEACH EARL WARREN said one. The towns we passed or saw signs for required strange movements of the mouth to say: Sopchoppy, Panacea, Arran, Medart.

Mick suddenly swung off the highway onto a road that was nothing but an unpaved track of ribbed sand. The car juddered and bounced, shaking us like a can of paint in a mixing machine. Nothing around us now but live oak hammock, dark stands of loblolly and slash probably populated only with wild hogs and snakes and bobcats and a black bear or two. I bolted upright in my seat as a bald eagle took off from the middle of the road, clutching in his claws some unlucky rodent that hadn't quite made the crossing.

He stopped, and took my hand, pulling me through an overgrown clearing. Spurge nettles and wild berry vines tore at my ankles as we cut through. I slapped mosquitoes as lizards wearing new-leaf green and orange-tailed skinks raced away, dove back into rotten-log homes. I tripped over something, maybe a rock. But Mick turned it over and it was a chunk of worn tombstone, the inscription no longer readable except for the dates: 1805–1829. He leaned the slab against a tree.

"Who was it?" I asked.

He shrugged. "Some northerner. Turned Floridian and died of it."

I slipped my arms around his waist. "So where we going?"

He kissed the top of my head. "To catch a gator."

Mick went first, cautioning me to watch out for gator holes. He'd concealed a huge flat-bottomed boat in the reeds, grasses, and tangled undergrowth of the edge of the river. We dragged it into the shallows and he shoved off, then jumped in.

He poled us up the run as fish splashed in the shallows and the sharp green smell of crushed reeds rose around us. Then he handed me the pole and unhooked a flashlight from his belt. He shone it down to light up the tannin-dark water and nearby gator holes. They were all empty. He took the pole again and sent us shooting out of the run and into a tiny concealed lake framed with thickets of hardwood and wild blueberries, which gators love to lie under. Then their dinners come right to them. Gators are lazy.

It seemed very silent all of a sudden. Not even the bobwhites were calling anymore.

Suddenly he raised a hand for me to keep quiet. He also raised the heavy pole, and now I saw it was sharpened at the tip like a spear. Our boat drifted forward inch by inch until I forgot to breathe. Mick raised the spear. Then I saw his prey clear, the dark eye mounds just above the surface of the water, a round bump of snout, and feet outlined below.

"How can you kill it?" I whispered, thinking how big it must be if you judged by the space between the eyes. And gators have bony armor all up and down their backs. The older ones are nearly bulletproof.

"I don't aim to."

I opened my mouth to ask what he did aim to do, but just then Mick's arm tensed. He struck, and the water churned to foam. I clung to the gunwales as we rocked crazily, then snatched my hands back quick as the alligator's lashing tail hit the boat, knocking out a chunk like it was wet cardboard. Luckily the damage was above the waterline. I looked up again in time to see the gator leap clear of the water, snapping and grunting in rage. If Mick had only meant to make him mad, he'd succeeded wonderfully. The thing thrashed and bellowed. It leapt again and again. And then, just as it seemed to tire and began to settle back and closed its jaws, Mick scooped up a line from the thwarts. I saw a noose in the end. He leaned out, and in one graceful motion, slipped that over the gator's head. Then he jerked back on the line and cranked a winch fastened to the boat.

Now the creature struggled desperately, his thrashing legs and claws tearing water hyacinths and duckweed and aquatic grasses loose from the bottom muck. Mick sat down on the front bench seat and lit a cigarette. He took one look at my face and laughed. "Here," he said, pulling the cigarette from his lips and slipping it between mine. "You need this more than me."

We just sat and waited until the big lizard was finally tired of putting on a show. Then Mick winched it up alongside the boat, slipped another thick noose over its tail, and hoisted his day's catch aboard.

"Lord God!" I leaped up, bracing my feet wide so as not to turn over the boat.

"Relax," said Mick. "He's gentle as a pup now."

The alligator snorted and rolled one evil, slitted yellow eye as if he'd like to show us just how many puppies he could eat, with us as a side dish. The old bull was at least twelve feet long. His bulk stretched from bow to stern. From over beyond the cypresses, I heard a hollow booming bellow. The gator grunted and strained at the ropes.

"Say good-bye to your old buddies," said Mick, swinging the boat around.

Sitting back well away from the thing, I began to feel a little sorry for it. "Why this one?"

"He tried to pull a boy under while his family was swimming down the way. Kid needed thirty-five stitches in his arm. It won't ever be right."

"Oh." I thought a minute. "But how do you know he's the right gator? They look pretty much alike."

Mick shook his head. "To you, maybe. See that fresh scar on his head, the mark that drops down between the eyes?"

I nodded.

"Tried to get him before, one night, but he got away. Then he rushed the boat. Getting big and ornery enough to cause trouble. They got more tourists coming up here now that don't know better than to swim in gator ponds." But he looked disgusted and tossed the butt into the water, where it sizzled, then sunk.

I reached out and touched a plate on the alligator's back. I knew what it was like to be locked up. I didn't like this gator, and I didn't feel sorry for him exactly. And yet I didn't want to think of him in a pen somewhere, too far from the others to join the chorus and sing his loud, terrifying songs at night. Then I looked at my fingers. "He's bleeding."

Mick snorted. "A scratch. He don't give a shit. You gonna nurse him?"

Then something else occurred to me. "What'll happen to him after?" Not shoes and handbags and belts, I prayed. Though why it mattered so much I couldn't have said.

"Sell him to that big gator farm in St. Augustine. They had one this size died of old age."

When we reached the bank again there was a big flatbed Ford parked next to the car. It took Mick and the two guys who got out of the cab to haul the gator over the ground and hoist him onto the flatbed. They tied him down like a load of logs and covered him with a tarp.

"He'll like it better if he don't have to look at all the traffic," cracked the tallest man. He handed Mick a wad of bills. They climbed into the truck cab and backed out, tires spinning in the sand, throwing up clods of grass and weeds.

Then Mick drove us on down to St. George Island, and we had dinner at a place called Posey's, a glorified shack on stilts over the Gulf water. We watched the sun set and had beer and cloud-light hushpuppies and fried shrimp and fresh oysters on platters big as hubcaps, but somehow I didn't enjoy it as much as I'd expected.

On my nineteenth birthday, Clayton threw me a party. When he asked who to invite I said Sweeney and Rose and Peggy and a couple local truckers and their wives. And Mick. He looked kind of disgruntled at that, who knows why. I ignored him.

He hung a sign in the window, CLOSED FOR PRIVATE PARTY, and laid on a feast of barbequed ribs and chicken, sweet corn, and baked beans. After everyone had eaten their fill, he made me close my eyes while Sweeney and Peggy carried out a red velvet sheet cake with my named in icing script — my favorite dessert, flaming with nineteen hurricane candles.

There was beer and wine, and I'd had a glass or two. I blew out all the candles on the first try, then Mick gave me a kiss.

"Here, sweetie," I said, setting Rose up at my place, handing her the first slice of cake. She scooped it up with both hands, gleefully cramming fistfuls of crumbling red cake and sweet vanilla icing into her mouth.

Clayton and Peggy took Rose over to her house when the sun set. I looked up the road just in time to see Clayton put his arm around Peggy's waist. They looked so much like a family — father, mother, and child — that I couldn't look away. It felt strange to see them with my daughter, looking more like her parents than perhaps I did. To make myself feel better, I tried to imagine Mick and I and Rose together, the three of us living in a little house on the water. But the picture wouldn't come clear and complete — one of us was always missing. The things he and I did together had nothing to do with family, really, but with having fun and taking risks. Having our own way, and getting as much pleasure as we could. I didn't think that was wrong, exactly. Yet at the same time, it wasn't quite right, either.

The party got wilder. Everyone insisted I dance on a table, and at last I did, feeling foolish but happy. I was just about to climb down into Mick's outstretched arms when some more folks came in to the diner, including Scilla, the midwife who'd helped me birth Rose. She wore her full, rainbow-hued traditional skirt sewn of countless strips of fabric. Her straight black hair was shining, freshly combed and pinned over the little board piece Seminole women used to make their upswept hairdo. And she'd brought six or seven kids of all ages along; I'd never realized Scilla had so many children. She surely should have been invited, and I wondered why this had been overlooked. We had plenty of cake and food left over.

"Ah, shit," said Mick, but he didn't sound upset or surprised. I gave him a look, wondering, then started forward to welcome her. But he grabbed my arm and held me in place.

I didn't like that one bit. But then thought better of making a fuss: He'd had a lot to drink, and I didn't want to spoil everyone's night. Maybe he and Scilla knew each other and didn't get along. But surely he'd forget any differences for an hour or so. We were having fun on the night I'd been waiting for. A good time with folks I cared about and who wished me well. My life was a gift again. Maybe God was making up for the fun and friendship I'd missed as a kid. My teenage years were all but over, and some of them best forgotten. So I felt entitled to enjoy myself, to act up a little, to welcome such surprises as a whole family of Indians on my doorstep for birthday cake.

Earlier we'd pushed back all the tables and shoved handfuls of quarters in the juke box so it blasted out all sorts of things: country western songs, Elvis, Sinatra ballads, Mac the Knife, some brand new stuff, rock and roll from England I still hadn't gotten used to.

"What's the matter?" I shouted in Mick's ear, because the song that'd just started was loud.

He shook his head. "Sorry," he said. "Got to go." He leaned down and kissed me, but on the cheek this time. Then he headed toward the new arrivals.

Confused, I started after him. Someone grabbed my arm.

It was Sweeney. "Give it up, Vera," he said. "Man, don't you get it? That's his wife. His kids."

I looked at them again. Mick had

reached Scilla. I expected tears, shouting. Maybe that she'd slap his face. But Scilla only regarded him calmly, appearing neither angry nor happy to see him, as if they'd played this scene out fifty times before. Oh God, I thought suddenly, shame and anger flooding me. Maybe they had. And everyone had known but me.

"Why didn't you tell me?" I said to Sweeney, jerking my arm away. "Why didn't anybody tell me?"

"Ain't my business." He let go of my arm. "And you, you didn't ask."

Mick picked up one of the smallest kids, a solemn-looking little girl in a skirt that was a tiny replica of her mother's. He lifted her to his shoulders, and the Poteke family left. I heard the rumble of his truck starting up.

He hadn't said good-bye. He hadn't even looked back.

I turned away. For lack of a better target, I swept plates, silverware, and the ravaged remains of the cake off the table. Then dropped into a booth, my sticky hands clenched into fists. But though I wanted to cry, needed to, my eyes stayed dry and hot and staring. My guests began quietly gathering their things to leave. Except for Sweeney. He came over and sat down across from me. Folded his arms and waited.

I slammed my fist on the tabletop. "When he comes back, I won't answer the door. If he comes in here, I'll tell Clayton to throw him out."

"He won't come round your house again," said Sweeney flatly. "At least, not for a long while. And he been Clayton's business partner for ten year. Don' make the boss choose between you."

Then he got up and came back with a broom. Held it out to me. And together, we cleaned up my mess.

The next morning I was subdued and apologetic, putting myself on probation. It was true I'd never asked Mick, or anyone else, why he disappeared for so long at times. I'd never asked about his life away from me. The people around me had understood all too well what was going on. Perhaps the worst was that they had known how it would end. I hadn't been able to see because I hadn't wanted to.

The worst part was, I still wanted him. Even knowing what I did. Was this how my father had felt, coveting his neighbor's wife? Was it the same way my mother had reasoned, had made excuses for her own selfishness, for abandoning her family? I didn't want my daughter to grow up thinking such things were normal, to be expected, even right. I did not want to sink to a level of behavior even the most jaded cocktail waitress could shudder at.

Before I came in the door, I took a deep breath of fresh air, bracing myself against the greasy aroma of frying bacon and the faint sulphur stench of heated egg yolks. Sweeney was framed in the order window, industriously scraping the grill. Clayton sat at his usual spot at the counter. When he heard the door shut behind me, he spun around on his stool and handed me a cup of black coffee.

"Good morning, birthday girl," he said, but kindly.

"Morning." I smiled a little and took a sip of the bitter, steaming liquid. Then set the thick mug on the counter and rushed to the restroom. After that I felt better.

All through breakfast shift I squinted hard against the overhead lights, nursing a hangover with aspirin and cool wet dish towels. The other waitress took over at lunch, and I went in the back to force down a sandwich and black coffee. I picked up two newspapers, the *Tallahassee Democrat* and a two-week-old copy of the

Ocala Banner. I'd never read it when I lived in Ordinary Springs, but now and then I came across a copy here and skimmed it for any doings back home. Generally there were none. The Springs had never really been a newsworthy place. On the back page of the local section was one two-inch article about a big fish kill in Lake Panasoffkee. Even a passing mention of the neon darter, those colorful little fish in the Springs who used to swim up and nibble my fingertips if I held still long enough.

Not exactly my backyard, but pretty close. Suddenly I felt an overwhelming rush of sadness, of longing for home. No way could I go there. And yet — I was nineteen now, too old to send back to juvenile detention. I'd never been charged with anything except being incorrigible, a juvenile offense. So I didn't think I'd be risking trouble with the law anymore. But it was hard to imagine walking in the door of my old home again, to imagine making peace with Dad. Clearing up old ghosts.

I'd hidden away at the You Better Believe It, a roadside fantasy stop, a poor man's vacation escape, for almost three years. Now it was the outside world, my old ordinary life, that'd come to seem fantastic, impossible to negotiate, hard to imagine inhabiting again. How to return and fit in among folks who might stare and point, might still recall that Tom Burney had hustled me out of town one night like a wanted criminal?

I had no good answer. After folding the newspaper and stowing it carefully in a drawer in my room, I went out to feed Pasha, to scratch his head and ponder my choices.

18

I did nothing about it at first, but still the idea remained. That somehow my father might welcome a chain-smoking single mother with child, a daughter who'd defiantly renamed herself after the faithless, runaway wife who'd left him. Owen Gamble had always been a pleasant package on the outside, but inside, at least to me, he'd come to seem hard, rough and twisted as the stunted water oak in the backyard. The one I used to climb with Pearce McMillan in that old, lost life.

But I'd read it in a poem in Mrs. Hawks's English class, years ago: Home is the place where, when you go there, they have to take you in.

In a small town, people gossiped, yes. But they always took care of their own. The talk if Dad rejected us, his own kin, one a helpless baby granddaughter, would ruin him and his store. He'd be shunned. And we would need a place, Rose and I. Not a motel room, but a home with a real yard, where she could have a real, ordinary childhood.

If I stayed here, could I trust myself when and if Mick Poteke did come around? I couldn't answer yes to that. But if we left the You Better Believe It and went to a strange new place, I'd have to work somewhere to support us, in a diner, a laundry, a dime store. Minimum-wage work, or maybe hustling for tips. Other women often had to do this. I wasn't so foolish as to believe myself more special, more deserving than them. But with rent and groceries and all, I'd be too poor to do anything but leave Rose alone in a rented room to cry all day, hungry and frightened, tied with a rope and no Owen Gamble to watch over her.

Perhaps Clayton would miss us, but he had Peggy to keep him company now. And the new waitress trained by me, in just the ways Ruby would want things done. Really, I had no more excuse to not head south and fix up my past, to swallow my pride and go home. Clear our name so my daughter didn't have to grow up under a dark cloud. I could show Rose to my father; living proof I'd done something worthwhile at last.

I didn't want to think about Myra or what she'd say.

Plenty of evenings I sat by the bear's

cage, thinking all this out in detail. Until at last I would have to get up, get some fresh air, and get my blood going. Until I could no longer deny that forward motion was good. That yes, I needed to move, to shake off this slump and pack. Get ready to go home again. Once I admitted it, relief set in.

"Come on, Pasha." I unhooked his chain and he rose, stiff and creaky as one of the geezers on the liar's bench back at Gamble's Hardware. He shuffled along after me, snuffling at the back of my knees. Late at night it was safe to take him for a walk down the highway, with no tourist traffic around to run themselves off the road staring.

We went up about a half mile and back again. Then I locked the old bear in his pen with a good hunk of leftover pot roast, and he happily set to chewing. Back at the diner I leaned against one of the giant painted gator teeth at the front entrance, looking up at the stars and all around me at what I'd soon be leaving behind.

Back in our room Rose slept, arms flung out as if in wonder at some amazing dream. Peggy, worn out from baby-sitting, had dozed off in the rocker next to her crib. When I touched her shoulder gently she woke and stretched, pulling a kink out of her neck. I pushed some folded bills into her hand even though lately she protested about that, claiming she didn't need the money.

"It's not really work," she kept saying. "I enjoy Rosie too much to be paid." And then I would tell her that was nonsense, she had earned every cent and had to take it.

After she left I sat in the rocker for a minute, too, listening to my daughter's even, innocent breathing. A wave of anxiety washed over me again. Was I doing the right thing, leaving?

At last I gave in, took a pack of cigarettes and went to sit outside on my concrete bench overlooking the parking lot. The moon rose higher and I pondered why I'd even want to stay at a place where I'd been deceived by a man it seemed no one could resist or be angry with for long. Not even his betrayed, long-suffering wife.

A shadow fell over me, and I looked up. Clayton had Ruby's crippled old greyhound on a leash. Although in the diner earlier he'd seemed fine, now his eyes were lost in dark, grieving shadows.

"Mind if I join you?"

"Don't mind at all." I scooted over to make room.

"Nice night."

I looked around at the trash on the side of the highway, the tromped-on mud, the cloudy night sky, and smiled. "Yeah, I guess."

"You still happy here, Vera?"

I shrugged and lied without crossing my fingers. "Happy as anywhere."

He cleared his throat and looked off toward the shuttered stands. "You know, Vera, I'd be happy to give you and Rose my name. I'd look after you both like my own. Why, we could even, you know . . ." He trailed off.

My mouth dropped open. I turned to face him, but now he was staring at the ground between his feet. Clayton Sebring was proposing. To me. No one had ever even suggested marriage before. But maybe he thought it was what Ruby would've wanted.

At last I recovered my voice. "I'm fine, Clayton. I don't need a husband anyhow." Then I smiled wryly. "I mean, my own or anybody else's." He laughed at that, and I draped an arm around his thick shoulders.

"Besides," I went on. "You know you don't want me. You ought to be asking Miss Peggy down the road the same thing."

He sagged a little, probably relieved.

"Yeah, well. Maybe." But I saw him smiling. He glanced over, then gave me a funny look. "Penny for 'em."

"I was just thinking about going home. I mean, back where I came from. Looking up family. Old friends."

"Huh." He nodded slowly. "Some writer, I forget who, says you can't do that. You know, go back. But that's bullshit. You can do anything if you want it enough and don't mind working for it."

"Yeah, maybe so." I thought I knew what he meant. People like us were strange fish who'd somehow drifted too far downstream and gotten lost. But we kept trying hard to swim back up against a raging current, because somewhere upstream were the others, the ones who'd managed to stay in place, who hadn't gotten lost at all. And maybe, just maybe, we could join them sometime if we kept swimming and didn't get too far off course.

Suddenly I felt so tired I could have toppled off the step, to just lie there on the concrete.

He frowned, his eyes vague and clouded. Then he sighed heavily, pushed himself up off the bench, and whistled up the dog. Then he patted my shoulder.

"Better get some rest, kid. You know,

349

Ruby loved you. And Rose, too. We never had no kids of our own, but she's probably looking down right now, as proud as hell. I just wish —" He stopped, pulled a white handkerchief from his pocket, and blew his nose. I reached out, but he lifted a hand to ward me off.

I watched him totter off down the sidewalk to his own place, the dog skipping all wobbly at his heels. I hoped Clayton was right. I thought I was ready to work and to fight, to do whatever it took to make a life for us, Rose and me. And to find out what had happened between my parents, where they'd gone wrong. I'd made enough of my own mistakes, so how could I fault them for theirs? Still, I wanted to know the truth.

Whatever happened, I wouldn't give up Rose. I would never disown her, or leave her behind, or tell her she was no daughter of mine. Not if they locked me up for a hundred years. I wanted her to have a nice, normal place to grow up in. A regular house instead of a motel, even one that had been this good to us. I wanted her to know her real grandfather, though Clayton Sebring was a wonderful man. I only wished I'd given her a complete set of parents, too.

Wondering what lay ahead kept me

awake. Then I remembered: My fate was all laid out in my own hand. Ruby had taught me that, along with prepping for a lunch crowd and consolidating my trips.

I lay back on the bed and held my hand up to the light. The *Linea Vitalis* outlining the pad of my thumb was short, a sign of fickleness, changeability. Prone to the influence of others, that was me. The many knots and cross-hatched lines? Obstacles and big events, more to come, when I figured I'd had enough to last a lifetime already. But then knots and cross-hatches can also mean a short life. The *Linea Hepatica* was branched like an oak sapling. That signified wit, a sharp mind, but also mischief and falseness. My face burned at that unfortunate truth. Next, the heavier lines crossing the *Naturalis* warned about my bold and reckless behavior. But why go on? Just pull out the memory file and the cardboard one in the Pine Hills School office, to see what a fool I'd been.

If I'd known about palmistry earlier, could I have predicted Frank Fitzgerald's death? Or that I'd end up here, a runaway kid with a baby, a girl who needed to clean up her act, ditch her charming married boyfriend, and go on home?

Yet despite pain and guilt, I didn't want

to have known everything in advance, to have avoided my fate. Because then there would've been — for me, at least — no green-eyed Frank Fitzgerald, no Clayton and Ruby Sebring, no Letitia or Ardis . . . and yes, even no Mick Poteke, to whom I owed a couple valuable lessons. All of them had given me something useful, more knowledge of myself or the world.

If I hadn't made my own stupid mistakes, if I'd been forewarned, perhaps there would've even been no Pearce with me in that silly jerking car in the Tunnel of Horrors, covering me with kisses under a carnival truck — the first man I'd ever loved, however brief a time it lasted. If I'd been forewarned of the cost, then maybe there'd be no Rose. That was truly unthinkable.

So I'd go home and face the music, even if it was loud and harsh and unpleasant. We'd have that life, that house, maybe someday a real father for Rose. I'd do it myself, on my own. Go see my father again, get things straight between us. I wouldn't let him off lightly, either. Now I was grown, he had no excuse not to tell what'd happened between him and my mother. Even if by now maybe she was dead.

Because when I put the few pieces together, it seemed impossible she'd never even written, or let anyone know where she was, how she was doing. That she'd never asked about me, what kind of person I had grown into. Maybe she had her own unmailed postcard tucked away. She would've done at least that much, I knew, from the gentle way she'd held me as a baby and rocked me to sleep. From the way her tears had fallen on my sleepy head, I knew there had to be more to all that'd happened. Because I was a mother now, too.

My father insisted she left us. So had everyone else I knew. So the possibility that my mother, the real Vera Gamble, was dead, and could have been so for more than a decade, suddenly made a great deal of sense.

19

The morning Clayton drove us to Talla-hassee, the Greyhound station was a shouting, grimacing mob that seemed to have it in for me. At least that's how it felt, being hurried and jostled by grim-faced, sweating strangers and snapped at by bored ticket clerks, after three fairly quiet years in Midway. Rose clung to my neck, too terrified to get down and walk. I hugged Clayton, with Rose sandwiched awkwardly between us.

"Now if you don't like it there, you just turn tail and come right on back," he said.

"I will," I promised.

"Oh, wait one." He fumbled in his coat pocket. "Here. Ruby would want you to have these. And they won't do me no damn good," he said gruffly. He thrust two things into my hands: Madame Le Normand's fortune-telling book, and the crystal ball he'd once mistaken for a paperweight.

He gave me another rough, awkward hug, and then was gone, too sad to stay to see us pull away.

I thrust the gifts into my duffle, hitched Rose higher on my hip, and climbed the steps to the bus. Our bag fit overhead, and I got settled in a lumpy window seat, her on my lap. When I turned back, an elderly lady in a rayon print house dress and blue-rinsed Baptist perm was squeezing into the aisle seat next to us. She eyed my long, untamed hair, the faded work jeans I'd chosen for a long, uncomfortable trip with a child clinging to my neck. We stared at each other for a frozen moment from either side of a stunning valley.

"Hey there," I said quietly and just waited, sure after a good look she'd move on to the next row.

But she smiled, dug deep in her pocketbook, and handed me two peppermints. I almost broke down and cried.

At last the bus lurched backward, turned, and set off. My permed lady laid her head on the paper-covered headrest and went off to sleep like one of those babydolls that close their eyes when you tilt them back. After a few minutes of the bus rocking away, so did Rose. That left me to brood about what I'd find in Ordinary Springs.

For most of my life I'd set my heart on leaving the place I was now hurtling back to on a silver Greyhound. I hadn't written to my father, so he wouldn't have a chance to turn us down ahead of time. Would home look the same? In my mind Ordinary Springs was the place I'd inhabited as a child, timeless and unchanged. But in my absence the town might've passed judgment. Folks could snub me, pretend not to know who I was. Or look square in my face and say they knew damn good and well and didn't approve.

I shifted my tingling arm from under the peppermint lady, whose carefully inked tag on her Samsonite vanity case said *Mrs. Samuel (Dottie) Harris.* She mumbled in her sleep and leaned the other way, till I was afraid she'd fall into the aisle. But Dottie found her center of gravity at last and hung there balanced, chin tucked on her chest. We passed by Chaires and Capitola and Waukeenah. By then I already needed to use the bathroom, but hated to wake her. I hoped we'd be stopping for a break soon.

By the time we'd rounded the Big Bend and left the Panhandle, I'd had time to develop a philosophy, something to sustain me in the land of my ancestors. A simple one, just this: that mostly life seems to go along fine. But time to time, the ride operator feels like a wild carnie at the switch and twists and turns and scares us one minute, then thrills us silly the next. While we're suspended in flight, there's no telling what will pop up around the next corner — a betrayal, a new husband, a lost child, a death in the family. Nothing to do then but get out and plod on a ways, until the next empty car pulls up with our name on it.

Yet what most people seemed to want to turn life's ride into was simply *waiting,* as if real living would always be located somewhere down the track. But to just sit and wait is to miss what's smack in front of us — life, even the boring parts — all we'll ever get of it. Running away, the Pine Hills School, the grabby fruit tramp men, and Sadie and Ruby and Clayton, the good between me and Mick as well as the bad, my sweet baby Rose and iron-handed Matron Camber and my poor crazy friend Ardis. Loss and hurt and pain were as much a part of my particular ride as love and friendship and good deeds. My job was to keep my eyes wide open, right to the end, or risk missing what really matters.

Of course it was a hell of a way to travel, all alone in the dark and scared half to death. But what choice did we have, in the end?

★ ★ ★

At Perry, a sprawling, industrious-looking town filled that afternoon with cheerleaders and majorettes marching in some sort of victory parade, we jogged east. Crossed the Suwannee River at Branford and, to my relief, stopped for a restroom break and to pick up new passengers. Then came Mayo, Fort White, Mikesville, and High Springs. I read road signs for entertainment, recalling how the tongue-twisting Indian place names used to knock Pearce and me out with dopey laughter on the playground — Arredondo, Wacahoota, Micanopy. Now they sounded musical and lovely, bringing tears to blink away, the green-and-white signs viewed through a watery haze that felt like lost time itself.

The red-haired woman in front of me had a baby draped like a shawl. The fat-cheeked, fuzzy-skulled child could be male or female; no telling from the sexless old-person face. It whined and fussed, reared back and danced angrily in its mother's lap, then flung itself down. Glared at me over the burp cloth, recognizing an inept mother when it saw one.

"That baby ugly," said Rose loudly.

I said, "Shh. It's tired, is all."

358

"It look funny," she insisted.

The mother frowned over her shoulder. I smiled and shrugged. "We're all a little tired."

The woman endured the squirming and fretting silently. When she stood once to straighten her clothes, I saw that her belly filled a gingham maternity smock. She cooed sweet nonsense at the ugly, miserable child, even while it grunted and strained and turned strawberry red, made gaseous noises, and filled its diaper with a mess so foul the stench woke Mrs. Harris. This mother looked comfortable in her smock and stretch pants and baby neckwrap, as if she'd been born to ride this bus forever, enduring on, adding more and more children to her ample lap. I wondered where I might tap the secret well her tranquility sprang from.

At last we pulled into the station in Ocala to let off an old couple with a huge cardboard box. I was starving, and Rose was squirming in her seat, tired of her Raggedy Ann cloth book and Baby Tears doll. So we went to the snack bar and bought flimsy paper cups of flat cola and cellophane packs of Nabs. But as we turned to go back to the bus, I was seized by a sudden floating fear, a giant fist squeezing my chest so I couldn't breathe. I wanted to run away and not get back on that Greyhound. My body screamed at me to flee, or I would die.

I was panting as if I'd run a mile, yet standing still, halfway to the door, a soggy cup in one hand, holding Rose's arm in the other. People streamed around us to get to the ticket counter or out the door. I looked up blindly, and there was a map on the bus station wall. I leaned closer and saw we were inches from Ordinary Springs, which was only one tiny black dot in among many other dotted possibilities. That put things in perspective.

I would not run from Myra or my father, my mother's fate or my own. If I was ever going to be a sensible person, a good mother to Rose, I had to face the music, the questions, even the smirks of people I loathed. I'd screwed up, and no doubt hated for anyone to know how thoroughly. Well, too bad. Maybe I'd be pointed at on a sidewalk, or in front of the Confederate memorial downtown, or perhaps on the cramped little spiral stairwell at the Leader Department store. I could be shunned before the dairy case at the Corner Market. Well then, bring it on, I thought. Do your worst, cut me dead. I had a beautiful little daughter, a few gypsy scarves, a crystal ball and a pack of cards. I could set up shop anywhere if I had to.

I picked up Rose and ran for the bus like a refugee.

But as I slammed through the glass doors, a sheriff's car pulled up in the back lot and I froze. I'd never see one again without remembering being dragged away in the middle of the night, barefoot and terrified. Or how I'd struggled and screamed myself hoarse while a deputy held me so tight for Matron Camber's convenience that my arms showed his fingerprints for weeks. I could review these scenes as if from a great height and feel shame and despair for my foolish behavior, my bad choices. But now I also knew for certain I'd been in the clutches of adults who hadn't done much better.

"You okay, ma'am?" The softly slurred voice was close to my ear, deep with concern. I turned and saw myself twice-mirrored in a cop's sunglasses. He touched my arm lightly, as if ready to catch me in mid-faint.

My mouth opened but no sound came out. Then, "Fine," I said, laughing a little to disguise the way my knees were shaking. Nodding and turning for the open door of the bus as he tipped his hat. "We're fine, thanks," I called over my shoulder, heaving myself and Rose back aboard. "Just the heat."

All right, I thought as I settled back into my seat, handed Rose her drink and crackers, and smiled over at Mrs. Harris. All right. I can do this.

Ordinary Springs didn't appear to have changed much in four years. Certainly not as much as I had. I walked down the bus steps, holding Rose's arm and waiting for her to climb down on her own, as she'd insisted. Ignoring the impatient grunts and sighs of the driver behind her. We made it to the sidewalk, where I stretched to unkink my back. Then I shouldered our bag, and looked around.

The main difference at first was that I didn't know everyone in sight. Even here, the older women had adopted shorter skirts and teased, Dolly Parton dos, while the younger ones had long, ironed-looking hair. Here and there were even a few flabby, sunburned tourists, drawn here for who knows what reason, or perhaps just lost. The leathery, creased-necked, crewcut farmers in shirt sleeves gave mildly disgusted glances to the occasional mop-haired teenage boy. Older ladies in polyester and Red Cross shoes smiled misty-eyed at Rose. A truck driver spat a brown stream out the window while he waited for us to cross.

I stopped at the Sinclair station to use the restroom and comb my tangled hair. Tried to wash Rose's sticky face, but she kept pushing my hand away. Her grandfather would have to take her in her natural state. My blouse was grimy with road dust and sweat, but it was too hot to rummage for anything else. I washed my face with strong green liquid soap from a wall dispenser, lifted my shirt and splashed water on my armpits, then squinted at the effect in the cracked mirror. The bare bulb hanging from the ceiling, twenty-five watts at most, cast a shadow over my face. Surely I'd looked worse in my life, but I couldn't summon the memory.

We went slow as an almost-three-year-old walks. The old bakery was now painted orange, the door purple, and the sign above called it Groove Record Shop. I stared a moment, remembering Mrs. Tucker's thick arms lifting trays of cakes and pies the two kerchiefed black ladies had mixed, beaten, and baked all from scratch. My sixteenth birthday cake had come from there, but I'd never gotten to eat it.

I carried Rose a couple blocks, shifting her between hips, but finally had to sit down on the curb for a minute. Heat rose off me in waves. My chest hurt, tight and sore from coughing with some cold virus I'd barely shaken before the trip. Why hadn't I thought to bring a stroller?

Gamble's Hardware wore the same old green wood and brick storefront, same old double screen doors and oversized black rubber doormat. It might've been the same window display I'd fixed up last. Hardware is pretty timeless. But when I tried the front doors, they were locked. I rattled the knobs, pressed my face to the glass. Closed at three o'clock on a Thursday. I cupped my hands to the front window again but it was dirty, and too dark inside. Why would the store be closed? Who helped out there now; surely not Pearce?

Old friend, I thought, where are you, what are you doing? Long gone, shaking the dust from this town off years ago, following his dream. Maybe sometimes recalling our last night at the carnival, the heat and stickiness and sudden pleasure of two bodies wedged into a small space. Then me, a shadow disappearing down the midway. No doubt he heard lots more about me, later. Probably he wouldn't even want to see me again, much less take credit for some baby I said was his.

I shouldered my bag and walked on, past the drugstore. Past the Cut 'n Curl, the market, and the post office. A few people passed, some glanced at me. But no one smiled and stopped, or said, "Hey, Dory." I was glad, not feeling like giving anybody a quick run-down of the past few years just yet.

After I got my breath back, we crossed Water Street and headed down Springhill Road, out of town. At first things looked unchanged. The old trees still arched a cool green canopy over the road. The neighborhood still smelled welcoming, like baking and clean laundry and cut grass and the scent of some sweet flower — confederate jasmine or a gardenia bush from the McMillans' garden, all mixed together. But I saw here and there, where before it had been only woods, now small concrete block houses stood, the trees shaved back to postage-stamp lawns and flower beds.

After a half-mile of carrying Rose, shifting my duffle from hand to hand, I passed 25 Springhill Road, Pearce's old house. The clapboards were faded, the paint powdery but not quite peeling, the front porch still furnished with the same rusted metal glider and bouncy, round-backed chairs we used to sit on eating boiled peanuts, hatching plans, bedeviling the cat. Pearce was probably married to some Ordinary Springs girl, maybe that blonde cheerleader, what's-her-name. I could barely recall, though once it had seemed real important. Sure, they'd have a pack of kids already and budding beer bellies. It helped to think so, anyhow.

The end of the McMillans' woods meant the beginning of our yard. On impulse, I turned onto the clay path that followed the property line down to the Springs. Set Rose and my duffle on the grass, and walked to the edge. The mud along the bank was churned up; someone had been doing wheelies.

I coaxed Rose over to the water. "Come look at the fishies." If only the old manatee would pop up, it would seem like someone familiar to welcome me back. And where were the boat-leafed water lilies that had drifted on the surface before, unfolding huge white blossoms to the sun? The water smelled rank up close and in the afternoon light mimicked the pale, diluted yellow of an unflushed toilet bowl. Maybe this strange hue was from the new Florida-Atlantic Paper Mill complex upstream; I'd seen its white smokestacks, smelled the eye-watering sulfur even through the closed bus window. In fact, here there were no fish at all, and Rose looked up at me, disappointed. The old scar-back manatee I used to feed heads of wilted lettuce could be long dead, or likely moved on to better pickings.

I leaned out and looked downstream, distracting Rose with a cattail plucked from the mud so she wouldn't try to wade in the water. There, around the bend, sat the pilings of our dock, listing a little, silver rot in the planks. The worn narrow track through the woods that connected our acres to the McMillans' was so overgrown I'd have needed a machete to hack my way home. So I collected my bag and trudged back to the road. We toddled on, slowly.

I stopped at the edge of our lawn to take in the house. Its white clapboards were mildewed black at the corners and under the sagging roof gutters. The windows were eyes closed against us, the curtains drawn tight. A stack of rain-swollen cardboard boxes and newspapers lay tumbled over the brick porch. The whole place looked unkempt, unloved, the unpopular kid in a corner at recess.

The driveway demanded attention as we worked our way to the house. It was potholed so bad I had to watch Rose's step and mine, stiffen my ankles to keep from twisting one or skidding on the loose gravel that rolled and crunched under our heels. Dad's old Ford truck wasn't in the drive, or in the open garage beyond the house. He probably had a new car by now.

But if he wasn't home, or at the store in the middle of the day, where was he?

The yard was overgrown with centipede grass and tangled creepers. No one had trimmed the rangy azaleas in a long time. I told myself it'd be smart to go slowly, calmly, not rush things. To knock politely, have explanations ready. I was coming back like a dead person after more than three years away, three years of silence.

But as I climbed the front steps, euphoria crept over me. With each riser my spirits rose a little, too. I knocked on the door, doing good by then just to keep from shouting, "I'm back! Hallelujah, here at last!"

"Mama." Rose tugged at my hand. "Who lives here?"

Perhaps I shouldn't have said it so soon, but the words just tumbled out. "We do, sweetie. This is our new home."

I lifted a hand and knocked again.

After a half-minute or so I heard the creak of springs, shuffling footsteps. The side window curtain twitched. I turned my head and aimed a smile that way. Then, nothing. I waited, legs jittery, knees weakening, and knocked again. Finally, the door opened about four or five inches, slowly. Then widened to halfway.

The man who stood in the gap was stoop-shouldered. His dark hair, streaked with gray, needed cutting. He was too thin, his chest hollow beneath a billowing flannel shirt. Stains on the front of his khaki trousers could have been food, or worse.

"Yeah," he said dully, as if he'd only expected to see me standing there and hadn't particularly been looking forward to it. Before I could open my mouth, a skinny gray tomcat leapt from the bushes, streaked across the porch, and wove itself round and round his ankles. It had the biggest set of balls I'd ever seen on a cat, which explained the musky reek that hung over the porch.

"It's me." I set my bag on the bricks. Rose hid, pressed her face into my pants leg. "It's me, Dory," I said louder. What came next? A hug or kiss seemed too sudden and personal. And this man wasn't . . . he didn't look like my memories. The face he turned to me, the gray eyes that wouldn't meet mine belonged to a much older person than my father. The eyes of a man who'd soaked up so many disappointments that living on was simply an inconvenience to be endured.

A stone settled in my belly. "Hey there. I — I know you weren't expecting me. We just got off the bus and —"

"If you come about the truck, don't have it no more." He stretched out a hand, waved it vaguely back toward the driveway, the garage. "As you can see."

I took a deep breath. Well, he wasn't the only one who'd changed. Obviously I looked different, too.

"No, no, it's not that. I guess you don't recognize me, Dad."

He took a step back behind the torn screen, frowning. "Who you say you're with?"

I put out a hand slow and careful, the way you would to calm an edgy stray dog. "I'm not with anyone. It's just me, Dory, come home. I'd like to stay a while, if that's okay."

He blinked at me, his eyes going

swimmy. "Dory? But, she's just a girl. And you, you're not . . . Dory, is that you?" He sounded weak and querulous. At last I took one step forward and he did, too. We hugged stiff and awkward, my nose bumping his chin, then pulled back at the same time.

He pushed the screen wider, stepped back, and noticed Rose for the first time. "Who's this? You all better come on in. I didn't expect you, you see. I didn't —" He waved at the living room beyond. His lower lip trembled, and he began to sob, loud harsh gasps that racked his whole body.

In two quick steps I had my arms around him. "Oh, here. Don't cry, Dad." I tried to see everything at the moment, all that I felt. To *live it* as I'd promised myself. But this meeting was so odd, it neither hurt nor soothed me. I didn't know exactly what I felt, except it wasn't what I'd expected — either real joy or bitter anger. "Let's just go inside."

The living room was nearly empty, not the comfortable, roomy place I recalled, but a square box with a low ceiling that smelled of dirty laundry and stale beer and something sour, spoiled. What I took at first for hideous flocked velvet wallpaper

— trust Myra to choose the weirdest possible pattern — was actually powdery stripes of mildew. I noticed some of her old furniture; the blond, knife-edged Danish modern coffee table, its sole ornaments now a huge black dog-eared Bible and a ceramic trapezoidal ashtray heaped with butts. Behind it, nicked and pocked with cigarette burns, the nubby beige couch upholstery's metallic threads had sun-blanched to a tweedy noncolor.

My father slumped into a chair and fumbled a hankie out. He blew his nose, rubbed it hard, then jammed the wadded cloth back in his pocket.

I set Rose on the couch and knelt in front of him. "There. Better now?" Then I clamped my mouth shut in horror. My voice had gone high, sing-songy, like he was Rose's age.

One side of his mouth lifted in a smile, then the other followed, slowly, like those muscles hadn't been used in a while. He reached out and touched my face, using one finger to trace my cheekbone, then higher. He hesitated, trembling at my temple. He reached out as if to touch my hair but settled for stroking the air. "My poor little girl."

"I'm not little, Dad. I have a daughter

now, see? This is Rose, your grandchild." I grasped his hand, took it away from my face, and held it between mine. I waited to feel like this was home, and I'd been saved. To feel something like love. Save the awkward details, like Rose's paternity, for later.

"And here I got no fatted calf to celebrate. Hold on." He sprang up, headed for the kitchen, nearly knocking me over. I heard him rummaging in there, swearing softly.

A new thing, a swinging double door like a saloon prop from an old Western, screened the kitchen from the dining room. I glanced back at Rose, who was inspecting plastic knickknacks on a bookcase. That seemed safe enough, and she'd never been one to put things in her mouth. I pushed the double door tentatively, because it felt like a wall, a heavy fortress gate. When it creaked open, the humped bulk of the old gas stove was the first thing I saw, its burners covered in cans and dirty pots, enamel crusted with dried, blackened food. Then the old deep sink, chock full of dishes. And in place of the black-and-white dinette we'd eaten our meals at for so long stood a beat-up card table crowded with cereal boxes, economy-size jars of cheap peanut butter and strawberry jam, knives standing sentinel inside. Here and there, like locust husks, crumpled chip bags. And propped against one jar, another dog-eared Bible.

The cat was on the table, too, purring loudly while my father banged things at the sink, licking a stick of bright yellow butter in a cracked saucer. The kitchen stank of old grease and spoiled food, of fermented garbage ready enough for the curb to walk itself out.

My father turned from the sink. "Here you go," he said, with that same faltering smile. "Lemonade. You always liked that." He held out a smudged glass of swirling, mote-speckled liquid.

"Thanks." I sniffed, then took a sip. It tasted like powdered lemon cleanser half-dissolved in water, and I swallowed it so fast I nearly choked. Dad would never have touched this chemical mess before. And how could they let the house get so bad?

"Where's Myra?" I finally asked.

He looked blank for a minute, then repeated, "Myra?" As if I'd asked him to produce Annie Oakley or Queen Elizabeth.

I laughed a little. "You know, your . . . wife, she must be by now."

He frowned and turned back to the sink. "She left. Left and didn't hardly say good-

374

bye. I don't know —" he broke off and sat abruptly in one of the kitchen chairs, as if admitting this treachery had cost all his remaining strength.

Myra, gone? It didn't seem possible. She'd been so crafty, so strong, like a force of nature. So sure of what she wanted. I patted his shoulder awkwardly. "I'm sorry, Dad." It wasn't entirely a lie. I knew a little more about wanting and betrayal now, myself. At least I felt no triumph. Only a cowardly relief that I wouldn't have to face her cool, mocking gaze.

"She left her damn dog behind. It wouldn't have nothing to do with me. Took sick one night, up and died." He dragged a hand over his face, to scrub away the thought. "But 'a righteous man regardeth the life of his beast,' " he whispered.

A dog? Myra? I never knew she cared much for animals.

"Recall when you were little, the time your puppy Rascal got hit by a car? I had to shoot the poor thing. You never forgave me. I used to wonder sometimes if that was why you ran off. No, no," he said, when I opened my mouth to object, waving me off. "I know, it happened different than that. When I tried to bury her damn dog, thing must've weighed seventy pound.

Could hardly lift the poor bastard."

He sighed and kicked at a grease-spotted paper bag lying near the chair. "Should've buried her things with the dog. I hate seeing the clothes, the jewelry she left. All her doodads. But I can't somehow, just can't."

"I could take them down to the thrift shop, if you like."

He glared. "So I can see her coming and going on some town woman? No, I'll toss 'em in the trash, not go digging more holes out back like a crazy man."

I stared at him. Was that a joke, or a reminder of how so long ago I'd seen him in a frenzy, trying literally to bury the past?

"Don't need her, anyhow. A woman just makes you crazy." He glanced at the Bible on the table in front of him, fingered the cover as if for reassurance.

"Crazy," he murmured again. "Been acting it lately. A man loses his kid, women all up and leave, pret' near loses his store — well, you had time to get a good look around." His face darkened and mottled. " 'How oft shall my brother sin against me, and I forgive him?' "

I backed up a step. Some nerve he had, to lecture me about forgiveness. "Well, I'm your family. I got sent off once, you know, but I'm back. We'll get the place cleaned up, and the store, too. Why, together we can —"

He rounded on me again. "Don't know what the hell a man's got to do to hold on to anything. Maybe I should dig up the stinking dog carcass, so we can pretend we're one big happy family."

He stopped inches from my face, his breath foul with stale cigarettes and cheap rotgut and dirty teeth. His cheeks were mapped with a million fine red veins. So were the whites of his pale blue eyes. Just as I was about to break and run, a tear oozed. He turned away, breathing hard and furious.

"Go on, get out," he rasped, his back to me. "Go back where you come from."

The outside of my father looked different, but inside he was much the same, now even more so the Owen Gamble who'd washed his hands of me. Why'd I even come back, his no-good daughter? We didn't need him, Rose and I. We'd manage. I hit the swinging doors with hands outstretched, stumbled over a footstool in the living room, and cursed. Rosie was cross-legged on the floor, engrossed in an old *Life* magazine, tearing a page out slowly.

"Mommy will be right back," I gasped,

wrenching at the front doorknob. The man was a bastard. Why had I ever longed for him to love, to notice, to care anything about me?

I stopped at the edge of the drive and caught my breath. Because where was I going? My daughter and my suitcase were still inside. But he had no right to lecture me, or anybody. Damned hypocrite. I stomped furiously around the yard, kicking up divots of dead grass. It all looked more neglected than you'd think possible in just four years, but in Florida the weeds don't wait. The Impatiens he'd planted a few years ago to impress that damned woman were all but gone. I'd always hated those stupid prissy pink flowers. So why did their choked, vine-strangled beds, the few hopeless buds they'd forced through, bring tears to my eyes?

Well, I knew something about loss and screwing up, too. If he thought he could just tell me where to go, I'd show him. I'd put up my mistakes against his any old time. And he had some explaining to do.

"Okay, you old bastard," I whispered. "We'll go. But not yet." I walked back slowly to the house, hands stuffed in my pockets, as if I'd meant to do just that all along. I looked across our big expanse of weedy side yard and noticed that next door, Violet Barrows's old cottage, the one Myra had transformed, looked neat, newly painted. The jungle was cut back and mowed. Someone else lived there now.

I stood in the open doorway again to see Rose still methodically tearing and crumpling pages, as if it was a job she'd been hired to do. I turned away and sat down on the steps a minute to cool off. To think.

We'd stay for a while, long enough to figure things out. How best to earn a decent living. I'd look up Pearce; I at least ought to tell him about Rose. And if he wasn't interested in her, in us, fine. If he was married, he might not be so thrilled to have us turn up now. So then again, maybe I'd just keep my mouth shut. We didn't need pity or charity, or to screw up anybody's life.

In any case, Dad could go to the devil. Nobody was sending me away again. Not before I was damn good and ready to go.

I looked around, speculating. First we'd air the place out, get a good spring clean going. I'd find out what the deal was about the store — find out by myself, if not from Dad. Had he lost it? Was it really closed? Even if he had, maybe things were not so bad. They'd certainly seemed worse before, to me. All this and more I could handle, if I had to. I flexed my fingers, which were stiff from being clenched, and slid my hands back in my pockets. Then took them out again. One thing I knew for sure just then: I hadn't smoked the whole bus trip. Boy, did I need a cigarette.

I turned around and went back inside, closed the door against mosquitoes. To find my daughter and my father sitting on the ratty old couch, reading a magazine together, like old friends.

20

The store wasn't that bad, if you liked dust, cobwebs, and the crisp shells of dead palmetto bugs. Dad hadn't been in for a while, that was clear from the coffee cup on the counter that held a thick scum of blue mold. There was still plenty of hardware left to sell, and I decided I was the woman to do it. Held up against slinging corn dogs in a fryer or feeding raw chickens to a twelve-foot alligator or evading the roving paws of drunk truck drivers, it'd be a breeze.

After a week, we were ready. Dad had helped clean up the place, after I'd nagged him into a shower, and clean clothes. We had to walk down to the store, because the truck was definitely gone. No matter, we'd save up and get a used one. It wasn't like we had anywhere fancy to go.

I actually enjoyed setting things to rights again, despite the cracks in my hands I got from so much hard scrubbing and the dust that caked my nostrils so I nearly sneezed my brains to Kingdom Come. While Dad entertained Rose with scraps of wood, taught her all the different ways to tie a knot in clothesline, and let her sift gleefully through bags of whole corn and onion sets, I made a sign with black marker on an old piece of plasterboard, then propped it in the window: OPEN UNDER NEW MANAGEMENT. Which was no lie. Anyhow, it might get attention.

I'd also gone down to the library, intending to look up ways of finding lost people. I skimmed through back issues of the *Ocala Banner* from the year my mother left but saw nothing useful there. I'd gone so far as to approach the librarian's desk to ask where else I might look. But when I'd realized Miss Hennessy was still behind the desk — the same librarian who'd called my father when I was fourteen and tried to check out *God's Little Acre* — I turned away and left.

What felt strangest was that no one seemed to much notice I was back. While the town had figured large in my mind, in my dreams, apparently I hadn't made as much of an impression, disappearing suddenly. Not that I wanted to be pointed out — the looney, the girl who'd killed her neighbor and got sent away. When I went out I hardly recognized anyone, and they didn't seem to know me. Passing Pearce's house I hurried my steps, not ready yet to spar with Miss Harriet and her acerbic tongue. I'd spotted a few old classmates in town who waved vaguely and returned a hello fast enough, but the casual way you did to a near-stranger passed on the street.

Then I ran into Mrs. Hawks, my old English teacher, in the Corner Market. I'd been wandering down the cereal aisle, trying to find something to feed Rose that fell in between sugar frosted puffs of air and rough squares of pressed hay. When an older woman ahead of me stopped abruptly to read the back of a box, I bumped her with my cart.

After I apologized she regarded me sharply over half-moon glasses. "Oh my. Dory? Dory Gamble?"

When I realized who it was I let go of my cart and rushed into her hug. "Mrs. Hawks, I think you're the first person who's actually recognized me. Guess nobody noticed I'd been, you know, gone."

She shook her head, smiling. "Oh, Dory. They noticed. But you know how it is. We all have our own little dramas we star in, which leaves only a certain amount of time to point and whisper and cast stones. Not to mention a short attention span, unless the scenes feature us."

Mrs. Hawks always had a way of putting things into perspective. She brought me up to date. A good many old people had left us. A good many new ones had moved in to work at the paper mill, mostly young families, and they'd built the identical shoe-box ranch houses that'd popped up on our road. There was even a tubing and canoe rental business down at the mouth of the Springs, for tourists. The thought of getting in that yellowed, tainted water made me shudder, but I supposed vacationing northerners who'd never laid eyes on it before wouldn't know it was supposed to be clear as gin. Or that the colorful little neon darters and the ponderous gray manatees had gone missing.

"You know, Dory, you left me without a mother for *Our Town*," she scolded mildly.

I looked down, sheepish. "Guess somebody else played my part, then?"

She smiled. "The only other actress who could do it justice. I was nearly as good in the role as you would've been, if I do say so myself."

It was nice someone had felt my absence. She hugged me again and made me promise to let her know if I'd be taking off on short notice again. Only after we'd wheeled our carts down opposite aisles did

I realize she hadn't asked why I'd left in the first place. No doubt she knew.

I saw folks occasionally who reminded me of the parents of kids I'd gone to elementary school with. Gradually I realized they actually *were* the kids I'd gone to school with and had started jobs and families of their own. This sent me to the mirror in the bathroom in back of the store, wondering if I was so much changed, too.

The first morning open I unlocked the front doors and unlocked the cash drawer, while Dad and Rose retreated to the back. Then I sat behind the counter with a paperback novel and a can of Fresca. If nothing happened in a week, I could amuse myself by setting up a card table on the sidewalk, offering free fortunes with every screwdriver or socket wrench or paintbrush purchase.

At first they didn't come. I wondered if some taint, a telegraphed knowledge of my family skeletons had arrived before my bus after all. If not the lingering grudge against my father, the whispers and gossip about his affair with Myra and Frank Fitzgerald's death, then perhaps some tiny, buried article in the *Banner*.

The third day a middle-aged man wandered in looking for a pipe wrench. I fixed him up and encouraged him to open an account. "No interest," I said. "Better than one of those plastic things, you know — a credit card."

The next afternoon a young mother came in who was having trouble with roaches and didn't feel the need to whisper about it. I told her nothing beat borax crystals, even these days, and they were safer for someone with small children. She stared at me round-eyed, as if I were psychic. I didn't mention the chocolate-tinted fingerprints all over her skirt.

By the next week the bell was jangling several times a day, and I'd encountered classmates and old neighbors who said they'd heard I was back in town. They peered at me with undisguised interest, obviously remembering I'd left real sudden, way back. Under some sort of cloud, their narrowed, speculating gazes told me. So anyhow, they'd ask too casually. What had I been doing with myself?

Oh, you know, a little of this and that, I'd counter. School. Work. A child to keep me busy.

Married?

I always waffled there. It wouldn't be smart to make Rose a fatherless love child in this small town. I'd cross my fingers under the counter and smile sadly. "But it didn't work out." I'd take on a longing far-away look, easy to do if I thought about Micco Poteke. That was usually sufficient.

On a hot Tuesday afternoon when we'd been reopened almost a month, a thin, well-dressed woman of about fifty walked in. She came straight to the counter and stood in front of me. "Dory," she said.

I smiled politely. "Yes, ma'am?"

"You don't recognize me, honey?"

I looked at her face. The neat bobbed hairdo. The narrow-bridged nose, the thin-lipped mouth bracketed with parallel lines. Then I had it, and felt foolish.

"Miss Harriet," I said, truly glad to see her. She'd aged a lot, her much shorter hair was all gray. I'd meant to come over, I told her. Maybe she had, too.

"What've you been up to, dear?" It didn't sound like an accusation, more like mild hurt, surprising me. "You left us so sudden." She blinked. "Mercy, we've got some catching up to do!"

"Well, after I went off, there was . . . school," I hedged. Lying outright to Miss Harriet was a losing proposition. She'd always seen right through me. "And then I worked in food service for a while. You know, restaurants and what-not. And then there was my, uh, Mick, but that didn't work out. He left us." Both sets of fingers crossed beneath the counter, I felt I'd committed a significant sin, a commandment broken. Yet I seemed to be getting away with it for a change.

"Oh, my. I'm so sorry to hear that, dear. You know, my Jack passed on, two years ago. And I suppose you heard about poor old Tom Burney?"

I felt a chill, but shook my head.

"Big Tom's heart gave out — let's see, it's been over a year ago. Massive coronary, gone just like that. A shame." Dad hadn't told me, and I'd been afraid to ask about Tom Burney.

I felt a surge of relief, followed by guilt. I hadn't been raised to gloat over people dying just because I didn't happen to like them. And Burney had had a family, sons and a wife who no doubt grieved. But I'd dreaded running into my old nemesis, even under better circumstances. I glanced away, hoping Miss Harriet hadn't seen all this in my eyes.

"Yes, a shame," I echoed lamely.

She laid a hand on top of mine, where it rested on the counter. "I know it's sad. And you've been off . . . waitressing, you say? Oh, Dory, you always had such presence on the school stage. I thought sure you'd end up — oh, I don't know — maybe on television!" She leaned closer, her tone more concerned. "Tell me, how's Owen doing?"

"He's in the back," I said. "Busy with Rose. Oh," I said, suddenly breathless with belated recognition. Because here in front of me stood Rose's paternal grandmother, it had only then struck me. I looked all around the store, feeling hot circles rise on my cheeks, as if I'd just been branded.

"You all right, sugar?" she said. "You look hot. Are you sick?"

"No," I said, when I got my voice back. No graceful way to blurt out the news about Rose right then and there. Miss Harriet smiled sadly, as if she knew more to our story than the usual person in town. I stiffened, hoping she wasn't pitying us. I didn't want that.

"Anyhow, Pearce will be so surprised to see you again," she said. "He's out on the Gulf right now. On the trawler, working with his cousins."

"I'd like to see him, too," I said, slipping my hands out of sight behind the counter so she wouldn't see how bad they were shaking.

"And his wife's a delight. You'll have to meet her." She looked me right in the eye, as if she were trying to tell me something telepathically.

Oh. "Well, good. That's real good." I felt a stab. Well, what'd I expected? One night we'd got carried away, that was all.

"I'm glad he's got himself a family," I finally managed.

"Oh, no children yet." She shrugged. "A rough patch lately, but they were made for each other. You'll see."

A copper-penny taste in my mouth. When I realized I was chewing the inside of my lip pulpy, I made myself stop. "So. You need anything today, Miss Harriet?"

"No, no. I'm canvassing for the annual school bazaar. It's in just two weeks. I'm head of the board, you know, and we always go out for donations this time of year from the merchants."

"Oh, right." Actually I hadn't known at all. Dad would've taken care of such things.

"Your father usually donates a hundred," she said helpfully. "And then you all get a quarter-page ad in the paper." She glanced around the store. "Of course, if it's too big a commitment right now . . ."

A hundred dollars. We didn't have half

that in the till. And less at home, left from my You Better Believe It savings minus our bus tickets and groceries. Then I had an idea. "You know, since I've been away so long, I'd really like to get involved in the community again." I braced my hands on the counter, making myself hold her gaze. "I'd like to sponsor a — a booth, or something."

"Why, what a good idea. What kind, Dory?"

I thought fast. Kissing booth was surely out of the question. Corn dogs and weiners? Ugh, never again. I wasn't much for baking, and I didn't want to spend the next two weeks sweating in a hundred-degree kitchen. I had more than enough left to do at the store.

"Well," I said at last, as if it was a daring idea that'd just occurred out of the blue. "Something fun, something different. How about fortune-telling? The proceeds could all go to the school fund."

"Why, Dory. What a novel idea!" She really did look pleased. "That wild imagination of yours, I should've known." She shook a teasing finger.

As soon as was polite, I walked her to the front door, then slumped against the nearest shelf and pounded my forehead.

Was I insane? Fortune-telling! Was this Ruby coming to my rescue? Not what I'd have asked for, but it was already done.

At least I had a few things — the fortune-telling instructions, the crystal ball, the cheap, bright colored rayon scarves from the Midway five and dime. I could whip up an outfit from odds and ends, maybe a trip to the Baptist thrift shop. I worked well under pressure. Damn good thing, too.

To pass the time after Rose was in bed and Dad gone to his room for the night, I began to practice fortune-telling, sitting at the kitchen table. Miss Harriet had said the school bazaar was only two weeks off, and I was a rank amateur. I studied Mademoiselle Le Normand's instructions again, then tried a reading for myself with a dog-eared deck I'd found in the kitchen junk drawer. They were only missing the ace of clubs.

Let's see, I thought, closing my eyes. I took a deep breath, glanced at the instructions one last time: *Use the two of diamonds to read a lady's fortune.*

I found the two and dealt eight cards around it. The inner ones to shape destiny, the outer square to represent the forces surrounding the subject. The idea was to weave a story around the person as you turned up cards. Of course you had to recall what each one stood for. This Mademoiselle Le Normand must've been good at it — she'd been sharp enough to predict Napoleon's downfall.

I turned all the cards, looked them over for my client — me. The four of diamonds was the Dog, which meant true friends. I smiled; perhaps Ruby *was* nearby. True friends, except . . . next to it was the five of diamonds, the anchor, symbol of the fidelity of the one you love. But the cards surrounding it could be significant, too. Which were unlucky? I shook my head and moved on to the next in the row. The six of diamonds: The Lion. My hand hovered, shaking. A lion made me think of a zoo or a circus, but the cards were never so obvious. Maybe a sudden shock, bad news. But I was having trouble making these things go together.

Though I'd shuffled the blasted cards thoroughly, all that kept turning up were numbered diamonds. And in order. Well, what else did I recognize? Ah, at last. Clubs. The two meant a railroad . . . a long journey, anyhow. I snorted. Yeah, been there all right. Maybe if I could find another I knew. There, the ace of spades, the Rapiers. Assault from somewhere threatened, and soon. No, wait. Had that already happened? Ah, nuts. I scooped all the cards up suddenly in a pile.

"Foolishness," I muttered. "Maybe I won't use cards."

I got up, went into the living room, and stretched out on the couch, a pillow under my head. There on the coffee table was Ruby's crystal ball. Had I left it out? I couldn't recall and eyed it like a ticking bomb. But I finally gave in, lay back, and balanced it on one hand before my eyes.

"We never got a chance to use this, Ruby," I whispered.

It made me angry, that perfect glass sphere. It was still here, would *always* be here, round and perfect and smug, never changing. While Ruby was turning to dust in an overgrown graveyard in Midway. This hunk of glass, dumb and forever the same, would outlive us all.

Even Rose.

That was too much. I snatched up the crystal and heaved it across the room. It was heavy as a cannonball, but I lobbed it right through the dining room. It hit the floor and rolled under the swinging doors to the kitchen. It clanged on something metal, then I heard it rumble off like a run-away bowling ball.

Ruby's crystal! What was wrong with me, trying to destroy what little I had of hers? I bolted to the kitchen, dropped to my knees, and crawled around looking under the chairs, the table, an old butcher block. A dent in the refrigerator's metal skin seemed to accuse me. I finally spotted the ball in the far corner, stuck beneath a cabinet.

I slid my arm under, groped through dust balls and dead bugs, and pulled it out. Turned the sphere round and round in anxious, fumbling fingers. Damn. A chip that hadn't been there before. In the dim light, this new flaw threw odd shadows into the wavering center. I carried it back into the bedroom, hugging the cold glass to me as gentle as you would a baby bird. I sat on my bed and nested the crystal gently in a pile of quilt. Polished it all over with the hem of my robe, then turned it this way and that, wishing for some guidance, some direction, a small switch to flip, a button to push. I cradled it and stared, unblinking, until first quilt and then crystal blurred away to something else.

A dull pain began, a headache coming on, but I kept squinting. Maybe I did see something there in the watery center. Little whirling specks, two figures. Small as ants, two people dancing. Or were they struggling? Little figures under water. Moving to a music I couldn't hear.

I blinked, and they were gone.

The night before the bazaar I got out my hastily assembled costume to try on one last time. A yellowed antique camisole. A long, full skirt striped with lines of red and blue and green and yellow, its thick brocade darker, more intense than a rainbow. I slipped my arms into a sheer organdy blouse, then settled a rose-embroidered shawl over my shoulders. It only had one bad stain, and the fringe fell nearly to my ankles.

I folded a scarf for my head, then picked up a comb and began to untangle my hair before the full-length mirror. When I at last stepped back to look, it seemed gangly Dory Gamble might not be that unconvincing as Madame Vera. My hair was long and straight, black and shining as any Seminole's. I hadn't cut it once since I'd been gone. My skin was tanned from spending time outside in the yard. When I straightened and lifted my chin and half-closed my eyes, I didn't look quite like the Queen of the Gypsies. But I thought it would do.

21

The Saturday of the bazaar was typical August in Florida. Sweltering, sun-baked, humid: a good day to swim at the beach or sit immobile under a ceiling fan. To be anywhere but on an unshaded school athletic field under the sun. Yet there I was, tacking up scarves and crepe paper, sweat running under my heavy skirt and woven shawl.

The air was scented with hints of charred meat and hot grease and burnt sugar as the vats and grills began to heat up. Long folding tables held white-oak baskets and handmade silver jewelry and antique doodads from closets and attics. My striped fortune-teller's booth — bedspreads draped over old tent poles from Dad's shed — was on the main aisle, easy to spot. It sat between Lady Godiva's Goodies and a raffle booth selling chances on a weekend cruise to the Bahamas. I set up a folding chair and card table, then draped the embroidered shawl over the tabletop. Too bad I couldn't walk old Pasha up and down the aisle on a jeweled leash to impress the crowd.

I took a deep breath and sat down. Laid out my cards, set the crystal in its carved ebony stand, and waited.

By ten o'clock the parking lot was full. People swarmed over the field. Smaller kids ran ahead, screeching and pointing, jumping like fleas on a griddle. The older ones hung back, strolling in cool, ironic groups of three or four. Some gave my booth a look, then smirked and slunk on past. At first everyone passed by, throwing me a glance then quickly looking away. A pack of teenage boys would stop, snicker, and elbow each other. Once, egged on by the others, a pimply fat one crossed his eyes at me. I smiled coldly and flashed the ornate silver letter opener I had tucked into my belt. Their eyes widened; they scooted off with long, water-spider strides.

Overalled farmers with wives and kids in tow gave the tent a wide berth, practically tripping over themselves in their haste to get away. On the other hand, teenage girls gazed longingly, something like lust shining in their eyes. At last a giggly trio in shorts and halter tops all plopped down for a reading, laughing and squealing at each others' futures.

Just like that, I was in business. A line

even formed off and on, and I had to hustle. One girl came back three times. At last, alarmed by her devotion, I said I could only see so much about one person on a given day and she was risking cosmic overload. I held out a hand for her dollars and promised a free reading the next week if she came into the store.

When there was finally a free moment, I realized I was thirsty and hungry and feeling beat. A cold drink, maybe popcorn — even a corndog sounded good. Whiffs of the deep-fryer had stirred memories of the diner's kitchen; of Ruby's endless patience with my first clumsy efforts at food service. I should have packed a sandwich or at least made a CLOSED FOR LUNCH sign.

Then a middle-aged woman passed. She backed up and stopped in front of the sign, hands clamped on a white pocketbook. I smiled, not too eagerly, from within my rainbow fall of satin skirts and silk scarves.

You always watch their faces, Ruby had advised when she'd begun instructing me in fortune-telling for tourists at the You Better Believe It. *Whether they look back, or away. Check jewelry and shoes — cheap, expensive — to know how much to charge. That's all ya need, sweetie. They already know the damn answers.*

When she'd said this, I thought she was joking, or at least exaggerating. But she was right. It was all there on that beaten, hopeful face.

"Please, come in," I said. "If you'd like to talk."

She teetered, Sunday high heels wobbling, sinking into the turf of the football field that just for today had been turned into a cheap crepe-paper fairyland. "Oh, dear. I don't know."

"Have a seat and rest then. No need to decide now. I'm not so busy, as you can see."

"Well. All right." She ducked under the tent flap, spotted my dagger, and stifled a thin shriek.

"Ah, it's nothing," I said, shrugging. "I only use it on past due bills."

She looked doubtful but edged in around the table, gripping the plastic pocketbook as if it held a fortune. Or at least the butter and egg money. I coughed into my hand to hide a smile.

She sat abruptly. "How much?"

"Two dollar." I said, imitating Sadie's vaguely Eastern European professional accent, as I'd been doing all day. "Tell you what, though. For you, I give ten-dollar reading. A slow day. So hot."

She brightened at a bargain, fumbled in

the depths of her pocketbook, and pushed two grimy bills across the table.

"Crystal ball," she said, jerking her chin at it. "*That's* what I want. Not that funny card business. Our church don't hold with card playing."

I shrugged, spread my hands before me: *I understand. Of course.* Then I gazed into the curve of heavy glass, squinting the way I had the night before.

Nothing. I felt panic until I understood what was wrong. I turned the ball to the cracked side and focused on the flaw, the chip I'd made with one moment of pure rage. The woman frowned and fidgeted on her chair, but I ignored her. And after a minute or so of staring, the edges blurred. I hoped my eyes weren't crossing. Tried not to blink.

They came again, swimming slowly to the surface. So far away I first thought: dust specks. Or gnats trapped in the glass like ants in amber. The little figures under water, moving, circling each other. As they came closer, they grew larger. I thought I finally understood who they were. Mick and me, pressed together, a naked sandwich of flesh. I squinted, my nails digging moons into my palms, barely aware of the woman across the table, though I heard her clear her throat, heard as if from a mile away the rustle of her clothes. She smelled of laundry soap and peeled onions and white shoe polish.

The figures in the glass turned slowly, feet barely moving. When I focused on just the woman, my mother's face flashed in my mind, laughing as it had been in the charred old scrap of photo. The real Vera. They were dancing close. Fondling each other like lovers. But was the man my father, or someone else?

I whispered, "Son of a bitch."

"You mean it's true?" cried the woman. I looked up, surprised, having forgotten all about her. She was twisting a thin gold band on her finger, staring as if her whole life depended on me alone. "It's really true, he's cheating on me?"

I closed my eyes, nodded. *Lying, cheating bastard* had been clearly etched in the creases of the woman's forehead, over her burning, crumpled face, the first moment I saw her. She slapped down another bill. I heard the tent flap drop, heard her plod away.

I hadn't been talking to my customer at all. The woman I'd seen was my mother, I was sure of it. But the other man, had it been him she'd left us for and never even looked back?

I was sliding the woman's crumpled bills into my cash bag when a man walked by and glanced in. Broad shoulders, short auburn hair under a ball cap, black Wayfarer shades, face deeply tanned. His hands were blunt-fingered, workman-practical, not the usual mark for this line of work. But when I looked up again he was making a second pass.

The third circuit he came inside, ducking under the bedspread flap. The hat bill shaded his face, but he was smiling crookedly as if to say, *Yeah, I know. But what the hell.* Something about the way he walked, the coppery hairs on his tanned arms, his squarish jaw, looked familiar. But so did half the other people I'd seen on the field. It was my home town, after all.

He glanced away to where a little boy was trying his luck at the Win a Goldfish booth. "I've been watching you this morning," he said, voice low.

As if I were a shoplifter, a dope dealer. Great, so that was it. A small-town cop, some bored Deputy Dawg on my case. This was a charity gig, for God's sake.

"Yeah, so?" I picked up my smoldering Kool from the paper cup ashtray and blew a little smoke his way. Since I came back I'd already quit and started up again.

He waved the smoke away with his left hand. It was missing most of the last two fingers, ring and pinkie. Huh, a serious customer. He gestured at all my trappings. "You look good. Like the real thing."

Oh. Not a cop, then. Just a come-on line. Hard to believe, with all the exposed young flesh jiggling around in halter tops and short shorts, that he was hitting on the only woman here dressed like someone's eccentric Romanian granny. I tugged my scarf lower and shrugged to show I wasn't interested.

"Dory," he said then, sounding exasperated. "You don't recognize me?"

I froze with the cigarette halfway to my mouth. Of course I knew that voice, knew the mouth, wide and smiling, the full lower lip dry and peeling from too much time spent outdoors. Pearce had obviously been out in the sun a lot, which explained the lines around his mouth, deep and bitter-looking for a guy his age. But his mother'd said he'd been working outside, on a fishing trawler.

Our hands collided halfway across the table. I grasped his, which felt odd for a minute because I'd forgotten about the missing fingers. But they were warm and dry, and mine were sweating. I laughed at myself. "I should've recognized you. But the hat and dark glasses and all."

He took off the cap. "Better?"

I nodded, waited, but he left the sunglasses on. "So." I had so much to tell, yet . . . where to begin? "Your mother says you've been out fishing."

"Yeah, commercial, with my cousins. We bought shares in this scallop boat. I got a quarter interest in a shrimper, too. You know, like I said back in school? It's what I wanted to do."

"Right, wow, a long time ago." Really, barely four years. Yet so much had happened in such a short time I now felt tongue-tied, a stranger. And why did he have to hide behind those damn glasses so I had to watch my own face reflected double, like tiny dual TVs? I wanted to see his eyes, otherwise who knew what he was really thinking.

Pearce and I had never been shy with each other, at least up until that last night at the carnival, right before I was hauled off by Sheriff Burney. So maybe I was annoyed at him for leaving the shades on, for acting weird. Whatever the reason, I laid my cigarette in the ashtray, leaned over, and whipped the damn dark glasses off.

I'd planned to say something smart-ass,

like, "Oh, good. You still have eyes. I just wondered." Instead I sucked a quick breath and gripped the thick-framed Wayfarers so hard it's a wonder they didn't bend.

On the left side of his face, bisecting his eyebrow, snaking over the closed, sunken lid ran a flat, red, twisting scar that ended just above his cheekbone. A little of that mark must have shown below the glasses, but in the dim tent I hadn't noticed.

His right eye was fine; it looked back at me clear blue and unblinking, judging my reaction. Maybe he wasn't surprised; maybe like a stupid endless pun, this happened to him all the time.

"Oh," I said, feeling petty and mean and stupid, trying not to look away or even blink. God, it was a terrible scar. Still red and new looking. I didn't even want to imagine how he'd gotten it. How it must've felt.

He smiled then, and the lines bracketing his mouth etched deeper. He reached over and took back the sunglasses. "They gave me an eye patch at the hospital," he said. "But I always felt stupid wearing it, like some idiot playing pirate. The fingers? They got crushed bad. Pretty common on fishing boats."

I wanted to say, Take them back off.

That it didn't matter, none of it. That the scar didn't bother me. But I'd have to mean it, because this was Pearce I was talking to and he'd know the difference. No, this would take getting used to.

"I'm sorry." I said. Then felt sorry again because he frowned. "I mean, I'm sorry you had an accident, when you — I guess, were out on the boat? That is —"

He smiled and shook his head. "Yeah. See, while you were gone, the place still changed. Things happened."

He sounded kind of bitter. Even mad. That'd never occurred to me, that he'd be angry at me for leaving. Not that I'd gone voluntarily, at least in the end.

He barked a harsh laugh. "Besides the eye and the fingers, everything else is attached and still works, though." He reached over suddenly and picked up my smoldering cigarette. His hand was steady. "Shit. I just quit these," he said, taking a long, hungry drag. He laid it back in the ashtray and smiled again. "You're still a bad influence."

"Me? Hey, I'm not the one who —"

"There you are." A blonde woman was leaning into the tent, talking to Pearce. She was short, slender, and tanned, wearing white shorts and a sleeveless blue blouse.

"Your mama said you'd be helping her, but then I looked all over the place. And here you're getting your fortune told."

"Not exactly," he said. "This is Dory, an old friend from school. We're just catching up. Dory, this is my wife, Caroline."

"Oh." I gave her a smile, hoping it looked more genuine that it felt. "Nice to meet you."

She looked me up and down without much interest, then her eyes flicked away. "Yeah, great. You, too."

"I'll meet you at the truck in a minute," said Pearce.

"But I'm ready to go." She folded her arms. When he didn't say anything else, she huffed a sigh and walked off.

"So, I predict you'll meet a beautiful blonde in the very near future," I joked. "How's that?"

"Real good, Dory. But I'd rather talk about the past. I'm not that interested in my future right now."

I cocked my head, interested. "No?"

"Nope. It seems all laid out anyhow. Caroline hates it here," he said, leaning back in the folding chair. "She left me last year and went back to school in Tallahassee."

I nodded. "But she came back."

He sighed and looked off toward the

bake sale tables. "Maybe. She wants to live in a city, maybe Miami or Atlanta. But there's more to it than that. There was this other woman."

I held real still then. Jesus.

He laughed. "It was like . . . I never got to tell her how I felt. She never took me seriously anyhow. And then," he snapped his fingers, and I flinched. "She was gone."

I stood and started packing my stuff. "Maybe you need a detective."

"So what do you predict, Madame Dory?"

"That you're married, and you love the water. And you . . . you have no children," I said softly, not looking up.

"As far as I know," he joked.

"You could see Reverend Hardy. I don't do marriage counseling."

He glanced away and shrugged. "She wants stuff, I want stuff. But none of it's the same."

"Yeah, well, people rush into things," I said.

"No kidding." He got up.

I pulled my shawl tight against a shiver, as if something was creeping up behind me, a thing I couldn't hear or see with only a crystal ball and deck of cards.

"How's your dad?" Pearce asked, suddenly

brisk and businesslike.

"Fine, he's fine. I'm real sorry about your father."

"Thanks," he said. "It was quick, we didn't expect it. Maybe that's good, in a way."

"And how's your mother doing?" I returned — stupidly, since I'd just seen her fifteen minutes earlier as she'd swept by with ribbons for the pie contest.

"Oh, she's fine. Yeah, getting along."

"That's good."

Our conversation had begun to sound like a practice dialogue from one of our old high school Spanish textbooks. Formal, stilted sentences. Long pauses while one waited on the other to work out the right translation.

"You glad to be back?" he asked, pitching in to help take down and fold up the sheets that had made up my tent.

I thought about it. "Yeah," I said at last. "I think I am."

Pearce leaned on the table. "Your dad was strange after you left. After that whole thing with your neighbor dying. The sheriff questioning people, weird shit in the newspaper. You going off to a private school or something."

I laughed. "Private school. Is that what

you heard? What else did they say?"

"For a while some folks thought your father had something to do with that guy dying. That he'd had this thing with the wife."

"Huh."

He turned back from stacking stuff in my wagon and faced me. "You know, Dory, I always thought I'd hear from you," he said quickly, as if he had a lot to spill and time was limited. And considering the wife waiting by the truck, I suppose it was. "Your dad said it was a strict school, you couldn't call or write anybody. And no holidays home. What kind of school is that, Dory? I thought we were friends, that I'd get a letter. Something."

I shook my head, pressed my lips together. "No. I couldn't."

"You couldn't?" He sounded skeptical. "Sometimes at night I'd think about you." He looked up, as if he were lying there in the dark all over again. "At first I felt like it might be my fault. And your dad got stranger and stranger, especially after that Fitzgerald woman picked up and moved back north. A leaky faucet or a slammed door, the tick of the clock, anything seemed to set him off. But maybe, when a lot of bad shit happens, one thing adds to another, till the whole pile just topples over. And then you lose it."

"It's not just that," I said.

A couple of high school students came up, pulled out money to have their fortunes told.

"Sorry, I'm closed." They rolled their eyes and wandered off, grumbling.

"Coming back was my idea, kind of a surprise," I said. "I didn't realize he'd gotten so odd. So, I don't know, religious. Not that there's anything wrong with that, but he's always *quoting* stuff at me, really deep into it. Like his life depends on it." Then it hit me, what I'd said, and I laughed. "Oh, well. Maybe it does."

"I guess you going away, then that woman leaving, it all broke him up. He was stuck on her bad. First he stopped working afternoons. People had been staying away from the store anyhow — you know how it is in a small town. Finally he'd only show up some mornings. I used to help out, until I bought the boat. And then that big Scotty's store opened in Ocala."

All that energy I'd spent hating, yes, even fearing Myra, had been wasted. She'd been back in New York the whole time, probably collecting more terrible art. And maybe I couldn't save the store anyhow.

412

The last thing I wanted to do was stay here with no money and no job and take care of a cranky old man who barely spoke to me, who spouted Bible verses and never thought to apologize for letting Tom Burney drag me barefoot from my own house like a criminal. But I was beginning to see nothing binds two people tighter than all the wrongs and hurts and slights they've inflicted on one another. Mick Poteke, my father, even Frank Fitzgerald. I'd learned from them all.

"I have to go," I blurted out. "Got to pick up my daughter." Then my face heated up. Shit. I hadn't told him anything about Rose. That she was his. Could I, now — should I? I saw the interest in his face; he was gearing up to ask about her. So I bundled the rest of the stuff up fast and grabbed the handle of the old Radio Flyer wagon I'd rolled there with. "It was great to see you again," I called over my shoulder, making sure not to look back.

I found his mother by the bake sale table, poking at some blueberry muffins. When she noticed me hovering, she turned, and I dropped the fat envelope of cash into her hand.

"A hundred ten dollars," I said.

"My goodness! Thank you, Dory." She

sounded like she meant it.

Still I stood there, mulling over her tone, ready to lash out at anything. All my life she'd been kind to me, but it had been the cool, polite sort of kindness that was quick to correct and judge, the sort that always felt like charity. Now at least I'd turned the tables, if only for a moment. "You're welcome. No problem."

I headed out, pulling the rusty old wagon. I'd oiled the wheels before I'd left the house, but from the way it screeched you'd never know. Once away from the school grounds I took off my shawl and hiked up the skirt a little but still must have looked a sight to the traffic on Water Street. I stopped at the sitter's — Miss Alma's — house to get Rose. It was no sweat to convince a three-year-old it'd be fun to ride home in a wagon.

I rolled up to the edge of the front lawn, then stopped. "Let's go down by the Springs, Rosie."

I was in no mood to talk nonsense with Dad, to endure quotations or demands that he'd forget before I could do a thing about them. So I took her hand and we walked down to the water, all the way to the end of the dock. We took off our shoes and dangled our feet. I patiently answered

Rose's questions about the fish that lived there: How big they were, how many colors they came in, whether they had mommies and daddies and aunts and uncles. The manatee had probably gotten in the way of someone's boat propellor. I missed him bumping the pilings below like a log of gray driftwood. That was why my eyes were burning.

What was I going to do with Owen Gamble, a ghost of the father I remembered? Or maybe he'd never been that man, and I only realized it now. Maybe nothing in my childhood had been the way I recalled it. Perhaps Harriet McMillan had never actually disliked me, but only felt sorry for a poor, motherless neighbor girl. Perhaps her crankiness, her willingness to find fault, her true argument had been with my father. Maybe even Myra had had her good points. Though I wasn't eager to imagine that yet.

I was frightened, I had to admit it. Dad wasn't real old yet. Could he be getting senile, a word I couldn't make myself say out loud? I'd seen old people around Midway and here in town, too, shuffling down the sidewalks or pushed along in wheelchairs by a hired minder. Their unfocused eyes seemed to already stare at eternity. They made little darting grabs at your hand if you passed by and called you by dead people's names. Begged to be taken home with you. To their cataract-shuttered eyes, maybe everyone looked like a lost husband or parent or child. These addled folks ended their days, Ruby had once remarked on one of our walks in Midway, curled into a ball like babies not yet born. "All the way back to the womb," she'd rasped, taking a drag off her Camel. "Only the womb ain't there no more."

At last I picked up my shoes and took Rose's hand. We went back up the lawn, in through the back door.

"We're back, Dad!"

I heard water running. Early for a shower, and anyhow that seemed unlikely. I'd had to wage a real campaign just to convince him to bathe twice a week. The gushing sound came from the kitchen, where the leaky faucet ran full blast. I turned it off, then tightened it to stop the chronic drip. Across the room a burner glowed blue on the stove. But where was he? Did I need to take him with me every-where, or send him to Miss Alma's with Rose?

"Dad! Where are you?"

He came up from behind and touched

my shoulder, making me jump. And he was definitely shuffling, though maybe you could blame it on the ratty old slippers.

He said testily, "Where you been? Dinner's late."

"It's not time for dinner yet."

He glowered and went into the living room. A burst of canned laughter, the TV coming on.

I went to the swinging doors. "Dad!" I said, more sharply than I'd meant to.

"What? I ain't deaf."

I took a deep breath; it did no good to flare back. "You forgot to turn the water off," I said calmly. "And see here, the stove —"

"Ah, you do it, Vera," he said, waving me off.

I stopped with my hand halfway to the knob on the stove front and went back to the doorway. "What'd you just call me?"

He stared at me. "*Vera*. Vera, Vera, Vera. Your name, ain't it?" He shook his head, wiped his nose on one sleeve, and turned back to the television. Rose came in and lay on the floor, on her stomach. She got him to change the channel to a cartoon, then eagerly started explaining the good parts to him.

I went back to the kitchen, a hand over my mouth. He'd used the forbidden word, my mother's name. I'd never heard it pass his lips before. I dropped into a kitchen chair. That misused name seemed to prove beyond a doubt I was no longer the child here. What if he was that confused; what if one day he no longer recognized me at all? I hugged myself in a sudden sick panic. My father and Rose. How could I run a store and still care for them both?

I stayed up late that night, hugging the crystal to me, waiting for the little figures to appear. I stared until I believed I saw them, stared until by all rights they should have been etched on the glassy curve of my own eyeballs. When I finally staggered off to bed at last, practically cross-eyed and blind, they seemed to turn and float before me. I wanted to know if the woman in the glass matched the scrap of photo still in the dusty cigar box under my old bed. But she was so tiny and never held still long enough. During the day I looked around the house for anything else that might've been my mother's, for some clue to another man's name, for any other piece, no matter how small, to the puzzle of our lives.

After weeks of gazing into that chipped glass globe, what I finally did begin to see was bits and pieces of the lives of people in town. Like Pearce standing on a deck, his legs braced against the swell of the sea, cranking hard on a winch, lifting a net of wriggling silver shrimp from the waves. I knew Thea Berry, who did the books for some local businesses, was sad. Her daughter had gone off to college and she hadn't gotten a letter in months, though if you saw her in the Corner Market she'd smile and tell you the girl was doing fine, pulling down all As and in a high-class sorority. And poor, tongue-tied Bill Hodges, the postmaster, who ate alone each night at the diner, was hopelessly in love with Barbara Downs, the math teacher at the high school. But she was slipping into the gymnasium office after school hours. The football coach was a hairy-chested Midwesterner a full head shorter than her who liked to wear her shoes and underwear.

I was going insane. It was the only explanation.

I didn't mean to spy on these people, my friends and neighbors. Each time I saw things I swore I'd lock up the crystal, put it out of sight, unless I could use it for some good, or at least raise a little cash again for some local charity. But nights I still crept back after Rose and Dad were in bed. I took the globe out of whatever new hiding place I'd decided on, the kitchen junk drawer or the produce bin in the refrigerator, drawn to it like a wino to drink. But no matter how long I gazed, I couldn't make the chipped glass ball show me my mother's face, or where she was or what had happened to her.

The one person I never saw was myself.

I thought I understood the depth of this obsession and made a solemn promise to myself. I vowed to never do anything I couldn't tell my own child about later. I'd never use what I was shown to hurt someone or to better myself unfairly. I'd keep to a certain standard, or at least do no harm, even if it cost time or money or my dignity.

And I wouldn't damage Pearce's marriage, even if that meant I couldn't tell him Rose was his daughter. He'd made a life of his own, and I'd made my choices, too.

I nodded to myself, turning over these solemn promises. Yet even as I did this I couldn't stop my mind from darting ahead like a wayward child, imagining how easy it might be to just happen to turn up. To accidentally put myself in his way.

22

On a warm afternoon in late October, I was in the store window, arranging a display of rakes and bushel baskets, autumn squash, and fat orange pumpkins. As I was hunting for a gourd to fill out a gap in one of the baskets, Pearce walked by outside, hands in his pockets. That glint of sun-bleached hairs on tanned arms, the tilt of his head, his long-legged stride all briefly made me feel fifteen again. As if none of our adult complications, good or bad, had come to pass. With that came a lightening of heart, an expanded feeling of possibility. Or maybe it was only the sun beating down through the glass, the heat getting to me.

I bent back to my work, trying to ignore the expectation that made my hands tremble. Only Pearce, after all. The front doors opened and he came in, brass bell ringing like a sailor's welcome. I'd only seen him once since the school carnival, with his wife, in the Corner Market. Rose had been talking a mile a minute to Dad as he pushed the squeaking cart slowly,

slowly through the narrow aisles. We'd all smiled and nodded and moved on. After that I'd figured he was off in the Gulf of Mexico again on the scallop boat or the shrimp trawler with his cousins.

"Hey. Over here," I called.

He looked around, and on a whim I ducked behind a bushel basket, one of our oldest games. Childish, but I did it anyhow. When he quickly spotted me crouched in the bay window, still holding the squash gourd, I felt silly.

"Home is the sailor," I said, looking down to hide my smile.

"That's right." He thumped a package down on the counter. He was wearing the eyepatch today, its thin strap nearly invisible in his thick hair. "And that's when a sailor gets his pay."

"Better than a kick in the pants." I crawled out of the window and beat dust off my jeans. "What's this?"

He handed it to me, a small, weighty, oddly shaped bundle in brown paper.

"Go on," he urged. "Open it."

I tore the wrapper off a flat hip-flask bottle of Wild Turkey. I frowned, looking puzzled, from him to the amber liquor. Then recalled the nearly full bottle I'd filched from Dad's liquor cabinet that night more than four years ago, a gift to surprise him with on our first and only date. The flask of whiskey a dare, a grown-up gift to share with Pearce, at the carnival.

"Thought we oughta replace the one you took way back, from your dad's supply. Think he missed it?"

I laughed. It was funny, this solemn paying-off of doubtful old debts years later. As if such a thing mattered now. But I suppose payment makes a debtor feel like a new person, like everything is as square as it ever will be.

His tense shoulders relaxed at my laugh.

"We may have to drink this one, too," I said without thinking. Then my face heated up. Of course we wouldn't, he was married now and when was I going to get that through my head?

He grimaced. "No way, I quit last year. Haven't had a drink in —" He looked at his watch, which made me laugh again. "Six months, two weeks, and three days."

That was surprising. I could still recall the way he'd put down amazing quantities of beer, and that purloined whiskey, like there was no tomorrow.

"I know, I know," he said, fingering the eyepatch. "It was getting to be, I mean it *was* a big problem. I liked it too much. And after something so stupid costs you an eye —"

I waited, but he didn't finish. "Well, I'll slip this back into the liquor cabinet then," I said.

"Great." But he stood, still looking at me.

"What," I said at last.

"I wanted to invite you to dinner at Mom's on Friday. Nothing fancy. Pot roast."

Did he think I was looking for more complications? Wasn't there enough on my hands with my father, the store, with trying to think of ways to keep Rose fed and clothed and safe while I figured out our futures?

"Well, gosh, but Dad's not really up to watching Rose by himself. She wears him out."

"Mom says bring them both. It was her idea."

"Oh." So it wasn't Pearce. He didn't want to see me in particular. I felt deflated then. I guess there was just no pleasing me.

He turned away and examined a rack of garden tools, as if they were the most interesting thing he'd seen in months. "Caroline won't be there, though. She's gone back to Tallahassee for . . . for a while."

Sirens and fire bells were going off in my head. I couldn't make my mouth work for a minute. Pearce was my friend; he had a wife, even if they weren't on the best of terms. He was all the good memory I had left of a botched-up childhood. The more I thought about it, the more I knew I should refuse.

Even as my brain was reasoning this all out, warning me off, I heard my mutinous mouth working on its own. "Well, sure, okay."

Lord God.

His face was a curious study of pleasure, cynicism, and resignation. "Good. Come on over at six, then."

I slumped against the counter. *Oh Dory. What a fool, what a fool you still are.*

When we arrived at the McMillans', Miss Harriet met us at the door, which made me think things weren't going well, because though she had an apron on over a nice print dress, her hair was still wound up on sponge curlers. I tried not to stare, but in all my life I'd never seen her anything but dressed, combed, powdered; hairsprayed past perfect. Even at a cookout or picnic.

"Oh my, you're here." She was breathless. "Well, of course you are, look at the time! Come on in."

Dad walked straight to the living room. He sat, hands flat on his thighs, at attention on the edge of her camelback sofa, his air of resigned patience so intent he might've been waiting for a bus to the Second Coming.

"This is Rose," I said. My daughter was clinging to my skirt, and I drew her forward to meet Miss Harriet. I'd labored to make her look presentable, brushing her hair up in a butterfly clip, putting her in a full-skirted plaid dress from the Leader Department Store sale rack. Thinking somehow if we made a good impression, maybe I'd find a way to tell them who she really was.

"Oh, aren't you precious!" gushed Harriet, bending to smile at her.

Rose leaned hard against me and regarded the curlers doubtfully, maybe scared, since I never used any. "Pink things on her head," she announced loudly.

Harriet clutched suddenly at her hair and turned beet red. "Oh my Lord," she moaned. "I forgot, I've been so — I must look a sight!"

"Nonsense," I said. "You look wonderful."

She waved me on in. "Please sit down, honey. I'll just —" She turned and rushed off.

We came in, but before I could shut the door behind us the gray cat brushed by, meowing. Rose shrieked with glee and grabbed the loose skin on his back like a suitcase handle.

"No, honey," I said. "You'll hurt kitty. What did I tell you?"

She let go, and the cat dashed off under the sofa.

Pearce came in and handed me a short glass filled with what looked like a whiskey sour, complete with a cherry and orange slice. Miss Harriet had gone all out. He also had a Shirley Temple for Rose in a fat plastic tumbler. She accepted it gravely, without surprise, as if she'd ordered ahead.

"What do you say," I prodded.

"Tank you," she mumbled, then wrinkled her nose. "Know what?"

He shook his head. "What?"

"Cats have prickers in they feet," she informed him solemnly. She regarded the eyepatch a long time, but didn't say anything about it.

He grinned. "That's right. Been pricked a few times, myself."

Dinner was pot roast, little new potatoes, greens, and corn muffins. Rose was perched on some phone books, and we began a bit stiffly. But halfway through everyone seemed to loosen up, talking and laughing as if no time had passed at all. As if we hadn't gotten any older, grown up, been imprisoned or maimed, been married or had a child. I caught myself glancing between Pearce and Rose more than once. She had his small, neat ears. Her eyes were the same shade of blue. And there was the identical cleft, same as in his chin. How could I be the only one to see it?

Things went well until it was time to go home. As we were heading out the door, Dad suddenly turned to Miss Harriet.

"Why you wear red is beyond me. Makes you look like the side of a barn." He shook his head and went on out.

I stammered an apology to poor shocked Harriet and scooted after him. As we reached the last step to the walk he stumbled. Pearce caught his arm, and they both nearly went over before he managed to straighten things out at the sidewalk.

"Whoa, watch it, Mr. Gamble." He called back to his mother that he'd walk us home, make sure we got there okay. She nodded wordlessly and shut the door. I suspected we wouldn't be asked back anytime soon.

At home I stepped in first and snapped on the hall light. Pearce and Dad sat on the couch, and I took Rose back to bed.

"Not sleepy," she whimpered but settled down when I promised a condensed version of *Green Eggs and Ham*. She sleepily patted my face as I tucked the covers all around. I waited a minute, then closed her door, leaving the nightlight burning.

In the living room, Pearce was alone. "Your dad went on to bed. He seems okay now. Mind if I use your bathroom?"

He came back shortly. "Afraid I knocked some stuff off the shower rod. I picked it up."

My underwear, the elastic-shot pairs I'd washed out the day before. It made me feel edgy and self-conscious that he'd been in our bathroom, seen the unscrubbed tub, manhandled my shabby panties back onto the rod.

He sat on the couch. I took the other end.

"Dory." He touched my hand, which lay on the cushion near his leg. Before I could jerk it away he slid higher, stroking my arm with his fingertips. I hoped he couldn't read my mood, what I'd really like him to do next. It felt like the words were printed on my skin and glowing.

I thought to change the subject. "That Wild Turkey. Should I get you some?" I asked, before I remembered.

"No, thanks. A Coke would be okay. Or ice water, even." He withdrew the hand and crossed his arms.

I returned with two glasses, mine spiked, his plain. Really, he should just go. That'd be best. But I didn't want him to leave, so I handed over the glass. "Remember when we did that project together for my science class, and you dropped the test tube? How bad it stunk?"

His face brightened. "Yeah. And the play, the time you keeled over right after your speech. They called me and Buddy Swinson to come carry you to the nurse's office." He laughed. "You sure put a lot into that part."

We stared into our glasses and slowly loosened up. Began to talk. I drank my Wild Turkey and cola, which was too sweet, in fact awful, but soon gone. Ice cubes rattled in my glass. "Want another Coke?"

His hand, the maimed one, trembled a little when he held out the glass. I pretended I hadn't noticed.

When I came back we laughed, recalling how, when we were eight or nine, we'd hauled scrap lumber from the hardware store and some bent nails twisted up in a paper sack and made a tree fort in my backyard, on the big oak branch over-hanging the Springs. We'd not done such a good job of finishing the floor, though. Pearce fell clean through, into the water.

When I threw my head back to laugh it made me feel dizzy, a little woozy. "Oh boy," I said. "Maybe you got the right idea. Too much of this stuff, I think." I thumped my glass down on the coffee table.

"Feel sick?"

I nodded. "A little."

He stood. "Here, stretch out. And lower one foot to the floor. Then the room won't feel like a tilt-a-whirl."

I did, then squinted up at him. "It's not just the room."

"No?" He leaned over, looking con-cerned. I reached up, pulled his head down, and kissed the hollow of his neck.

He scooted up beside me, smiling a little. "Guess you been drinking, Dory."

"Mmm." I ran two fingers down the line of buttons on his shirt, then slid them in-side and hooked them into the cloth. I tried to pull him down again, but he resisted.

I let go. "Sorry. Shouldn't have done that."

"I don't need sympathy," he said. "If that's what you think."

I frowned. "What?"

"Come on. My own wife won't look me in the . . . in the eye." He barked a short humorless laugh. "Says my face is scary now."

"I'm not scared of you." I touched the edge of the eyepatch. "But what happened, Pearce? An accident on the boat?" I folded his left hand, the one missing fingers, in mine.

His lips compressed into a line thin as a scaling knife. He nodded. "Yeah. Something real stupid. Like I said."

"Maybe I can relate," I said. "In fact, I'm sure of it."

He raised an eyebrow and glanced at me. Sighed. "I doubt it. But okay, it went like this: six months ago my cousins and I and a hired deck hand bring in a huge haul of shrimp. Get top dollar, too. Me and Rick and David and this guy, after work, decide to celebrate. Really tie one on. Find a jook in Steinhatchee, bring back a few cases, and start working on them.

"At some point, I got to take a leak. To impress the cousins, who're too blasted to stand, I stagger over to the rail, unzip, and so on. That part goes okay. Then I turn to go below, lose my balance, slip, and go over the side."

"Ah." I winced. "You hit a piling or something?"

"No." He ran a hand lightly over his face, as if still checking for damage. It was tense with remembered pain. "No. I fall in, yeah, no big deal. I'm a great swimmer, even drunk. But then I yell out to them, because I can't reach the ladder. So Rick gets up and decides he'll pull me out with the gaff. You know, hook my suspenders in the back? Only he's so drunk, he can't tell I'm floating face up. He . . . he gets me in the eye."

God. I drew in a sharp breath.

He gave a crooked smile without any humor in it. "See? Pretty stupid." He pulled his hand free, held it up. "The fingers are more boring. Got crushed so bad one time between the boat and the pier, they had to amputate. Doc said he sees that kinda thing all the time, with commercial fishermen. But the eye —"

I stroked his cheek. "I've heard worse. Maybe done stuff more stupid."

He snorted in disbelief. I pulled him to me again; this time he seemed more enthusiastic.

But when I let go of his collar, he sat back. "You don't have to do this, Dory. I don't need pity, like I said. No way you can tell me you find this attractive."

He jerked the patch up.

I looked, longer this time. Oh, it was

awful, no way around it. And yet it was part of Pearce now, so how could I reject it, or the rest of him? I raised a hand and gently touched the lower half of the scar.

He flinched, but only a little. And when I didn't pull back or gag or shudder, or whatever it was he'd been expecting, he pulled me onto his lap, and we just stayed that way, not moving. It was so nice, I started to cry.

"Hey. What's wrong?" His fingers tried to get hold of my chin, but kept slipping on my tears. Finally he tilted my face up so he could see.

"I'm scared," I said. "We'll ruin everything. It'll all turn bad. I mean, there's your wife —"

"She left," he said. "I told you. This time she's not coming back."

But did he want me, Dory Gamble? Or just to feel again like the teenage boy with two eyes and all ten fingers, when the most dangerous thing we knew of was a shouted dare? But by then I was kissing him again anyway. His mouth tasted sweet, like Coca-Cola and the caramel cake we'd had for dessert. I hoped mine wasn't stale from cigarettes. I slid back down onto the couch, and he did, too. Then he raised his head again to kiss my neck, shoulders, the shadowed hollows of my collarbone. His breath warmed my skin like the sun on a dock at noon. What in God's name were we doing?

But I couldn't make myself worry anymore. Because wasn't it just the thing I'd sworn to do, to live in the minute, really live it? Not waiting for any trains, or a bus out of town. Not sitting on our butts expecting life to arrive here on its own and start up like a movie. Yes, right here on Myra Fitzgerald's ugly old couch, God bless her black heart, we were rolling around like dogs in the road.

A shaky querulous voice from down the hall. "What time's it?"

I heaved up in sudden panic, and the top of my head cracked Pearce. He clamped a hand over his mouth, and I saw a smear of red on his fingers.

My father stood down the hall, swaying in the light from his room, outlined like the silhouette of a distant God. And here I was, fifteen years old again, caught in the act. Until his quavering voice said, less certainly, "Vera, what you doing?"

I got up, pulling my blouse together. "Nothing, just . . . helping Pearce, because he . . . hurt himself." I whispered back, "I'll get you a towel."

Dad turned and shuffled to his room. I'd forgotten he slept less soundly even than a three-year-old. When I came back to the living room, dishcloth in hand, Pearce was sitting up. Bright red drops dotted the front of his white shirt. He watched my face while I dabbed blood from his swelling lip with the cold, wet cloth. Then I stood there, looking down, actually wringing the washcloth, because if possible I wanted him even more than when we'd been all over each other.

At the same time, I wanted him to just be my friend again. Safe, reliable Pearce. And I still hadn't told him about Rose. This seemed like a good time. But before I could open my mouth he stood.

"I better go," he said dully. "Got to get up early and go back to the coast. And my mother will worry if I'm not back. She worries a lot, especially since Dad passed." He shook his head. "I got to find her a new hobby besides me."

Fine, maybe we'd had enough revelations for one night. I took his hand. But still hated to lose the moment. "I have some things to tell, too."

"Okay." He waited.

"Actually, several things," I began, looking away. "But I guess I'd like to get a fresh start." Damn. *See Dory, the amazing yellow-bellied coward.*

"Okay then," he offered. "I'll come over when I get back in."

I nodded, as eager to see him again as I was eager to postpone the telling. Because who knew what would change, what would happen then?

After Pearce left, I went back and splashed water on my face, which in the unshaded bathroom bulb's light looked as bloodless and tired as his had. Maybe it was as hard to get to sleep out at sea as it was in a house with an angry, confused old man who sometimes prowled at all hours, who still raged at women long gone.

I yawned and stumbled to my room, feeling the drag of fatigue and too much whiskey on my arms and legs. The crazy gray cat had followed us home again. He jumped on the bed, kneading the covers.

"You're confused," I whispered in the dark. "You don't live here."

He meowed, seeming to disagree. He butted my leg with his head and settled purring at the foot of the bed.

Now that it was safe, I allowed myself to feel cheated. I kicked off the chenille spread and whacked my pillows into different shapes. By the Big Ben on the night stand, a few minutes passed. I gazed into the dark, hoping for sleep. But not until a faint orange glow announced the coming sun, turning the world beyond my blinds rosy orange, did I begin to drift off. A mocking-bird whistled from the oleanders.

"Damn catbird," I muttered. Only then was it possible to close my eyes and finally fall asleep.

23

When I got up it was late, but fortunately also a Saturday, when we didn't open till ten. Dad was already stirring and had gotten himself a glass of milk and some cereal. But he'd also turned on a burner and left it going, no pan or anything on it.

I turned off the flame and sat across from him. I dragged my fingers through my hair, rubbing my face hard. I was somehow mothering Rose and a sixty-one-year-old man, and running a store that took in fifty dollars on a good day. Did that prove I was responsible and sane, or crazier than a loon?

"What should we do about billing, Dad?" I asked. "Statements at the end of the month?"

He turned to look at me, blue eyes clear this morning. "Money answereth all things."

I stared at the wrinkled oracle eating cornflakes across from me while Rose prattled on about the cat. After a minute or so his eyes lost focus. Why couldn't he just talk to me? Were a few simple words too much to ask? He began humming a tune I didn't recognize.

When the percolator hissed, I jumped. "Dad."

No response.

"Whatever happened to Vera?" I asked.

He stopped chewing.

I waited a minute. "You hear me, Dad? I want to know what happened to my mother. Why'd she leave and never come back, never even call?"

He sighed and laid his spoon on the table, hand shaking so that it beat out a quick little march in the process. "Let the dead bury their dead," he muttered, as if to prove he'd never tell, would always fob me off with verses and scripture. A more stubborn man than Owen Gamble had yet to be born.

But then, I was the daughter of Owen Gamble. I wouldn't give up easy.

"All right then, Dad," I said cheerfully. "We'd better go render unto Caesar. Another day, another dollar. Sufficient unto the day is the evil thereof. It never rains but it pours." Baptist Sunday school classes had done me some practical good, after all.

He made a sour face, being caught out at his own game. Then got up and shuffled out.

"All done, Mama," said Rose. I untied the napkin from around her neck, brushed toast crumbs off her shirt, and all of us Gambles went out to sell hardware.

I was moving bags of grass seed to make room for winter rye when the bell over the front door jangled and Pearce came in, carrying a duffle.

"I'm running late," he said. "Can you come in the back a minute?"

I followed him to the storeroom.

"Where's your father?"

"Over at the Cut 'n Curl. I sent him to Betty for a trim. Rose is at Miss Alma's."

He backed me against the shelves of grass seed and mulch and tried to kiss me. I turned my head this way and that, then finally kneed him. Not hard, just enough to show I was serious.

He looked hurt and puzzled. No wonder, after our interrupted wrestling match on the couch. Like there was Dory's nighttime self, the one who kissed back and tried to peel off his clothes. Then, this daytime woman, all hard knees and business. Well, I couldn't help it.

"Dory, what's going on? I thought about you for years. If you hadn't left —"

"Then what? You'd have married me and

everything would be perfect?"

"I don't know," he said, running a hand over his face. "At least it'd be different. What do you want me to say?"

I sighed. My problems weren't his fault. That it never seemed the right time or place to confess wasn't, either. "Nothing. I've just made some big mistakes already. Have some problems to work out. I don't want to make things worse, complicate them more. For you or me."

He slammed a hand into the nearest bag, and it burst. I jumped, but then we both pretended not to notice the seed cascading onto the floor. "Yeah, well what's so damn complicated? Why can't you give a straight answer? Just tell me."

I shrugged. "I guess because I wasn't raised that way," I said lamely.

"How hard can it be? You can *tell* me," he said, but softer. "Everyone makes mistakes. Look at me."

The bell over the door jangled. "Dory," called my father, as he came in the front.

I started up, but Pearce grabbed my arm. "Don't use him as an excuse. Come on. What's the worst thing you've ever done since I've known you?"

It sounded like one of our old childhood dares, and I didn't want to take it. I had to confess about Rose, most important, though maybe not tell about Micco Poteke. But then there was Frank Fitzgerald and the pills. The delinquent girls' school I'd broken out of by stealing a state car. If we came burdened with all this, he might reject one of us, his daughter or me.

But I'd forgotten how stubborn Pearce could be. He stared me down, as he'd managed only a few times before. Way back.

I bowed my head and sighed. "Fine. Let's get it over with." I lifted his hands from my shoulders and folded them in front, like an undertaker's. "Wait here a second, all right? Don't break anything else."

I went up front and turned the sign in the door to CLOSED. Then scooted into the side room where the nail bins, hammers, and sledges were kept. My fathered had started dusting, and he'd spilled a huge bin of screws. They rolled around his feet like shiny silver insects. "Can you pick those up and get them all back? I've got to take care of something." I handed him the lid.

He nodded, and on a whim I kissed his leathery cheek. He looked surprised but not entirely displeased. For a change, no

Bible verse dogged me back to the main aisle.

Pearce was still posed, waiting: The Patient Man. I pulled up a wooden crate and sat. "Okay. The Story of My Life So Far. How long do I get to tell it?"

"As long as it takes. Till Kingdom Come." He pulled a cardboard box across from me.

I took a breath, then let it out. Maybe this was the last I'd ever see of him, and I was in no hurry for that. So I made him wait while I went and got two dusty folding lawn chairs from the patio aisle so we could sit across from each other. Then slowly, with lots of pauses, I filled him in.

I decided to tell it in order, hoping that everything, especially the bad parts, would make more sense that way.

He looked shocked when I told about Frank Fitzgerald and the pills but then interrupted, surprising me. "So this Fitzgerald guy, he knew what was happening. Wasn't denying it anymore, ready to get on with dying. You were only a tool, Dory. See? It's bad that he used you, a kid, to do it. But maybe when you're trapped in a bed, dying by inches, any chance that falls your way looks like fair game."

I nodded, speechless.

"Go on," he said. "What else?"

I told him about the Pine Hills School in Marianna. About Matron Camber and the cop who'd laid hands on me so she could do her job. "Jesus, Dory," he said, swallowing. He took my hand and turned it over, staring like it was a work of art.

Then how I'd planned my escape with my damaged friend, Ardis. And that when she'd backed out I'd felt glad and at the same time guilty, like I'd failed her. Then my strange run for it, my meeting up with the fruit tramps. How nervous I'd been of the drunk, taciturn men with quick, roving hands. Until Sadie McElroy had taken charge, had encouraged me to keep going.

Then the Sebrings, Clayton and Ruby, who'd taken us in and loved us like their own children. It hurt all over again to tell how Ruby had died, and how afterward everything wanted to slide toward chaos at the You Better Believe It. As if it was a test, I made myself tell about Mick Poteke — though not every detail. Some things are not only hard to explain, but so personal they ought to stay private.

I could tell that disturbed him; he kept frowning. "A Seminole, huh?" he said at last, as if I'd been keeping company with an Arab sheik. "Well, sure. I figured a girl

445

like you would have, you know, boy-friends."

"What does that mean — a girl like me?" Then I wondered, *Does he still see me that way. A girl?* Because despite my age I no longer felt all that young and carefree, or girlish.

"You know." He squeezed my hand. "Somebody so . . . alive. Who's not afraid, who's beautiful and doesn't even know it or care. So why would you be interested in a scarred-up loser like me?"

Well, that set me back, making me speechless for once.

He was watching me still, as if waiting for more.

"What now?"

"One thing you haven't said, about Rose. So is her father this, uh, this Mick guy?"

My turn to squeeze his hand. "Oh, Pearce," I said, shaking my head. "She's three and a half. You haven't counted back yet?"

He was quiet a moment, doing the simple math. "That night at the carnival?"

I nodded, watching his face. The right answer would either appear there — written on the face, as Madame Ruby would say — or it wouldn't. I was all but crossing my fingers. Nobody was going to slight my beautiful girl, not even Pearce McMillan. Especially not him.

He stood suddenly and walked in a slow circle around the store room. He stopped with his back to me, all the while looking down, as if his next lines were written in the dust on the floorboards.

"I hear there's a fast boat out of town," I said, trying to make it sound light, a joke.

He looked up then, smiling, pleased wonder on his face. "You know, she's something else, that kid. I feel like I won some kind of lottery." He shook his head. "But how slow can I be? Damn, I should've figured that out. And you know what this means?"

I shook my head, struggling to keep from grinning, from jumping up and down.

"We can get married soon as I'm divorced."

I had all but forgotten he had a wife. Somehow bringing the past back to life, watching him take the time to absorb his new status as a father, had sent it winging right out of my head. Now I recalled the night of my last birthday, when stoic, poker-faced Scilla Poteke had brought all her children, hers and Mick's, to the diner. To show me, and everyone, what he'd been denying. And just who I'd be stealing from.

"I don't want to break up anybody's marriage."

"You aren't," he said simply. "Even if you'd never come back, that would all be over. We'd already decided to file."

It was a wonder I didn't pass out, the blood rushed to my head so fast. Everything had once seemed so impossible, so screwed up. And here maybe for a change I'd timed things right. Had hit on the perfect moment to set the record straight.

"She mostly sounded relieved," Pearce said, after he'd called Caroline to talk about making their separation permanent. I didn't ask what else she might've sounded like. To break up a marriage had to hurt, even if things weren't going well.

But Caroline was staying with her mother in Tallahassee and didn't want to come back to Ordinary Springs. She still hated small-town living; she wanted to work in a big law office and have a new Lincoln to drive. Who could blame her? People have been fools over much less, and I didn't think she was any kind of fool. Except, of course, for rejecting a good man for bearing the scars of old injuries in plain sight. But then I'd had the advantage of knowing Mick Poteke, perfect enough on

448

the outside to turn all female heads. Yet somehow still lacking, inside.

All Caroline McMillan asked of Pearce was a little money every month until she finished school. They'd see a lawyer in Ocala to get the papers in the works. Still, every now and then I got a sudden guilty flash, worrying I'd somehow broken them up. And Pearce kept patiently assuring me there hadn't been much left to keep together.

The night after he returned we sat out on the screened porch. Dad had gone to his room after I'd put Rose to bed. It was warm still for November, so we were drinking iced tea. Pearce was speculating about buying his own boat. I was wondering how I might persuade my future mother-in-law, who'd never seemed to care much for me, to look on our marriage kindly. All the while crickets and peepers sawed and croaked and buzzed around us like a premonition of doom. Miss Harriet would be the hard nut to crack. She'd always been polite before. But the past few days when I'd seen her out working in her flowers or at the Corner Market or on the street, I'd felt a chill in the air.

If it'd been hard to confide in Pearce, to explain everything, when we'd always been friends and close, how would we tell Miss

Harriet that Rose was his love child — her illegitimate, ready-made granddaughter? Would it turn her against a little girl, the fact she was conceived by two unmarried teenagers, in a scenario straight from Reverend Hardy's book of hell-bound sins? And what about the fact that Miss Harriet would be losing a daughter-in-law she was real fond of, in exchange for me, whom she only tolerated?

Oh, I'd never been able to read that woman. Being so proper and correct herself, surely she'd never understand how any person, especially a female one, could go so wrong. Could hand over death to a sick man, though maybe we didn't have to tell that part. But she must already know I'd been sent away in shame. Now I'd come back bold as brass with a baby and made everyone in town think I'd been married all along. And if we didn't tell, then everyone, even Rose herself, would go along believing a lie. That Pearce was her stepfather, not her flesh and blood.

He stopped talking about boats and bank loans and looked at me. "You're awful quiet."

I stubbed my cigarette on the sole of my sneaker and flicked it into an empty coffee can on the floor. "What about your mother?"

"Oh." He understood right away. "When I explain it all, she'll understand. She's a mother, too, for God's sake. I know what you think, but she really likes you, Dory."

Ha. And it snowed all the time in Miami Beach. But this was important to him, the notion that we'd all get along. And let's face it, he was getting no bargain for a father-in-law, either. When I'd told Dad we were getting married, Pearce and I, he'd shot me a fierce, disgusted look and said not a word. Who knew what it meant?

I wasn't banking on anybody's good will just yet, but I nodded anyhow. In six months, after the divorce was final, we'd be married. Rose would have a daddy, like the other little kids Miss Alma baby-sat at her house. That lack had begun to seem very important to her lately, and I of all people could surely understand.

We'd been doing an awful lot of explaining between the two of us, Pearce and I. When was I going to get any answers from my father? I wanted one for the old question, the one I'd finally gotten brave or defiant enough to ask: *What happened to Vera Gamble?* My father was a hard man sometimes, and a tiring, exasperating one. Despite the fact that he slipped up and called me by her name now and then, the old no-talking rule was still in effect. Maybe it wouldn't matter if I lived to be eighty and he was a hundred twenty-two. Or that she'd been gone so long hardly anyone else alive would care one way or the other if she'd run off stark naked with a tribe of cannibals.

Pearce sympathized, but I could see he didn't understand why I worried so. "People disappear in this state, all over the country, every day," he said. "You don't even want to know how many kids. All those faces. Now they're putting them on milk cartons. And up in the post office. Maybe your old man knows where and why, but it's a sore point he doesn't want to talk about. Some people's pride gets hurt, and they never get over it."

He was probably right. Dad seemed bound to take this particular hurt, and the sorrow or anger or whatever it was he still felt, to his grave. Yet I wasn't asking him to get over it, to forget or forgive anyone. Only to let me own the part that belonged to me: my history. My mother. Where and who I came from. Why she went away. Any child deserved to know that much.

Pearce moved our glasses around the patio table like he was playing chess. "What if you find out. Maybe even find her. Then you wish you hadn't?"

"Nothing comes without risk."

"That's true," he conceded. "Sometimes the sharks bite back. When I'm on the trawler now, I can't hardly stand the sight of a gaff hook. And there's storms, even hurricanes out in the Gulf. Did I tell you I was washed overboard once? So was another guy. He drowned. But I keep on heading out. Why? I wonder myself. It's just what I have to do."

"Then you understand how I feel," I said.

He hesitated, then nodded. Set his glass down with a thump, as if that settled everything.

I stood and held out a hand. "Come on. We have business to finish."

"What?"

"From the other night."

He looked surprised but agreeable. Enthusiastic, even.

"We'll have to be quiet." I led him down the hall to my old room.

I closed the door softly behind us and pushed in the lock button. Pearce looked around at the torn, faded Elvis poster, the old Bobby Darin albums, at the dusty stuffed animals still perched on a shelf, and started laughing. I knew why. It was like a stage set, as if I'd planned it all, kept the room in a childhood time warp just for us.

"Huh. Pretty cool," he said, staring at a saw-edged Polaroid of us in an old school play, one I'd thumb-tacked to the bulletin board on my closet door. The only new things I'd added were two: the damaged photo of my mother, carefully glued to a piece of shirt cardboard, and the dog-eared postcard I'd written to my father, but never sent, with a picture of Sebring's Original You Better Believe It Museum and Restaurant on the front.

I ducked down the hall to check on Rose, then came back and locked the door again, glad we'd had to wait until now. Because he'd know when I kissed his scarred face, his maimed hand, it was because I wanted to. Not some kind of bribe, a down payment to get him to do something: feel guilty, marry me, pay for Rose. All that had already been taken care of.

Pearce was setting a record on the player. When he saw me, he reached for the light switch.

"Let's leave it on," I said, unzipping my skirt.

He shrugged. "Okay."

Bobby Darin began to sing, softly, about

a lover waiting somewhere, beyond the sea. Then there was nothing left to do but pull him onto the narrow bed with me.

He looked me up and down and shook his head. "Yes. Perfect," he said.

I laughed. "What about the stretch marks on my stomach? These little burn scars on my arms from hot grease? Maybe we need a better light. Maybe you need glasses."

He shook his head. "You're getting the lesser end of this deal," he insisted. "Me, missing parts. And barely a mark on you."

I laughed again. If only he could see the inside! But I let it go, mindful of the fact that three-year-olds and fathers sleep light and have keen hearing when you least want them to listen. I was glad to be done with revelations for a while, to have nothing left to explain or regret. Only a future to look forward to. The past, stripped away and laid bare, wouldn't come up to haunt us anymore.

After Pearce left, I went into the dining room and found some stationery in the old secretary. I took out a few sheets and started a letter. The idea had come to me when I'd looked at the old postcard in my room. It got me to wondering again what it might've changed, had I ever sent it. To thinking of all the letters I might've written but hadn't, while I'd been banished. To Dad and to Pearce.

What if my mother had just once written? If only to say she was alive and well, maybe even missed us. Would a sheet of paper with her words on it have had the power to shock my father out of his dull anger, to make him talk? Maybe it would've set something in motion in his heart. Late now to imagine she'd ever do this, write or call or turn up on our doorstep. But even if she existed now only as bones in a grave somewhere, I could still try to write it for her.

Oh, yes. It was a lie and a deception, but that night I felt full of myself, cleansed anew with confession and flushed with love and pleasure. I felt entitled, because in the midst of this consummated love that was new and old both, I thought I could see past and present and future clear. Felt I could fix anything. So surely on paper I could find the right words and put them together in the right order, with enough love and humility and repentance to chisel a way into Owen Gamble's cold heart. The words that Vera, my mother, *would* have written — if she'd ever thought to send them.

There had been some penciled words on the back of her photo. I got it out and looked carefully. Not much there, just a scrawled "Me and" plus below that what looked like "beach." Enough to see that she'd written in a rounded, slanting hand not unlike my own. I laid the picture face down beside a sheet of paper on the desk and began.

Dear Owen,

I know you'll be surprised to hear from me. Please don't worry — I won't be coming back or making any demands. For reasons you know too well, I had to leave you and Dory, though I didn't want to go like that. Maybe I understand better now how it all went wrong.

Maybe you sometimes feel guilty, too, for how things worked out. Maybe you figured to be rid of me was for the best. I can see why it might have looked that way.

Some day I hope to come back. To meet my daughter again, get to know her a little. I'm sure Dory has grown up tall and strong and healthy, thanks to you. You were such a good father to her. Any fool could see that.

Sometimes keeping secrets seems necessary, to protect the innocent. But in the end, a child ought to know where she came from. She ought to know both the good and the bad. So I'm asking you to tell Dory all of it. Everything that happened.

My love to you both,
Vera

Yes, it was a fabrication, but one conceived in love and hope. My father was still punishing my mother and himself and perhaps me, too, by keeping everything — even my own history — forbidden. So I brushed aside misgivings and slipped this flimsy folded sheet into an envelope. I carried it like a beating heart in my shirt pocket all day. At a quarter to five, just before the post office closed, I jumped up and ran out the door. Imagining revelation and redemption, I pushed it through the slot embossed LOCAL MAIL until it disappeared. So what if I was reduced to trying to shock my father into doing what was right. In the not-so-distant future, I might get to meet my mother again, at last.

Not that I believed blindly in happy endings. I'd been around enough to know they mostly didn't pan out. Yet just then I could close my eyes and, without the help of a card or crystal ball, conjure Vera Gamble right there on the sidewalk in front of the Cut 'n Curl. She was taller even than me, and pretty, with light olive skin and long black wavy hair and a round, stubborn chin like mine. She was laughing, head thrown back, face turned up to worship the sun. Because she was coming home at last.

Too late, after the envelope had disappeared into the slot, it hit me: Vera's letter would have a local post mark. Surely that would be a dead giveaway, considering she'd left almost twenty years ago. But maybe it wouldn't be noticeable, get blurred or fade. Who checked postmarks, anyhow?

So I'd look on the bright side and assume it was possible. And when I met my mother, if I wasn't the baby she recalled, and she wasn't my patchwork ideal made up of skin and breath and scraps and scent, why that would be all right. It would be fine.

I left the post office feeling as if a weight had been lifted from my shoulders. As I walked home, I felt more of it falling away. The secret, buried past no longer hanging over me like a dark, lowering sky. I'd taken steps to solve the mystery that'd haunted my whole life.

24

A week went by. I began to think the letter was lost in the mail. A queer sensation, mixed relief and disappointment. Maybe some problems defied all solutions, no matter how creative. I mused over this, so distracted while making dinner one night I cut myself on the sharp-edged lid of a can.

I held my hand over the sink, watching blood drip on the white porcelain. I turned on the faucet to wash it down the drain. A sacrifice, an offering. If it wasn't enough, maybe God would tell me what else to do.

The letter arrived the next day, concealed in the middle of a rubber-banded swatch of bills and advertisements. My hand shook so when I saw our address in my own writing, I dropped the envelope in the driveway, then snatched it up and nearly ran inside. I left it propped against a vase on the hall table for Dad to find.

Dinner came and went. I'd told him he had mail but didn't want to seem pushy. I'd never taken a great interest in his correspondence before, only the bills. But not a word from him. I slipped into the hall twice, and there it sat, untouched, along with an advertising flyer for the Western Auto in Ocala.

In the evening, when it was time for Rose's bath, I took her down the hall to the tub.

"I like bubbles," she said firmly, snapping the elastic on her flowered panties like a rubber band. "Lotsa bubbles."

She liked the ones that smelled like pink bubble gum best. But we were out of those. "You know, I've got to buy more Mr. Bubble at the market. So how about some of this?" I held up a bottle.

She squinted dubiously at the economy-size Johnson's Baby Shampoo in my hand. "That for my *head.*"

"I know, but it makes even more bubbles than the other stuff."

Judging by the way her lip crept out and her brow furrowed, I had no future in marketing. But before she could open her mouth to list her objections, a strangled cry from the living room stopped us both cold.

I threw a towel around Rose. "It's okay, I'll be right back. Stay there, honey. Don't leave."

I ran down the hall, noting as I passed the table that the mail was gone. "Dad! You all right?"

But I couldn't find him. Not in his room, or the dining room, or the kitchen. He wasn't on the screened porch. I ran back down the hall and looked in his room again, then stuck my head in the bathroom to make sure Rose was okay. She was sitting in the dry, empty tub in her underwear, playing with plastic juice cups and rubber bath animals. "Mommy will be right back," I gasped and ran back down the hall, through the kitchen. Where, on the floor, lay a crumpled piece of paper. My letter.

"Oh, God." Somehow it had gone wrong. I grabbed a big flashlight and went out the back.

I shone the light around the yard. At last it spotlighted Dad down by the dock, struggling with the old wooden johnboat, the one he'd taken me fishing in ages earlier. After inspecting the bottom, which was spongy with rot, at the beginning of the summer I'd rejected even attempting to take it out. Decided it'd be safer to buy a new one, if we ever made enough at the store.

"Dad, what're you doing?"

The face he turned back looked wild. "It's a lie," he gasped, struggling and pushing at the boat's stern. "She's gone.

Never coming, can't come back here. Why, they told me —"

I grabbed his arm. "What are you talking about? Come back inside." Struggling against telling him I'd been the author of the note. If I only stood firm, for a little while at least, maybe he'd finally blurt the truth out at last.

"No! Got to get out there and see."

"See what?"

He stared at me blindly a moment, then something else came over his face, a look both crafty and terrified. He clamped his mouth tight and turned back to struggling with the boat again. I was afraid if he launched it in the dark he'd sink or fall overboard. The Springs were deep, twenty feet or more in places. If he made it that far. I'd have been surprised if the thing floated more than five minutes.

I looked from my father to the house, where Rose was alone. I yanked Dad's arm, but he shook me off. I turned and ran halfway up the slope to the house, then looked back. He was making progress. The boat was half-afloat, the stern digging a trench in the beach sand.

I ran inside and checked on Rose, who was whining now for her bath, a big change that under other circumstances I'd have welcomed. I gave her a handful of animal crackers and snatched up the phone.

I hoped Pearce would be at his mother's; he hadn't said anything about leaving early for the coast. I misdialed the number the first time, cursed, and redialed it.

Miss Harriet answered. She sounded distant and a little sleepy, though it wasn't even nine yet. "Oh. Hello, Dory."

I ignored her cool tone. "I hope I'm not bothering you, but it's Dad. Is — is Pearce there? May I speak to him?"

"Sorry, I can't put him on, honey. He left this evening to sleep over on the boat and get an early start in the morning. He was worried about something he saw on the TV. On the weather report."

It would've been nice if she'd sounded less pleased. And how was I going to keep my three-year-old and my father out of trouble tonight all by myself? I had to admit it by then; it was my own fault. That it would've been better if I hadn't gotten this wonderful idea to send that tricked-up letter. Though what the boat had to do with anything, I couldn't imagine. Or the Springs. And I needed help and Pearce was gone. "Damn."

"What!" gasped Harriet McMillan. "What'd you say?"

"I said — Miss Harriet, I need your help." It dawned then what would most put her in a benevolent mood. "I've made a big — no, a terrible mistake."

A pause. Then, "Well, tell me about it, sugar."

"Come on over and I will. Full details." I hung up.

It didn't surprise me when headlights spilled across our driveway in no time. Miss Harriet was not the sort of woman who'd scramble through the woods in the middle of the night. I waved her in, then ran back to check on Rose. She was asleep in the tub, looking flushed and totally bereft, bath toys clutched in one arm, head pillowed on the other. "Oh, sweetie. Mommy's sorry," I whispered.

I ran down the hall again and Harriet was coming in the front. I grabbed her sleeve. "Around back," I said. "He's out in the water."

She looked only mildly surprised. An unflappable woman, I grudgingly had to admire that. Fortunately she was wearing lace-up flats and a pair of slacks, not her usual heels and stockings.

"But what's happening, Dory?"

"Dad got a letter that upset him. And . . . and he ran down to the Springs."

"Well, for heaven's sake. What was in this letter? Was it an overdue bill, or taxes, or —"

I hadn't wanted to get into that. Well, too bad for me. So I told her everything while she stood in the middle of the back-yard, arms folded, nodding, as if we were discussing gardening tips.

But when I told what I'd written, even in the dark her face looked paler than usual. "Oh dear God," she whispered.

I flushed with shame. My bad judgment was always so obvious to other people. Why not to me? But then I'd never been trusted with all the facts, either.

"Well, of course you don't understand," she said, softly, shaking her head. "How could you? Oh, I told Jack back then it was wrong. A terrible, terrible idea! And now look."

"Harriet," I said sharply. "No more half-truths, no more forbidden names. Just tell me. Do you know what happened to my mother?"

She bit her lip, eyes brimming with tears. "I loved your mother," she said, shaking her head. "And she's out there."

She wheeled and ran down the slope, to where my father still struggled and splashed and cursed. I bolted after her.

Dad was knee-deep in the water, and when I caught up, Miss Harriet had him by the arm trying to bodily drag him out. A losing proposition, because she was just a little over half his size. So I grabbed his other arm. The boat was indeed sinking, the bow already submerged in the chilly water.

Dad bellowed, "Get off, you damn meddlers. Let go!"

"Oh, come on now, Owen," Miss Harriet wheedled, mindful even in an emergency about catching flies with honey, not vinegar. "You know you really don't need to go out there."

He dragged us both out a little farther. "She sent a letter, Harriet. From town! Says she's coming back. When everyone said it was all right. All over. Lies, damn lies!"

I shouted in his ear, "Never mind the letter, Dad. I'm the one wrote it. I just wanted to know, I have a right —"

He wrenched his arms away from both of us, then rounded on me, gaping. "You did it? You?" He stared, looked me up and down as if he'd never seen me before in his life. "Well then, Eudora Gamble. You got to know so bad? I'll take you to her!"

He gripped my arm, twisted it, and waded farther out, dragging me with him.

The shock of the cold water took my breath.

"Stop it, let go." I clawed at his hands but couldn't break his grip. As if we were all trapped in a slow-motion nightmare, over his shoulder I saw Miss Harriet coming up from behind. She raised something with both hands and swung at us.

Dad let go. He dropped into the water with a muffled grunt.

I wanted to call the doctor first after we'd dragged him up to the house and laid him on the couch. But Miss Harriet stopped me. "I didn't hit him that hard, honey. He'll be all right."

I wasn't so sure. And still trying to reconcile the sight of her, hair in its usual neat pageboy, the circle pin inlaid with a pearl winking on her shoulder in the moonlight as she'd cold-cocked my father with an old board pulled off the dock. This was no Harriet McMillan I'd ever known or hoped to see.

I lifted Rose from the bathtub carefully so as not to wake her. Bedded her down in the sewing room, then went back out. Harriet sat on the couch next to Dad, smoothing his hair back from his forehead. Checking on the damage, I supposed.

I went to the kitchen and put on a kettle for tea, then came back out. "So did I hear you right? I thought you said Dad was going after my mother. That she was . . . out there. In the Springs."

Harriet's hand stopped moving over my father's forehead. Without looking up, she said slowly, "You were just a baby, Dory. Jack and I were always good friends with your parents. You know that, I suppose. But Vera was my best friend."

She laughed a little. "Hard to say why! We weren't much alike. She was beautiful. So lively, always ready to have a party or go to one. She was funny, and loved to dance, to be admired. Well, why not? Things were never dull here while she was around."

I sat on the couch and drew my feet up under me, forgetting my wet clothes, the letter, my wounded father. I'd never heard anyone speak of my mother before, at least not willingly or at any length. Harriet might've been Scheherazade in a striped tent. I hung on every word.

"But the town was dull for her. She'd come over after Owen and Jack had gone to work and tell me things over coffee. There were men, even other women's husbands, who wanted to do more than admire her. And I think perhaps they did,

469

though she was always vague about that. But I'd heard rumors at the church thrift shop, at altar guild meetings." She grimaced. "I suppose I should've shunned her company, not even let her in.

"But she was *appealing*. So charming you just couldn't hold it against her. 'Sister Harriet,' she called me. Like we were that close. But really I was just the only one she had to confess to."

Now this wasn't exactly the mother I'd imagined, either. "You mean she went with other men. Did my father know that?"

"Not at first. Or if he did, maybe he thought it was the price of keeping her here. She'd grown up with money, had traveled all over. They met during the war; she'd been with a bunch of women in some program training to fly planes. 'Owen swept me off my feet,' she used to say. But when we were alone she sometimes laughed and added, 'But I wish he'd let me down.' After you were born, she seemed more settled. For a year or so, anyhow. Until this one man came along at a boathouse dance. A winter visitor. They danced a while, then went off together. Vera told Owen later she'd felt sick and couldn't find him, that the man had just driven her home."

"Had he?"

"No." Harriet sighed. "She was crazy about him after a week. They were going to run away together. By then I wished she wouldn't tell me so much. Owen was our friend, too. We'd known him longer. But I couldn't say no to Vera. No one could."

She laughed a little, but her face was bleak. "That's why I promised not to tell anyone she was going to meet this fellow at the end of our dock. I thought — oh, I don't know — that by then it might be good if she did go away."

The tea kettle screamed, and we both jumped. I sucked in a shuddering breath, and Harriet gave me a little lop-sided smile. I ran to take the water off the burner. Brought back the mugs, hot water slopping over the sides and my shaking, scalded hands.

Dad groaned. We both looked down at him, but his eyes were still closed. Harriet shivered and pulled her sweater tighter around her. I'd forgotten she was in wet things, too.

She took the mug I handed her. "Oh, thank you, dear," she said, as if we were having a nice get-together. She set it on the coffee table.

"I'm going to tell you the truth, Dory. By then I *wanted* her gone. Because for

Vera, no man was out of bounds. Not even Jack." She bit her lip again. "I kept glancing out the back window that night, you see. So I'd know. But she never came. Well, then I figured it'd been a fantasy, another of her one-week romances. But later, someone did come."

I thought I had figured out the ending. "The man?"

She looked surprised at that. "Goodness, no. Your father. He was at our door like a ghost, shaking, blood on his hands. He said Jack had to come over right away. That Vera was hurt."

"Well, nothing could've kept me away, either. Owen wanted to bring you over here, Dory. But I bundled up Pearce, went there, and laid him in the crib with you. He just fit; he was getting so big.

"Your father said Vera was out back. I thought he meant she was waiting, maybe she'd broken a bone and couldn't move. I said we ought to call an ambulance. But Owen said no, no. That it wasn't — but then we got there." She stopped and passed a hand over her face.

"He took us down to the Springs, shining a light all the way to the dock. A suitcase was lying next to the boathouse. And Vera was floating in the water by a piling, face down. I couldn't understand why he'd left her there, but he was too hysterical to answer questions. Jack jumped in and pulled her out and laid her on the beach. He knew artificial resuscitation; he was a volunteer fireman, you know. But it was no use.

"Only later he told me the back of her head had felt wrong. Soft, he said. That made sense, because when I'd gone to get the suitcase, to carry it up to the house, I'd smelled blood and saw dark patches on the decking. Owen babbled about how she'd fallen, her head had hit a piling. And sure enough, there was blood on one of those, too.

"I thought at first I'd faint. But when we got inside the two men looked even worse. Owen just kept mumbling that she'd run from him and slipped."

I glanced at my father, lying so still, then back at her. "But why was she running? What happened?"

Harriet shook her head. "The Lord alone knows, honey. But I wonder if even Owen recalls, now. In any case, I went for the phone."

"You did. But I stopped you," my father mumbled, wincing as he pulled himself up, until he was sitting. I wondered how long he'd been awake. Maybe he'd been listening all along.

"Why, Daddy?" I asked. "If it was an accident."

"Because everyone knew," Harriet said.

"I can tell the rest," he said sharply, and she pressed her lips together, nodding.

I set my mug of cold, untouched tea on the table. "Then damn well do it, for God's sake." They both stared; I guess they still thought of me as a child. But damned if I was going to wait another second.

"The whole town knew about it." He raised a hand over his eyes, then dropped it. "Everyone but me. Oh, I suspected. So that night I pretended to be asleep. Then got up and followed her out there. All she did was laugh. 'You don't want me, Owen Gamble,' she said. 'Don't you see? I'm doing you a favor.' But I didn't believe. How could a person could stop loving someone, just like that? 'What about the baby?' I asked. 'What about Dory?'

"She cried a little then. Said I'd be a better mother. That anybody would."

"Nonsense. She was a fine mother," murmured Harriet, sipping her tea.

My turn to stare. At her, then at him. I was in some kind of crazy house. "But how did she die, Daddy?" I realized I was calling him that, when I hadn't since I was five or six.

He closed his eyes and turned his face away. "She fell."

Harriet sighed, nodded.

But I wasn't done. "But if you saw her lying in the water, why didn't you pull her out? Then maybe she wouldn't have drowned."

His face was gray, slack. It had a faraway, wondering look. "I didn't want to. Right then, I just . . . she would have gone away."

I put my face in my hands. So my mother had never left us after all, though she'd meant to. He had stopped her from going. And then I was never allowed to speak her name because it reminded him of what she'd done. And what he had done, too.

"But how," I said, and then had to stop and swallow hard. "What," I tried again, "did you do with her? With the, with her body? Because there's no grave. Is there?"

My father shook his head.

"I can tell it, Owen," said Harriet. "Maybe that would be easier."

"A guilty conscience needs no accuser," he whispered. Then he lowered his head and stared at the floor. The old silent treatment again. He'd retreated into his cave, the walls chalked with knee-jerk Bible verses. I allowed myself to hate him fully, at least for the moment.

"We had a hard time making Owen understand she was dead," said Harriet slowly. "That there was nothing to be done except call the sheriff."

"You mean Tom Burney?" I couldn't help it, I shivered, though my clothes were getting dry.

"He'd just been elected the year before. So Jack picked up the phone, but then I had second thoughts."

"Why?"

"Because, Dory." A fervent light kindled in her eyes as she leaned forward to convince me they had done right. "If the law hadn't believed Owen, you'd have been an orphan. Of course we'd have raised you! But you'd still be the child whose father was a murderer, a wife-killer, forever notorious. Your life would be ruined."

"So instead I got to be The Girl Without a Mother."

She had the grace to look abashed, at least. "Oh, honey, I know. It's tragic for everybody. Owen was a quiet man who fell in love late with a beautiful younger woman. He doted on her so, people remarked on it. But in the end, something about the two of them together . . . well, some folks in this world simply aren't good for one another. But they come together anyhow, like magnets."

Her face reddened at the image this evoked. "But that sort of . . . attraction, it burns away fast. Maybe cancels itself out, like two poisons mixed in one vat. Do you know what I mean?"

Oh, yes. I thought so. There'd been Mick Poteke, anyhow. I'd had to leave the You Better Believe It, leave town to be sure I wouldn't take him back on any terms, take him from his family and not look back. Had my father craved my mother that same way? Then maybe nothing else would've mattered. Then maybe over the years he'd refused any comfort or compassion, any female attention as his punishment, his atonement. At least, until Myra Fitzgerald came along. And she'd left, too, in the end.

"So you didn't call the sheriff," I said flatly. "Then what *did* you do?"

Harriet looked away. "I told Jack to help me. We wrapped poor Vera in a sheet and then a shower curtain. Jack tied it all up with clothesline. I went to the back to check on you and Pearce. But I had to come out again and help carry her, because Owen was too broke up. I'll never forget . . . how heavy she was." Harriet's head trembled on her neck until she looked suddenly feeble, old. "How we had to drag and bump that terrible bundle over the grass because I couldn't lift my end well enough."

My father put his head in his hands and groaned.

"You have to face it now, Owen," she said, more sharply than I'd ever heard her speak to anyone before. Then, "I'm sorry, Dory."

I already knew what came next.

"I stayed here with you babies, while they took the boat out to the far end of the Springs, to where they merge with Lake Panasoffkee. Jack had taken along a concrete block for, you know, weight. They pushed everything overboard and used the paddle to wedge it beneath some tree roots. Then they came back."

"I found sleeping pills in the bathroom cabinet. Gave Owen two, then Jack and I cleaned up."

Proper, refined Miss Harriet, who'd depended on her maid, Delia, to clean up messes for all her married life. I tried to imagine Pearce's mother on her knees, scrubbing my own mother's blood off our oak plank floor. She must have taken a long time to do it. I knew how thorough, how house-proud she'd always been.

She gazed at me, wringing her hands. "What we did was wrong, though it seemed like the best thing at the time. For years I expected someone to . . . to find her. Sheriff Burney was a very ambitious young man in those days. Solving a murder would have been good for his career, for reelection. But after a while . . . well, it's surprising what a body can live with, even forget about, for months at a time."

Something else struck me. "But what about the man? The one she was going to meet?"

"I knew him by sight. From somewhere north. Tallahassee, or maybe it was Panama City. For three nights the same car drove by our house, a white Pontiac. Once it parked by the drive, but when Jack went out to see, the driver took off. So maybe that was him. Or maybe he wasn't as interested in Vera as she'd thought. Or maybe just a coward. Because he never got out or came up to the house. Just went away."

"When I wrote the letter." I stared into my mug of tea, because I couldn't look at Miss Harriet anymore. "When I did that, I was sure she was alive somewhere. For most of my childhood, almost, I felt sure of it. I thought Dad knew where, so maybe this letter would shock him, make him finally tell. But shouldn't I have known? That she was dead, I mean. Seems like I should have felt that. Why didn't I at least *feel* that she was gone?"

Miss Harriet laid a hand on my knee. "A death like that does strange things, not just to the people involved. My knowing Vera so well, and what happened to her, it made me see you differently, even as a child. You look so much like her. It got harder, the older you grew, to be reminded. Harder to pretend, to forget what we did and get on with things."

I should hate them all. Even poor, dead Jack McMillan. They hadn't ruined my whole life, just a big part of it. Instead I ended up kneeling on the floor, my head in Miss Harriet's lap, her arms around me.

"I'm sorry, honey," she whispered. "So sorry. You were the only innocent one. You had no choice, no say in anything at all."

She was wrong about that. We all make our choices. Some of mine had been very bad indeed. But I didn't want to think about all that right now. I wanted to understand how, even when I thought of her, when I'd seen her in Ruby's crystal ball and felt she was alive and that someday I'd find her, my mother had already been dead and gone for almost twenty years.

I'd told the future, half-serious, half-disbelieving, to others. And sometimes I'd even been right. Yet I'd watched the tiny dancing figures in the crystal, with never the least notion it might be my mother's last message, sent to me.

We got Dad into some dry clothes and put him into bed. Harriet stayed on, saying she wanted to make sure we were all right, as if such a phrase could be applied to the sorry, bedraggled, meddling lot of us ever again. At last she did leave, giving me a hug that felt honest and warm, like she truly meant it. I went to bed then, too, but lay awake, thinking about what to do.

Should I turn in my father now, twenty years later? There was no statute of limitations on murder, not in Florida. But had it been that? Dad claimed it was an accident. But even so, he hadn't pulled her out. She might have lived.

But then so might have Frank Fitzgerald, if I had taken away the pills or gone down the hall and told someone. The fact that he was sick, maybe dying already, did not absolve me. How would a jury of strangers see that?

I didn't know the answers to any of those questions. But one thing was certain. I did not want my own daughter to find out the world was a harder place than even I had ever imagined. That there were people you knew and trusted who'd lie to you, who'd tell tall tales and call it history and truth. Who'd steal anything that wasn't nailed down, not excluding your heart and soul. I didn't want to make Rose the grand-daughter of a killer, the daughter of a woman who'd helped a dying man do away with himself. Some day she'd have to lose that shy sweet smile, that open, trusting look. But dear God, must it be sooner rather than later? Lying there in the dark, I knew I held the power. That I was the stopper on the bottle and could hold it all inside or let go and take her childhood away from her. Either way, knowing or not, she would pay.

Miss Harriet had known this, too, when she decided to tell. Maybe she was tired of being the one and wanted me to take her place. So how could we escape from history and keep it from hurting us again and again?

I knew the answer to that well enough by then. So common sense said, *Tell it. And suffer the consequences.*

I dropped Rose at Miss Alma's in the morning. Dad and I went into the store. I caught him glancing my way more than once, his look a queer mix of hope and despair and something else I hadn't seen there before. Childlike, dependent. But after twenty years, there was no great hurry. So I ignored him and sold paint and sandpaper and putty, as if it were still possible to put a good face on things, to smooth and fill in the cracks and flaws in life.

Pearce returned from the coast two days later, and I told him everything. When I was done, God bless him, he put his arms around me and said, "What do you want to do? I'll back you up."

It wasn't just me we were talking about now, but his own mother. Still, he pulled me up tight against his chest and held me there. He didn't lie and say everything would be all right — a real blessing because how could it, ever? He just let me cry, squeezing my shoulder occasionally so I'd know he was still with me and paying attention.

I guess maybe I'd still thought of him as the boy I'd played with and sometimes bested at games. Not a man who knew when to keep quiet and listen, who knew better than to give advice or meddle when he shouldn't. What could top that? Perhaps he'd already figured out a thing I'd begun to suspect. That sometimes mere words don't have the power to hold and savor great joy or the size to support big sorrows. That in certain cases you have to let them go, all the words. Just let things be.

What I finally asked him to do, the following Saturday, was to take me to church. I had not, since leaving town, been what anyone could call a church-going person. But Pearce didn't look surprised or ask questions. We dropped Rose at Miss Harriet's, then he pulled out and turned down Council Bluff and headed slowly toward Ordinary Springs First Baptist, his eyes on the road, as if driving this familiar stretch required great amounts of skill and concentration. Only after he'd pulled into the shell-paved lot did it occur to me the church might be locked up.

But it was open. Two women were up front, putting flowers in vases at the altar, while a third polished the brass railing with a soft cloth. Dust motes swirled in the pastel light streaming through stained glass. I slipped into a pew in back, got down on that hard kneeler, and prayed for my mother. Then, for the second time in my life, I offered up a formal prayer for the soul of Frank Fitzgerald. Maybe God would forgive my hand in his death. I still didn't understand it all, but I knew He must. So then I asked Him to forgive my father, because I didn't know how long it would take me to. And to forgive Miss Harriet and everyone else for the tangled web of hurts and deceits and betrayals that I feared by then were not that remarkable or different from those afflicting any community, any town. For everywhere we are alike, under the surface.

All my life I'd been consumed with the wrongs done me, but I'd never properly considered what I'd done to others. So I did it then, while Pearce waited in the back, turned away, pretending to read salvation pamphlets and missionary news on a wire rack by the door. And though I would not have thought it possible, a huge weight fell away from me, leaving sadness and regret, but a sort of acceptance, too. I can't explain it any better than that.

When I came out, Pearce took my hand and drove me home.

25

In the end, we put the wedding off for longer than the six months it took for his divorce to be final. In fact, a year passed before I could say, *Yes, all right. Let's set the date.* I wanted to feel sure I could live with the past and the present in one house, merge two very imperfect families, and still stay friends, too.

I wouldn't look ahead in the cards or the crystal to see how it might all come out. I wanted to be surprised like the rest of the town at whatever fate was sending us, Pearce and Rose and me. I was so excited at the idea of not knowing, yet so thrilled at the normalness of it all, some days I nearly had to hug myself and gloat, *Just wait and see.*

The wedding was small but traditional at the Baptist Church. We had caused something of a stir in town beforehand, during our marital counseling session, when it got around that I'd asked to have the word *obey* taken out of the vows and Pearce had backed me up.

Reverend Hardy cleared his throat when

we told him. "It's traditional to acknowledge the husband as the head of the family.
The Southern Baptist Convention clearly
states that this is part of God's plan for a
blessed union, a life partnership —"

"But if we're going to be partners," I
asked, "why does one of us have to be the
boss?"

The reverend turned pink in the face. He
mumbled something about how the SBC
rules wouldn't let him budge on this
matter. But when Pearce picked up his hat
and suggested in that case we might ought
to go down the street to the Presbyterians,
Hardy grimaced and made a note, then
went on.

We had a notice printed in the newspaper that everyone was welcome. The re-
ception was in Miss Harriet's garden, with
a three-tier frosted pound cake and fresh
orange juice punch and then champagne
toasts. All the town ladies turned out to
wipe their eyes with little embroidered
hankies and eat the butter-frosting pound
cake with candied fruit and coconut inside.
And moreover, they all came to wish us
well. Even Dad seemed to enjoy himself,
sitting out under the grape arbor with the
gray-haired women who'd used to come
into the store and flirt with him in days

past. And it even seemed to me he might be flirting back a little. But now that he acted more available, no one asked me for his hand.

We had our honeymoon, with Rose along, in Atlanta. It wouldn't be all that far a detour on the way back to wing by Midway, I noticed on the road map. So Pearce asked if I wanted to turn west and head there, to see what'd become of the You Better Believe It. I shook my head. Sometimes it's best to move on. Someday I'd take Rose back to see her Uncle Clayton. But I wanted to start our new life first and not add in any more confusion.

The following spring, like a fool I chose a hot day in early April to put up strawberry preserves. I'd quit cigarettes again for the baby's sake, and it helped to have my hands busy. Still, a woman in my condition should've known better. My belly was so big I couldn't get too near the stove for fear of burning off my navel. But Pearce loved strawberry jam on biscuits for breakfast, and we were out.

He'd said so that morning, scraping out the dregs of the last jar. "A hundred times better than store-bought. Shame it's all gone." So I intended to surprise him with a fresh supply when he got home from the store.

He'd gone in early, because Dad was feeling poorly and had stayed home. Normally my father enjoyed being at the store most of the day so he could sit on the liar's bench and talk to his old friends, the ones who could still get around. But this morning he'd stayed in the dining room, reading the paper, though he'd already been through it once. He was leaving most of the work and all the decisions to us these days, anyhow.

Pearce had done wonders with the place; we carried all sorts of new things: patio furniture and textured wallpaper and organic cleaners and floor waxes that smelled like lime and oranges. Next week he'd be putting in a new section of housewares. Who'd have ever guessed a seagoing man would have such a gift for retailing?

I'd just screwed a lid on the last jar, wiped it, and turned it upside down to seal, when I heard the mailman coming up the walk. So I cleaned my hands on a dishtowel and stepped out onto the porch. Rose looked up from her paper and crayons and smiled at me.

"Mama," she said. "Look at my mermaid."

"Wow, that's nice. Don't you think she

looks like me?" Shamelessly soliciting flattery as I bent to admire the crayoned strings of black hair, the perfect red circle of mouth, the green fishy tail. This coming baby had me barn-big, reduced to awkward waddling. I needed a compliment from time to time.

Rose laughed. "Not you! I don't know who she is."

Oh well. I took the mail from our postman, an old classmate. When I came back, Rose looked up again. "I heard a big thump."

"Oh, what was it?" I asked, heading for the dining room, looking over the stack of bills, a postcard from Miss Harriet, who was visiting her sister in New Orleans, a *Highlights Magazine* for Rose. It all slid to the floor, though, when I saw Dad's chair tipped on its side. He lay there too, sprawled, head thrown back. I rushed over and knelt beside him.

His face was white. He seemed unable to catch his breath. I fumbled with his top button and loosened his collar. "I'm going to call somebody, Dad. You lie still."

At first I thought he hadn't heard me, because he kept struggling to raise his head. He gripped my arm much harder than I'd have expected from a man who looked deathly ill. "No." His voice raspy, weak. "Just hold on a minute. I want to say . . . sorry. Not good enough. Just . . . you look so much like her." He took a deep breath, winced. Then whispered wonderingly, "Ah. Hurts."

I didn't know if he meant body or soul. He only closed his eyes and let go of my arm. His hand slid away.

I went for the phone then, knowing it was too late, that he was gone. I got the county ambulance on the first ring and gave them the town and address. Next I called the store and told Pearce. He said he'd be right home.

Then I had no idea what to do next. So I hovered there, by Dad. He looked like he was sleeping, except that he lay on the floor and not in bed. He looked . . . not exactly happy, but, yes — peaceful. All the lines and furrows had relaxed a bit; you could see a shadow of the handsomeness that had once swept a younger woman named Vera right off her feet.

You look so much like her. They'd both said that, my father and Miss Harriet.

Perhaps my father had taken care of me as well as he knew how. Had even loved me, only it got harder as I got older. He'd begun to hold me at arm's length, then push me away. Myra Fitzgerald had only been incidental, a bit player. I was the one who'd endowed her with so much power. My father had been poised for years, ready to strike before anyone else got a good chance to hurt him. Even his own daughter. But Lord God, who had entered us into this contest to see who could abandon the other first?

Now the time for making it up to each other had passed. Owen Gamble was a mystery yet, despite the revelations about my mother. Perhaps children can never know their parents as real, separate people, because we are so closely linked: the yardstick by which we measure, the failures we vow to avoid, the guilt that prods at the most inopportune moments. And neither will understand what the other is saying, with so much history between them muffling the words.

Yes, my father was still mysterious, but parts of him were beginning to emerge, as if he was walking toward me slowly out of a fog. If my life had seemed hard at times, his could not have been much easier. It had taken him many years to find Vera, and he had loved her maybe beyond reason. Then, according to Harriet, my mother had taken that love and betrayed him, perhaps many times. Until the night, when in her passion to escape, she'd slipped and fallen to her death. Or else, in his rage to keep her with him, my father had killed her. I'd never know which, but the end had been the same. I was the changeling left behind. Vera's daughter, who looked and sounded, even acted like her more each day.

No wonder he'd been silent and distant. I must have seemed like a living rebuke. Yet in his own clumsy way, my father had tried to save his daughter from notoriety and shame by living out a lie. Atoned for his guilt by forgoing the simple pleasure and consolation of another relationship for fifteen years while he raised me. Myra Fitzgerald must've seemed like a pardon, a blessing. All that loneliness, those frustrated longings moving in right next door, sending out signals like a radio tower. If he hadn't answered in some way, he'd hardly have been human.

And what about my mother? I had a better idea of her as well. That she'd been neither a bad mother nor a she-devil who had coldly abandoned me. Because no one alive can say what might've happened if she hadn't died that night. Like me, she might've come to her senses and come back. Maybe even for both of us.

And just as the time for making it up had passed, so had the time for casting blame. I had my own collection of mistakes and missteps now to pore over in the gray hours between sleep and waking. That my father might've been wrong did nothing to alleviate the ache in my chest. I pressed a hand there, over my heart. Not hoping the hurt would go away, but to capture and hold it there. As long as that feeling remained, so would he, so would they both. Enough time wasted making neat columns of debt that could never be collected or paid in full. Oh, why after Harriet's revelations, had Dad and I still walked so tentatively, so carefully around each other, like polite opponents in a long, tiring game? As if it really mattered who would finally hold the upper hand, and who would lose.

I was still here, so I supposed that made me the winner. A sad, ridiculous notion. A waste. My laugh came out more like a sob.

I sat on the rug beside him. Touched his hand, which was rough-skinned, as warm as if he might still get up to read magazines with Rose or complain I'd made the coffee strong again.

"I'm sorry, too, Dad," I whispered. "Maybe we all did the best we could."

Then it hit me. Now I could call up the sheriff's office. Tell the whole story, set the record straight. Too many years had passed to think they could find my mother's bones now. But she could have some sort of memorial. A headstone with her name and the dates at least. Grasping at this, I went straight to the phone and dialed 0. Told the operator what I wanted and waited while she put me through.

I stood in the archway between living and dining room, waiting, twisting the telephone cord. What would happen, when and if they found her? Of course Dad was beyond the reach of the law, and Miss Harriet needn't be mentioned.

Then my gaze fell on my daughter, coloring in her book, oblivious to the turmoil about to be set in motion.

And I realized I'd forgotten the most important consideration of all. I knew well enough how a scandal played out in a place where everyone knew you and your history. If I told the police about my mother, my father, the events of that long-ago night, my words would be passed hand to hand, and soon it would be accepted fact that Rose's grandfather had murdered her grandmother in cold blood. And why not, for she'd been an adulteress and abandoned her baby. The newspapers would pick up on that, the kind of story they thrived on. Then they could rehash Frank Fitzgerald's death, poke around asking folks all about Dad and Myra.

On the fourth ring, someone picked up on the other end. "Marion County Sheriff's Office," said a woman's voice briskly.

A weight was slowly settling back on my shoulders. As long as we made a life in Ordinary Springs, I had to keep that stopper in the bottle. To protect Rose, who was innocent, from the sins and crimes and foolish mistakes played out long before she was born. Who could tell if I'd make a better job of it than those who'd gone before?

"I'm sorry," I said at last, slowly, not knowing whether it was right or not. Had my father felt this same guilt, this dread and despair, telling the first lie about the whereabouts of his suddenly missing wife?

"Hello," repeated the woman impatiently. "Can I help you?"

If only she could.

"Wrong number," I said at last. Then set the receiver back in the cradle so gently it might have been made of glass. I came back to the living room and dropped onto the couch.

Rose glanced up from her coloring.

"What's wrong, Mama?"

It was difficult with my pregnant belly, but I managed to get down and kneel on the rug beside her. "Grandpa's sick," I said, improvising as I went. She was only four and a half, what did she know of death yet? "So pretty soon a white truck will come, and they'll take him to the hospital. Doctors and nurses will take care of him there. But he's very sick, sweetie."

Instead of turning back to her coloring, she regarded me gravely, then dropped her red crayon. "I'll come sit with you," she said, climbing up beside me. "Don't be scared."

It was true. I was scared, because my father and mother were both gone. So often you are lonely in this world, and afraid, even when people you know are right in the same room. Because once again you're belted into that carnival ride, the one you don't recall even buying a ticket for. Yet there you sit, white-knuckled and terrified, hunkered down, wishing someone would turn on the lights.

Maybe sometimes it makes no difference that you've sworn never to make the same mistakes, never to repeat the old half-truths you were raised on. What did it all mean? Perhaps even fools are right, sometimes. I did cry then, because experience is such a hard teacher. And when would I ever get the lesson right?

I heard Pearce's truck turning into the drive at last. And then Rose reached out and took my hand. She patted it, squeezing my fingers gently, as if to say, *Don't worry.* That she'd been born for just such a moment as this, and now was rising to the occasion. That I could count on her to do her part. To help lead us, together, out of the dark.

READERS GUIDE FOR

Ordinary Springs

by Lenore Hart

QUESTIONS FOR DISCUSSION:

1. Dory tells us: "A freshwater spring makes a path nearly as twisted as the ones people choose. It flows underground, then above. Sometimes pure, sometimes tainted . . ." Is this a fitting metaphor for Dory's life? For everyone's lives? Do we all choose the paths we make? Are the problems in her life caused by her fate or by her choices? Does Dory take responsibility for her choices?

2. Why does Dory form a bond with her dying neighbor Frank Fitzgerald? Why does she agree to give him the pills? In your opinion, did she do the right thing?

3. Dory's father, Owen, and her neighbor, Myra, both bury their spouses' belongings in the backyard. What are each of their motivations for doing so? Why is it good or bad to bury the past?

4. From an early age, Dory feels betrayed by her mother. In what other ways

does she feel betrayed? In what ways has she betrayed others? Which transgressions are forgivable and which are not?

5. The carnival plays different roles in Dory's life and imagination. Why does she run away with the circus? What is she really afraid of in the Tunnel of Horrors with her friend Pearce? Why does a carnival ride ultimately symbolize life in Dory's mind?

6. Dory remembers her church reverend telling her, "The human soul's elastic." How does this apply to Dory? To the people in her life? To yourself?

7. Who are the real mother figures in Dory's life and why? Her absent mother, Vera? Her neighbor, Myra Fitzgerald? Her friends at the Pine Hills School? The vagrant Sadie? The waitress Ruby? Pearce's mother, Harriet?

8. When Dory meets Clayton and Ruby, she thinks: "People like us were strange fish who'd somehow drifted too far downstream and gotten lost." How is this an apt metaphor? Is it possible for these characters to find the way upstream?

9. What is the significance of Dory's interest in fortune-telling? Does she

really see visions in Ruby's crystal ball? Does the idea of fortune and fate conflict with her statement that "We all make our choices"?

10. Dory admits: "I have been the worst kind of fool imaginable. A walking, talking cautionary tale, a regular parable. Take a lesson from me." In what specific ways could Dory's life story be seen as a cautionary tale? What are some of the lessons she has learned? What are the lessons we all can take from Dory?

11. Should Dory — or anyone of us — regret our mistakes if something good ultimately comes out of it?